Hope Larson • Brittney Wi...

GOLDIE VANCE™

Volume One

BOOM!
BOX™

GOLDIE

ROSS RICHIE CEO & Founder
MATT GAGNON Editor-in-Chief
FILIP SABLIK President of Publishing & Marketing
STEPHEN CHRISTY President of Development
LANCE KREITER VP of Licensing & Merchandising
PHIL BARBARO VP of Finance
BRYCE CARLSON Managing Editor
MEL CAYLO Marketing Manager
SCOTT NEWMAN Production Design Manager
IRENE BRADISH Operations Manager
SIERRA HAHN Senior Editor
DAFNA PLEBAN Editor, Talent Development
SHANNON WATTERS Editor
ERIC HARBURN Editor
WHITNEY LEOPARD Associate Editor
JASMINE AMIRI Associate Editor
CHRIS ROSA Associate Editor

ALEX GALER Associate Editor
CAMERON CHITTOCK Associate Editor
MARY GUMPORT Assistant Editor
MATTHEW LEVINE Assistant Editor
KELSEY DIETERICH Production Designer
JILLIAN CRAB Production Designer
MICHELLE ANKLEY Production Designer
GRACE PARK Production Design Assistant
AARON FERRARA Operations Coordinator
ELIZABETH LOUGHRIDGE Accounting Coordinator
STEPHANIE HOCUTT Social Media Coordinator
JOSÉ MEZA Sales Assistant
JAMES ARRIOLA Mailroom Assistant
HOLLY AITCHISON Operations Assistant
SAM KUSEK Direct Market Representative
AMBER PARKER Administrative Assistant

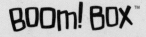

GOLDIE VANCE **Volume One, October 2016.** Published by BOOM! Box, a division of Boom Entertainment, Inc. Goldie Vance is ™ & © 2016 Hope Larson & Brittney Williams. Originally published in single magazine form as GOLDIE VANCE No. 1-4. ™ & © 2016 Hope Larson and Brittney Williams. All rights reserved. BOOM! Box™ and the BOOM! Box logo are trademarks of Boom Entertainment, Inc., registered in various countries and categories. All characters, events, and institutions depicted herein are fictional. Any similarity between any of the names, characters, persons, events, and/or institutions in this publication to actual names, characters, and persons, whether living or dead, events, and/or institutions is unintended and purely coincidental. BOOM! Box does not read or accept unsolicited submissions of ideas, stories, or artwork.

A catalog record of this book is available from OCLC and from the BOOM! Studios website, www.boom-studios.com, on the Librarians page.

BOOM! Studios, 5670 Wilshire Boulevard, Suite 450, Los Angeles, CA 90036-5679. Printed in Canada. First Printing.

ISBN: 978-1-60886-898-8, eISBN: 978-1-61398-569-4

VANCE™

created by Hope Larson & Brittney Williams

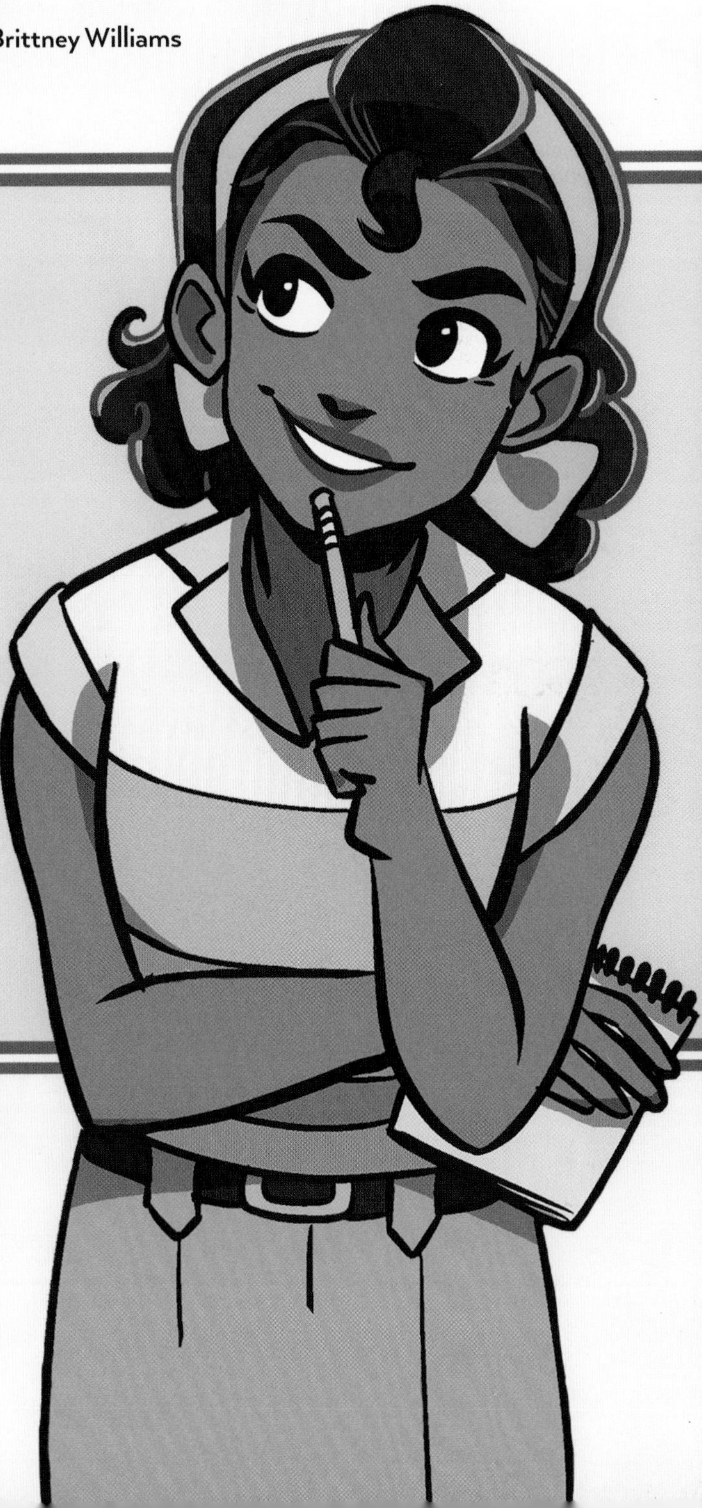

written by
Hope Larson

illustrated by
Brittney Williams

colors by
Sarah Stern

letters by
Jim Campbell

cover by
Brittney Williams

designer
Jillian Crab

editors
Dafna Pleban & Shannon Watters

chapter ONE

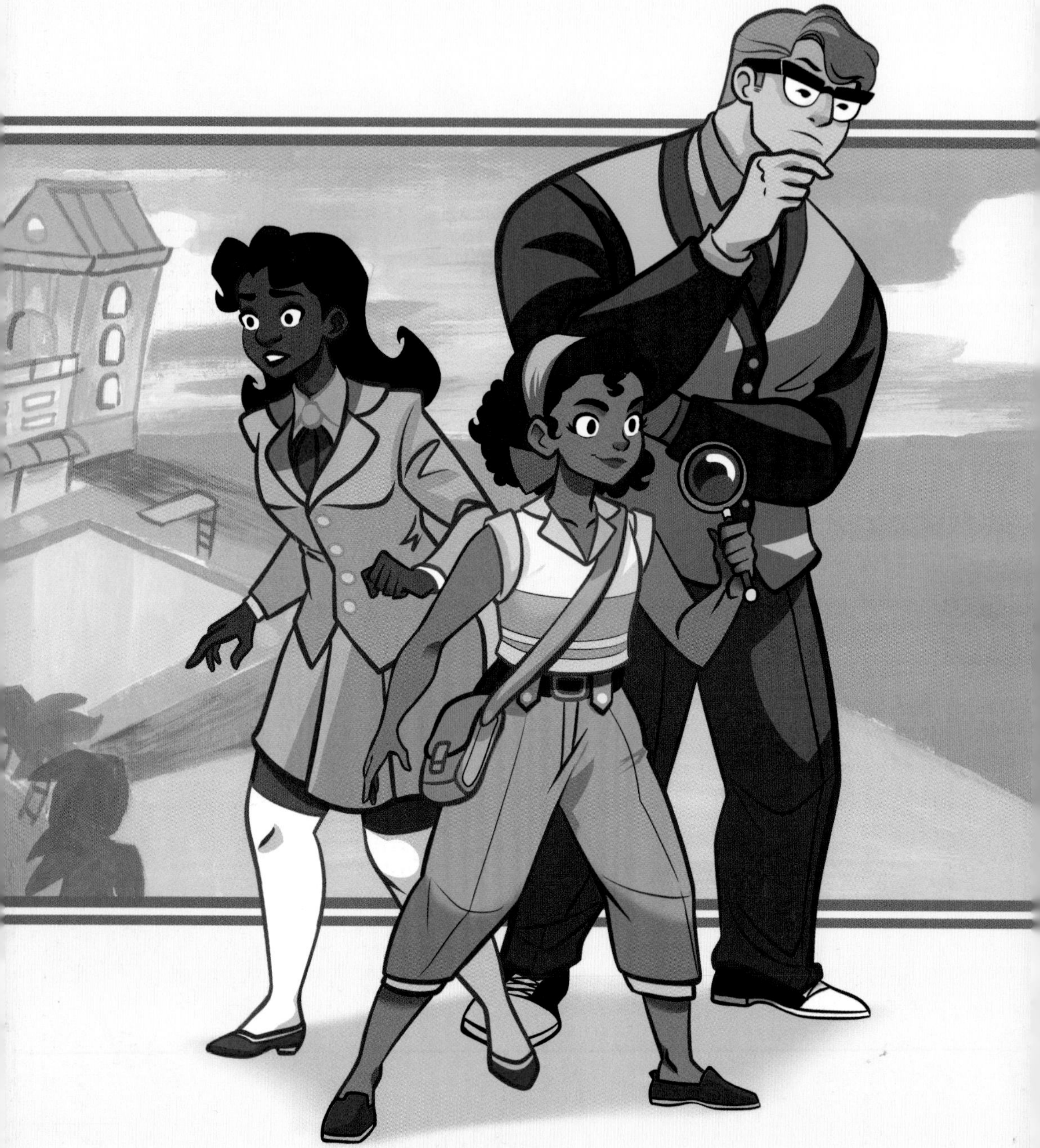

issue one cover by **Brittney Williams**

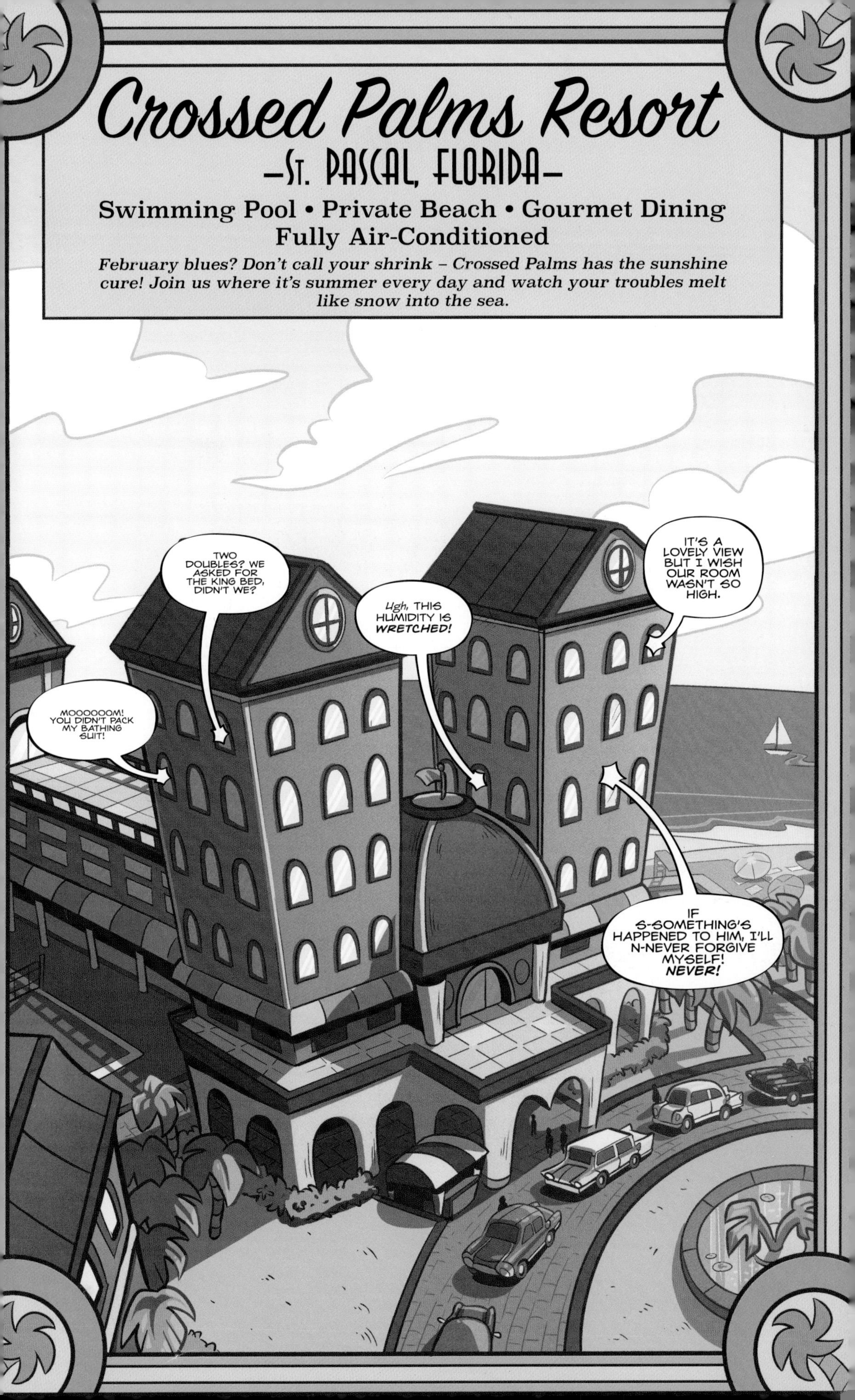
Crossed Palms Resort
–St. PASCAL, FLORIDA–
Swimming Pool • Private Beach • Gourmet Dining
Fully Air-Conditioned
February blues? Don't call your shrink – Crossed Palms has the sunshine cure! Join us where it's summer every day and watch your troubles melt like snow into the sea.
TWO DOUBLES? WE ASKED FOR THE KING BED, DIDN'T WE?
Ugh, THIS HUMIDITY IS WRETCHED!
IT'S A LOVELY VIEW BUT I WISH OUR ROOM WASN'T SO HIGH.
MOOOOOOM! YOU DIDN'T PACK MY BATHING SUIT!
IF S-SOMETHING'S HAPPENED TO HIM, I'LL N-NEVER FORGIVE MYSELF! NEVER!

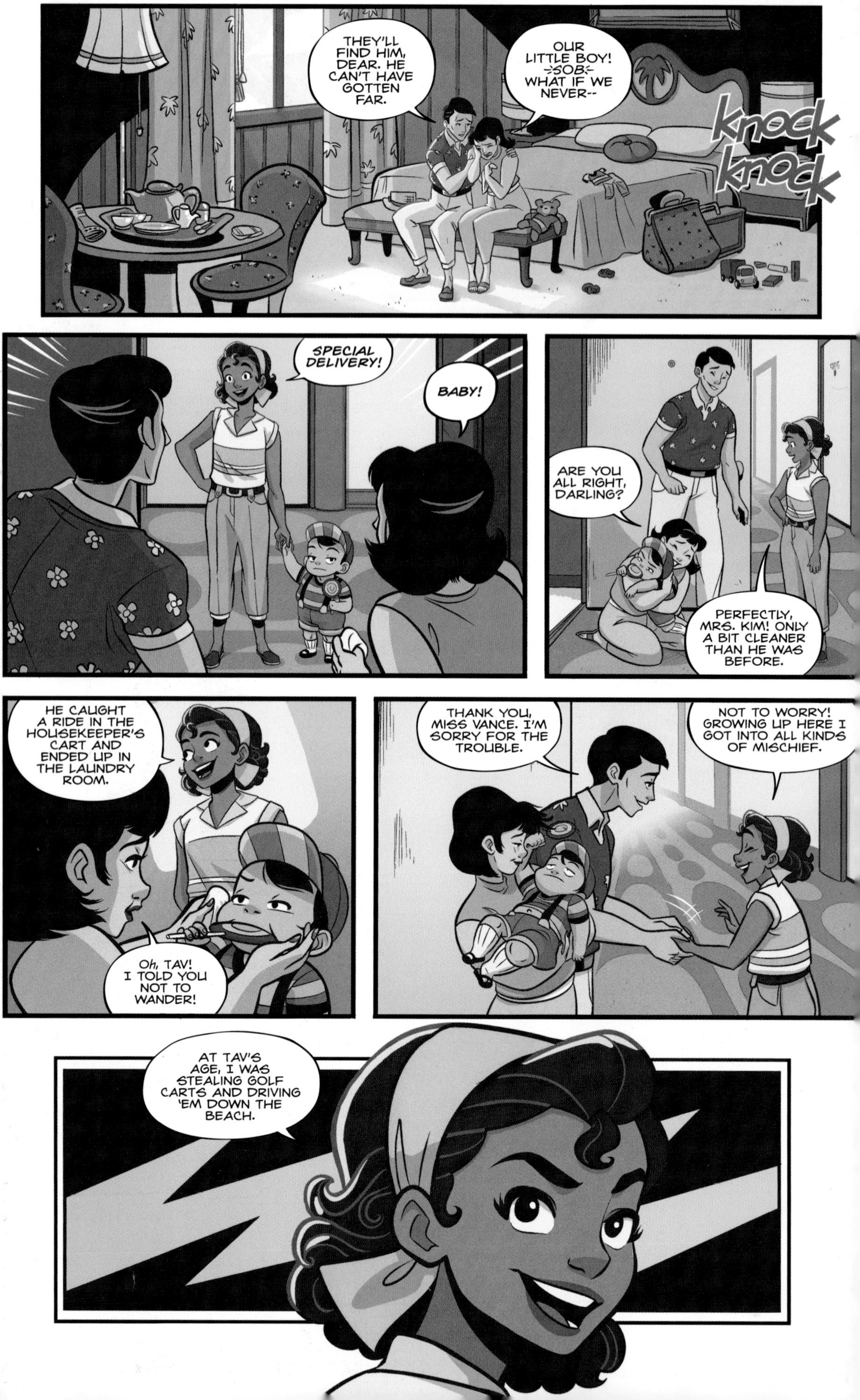
THEY'LL FIND HIM, DEAR. HE CAN'T HAVE GOTTEN FAR.
OUR LITTLE BOY! -SOB- WHAT IF WE NEVER--
knock knock
SPECIAL DELIVERY!
BABY!
ARE YOU ALL RIGHT, DARLING?
PERFECTLY, MRS. KIM! ONLY A BIT CLEANER THAN HE WAS BEFORE.
HE CAUGHT A RIDE IN THE HOUSEKEEPER'S CART AND ENDED UP IN THE LAUNDRY ROOM.
Oh, TAV! I TOLD YOU NOT TO WANDER!
THANK YOU, MISS VANCE. I'M SORRY FOR THE TROUBLE.
NOT TO WORRY! GROWING UP HERE I GOT INTO ALL KINDS OF MISCHIEF.
AT TAV'S AGE, I WAS STEALING GOLF CARTS AND DRIVING 'EM DOWN THE BEACH.

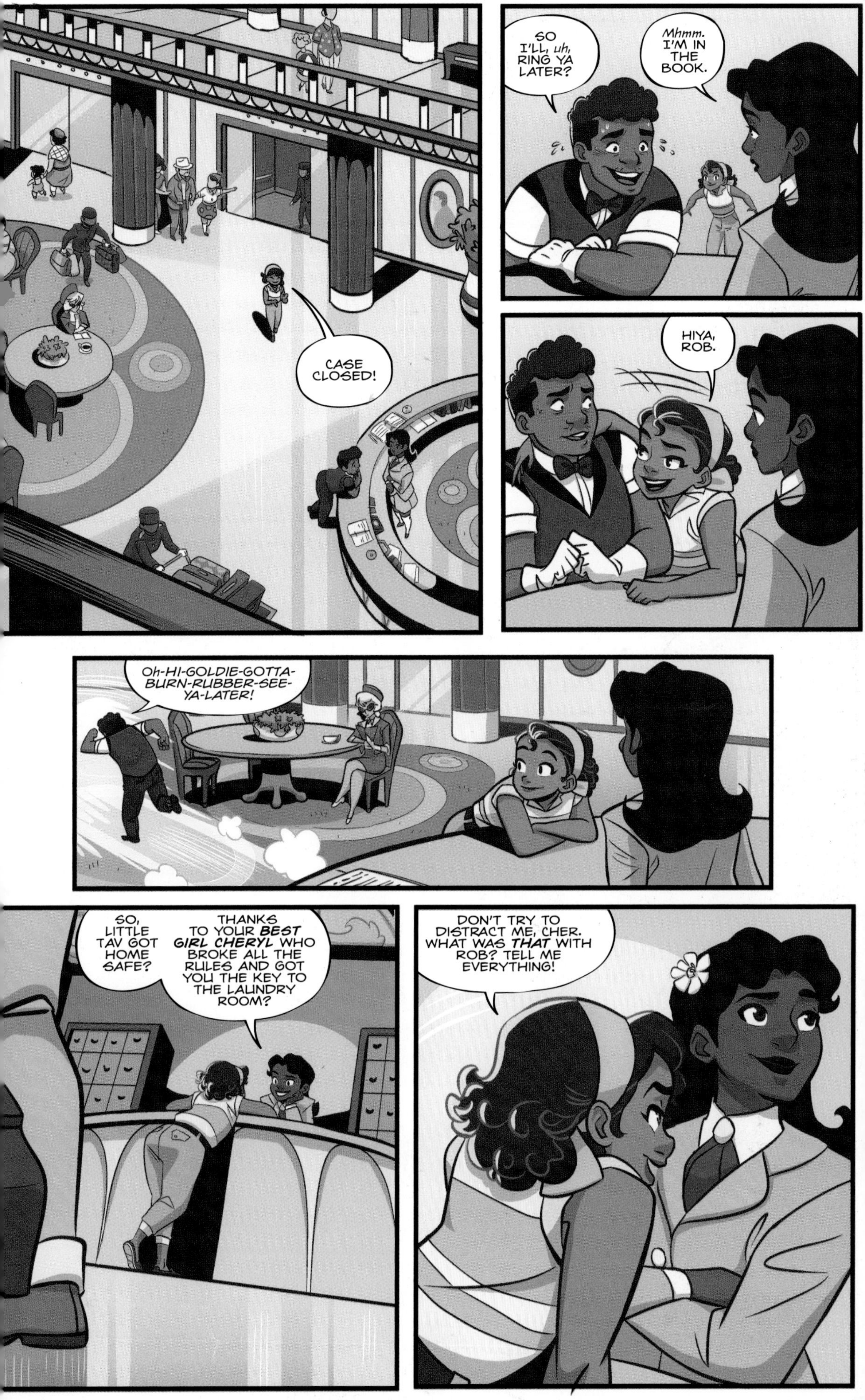
CASE CLOSED!
SO I'LL, uh, RING YA LATER?
Mhmm. I'M IN THE BOOK.
HIYA, ROB.
Oh-HI-GOLDIE-GOTTA-BURN-RUBBER-SEE-YA-LATER!
SO, LITTLE TAV GOT HOME SAFE?
THANKS TO YOUR BEST GIRL CHERYL WHO BROKE ALL THE RULES AND GOT YOU THE KEY TO THE LAUNDRY ROOM?
DON'T TRY TO DISTRACT ME, CHER. WHAT WAS THAT WITH ROB? TELL ME EVERYTHING!

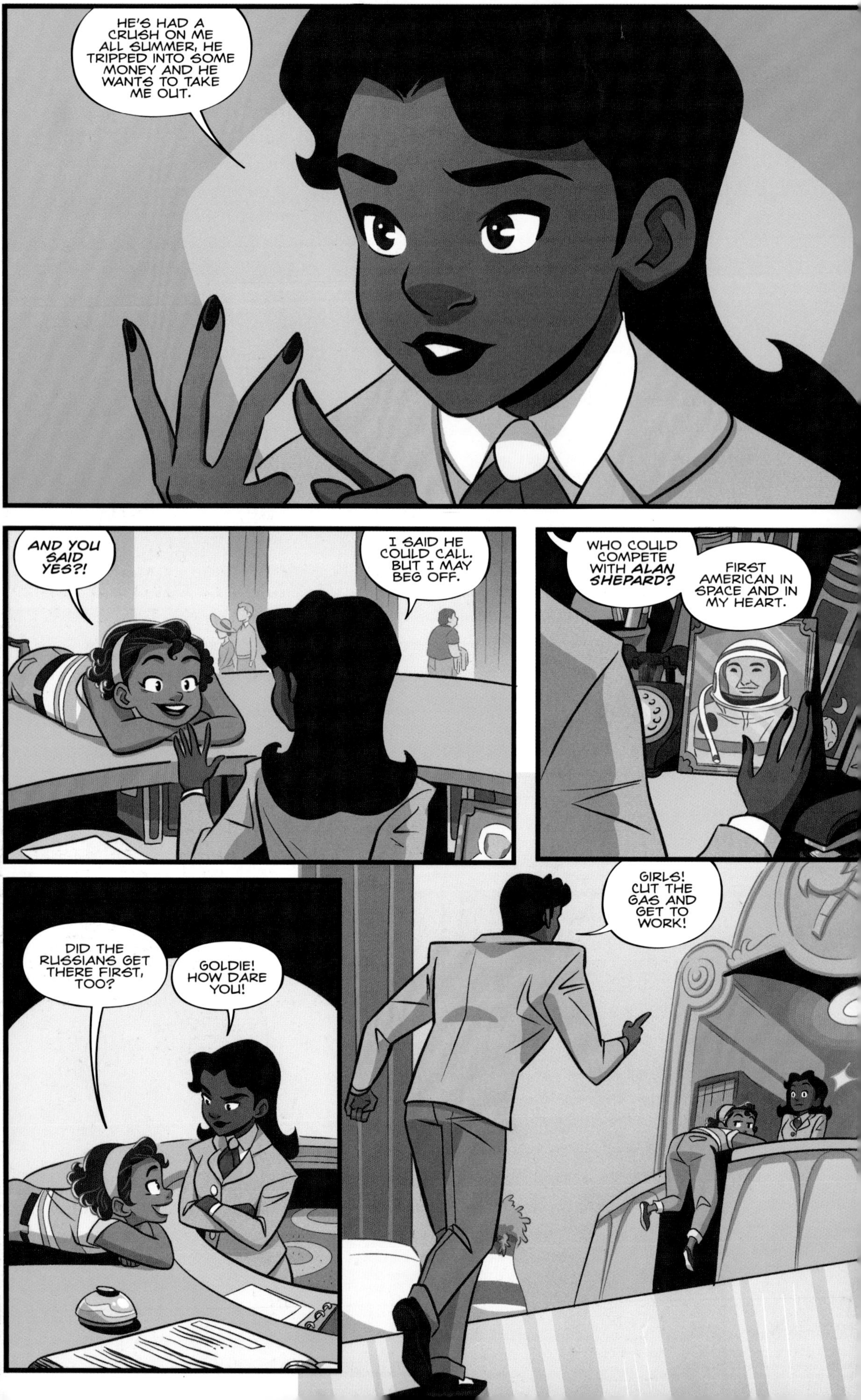
HE'S HAD A CRUSH ON ME ALL SUMMER, HE TRIPPED INTO SOME MONEY AND HE WANTS TO TAKE ME OUT.
AND YOU SAID YES?!
I SAID HE COULD CALL. BUT I MAY BEG OFF.
WHO COULD COMPETE WITH ALAN SHEPARD?
FIRST AMERICAN IN SPACE AND IN MY HEART.
DID THE RUSSIANS GET THERE FIRST, TOO?
GOLDIE! HOW DARE YOU!
GIRLS! CUT THE GAS AND GET TO WORK!

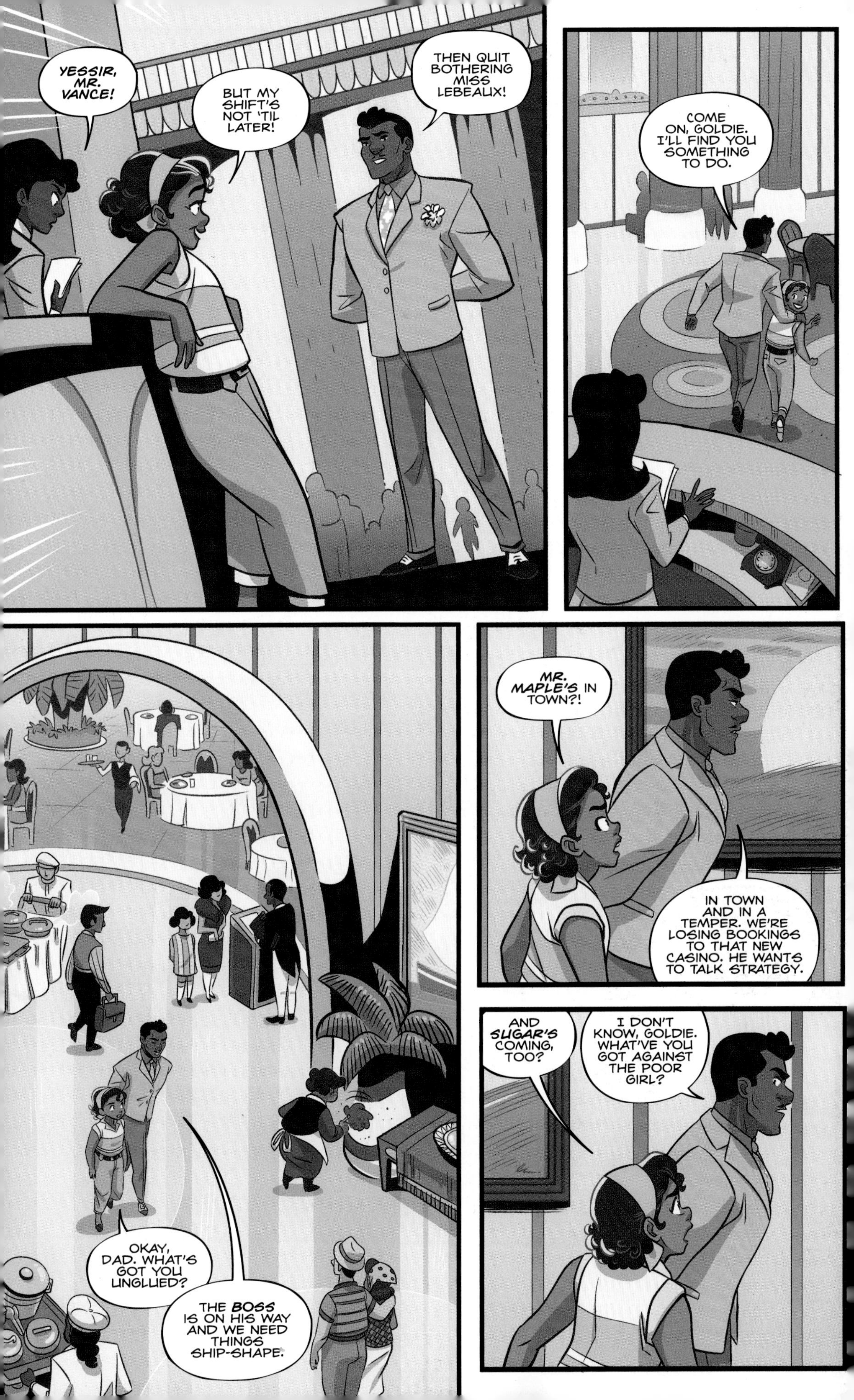
YESSIR, MR. VANCE!
BUT MY SHIFT'S NOT 'TIL LATER!
THEN QUIT BOTHERING MISS LEBEAUX!
COME ON, GOLDIE. I'LL FIND YOU SOMETHING TO DO.
OKAY, DAD. WHAT'S GOT YOU UNGLUED?
THE BOSS IS ON HIS WAY AND WE NEED THINGS SHIP-SHAPE.
MR. MAPLE'S IN TOWN?!
IN TOWN AND IN A TEMPER. WE'RE LOSING BOOKINGS TO THAT NEW CASINO. HE WANTS TO TALK STRATEGY.
AND SUGAR'S COMING, TOO?
I DON'T KNOW, GOLDIE. WHAT'VE YOU GOT AGAINST THE POOR GIRL?

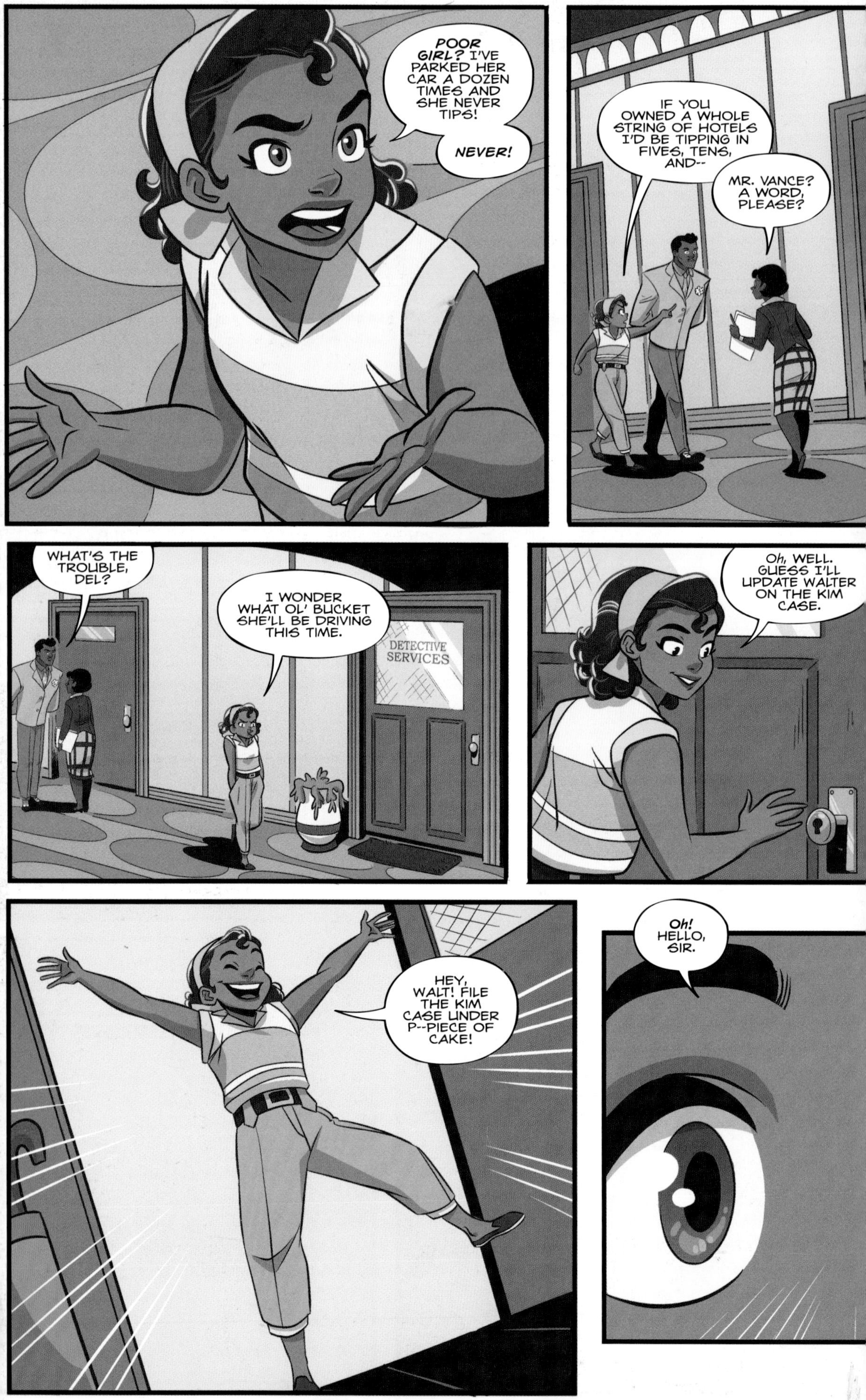
POOR GIRL? I'VE PARKED HER CAR A DOZEN TIMES AND SHE NEVER TIPS!
NEVER!
IF YOU OWNED A WHOLE STRING OF HOTELS I'D BE TIPPING IN FIVES, TENS, AND--
MR. VANCE? A WORD, PLEASE?
WHAT'S THE TROUBLE, DEL?
I WONDER WHAT OL' BUCKET SHE'LL BE DRIVING THIS TIME.
DETECTIVE SERVICES
Oh, WELL. GUESS I'LL UPDATE WALTER ON THE KIM CASE.
HEY, WALT! FILE THE KIM CASE UNDER P--PIECE OF CAKE!
Oh! HELLO, SIR.

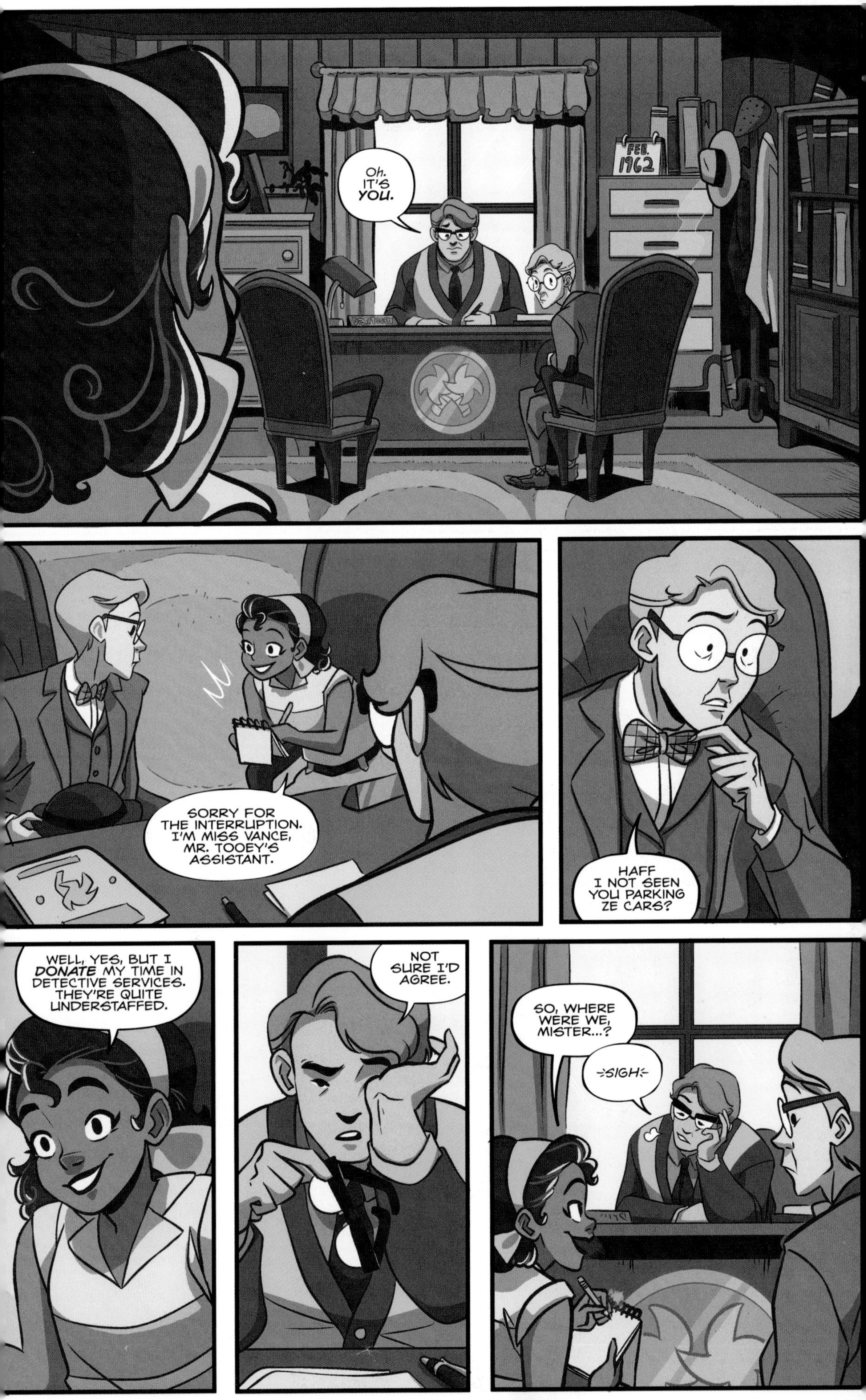
FEB.
1962
Oh. IT'S YOU.
SORRY FOR THE INTERRUPTION. I'M MISS VANCE, MR. TOOEY'S ASSISTANT.
HAFF I NOT SEEN YOU PARKING ZE CARS?
WELL, YES, BUT I DONATE MY TIME IN DETECTIVE SERVICES. THEY'RE QUITE UNDERSTAFFED.
NOT SURE I'D AGREE.
SO, WHERE WERE WE, MISTER...?
SIGH

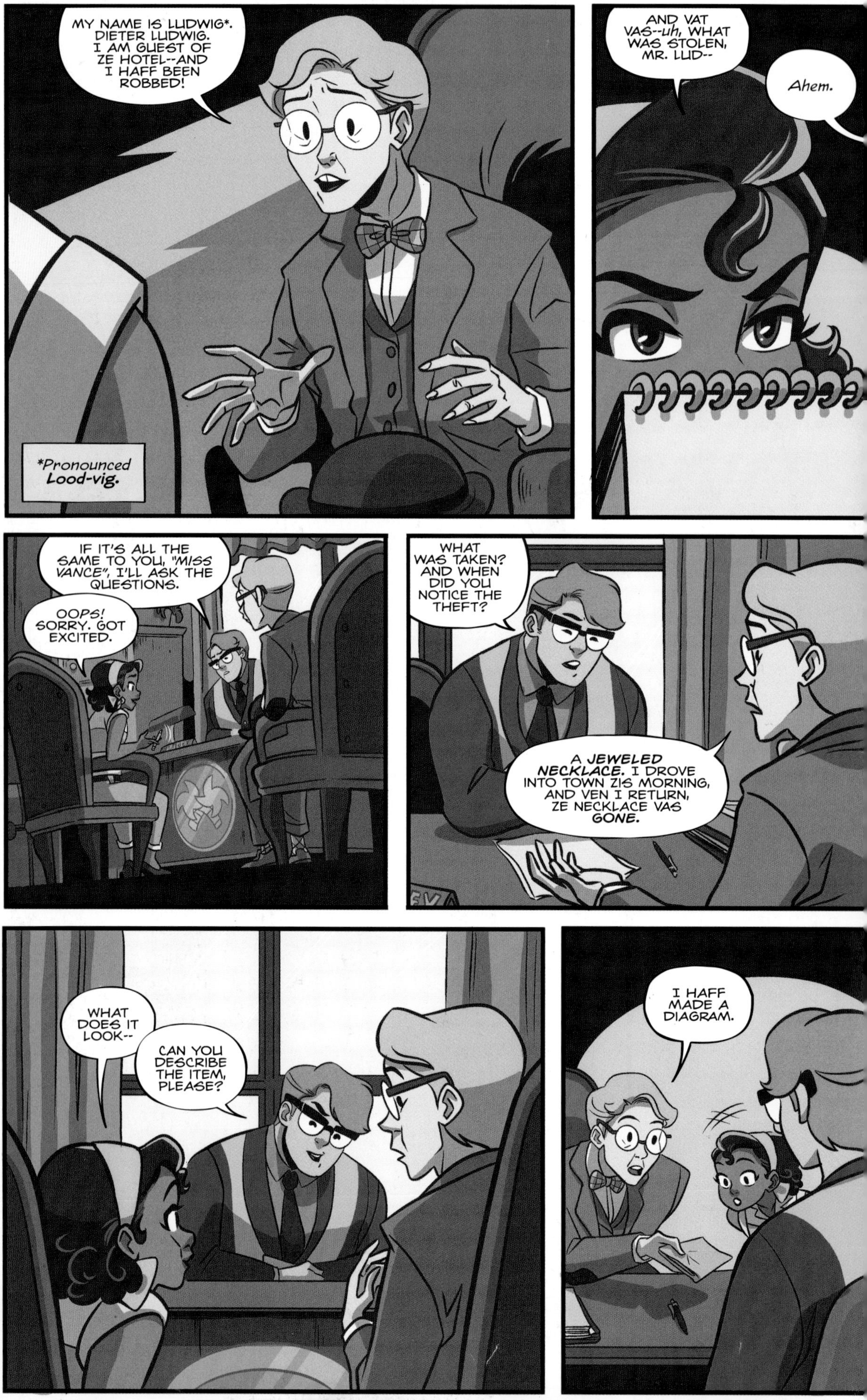
MY NAME IS LUDWIG*. DIETER LUDWIG. I AM GUEST OF ZE HOTEL--AND I HAFF BEEN ROBBED!
*Pronounced Lood-vig.
AND VAT VAS--uh, WHAT WAS STOLEN, MR. LUD--
Ahem.
IF IT'S ALL THE SAME TO YOU, "MISS VANCE", I'LL ASK THE QUESTIONS.
OOPS! SORRY. GOT EXCITED.
WHAT WAS TAKEN? AND WHEN DID YOU NOTICE THE THEFT?
A JEWELED NECKLACE. I DROVE INTO TOWN ZIS MORNING, AND VEN I RETURN, ZE NECKLACE VAS GONE.
WHAT DOES IT LOOK--
CAN YOU DESCRIBE THE ITEM, PLEASE?
I HAFF MADE A DIAGRAM.

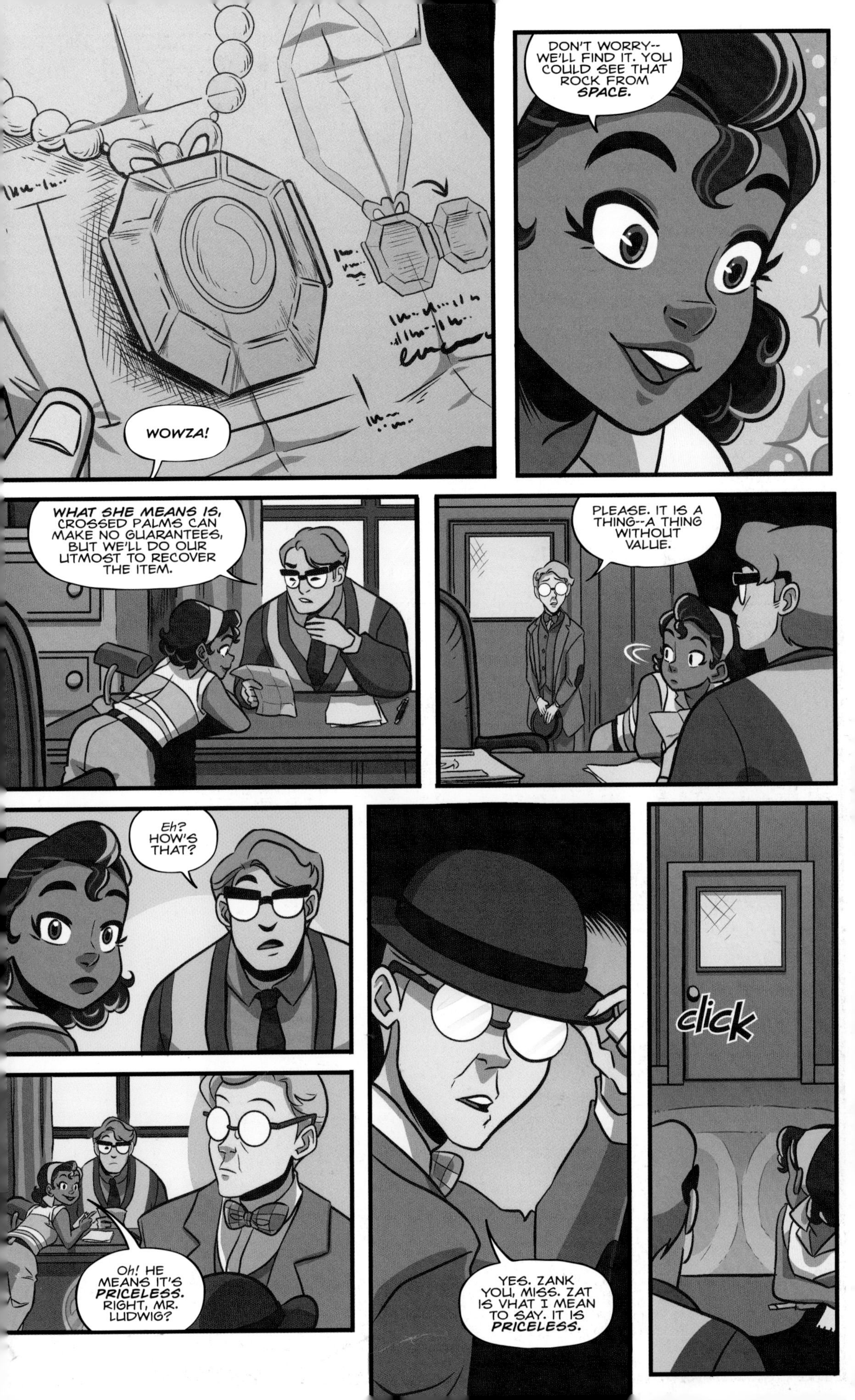
WOWZA!
DON'T WORRY-- WE'LL FIND IT. YOU COULD SEE THAT ROCK FROM SPACE.
WHAT SHE MEANS IS, CROSSED PALMS CAN MAKE NO GUARANTEES, BUT WE'LL DO OUR UTMOST TO RECOVER THE ITEM.
PLEASE. IT IS A THING--A THING WITHOUT VALUE.
Eh? HOW'S THAT?
Oh! HE MEANS IT'S PRICELESS. RIGHT, MR. LUDWIG?
YES. ZANK YOU, MISS. ZAT IS VHAT I MEAN TO SAY. IT IS PRICELESS.
click

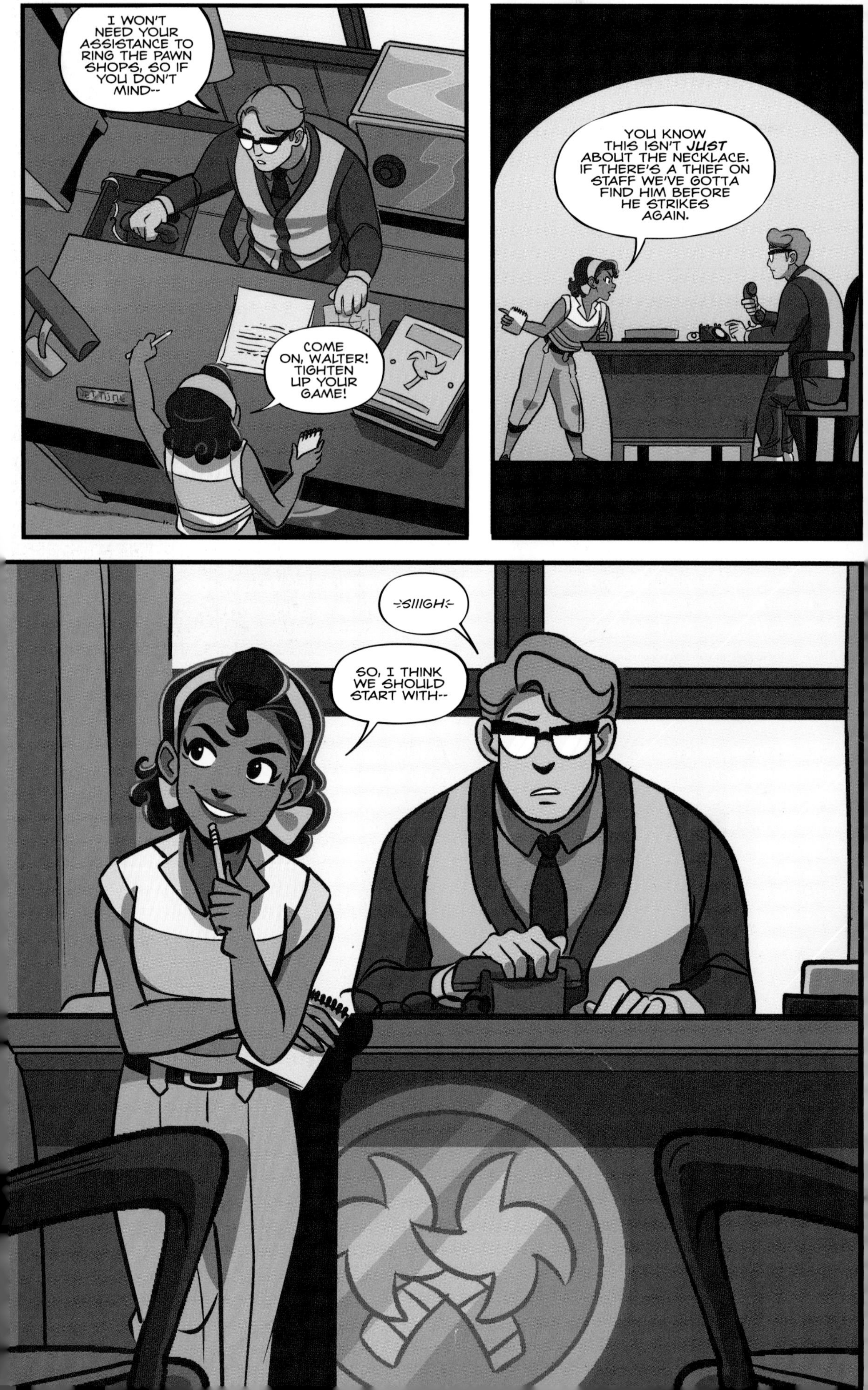
I WON'T NEED YOUR ASSISTANCE TO RING THE PAWN SHOPS, SO IF YOU DON'T MIND--
COME ON, WALTER! TIGHTEN UP YOUR GAME!
YOU KNOW THIS ISN'T JUST ABOUT THE NECKLACE. IF THERE'S A THIEF ON STAFF WE'VE GOTTA FIND HIM BEFORE HE STRIKES AGAIN.
-SIIIGH-
SO, I THINK WE SHOULD START WITH--

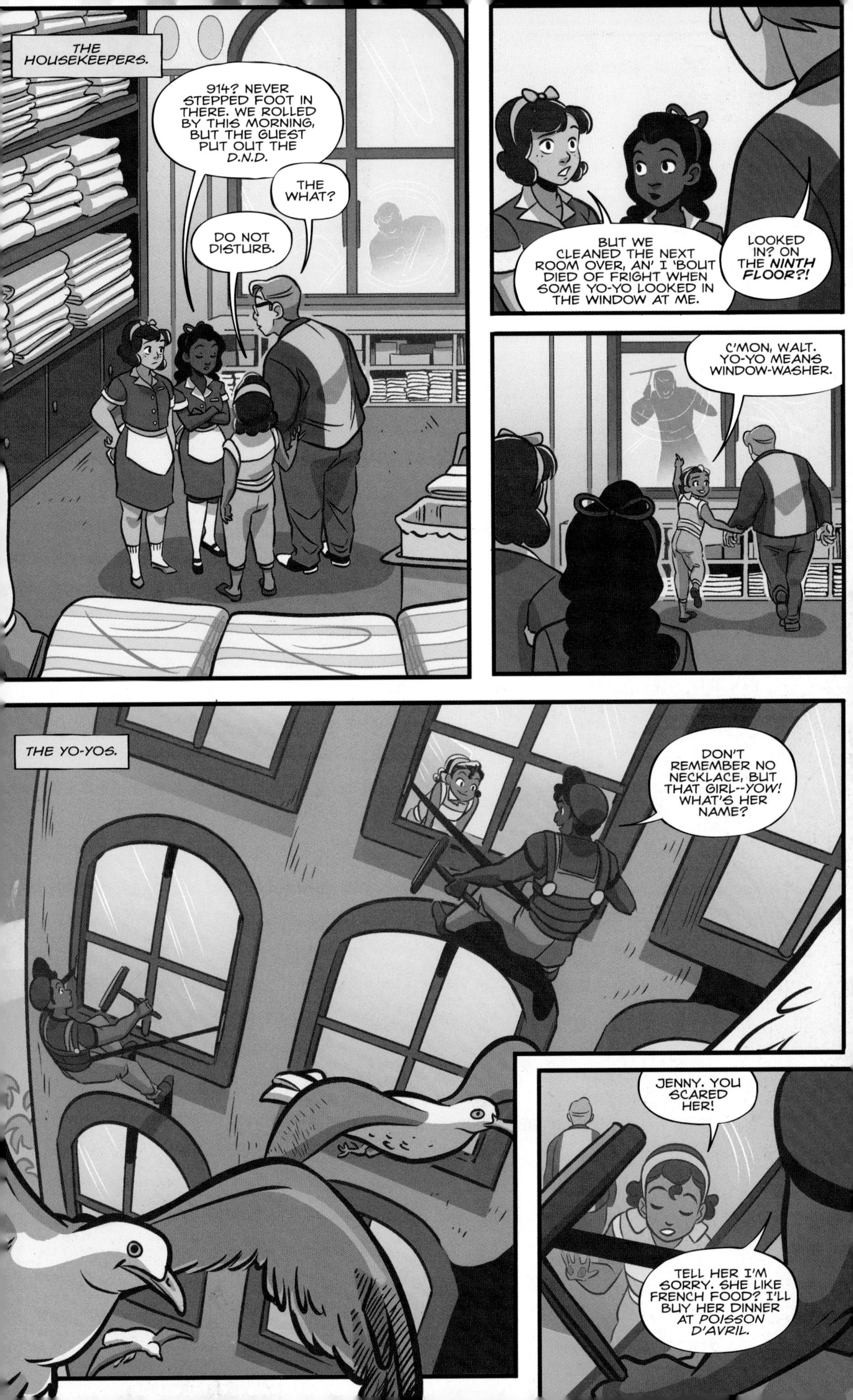
THE HOUSEKEEPERS.
914? NEVER STEPPED FOOT IN THERE. WE ROLLED BY THIS MORNING, BUT THE GUEST PUT OUT THE D.N.D.
THE WHAT?
DO NOT DISTURB.
BUT WE CLEANED THE NEXT ROOM OVER, AN' I 'BOUT DIED OF FRIGHT WHEN SOME YO-YO LOOKED IN THE WINDOW AT ME.
LOOKED IN? ON THE NINTH FLOOR?!
C'MON, WALT. YO-YO MEANS WINDOW-WASHER.
THE YO-YOS.
DON'T REMEMBER NO NECKLACE, BUT THAT GIRL--YOW! WHAT'S HER NAME?
JENNY. YOU SCARED HER!
TELL HER I'M SORRY. SHE LIKE FRENCH FOOD? I'LL BUY HER DINNER AT POISSON D'AVRIL.

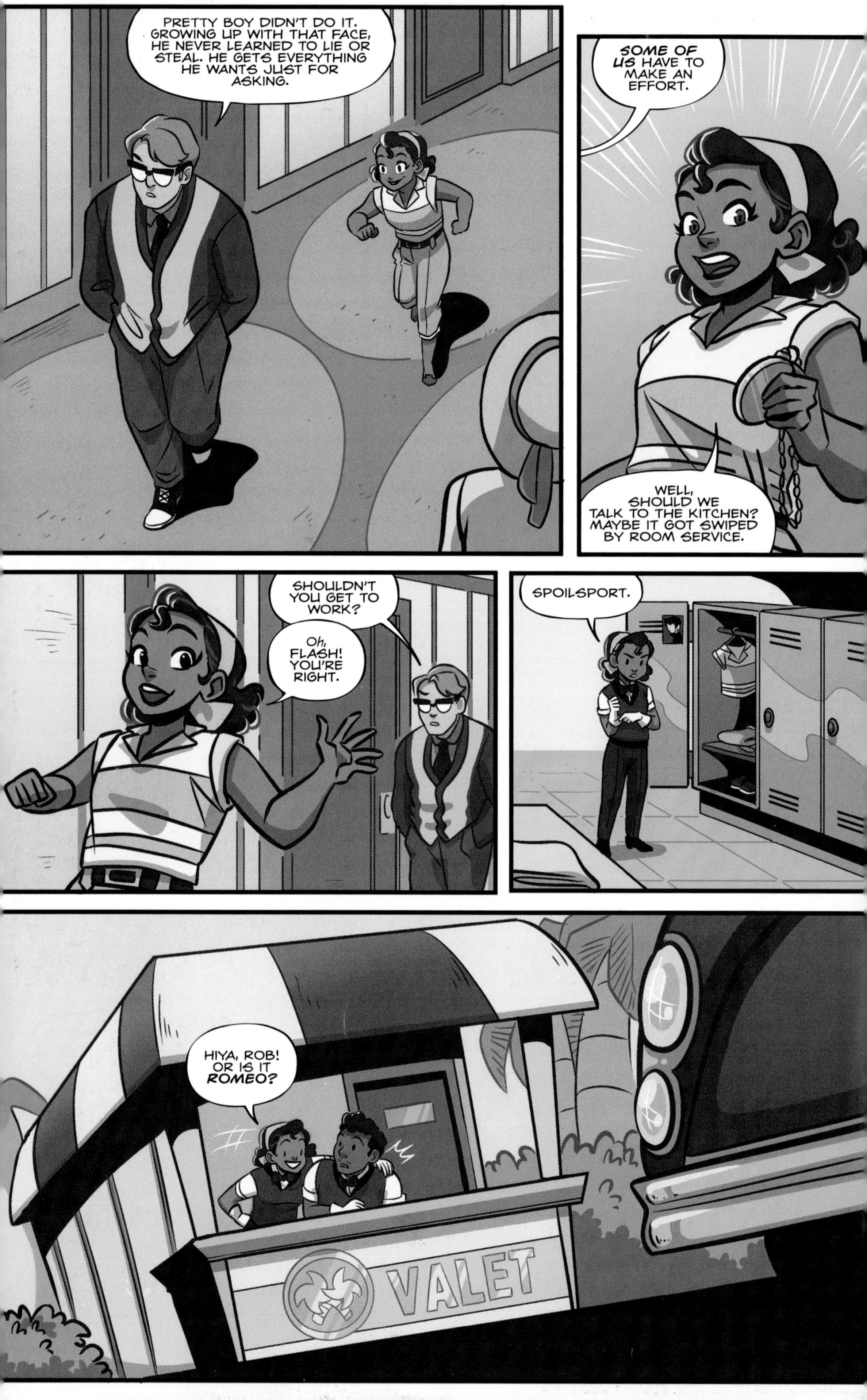
PRETTY BOY DIDN'T DO IT. GROWING UP WITH THAT FACE, HE NEVER LEARNED TO LIE OR STEAL. HE GETS EVERYTHING HE WANTS JUST FOR ASKING.
SOME OF US HAVE TO MAKE AN EFFORT.
WELL, SHOULD WE TALK TO THE KITCHEN? MAYBE IT GOT SWIPED BY ROOM SERVICE.
SHOULDN'T YOU GET TO WORK?
Oh, FLASH! YOU'RE RIGHT.
SPOILSPORT.
HIYA, ROB! OR IS IT ROMEO?
VALET

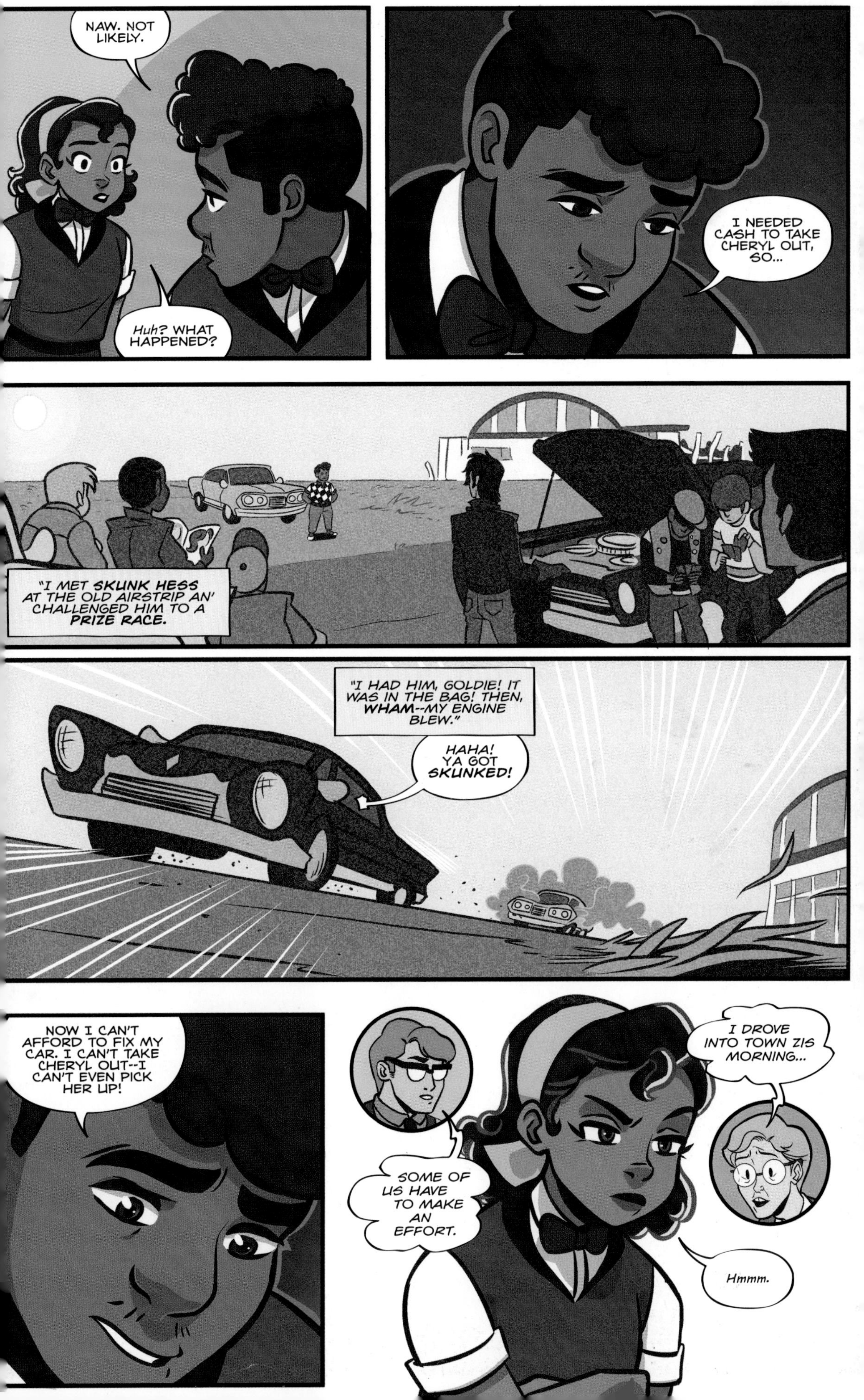
NAW. NOT LIKELY.
Huh? WHAT HAPPENED?
I NEEDED CASH TO TAKE CHERYL OUT, SO...
"I MET SKUNK HESS AT THE OLD AIRSTRIP AN' CHALLENGED HIM TO A PRIZE RACE.
"I HAD HIM, GOLDIE! IT WAS IN THE BAG! THEN, WHAM--MY ENGINE BLEW."
HAHA! YA GOT SKUNKED!
NOW I CAN'T AFFORD TO FIX MY CAR. I CAN'T TAKE CHERYL OUT--I CAN'T EVEN PICK HER UP!
SOME OF US HAVE TO MAKE AN EFFORT.
I DROVE INTO TOWN ZIS MORNING...
Hmmm.

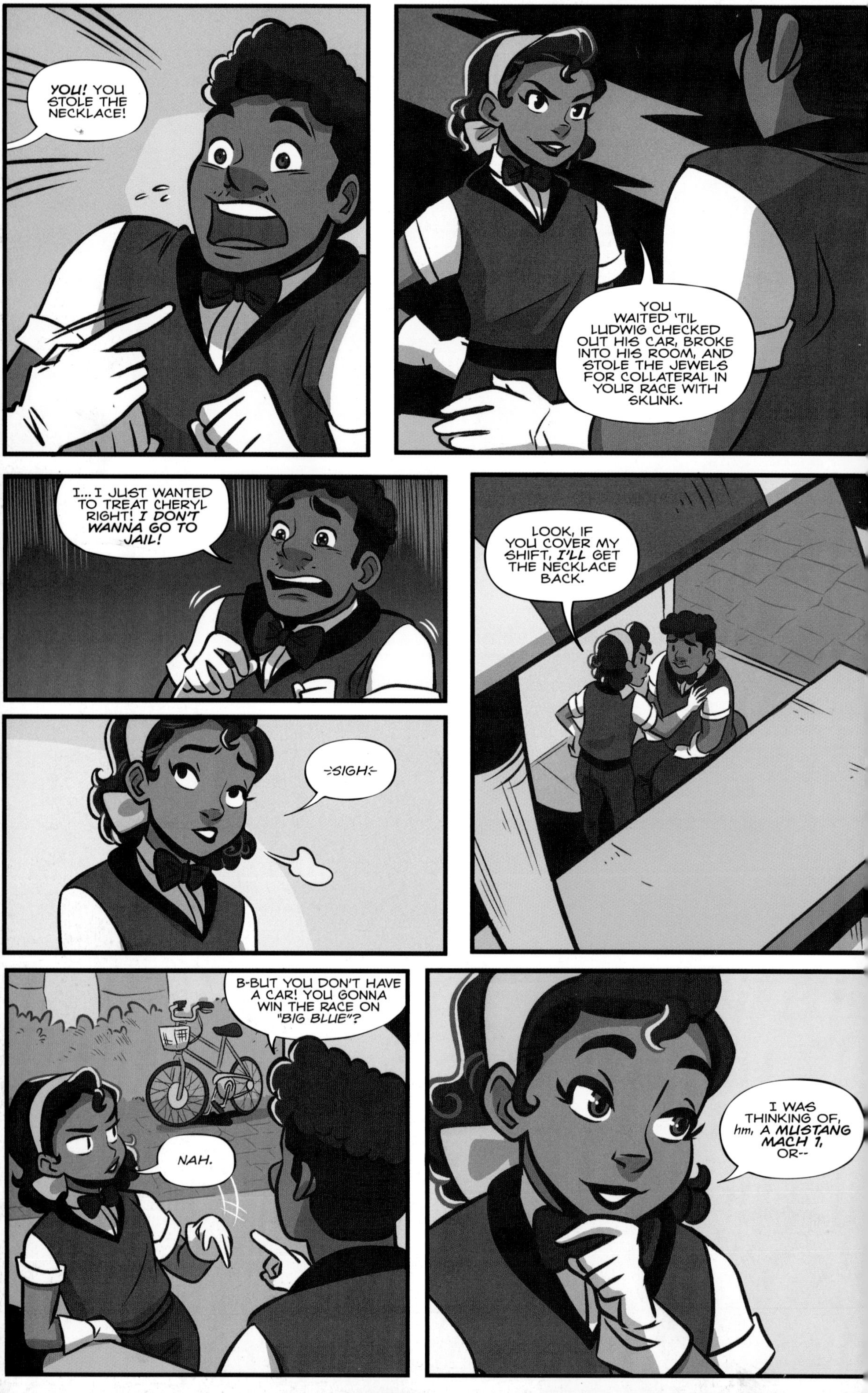
YOU! YOU STOLE THE NECKLACE!
YOU WAITED 'TIL LUDWIG CHECKED OUT HIS CAR, BROKE INTO HIS ROOM, AND STOLE THE JEWELS FOR COLLATERAL IN YOUR RACE WITH SKUNK.
I... I JUST WANTED TO TREAT CHERYL RIGHT! I DON'T WANNA GO TO JAIL!
-SIGH-
LOOK, IF YOU COVER MY SHIFT, I'LL GET THE NECKLACE BACK.
B-BUT YOU DON'T HAVE A CAR! YOU GONNA WIN THE RACE ON "BIG BLUE"?
NAH.
I WAS THINKING OF, hm, A MUSTANG MACH 1, OR--

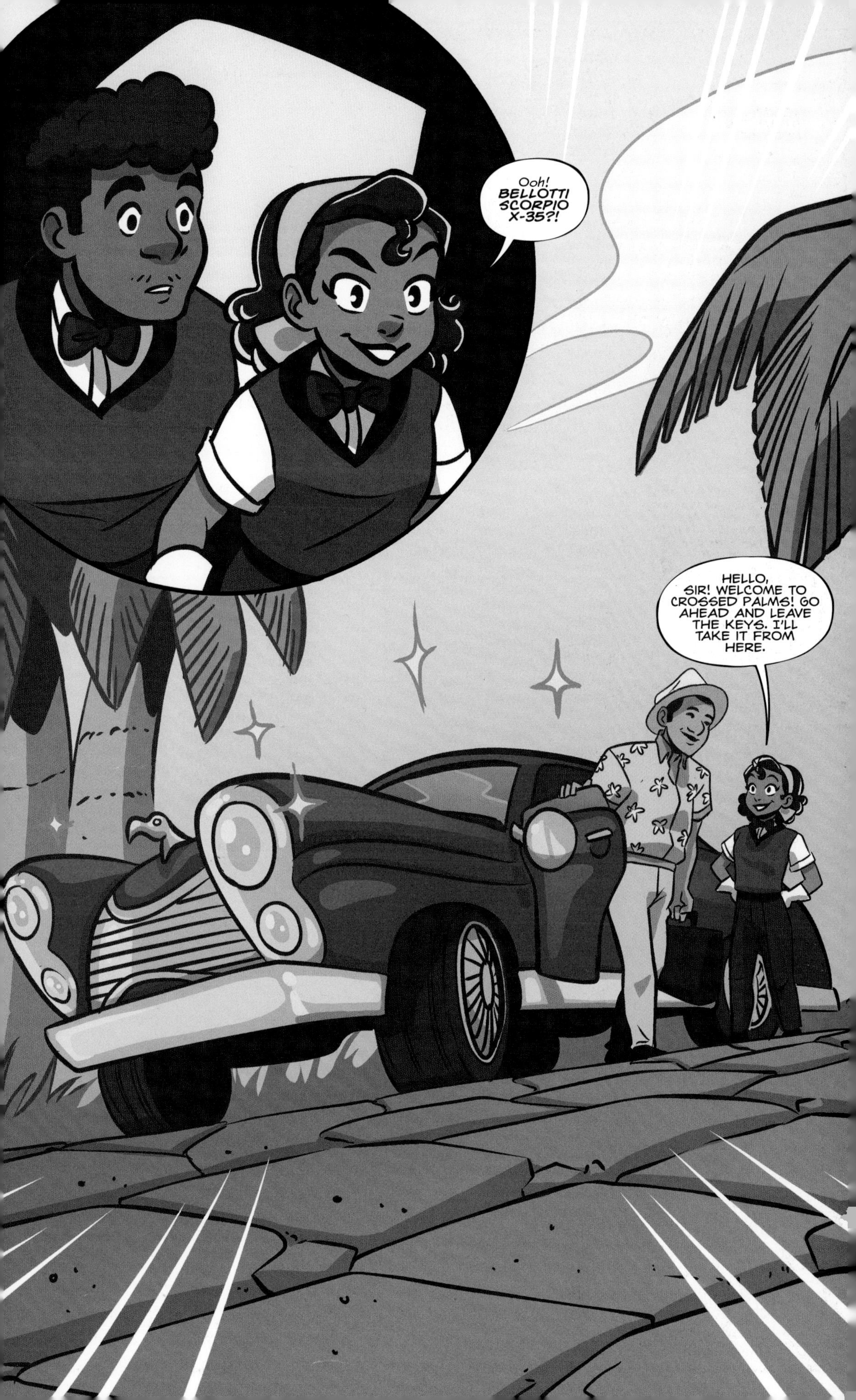
Ooh! BELLOTTI SCORPIO X-35?!
HELLO, SIR! WELCOME TO CROSSED PALMS! GO AHEAD AND LEAVE THE KEYS. I'LL TAKE IT FROM HERE.

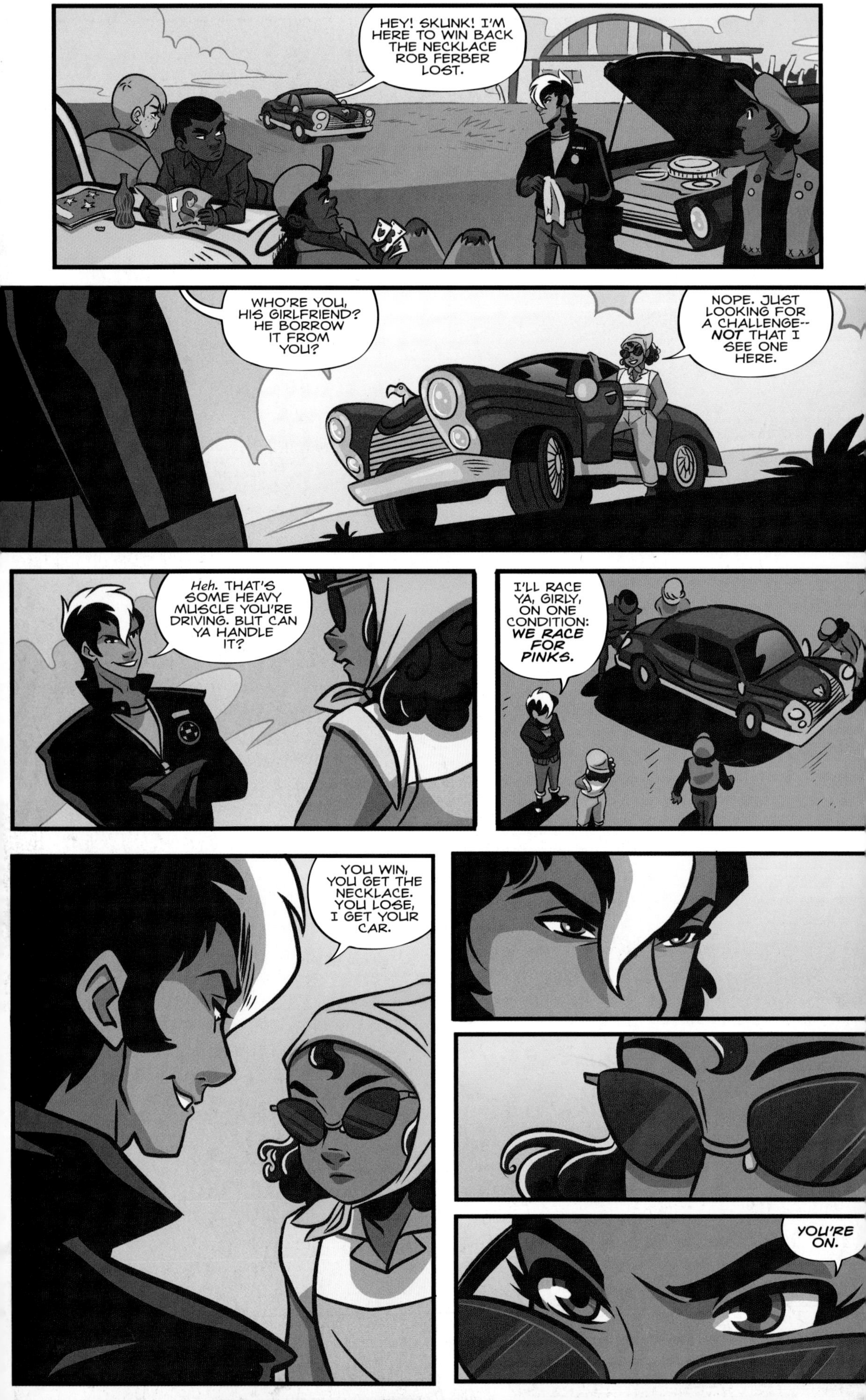
HEY! SKUNK! I'M HERE TO WIN BACK THE NECKLACE ROB FERBER LOST.
WHO'RE YOU, HIS GIRLFRIEND? HE BORROW IT FROM YOU?
NOPE. JUST LOOKING FOR A CHALLENGE-- NOT THAT I SEE ONE HERE.
Heh. THAT'S SOME HEAVY MUSCLE YOU'RE DRIVING. BUT CAN YA HANDLE IT?
I'LL RACE YA, GIRLY, ON ONE CONDITION: WE RACE FOR PINKS.
YOU WIN, YOU GET THE NECKLACE. YOU LOSE, I GET YOUR CAR.
YOU'RE ON.

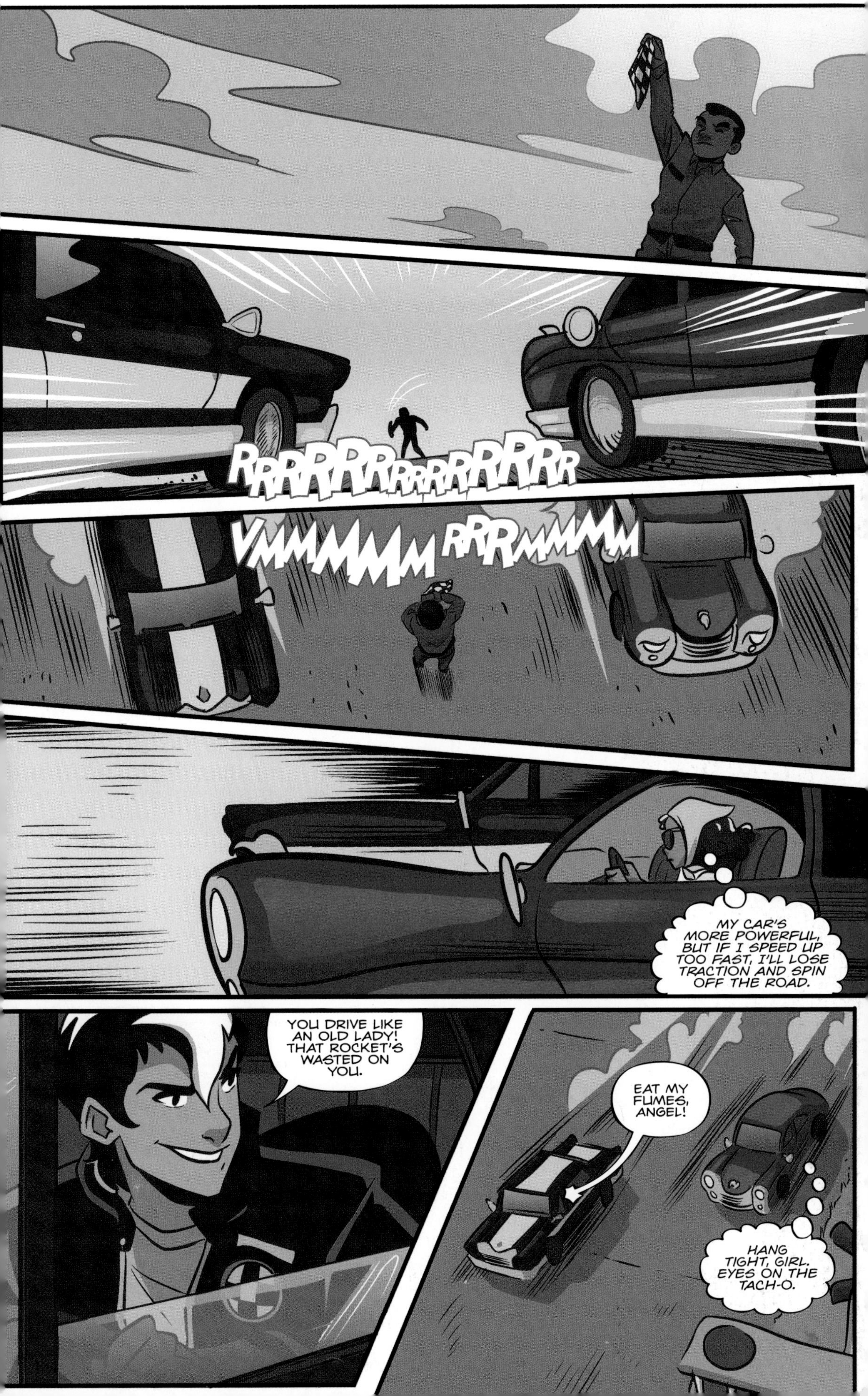
RRRRRRRRRRRRRRRR
VMMMMMM RRRMMMMM
MY CAR'S MORE POWERFUL, BUT IF I SPEED UP TOO FAST, I'LL LOSE TRACTION AND SPIN OFF THE ROAD.
YOU DRIVE LIKE AN OLD LADY! THAT ROCKET'S WASTED ON YOU.
EAT MY FUMES, ANGEL!
HANG TIGHT, GIRL. EYES ON THE TACH-O.

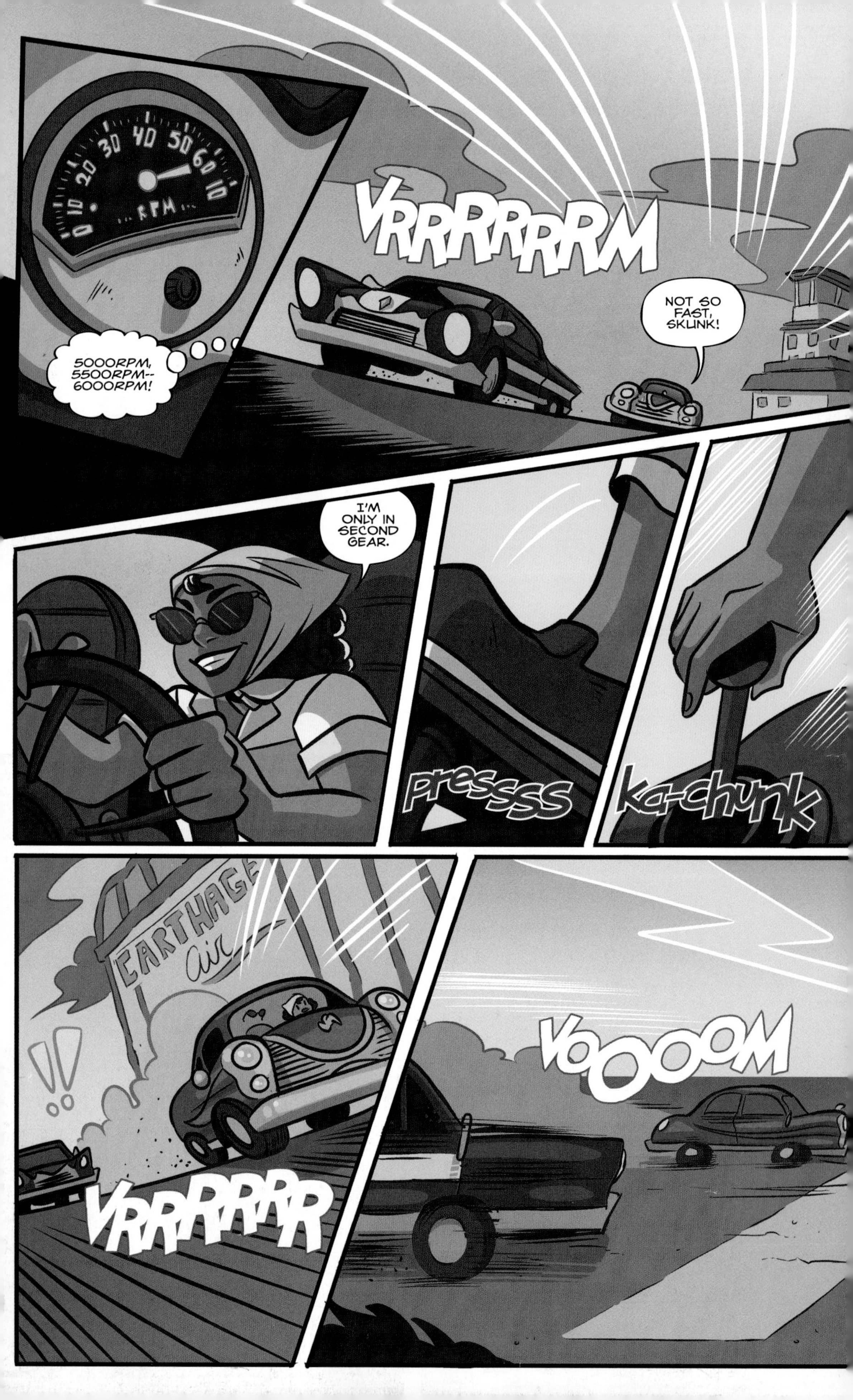

VRRRRRRRM
5000RPM, 5500RPM-- 6000RPM!
NOT SO FAST, SKLUNK!
I'M ONLY IN SECOND GEAR.
presssss
ka-chunk
CARTHAGE Air
!!
VRRRRRRR
VOOOOM

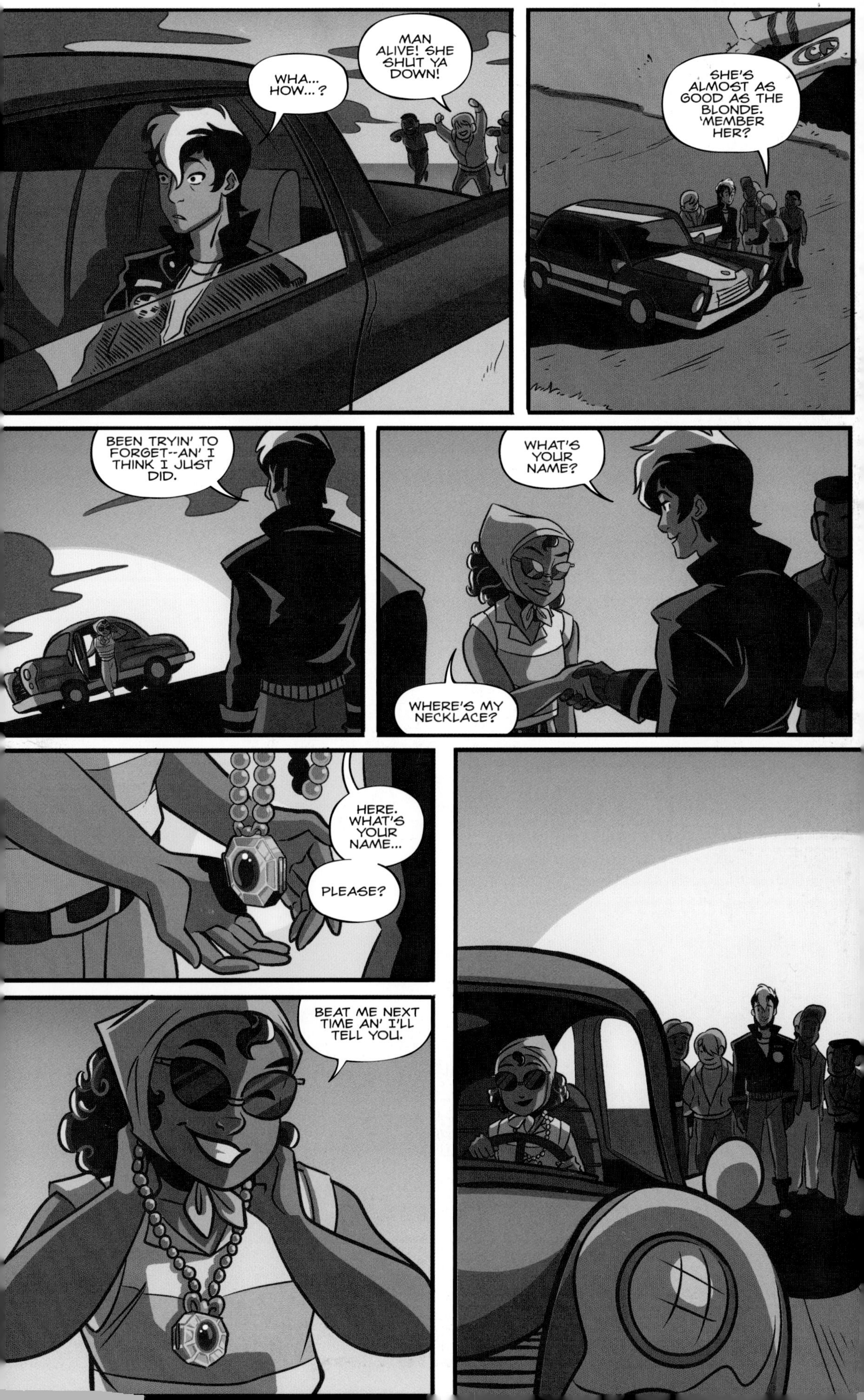
WHA... HOW...?
MAN ALIVE! SHE SHUT YA DOWN!
SHE'S ALMOST AS GOOD AS THE BLONDE. 'MEMBER HER?
BEEN TRYIN' TO FORGET--AN' I THINK I JUST DID.
WHAT'S YOUR NAME?
WHERE'S MY NECKLACE?
HERE. WHAT'S YOUR NAME...
PLEASE?
BEAT ME NEXT TIME AN' I'LL TELL YOU.

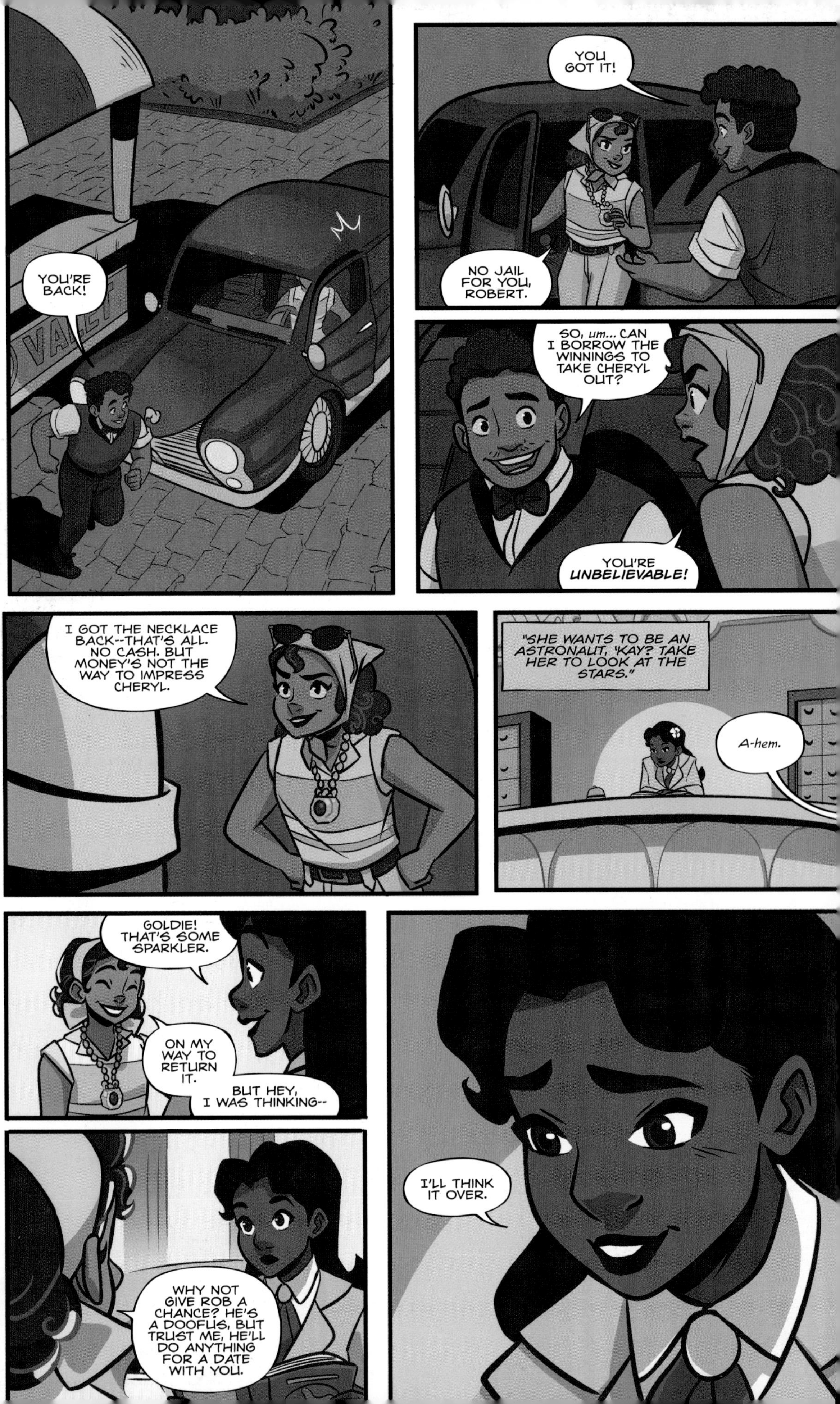
YOU'RE BACK!
YOU GOT IT!
NO JAIL FOR YOU, ROBERT.
SO, *um*... CAN I BORROW THE WINNINGS TO TAKE CHERYL OUT?
YOU'RE ***UNBELIEVABLE!***
I GOT THE NECKLACE BACK--THAT'S ALL. NO CASH. BUT MONEY'S NOT THE WAY TO IMPRESS CHERYL.
"SHE WANTS TO BE AN ASTRONAUT, 'KAY? TAKE HER TO LOOK AT THE STARS."
A-hem.
GOLDIE! THAT'S SOME SPARKLER.
ON MY WAY TO RETURN IT.
BUT HEY, I WAS THINKING--
WHY NOT GIVE ROB A CHANCE? HE'S A DOOFUS, BUT TRUST ME, HE'LL DO ANYTHING FOR A DATE WITH YOU.
I'LL THINK IT OVER.

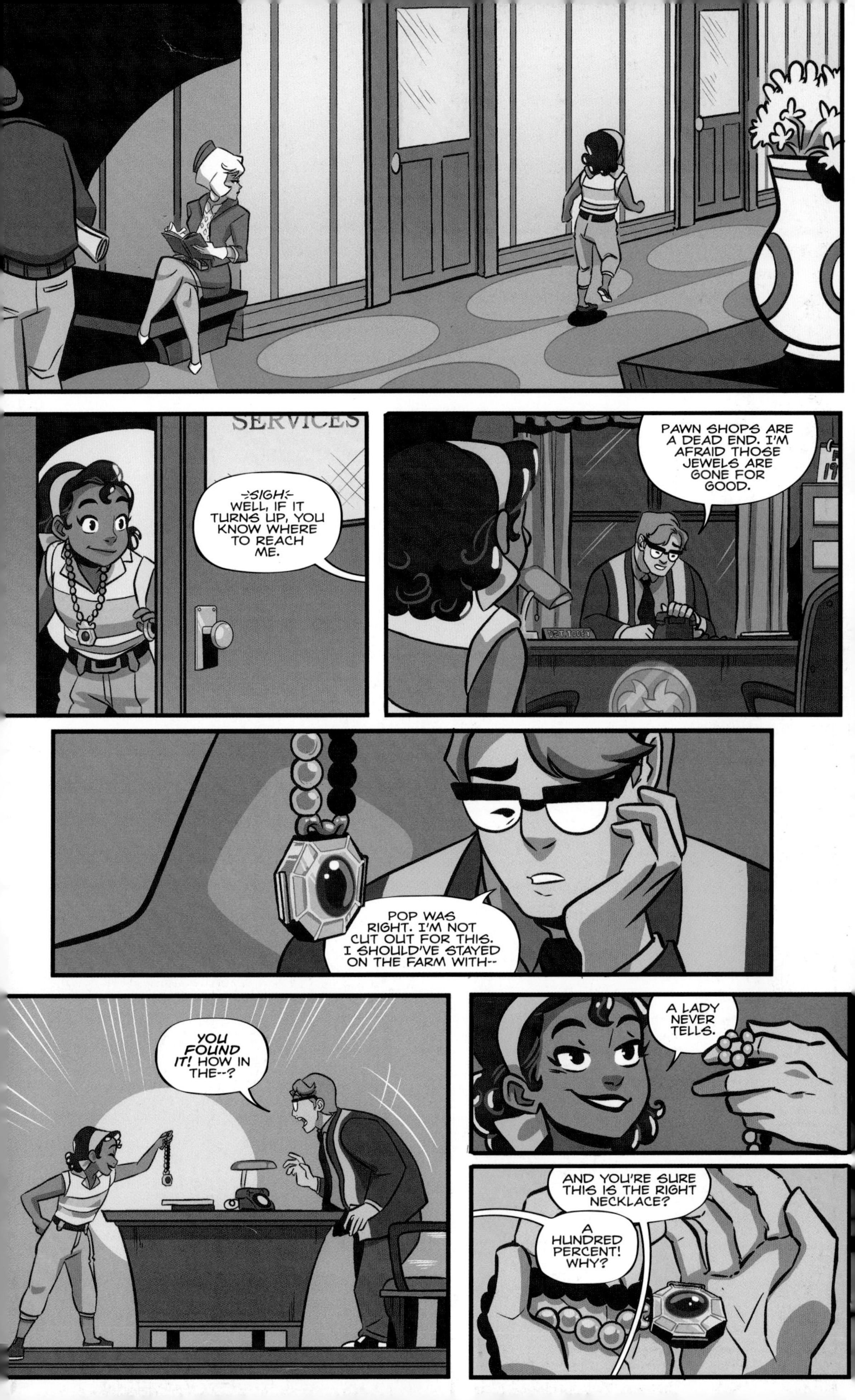
SERVICES
-SIGH- WELL, IF IT TURNS UP, YOU KNOW WHERE TO REACH ME.
PAWN SHOPS ARE A DEAD END. I'M AFRAID THOSE JEWELS ARE GONE FOR GOOD.
POP WAS RIGHT. I'M NOT CUT OUT FOR THIS. I SHOULD'VE STAYED ON THE FARM WITH--
YOU FOUND IT! HOW IN THE--?
A LADY NEVER TELLS.
AND YOU'RE SURE THIS IS THE RIGHT NECKLACE?
A HUNDRED PERCENT! WHY?

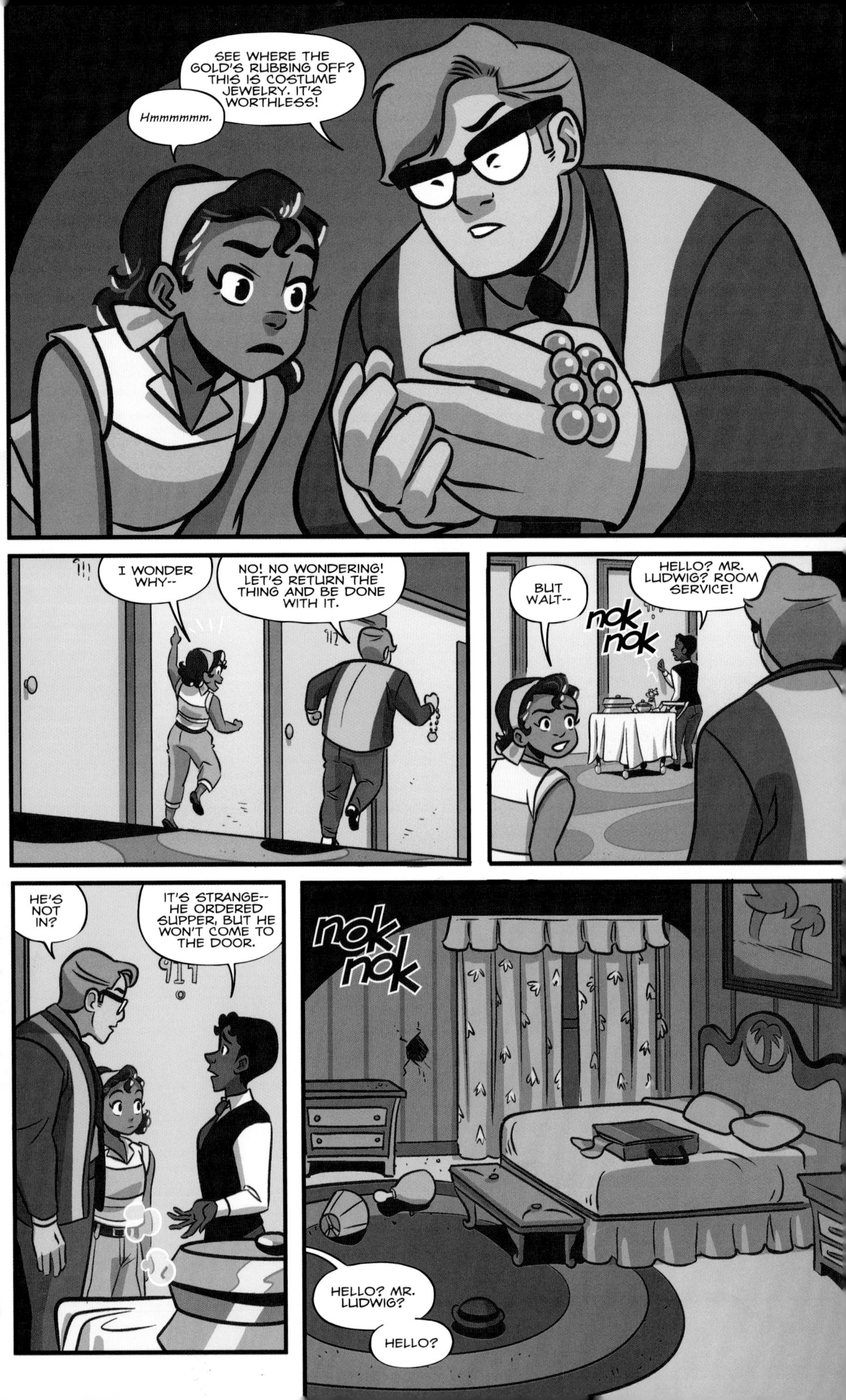
SEE WHERE THE GOLD'S RUBBING OFF? THIS IS COSTUME JEWELRY. IT'S WORTHLESS!
Hmmmmmm.
I WONDER WHY--
NO! NO WONDERING! LET'S RETURN THE THING AND BE DONE WITH IT.
BUT WALT--
HELLO? MR. LUDWIG? ROOM SERVICE!
nok nok
HE'S NOT IN?
IT'S STRANGE-- HE ORDERED SUPPER, BUT HE WON'T COME TO THE DOOR.
nok nok
HELLO? MR. LUDWIG?
HELLO?

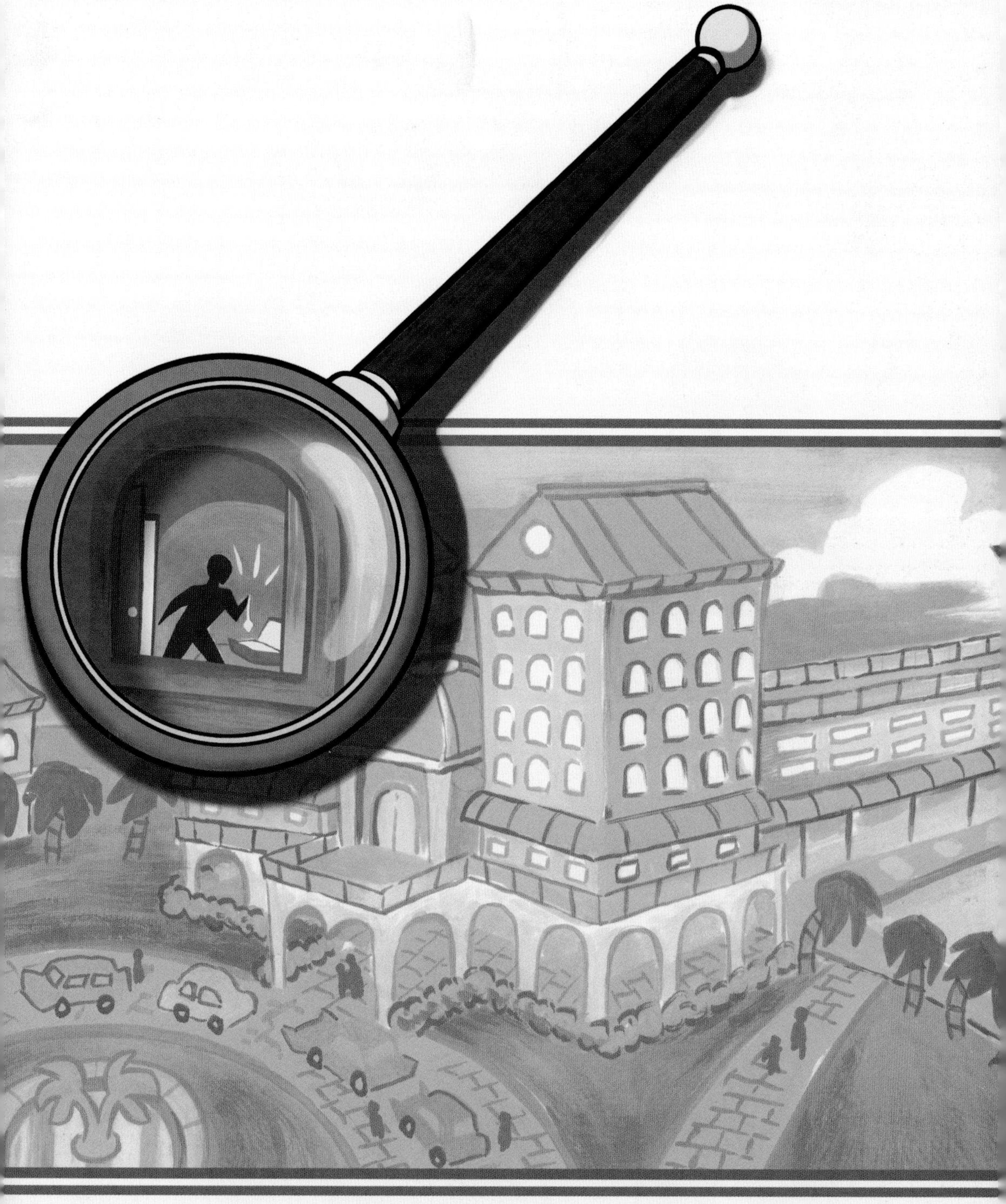

chapter TWO

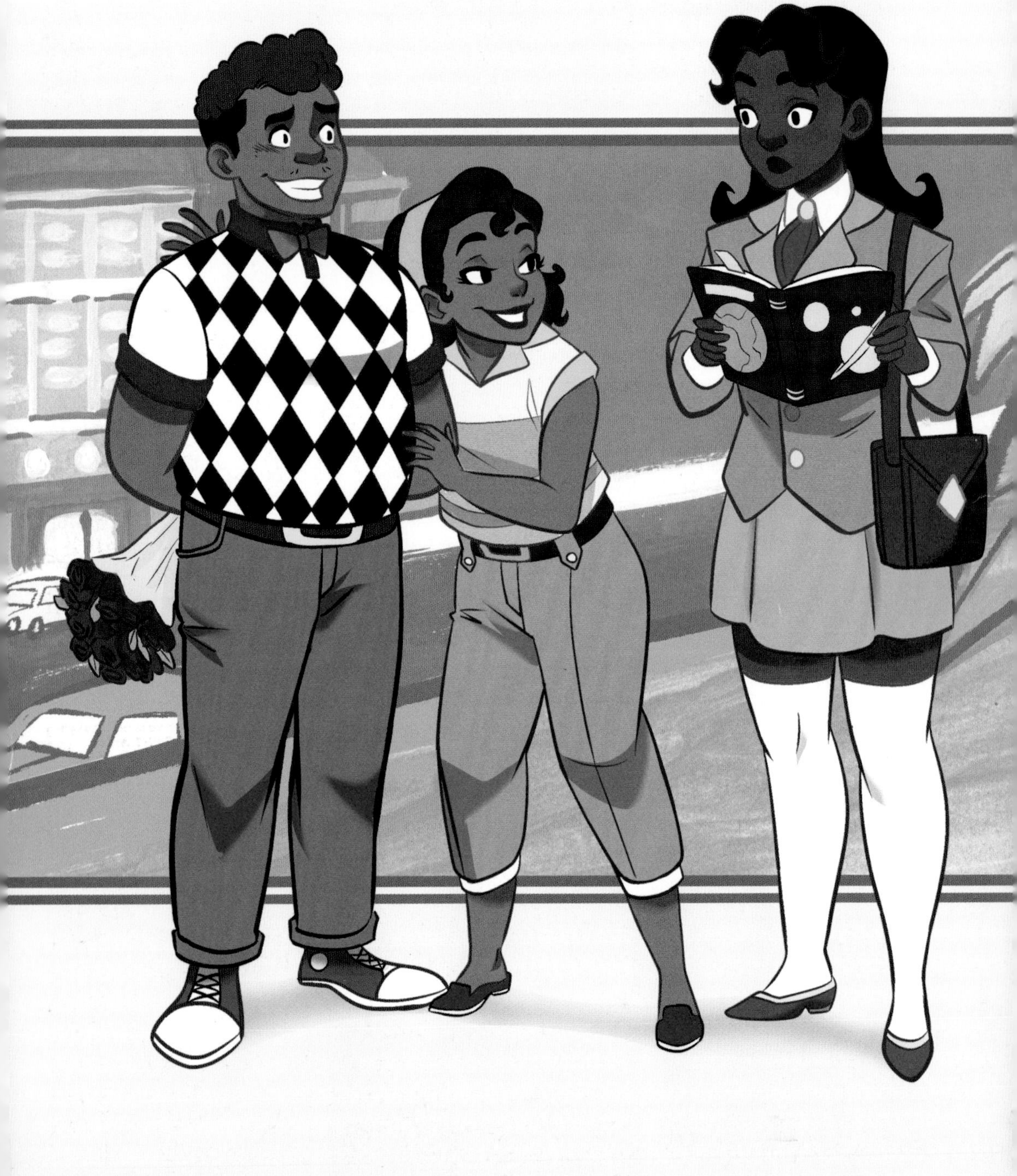

issue two cover by **Brittney Williams**

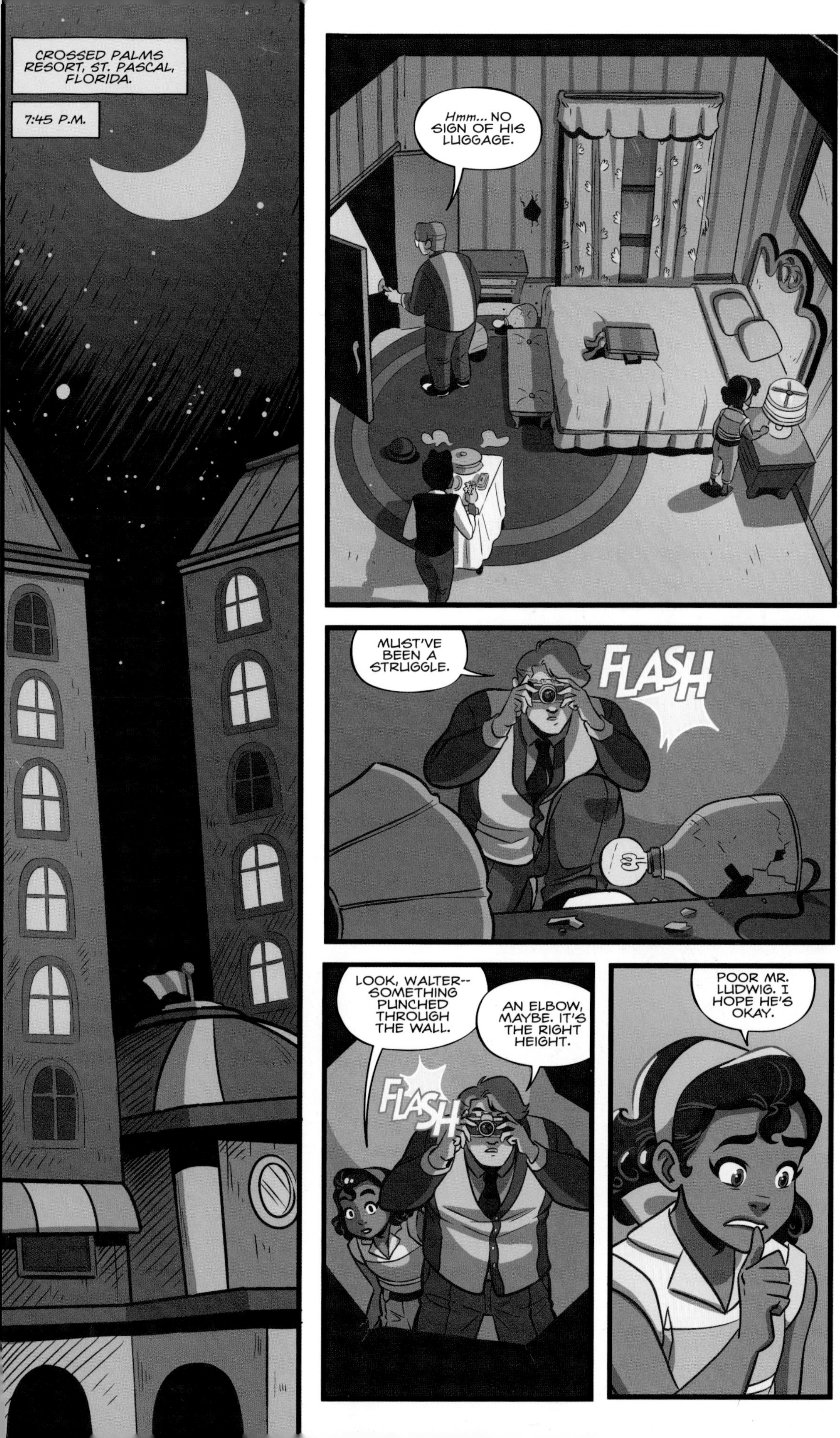
CROSSED PALMS RESORT, ST. PASCAL, FLORIDA.
7:45 P.M.
Hmm... NO SIGN OF HIS LUGGAGE.
MUST'VE BEEN A STRUGGLE.
FLASH
LOOK, WALTER-- SOMETHING PUNCHED THROUGH THE WALL.
AN ELBOW, MAYBE. IT'S THE RIGHT HEIGHT.
FLASH
POOR MR. LUDWIG. I HOPE HE'S OKAY.

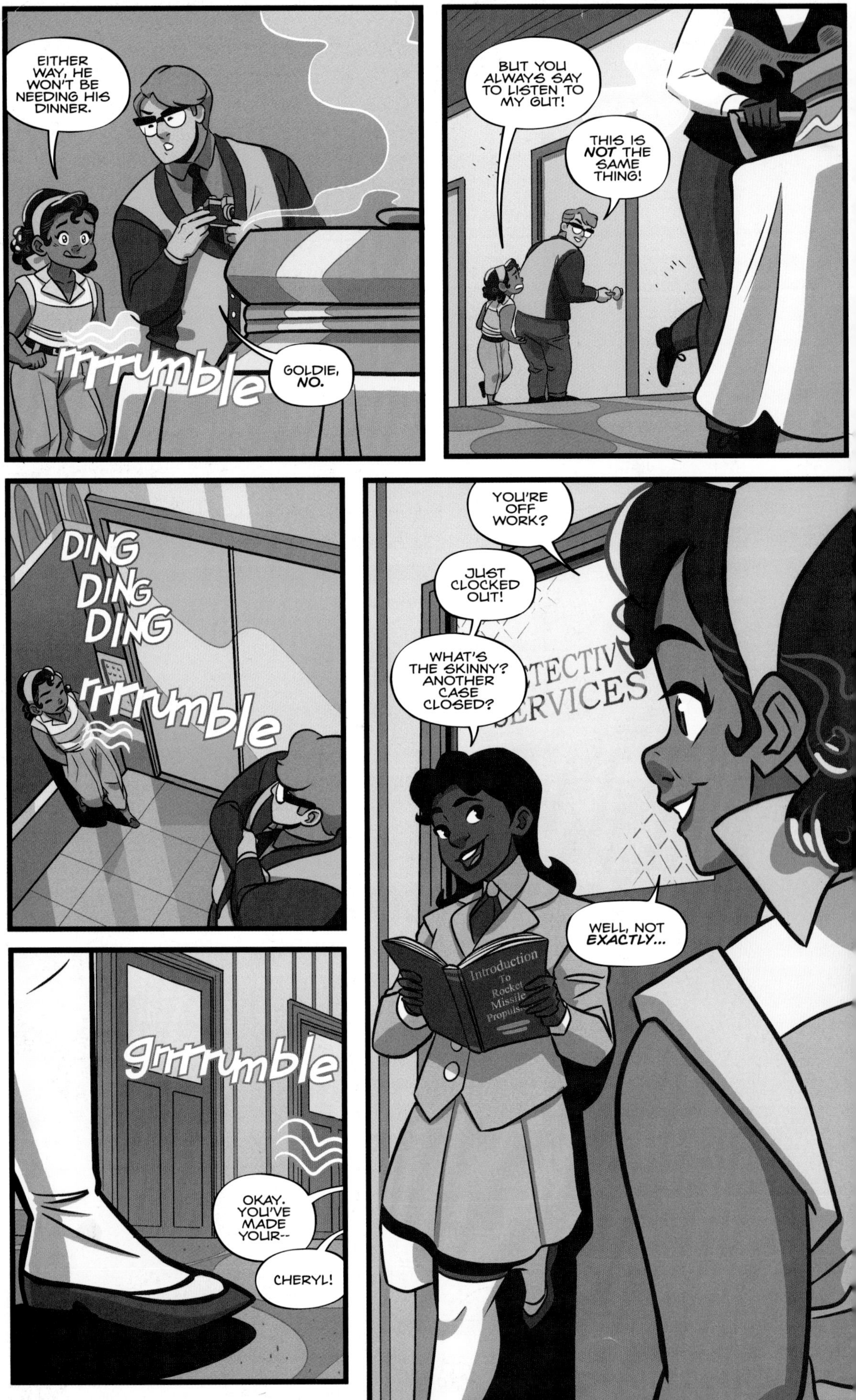
EITHER WAY, HE WON'T BE NEEDING HIS DINNER.
rrrrumble
GOLDIE, NO.
BUT YOU ALWAYS SAY TO LISTEN TO MY GUT!
THIS IS NOT THE SAME THING!
DING DING DING
rrrrumble
grrrrumble
OKAY. YOU'VE MADE YOUR--
CHERYL!
YOU'RE OFF WORK?
JUST CLOCKED OUT!
WHAT'S THE SKINNY? ANOTHER CASE CLOSED?
WELL, NOT EXACTLY...
ECTECTIV
SERVICES
Introduction To Rocket Missile Propuls

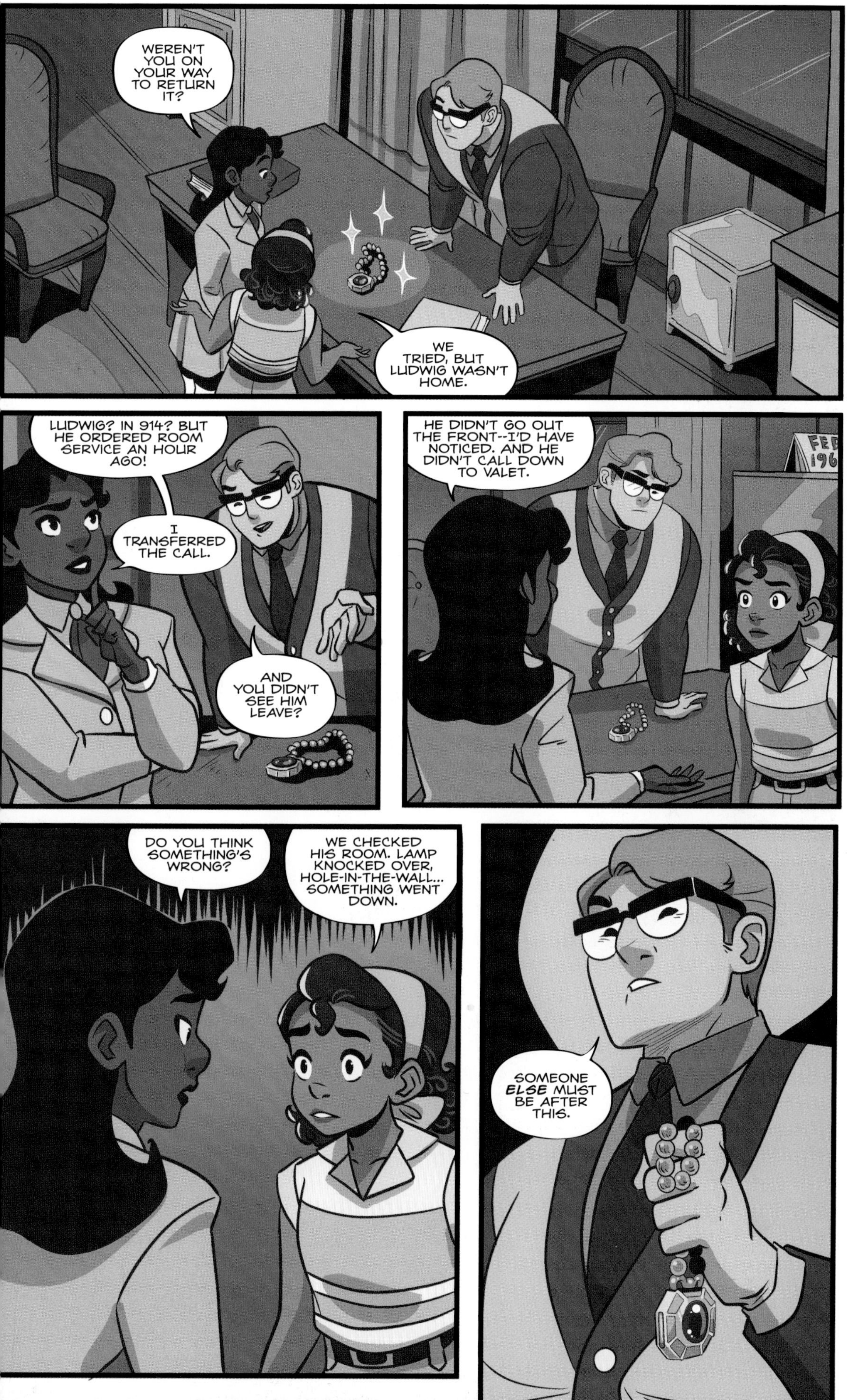

WEREN'T YOU ON YOUR WAY TO RETURN IT?
WE TRIED, BUT LUDWIG WASN'T HOME.
LUDWIG? IN 914? BUT HE ORDERED ROOM SERVICE AN HOUR AGO!
I TRANSFERRED THE CALL.
AND YOU DIDN'T SEE HIM LEAVE?
HE DIDN'T GO OUT THE FRONT--I'D HAVE NOTICED. AND HE DIDN'T CALL DOWN TO VALET.
DO YOU THINK SOMETHING'S WRONG?
WE CHECKED HIS ROOM. LAMP KNOCKED OVER, HOLE-IN-THE-WALL... SOMETHING WENT DOWN.
SOMEONE *ELSE* MUST BE AFTER THIS.

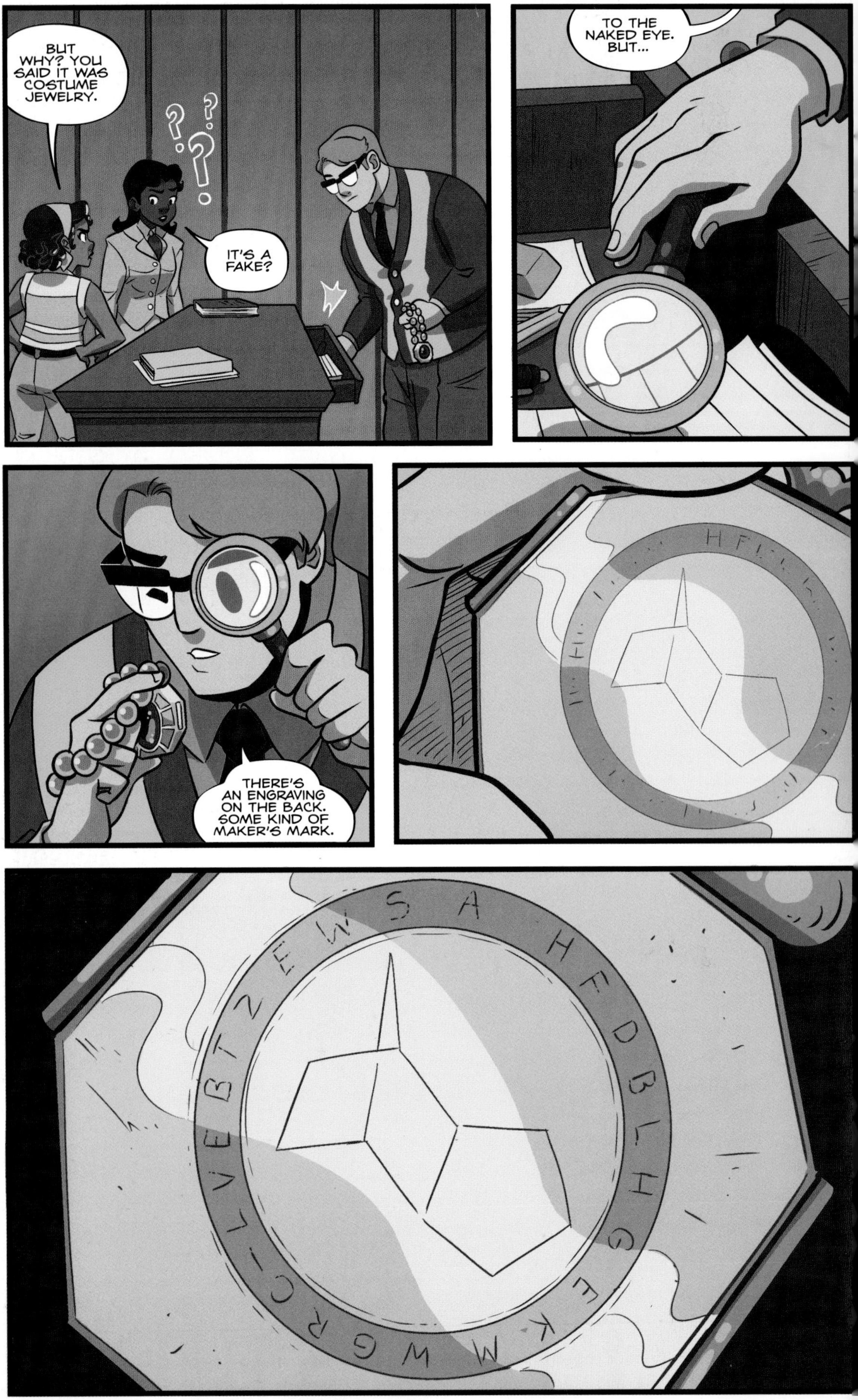
BUT WHY? YOU SAID IT WAS COSTUME JEWELRY.
IT'S A FAKE?
TO THE NAKED EYE. BUT...
THERE'S AN ENGRAVING ON THE BACK. SOME KIND OF MAKER'S MARK.
L V E E B T Z E W S A H F D B L H G E K M W G R C -

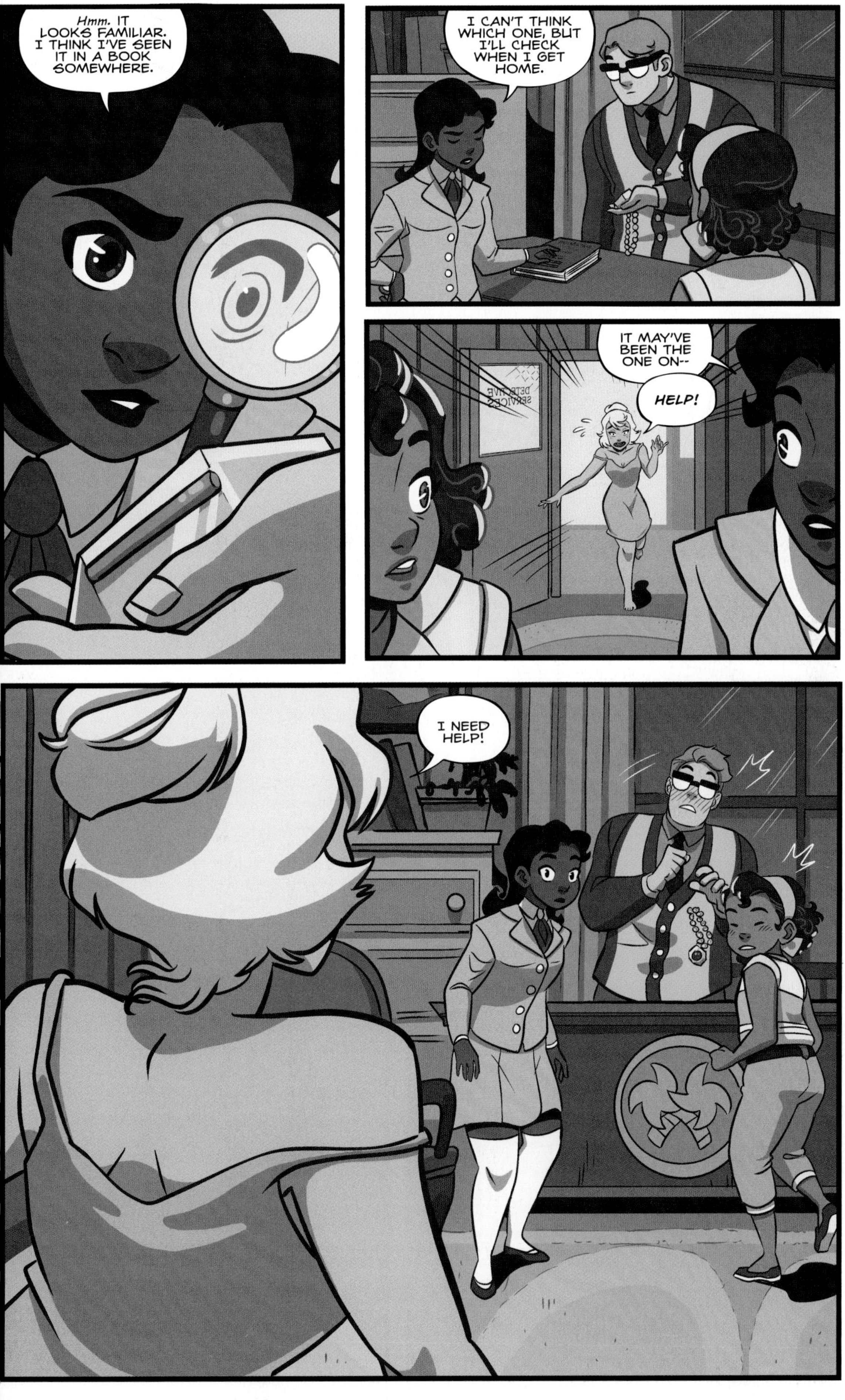
Hmm. IT LOOKS FAMILIAR. I THINK I'VE SEEN IT IN A BOOK SOMEWHERE.
I CAN'T THINK WHICH ONE, BUT I'LL CHECK WHEN I GET HOME.
IT MAY'VE BEEN THE ONE ON--
HELP!
I NEED HELP!

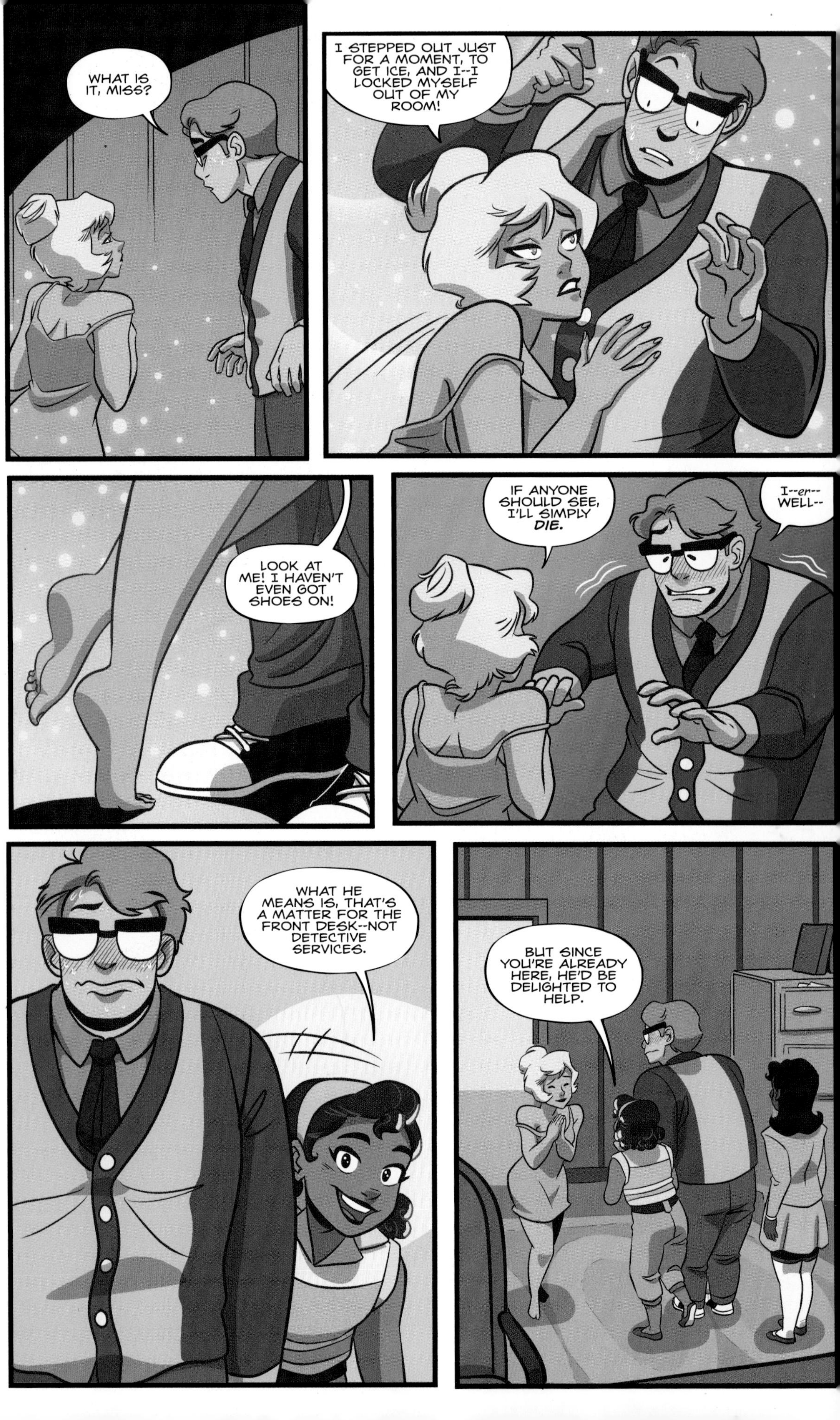
WHAT IS IT, MISS?
I STEPPED OUT JUST FOR A MOMENT, TO GET ICE, AND I--I LOCKED MYSELF OUT OF MY ROOM!
LOOK AT ME! I HAVEN'T EVEN GOT SHOES ON!
IF ANYONE SHOULD SEE, I'LL SIMPLY *DIE.*
I--*er*-- WELL--
WHAT HE MEANS IS, THAT'S A MATTER FOR THE FRONT DESK--NOT DETECTIVE SERVICES.
BUT SINCE YOU'RE ALREADY HERE, HE'D BE DELIGHTED TO HELP.

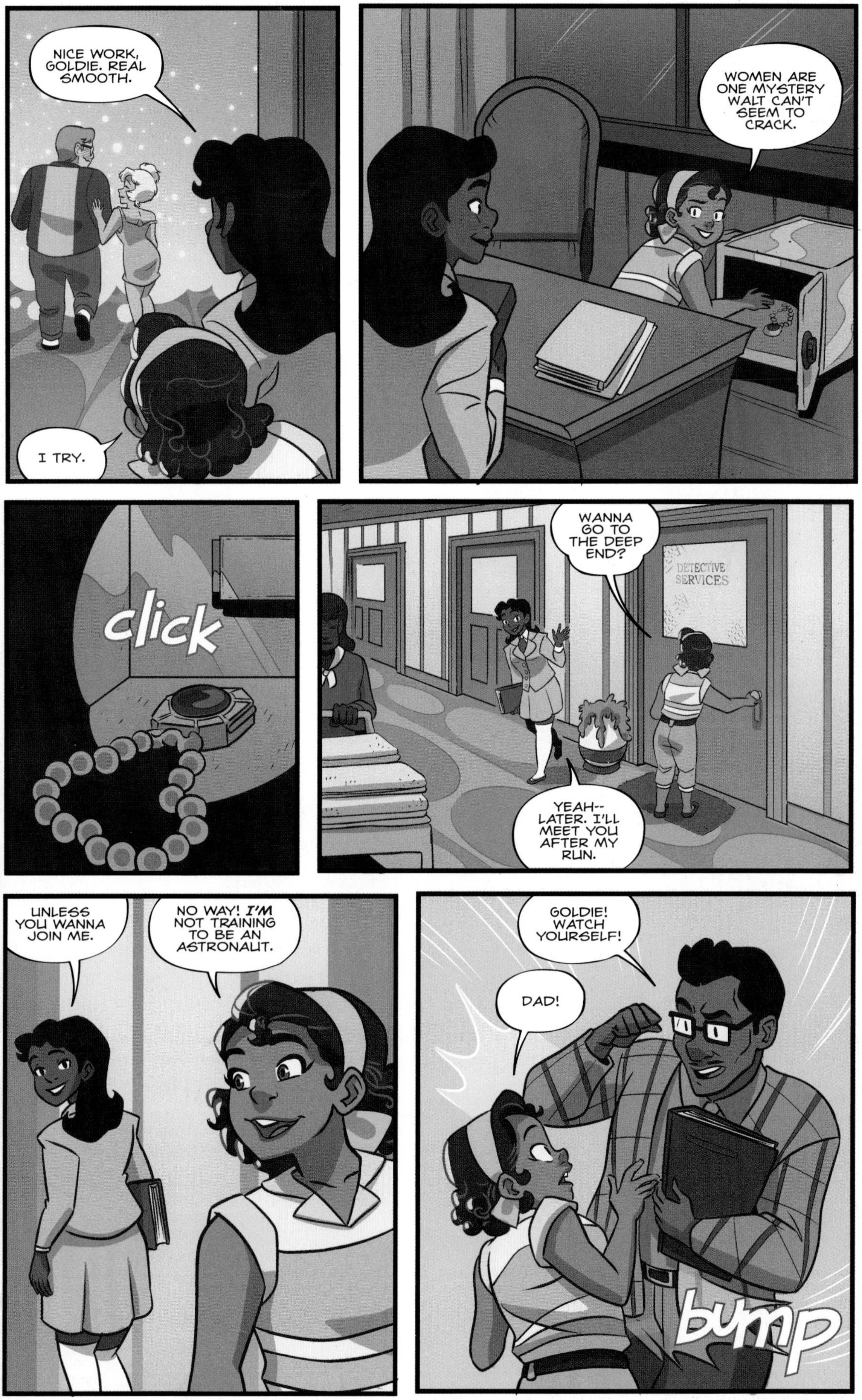
NICE WORK, GOLDIE. REAL SMOOTH.
I TRY.
WOMEN ARE ONE MYSTERY WALT CAN'T SEEM TO CRACK.
click
WANNA GO TO THE DEEP END?
DETECTIVE SERVICES
YEAH-- LATER. I'LL MEET YOU AFTER MY RUN.
UNLESS YOU WANNA JOIN ME.
NO WAY! I'M NOT TRAINING TO BE AN ASTRONAUT.
GOLDIE! WATCH YOURSELF!
DAD!
bump

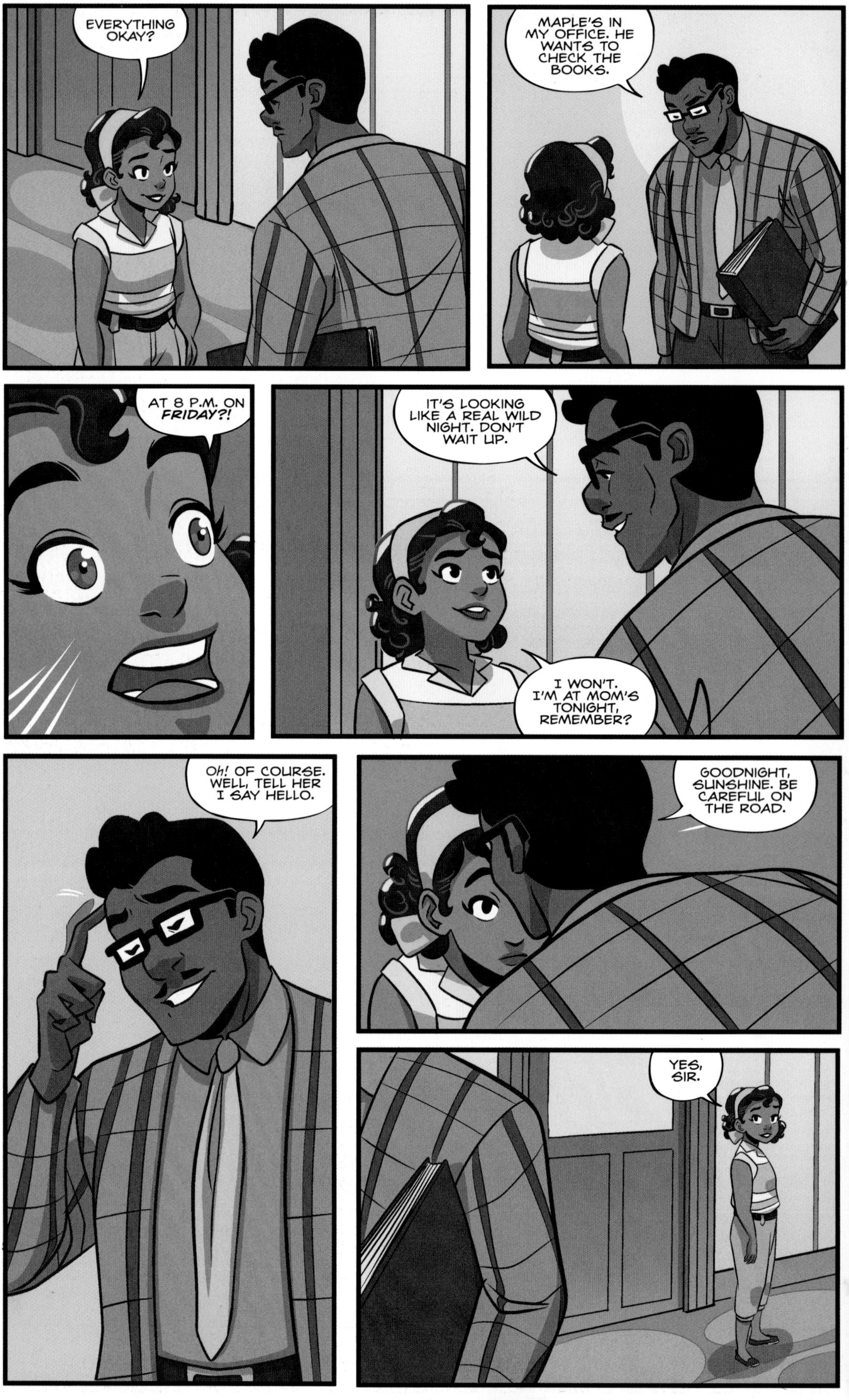
EVERYTHING OKAY?
MAPLE'S IN MY OFFICE. HE WANTS TO CHECK THE BOOKS.
AT 8 P.M. ON *FRIDAY?!*
IT'S LOOKING LIKE A REAL WILD NIGHT. DON'T WAIT UP.
I WON'T. I'M AT MOM'S TONIGHT, REMEMBER?
Oh! OF COURSE. WELL, TELL HER I SAY HELLO.
GOODNIGHT, SUNSHINE. BE CAREFUL ON THE ROAD.
YES, SIR.

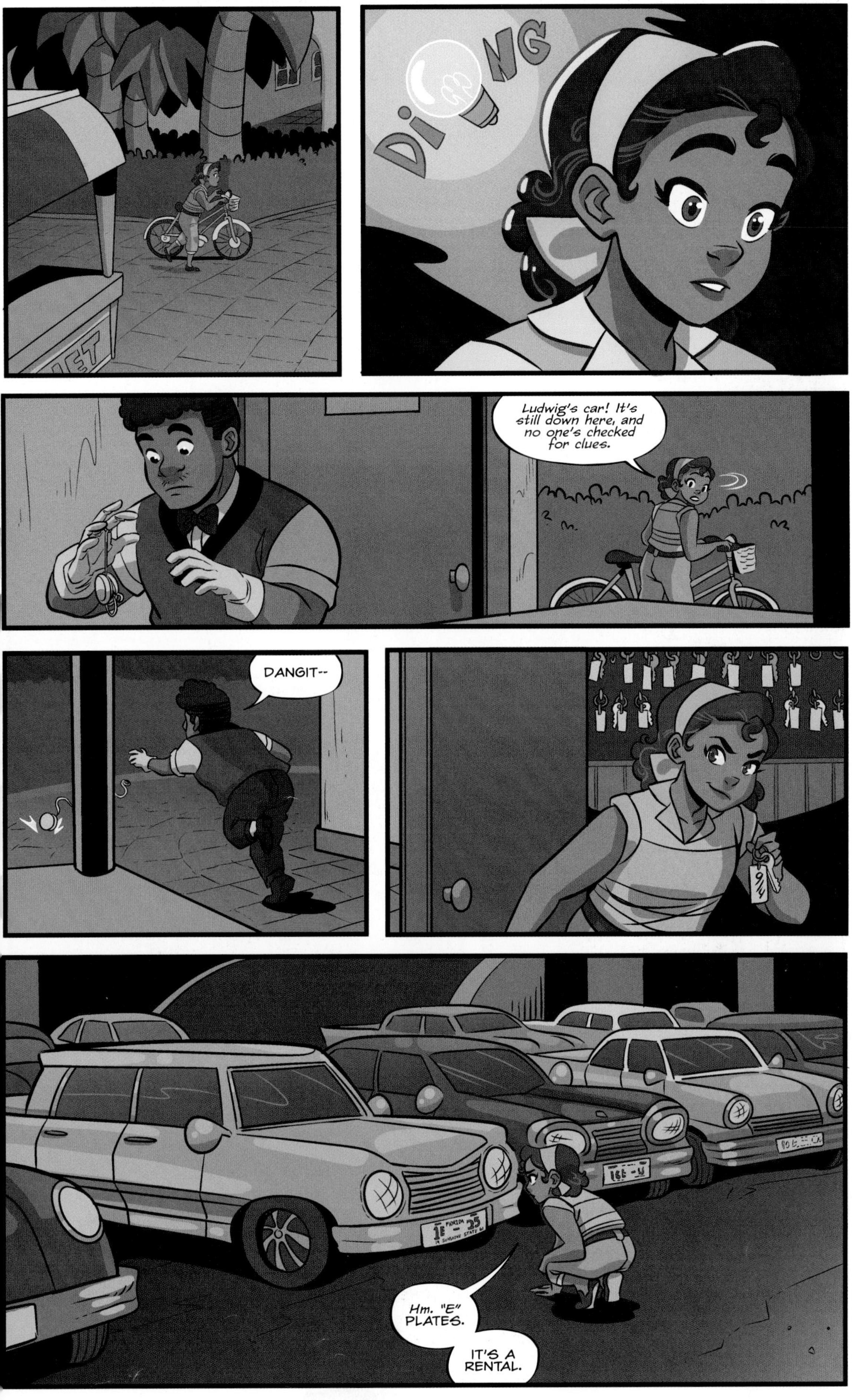
DING
Ludwig's car! It's still down here, and no one's checked for clues.
DANGIT--
Hm. "E" PLATES.
IT'S A RENTAL.

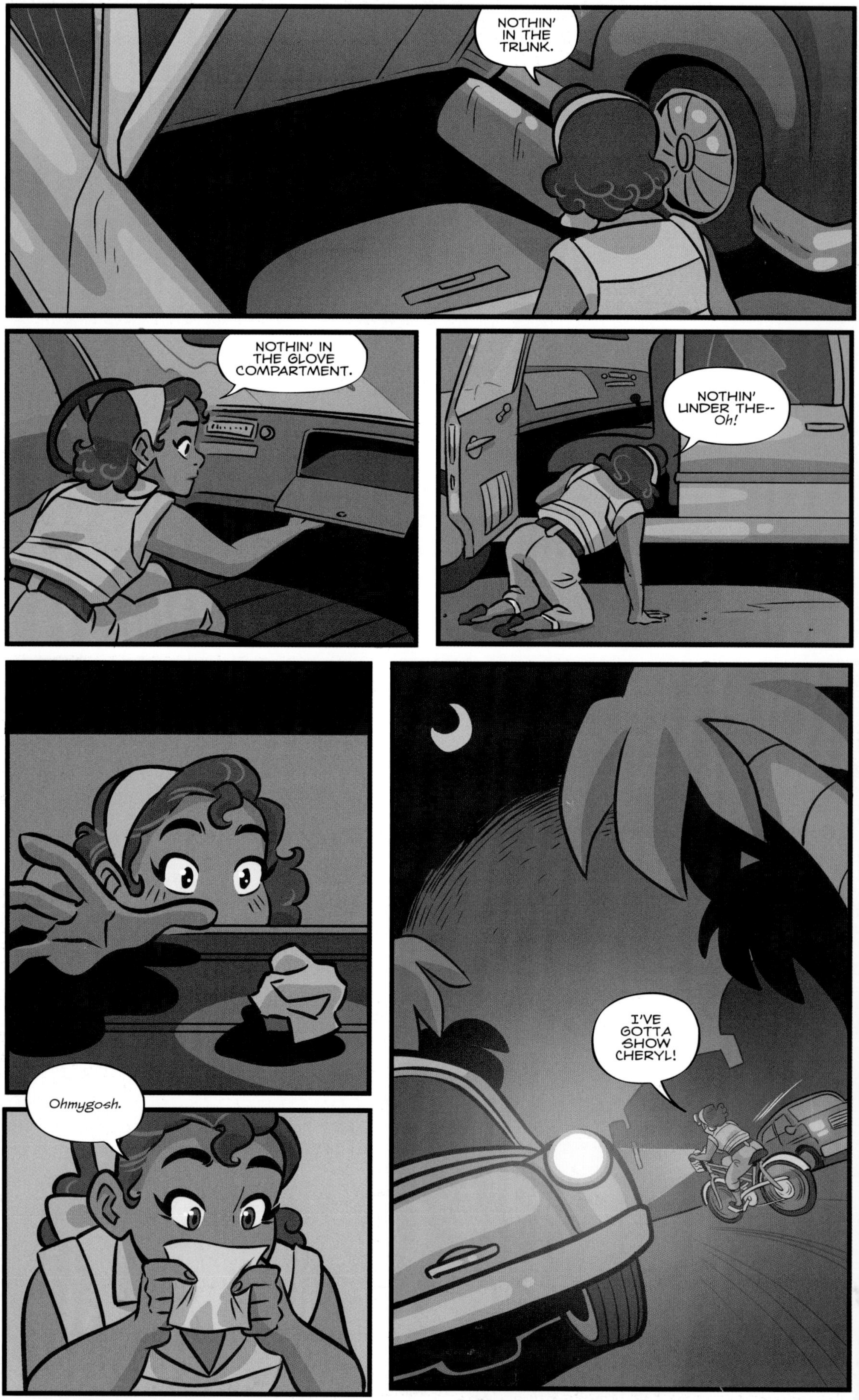
NOTHIN' IN THE TRUNK.
NOTHIN' IN THE GLOVE COMPARTMENT.
NOTHIN' UNDER THE-- Oh!
Ohmygosh.
I'VE GOTTA SHOW CHERYL!

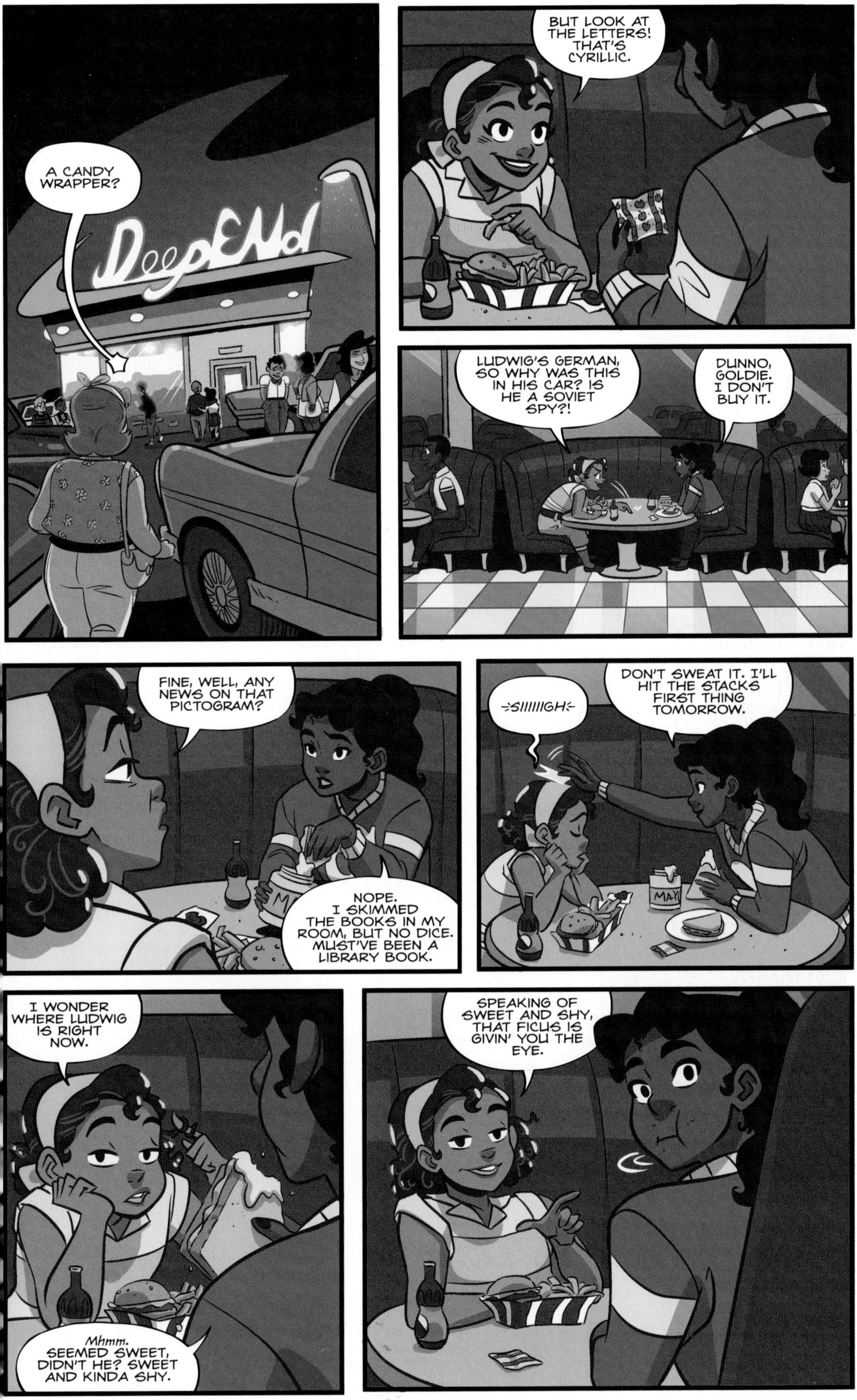
A CANDY WRAPPER?
DeepEnd
BUT LOOK AT THE LETTERS! THAT'S CYRILLIC.
LUDWIG'S GERMAN, SO WHY WAS THIS IN HIS CAR? IS HE A SOVIET SPY?!
DUNNO, GOLDIE. I DON'T BUY IT.
FINE, WELL, ANY NEWS ON THAT PICTOGRAM?
NOPE. I SKIMMED THE BOOKS IN MY ROOM, BUT NO DICE. MUST'VE BEEN A LIBRARY BOOK.
-SIIIIIIGH-
DON'T SWEAT IT. I'LL HIT THE STACKS FIRST THING TOMORROW.
MAYO
I WONDER WHERE LUDWIG IS RIGHT NOW.
Mhmm. SEEMED SWEET, DIDN'T HE? SWEET AND KINDA SHY.
SPEAKING OF SWEET AND SHY, THAT FICUS IS GIVIN' YOU THE EYE.

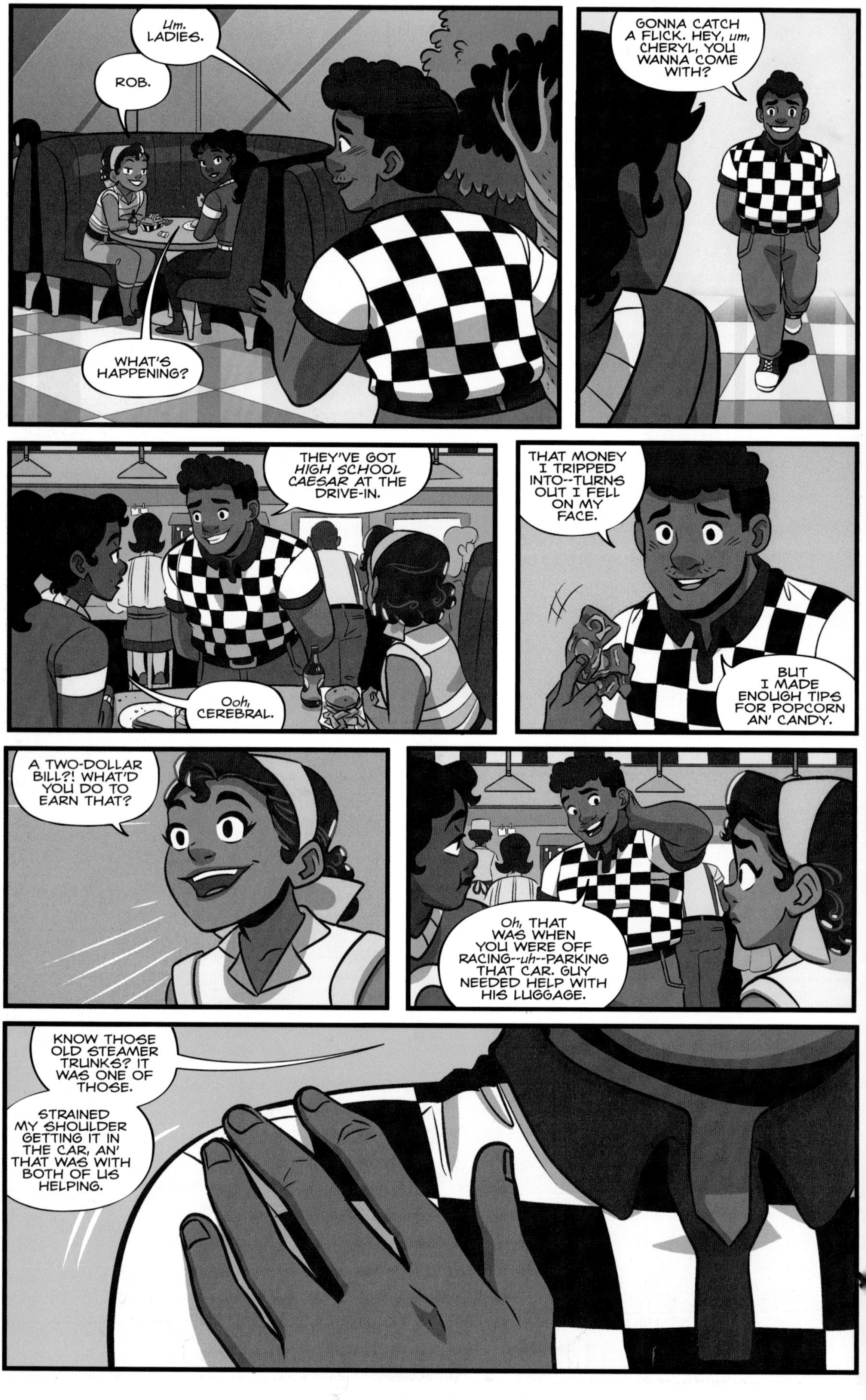

Um. LADIES.
ROB.
WHAT'S HAPPENING?
GONNA CATCH A FLICK. HEY, um, CHERYL, YOU WANNA COME WITH?
THEY'VE GOT HIGH SCHOOL CAESAR AT THE DRIVE-IN.
Ooh, CEREBRAL.
THAT MONEY I TRIPPED INTO--TURNS OUT I FELL ON MY FACE.
BUT I MADE ENOUGH TIPS FOR POPCORN AN' CANDY.
A TWO-DOLLAR BILL?! WHAT'D YOU DO TO EARN THAT?
Oh, THAT WAS WHEN YOU WERE OFF RACING--uh--PARKING THAT CAR. GUY NEEDED HELP WITH HIS LUGGAGE.
KNOW THOSE OLD STEAMER TRUNKS? IT WAS ONE OF THOSE.
STRAINED MY SHOULDER GETTING IT IN THE CAR, AN' THAT WAS WITH BOTH OF US HELPING.

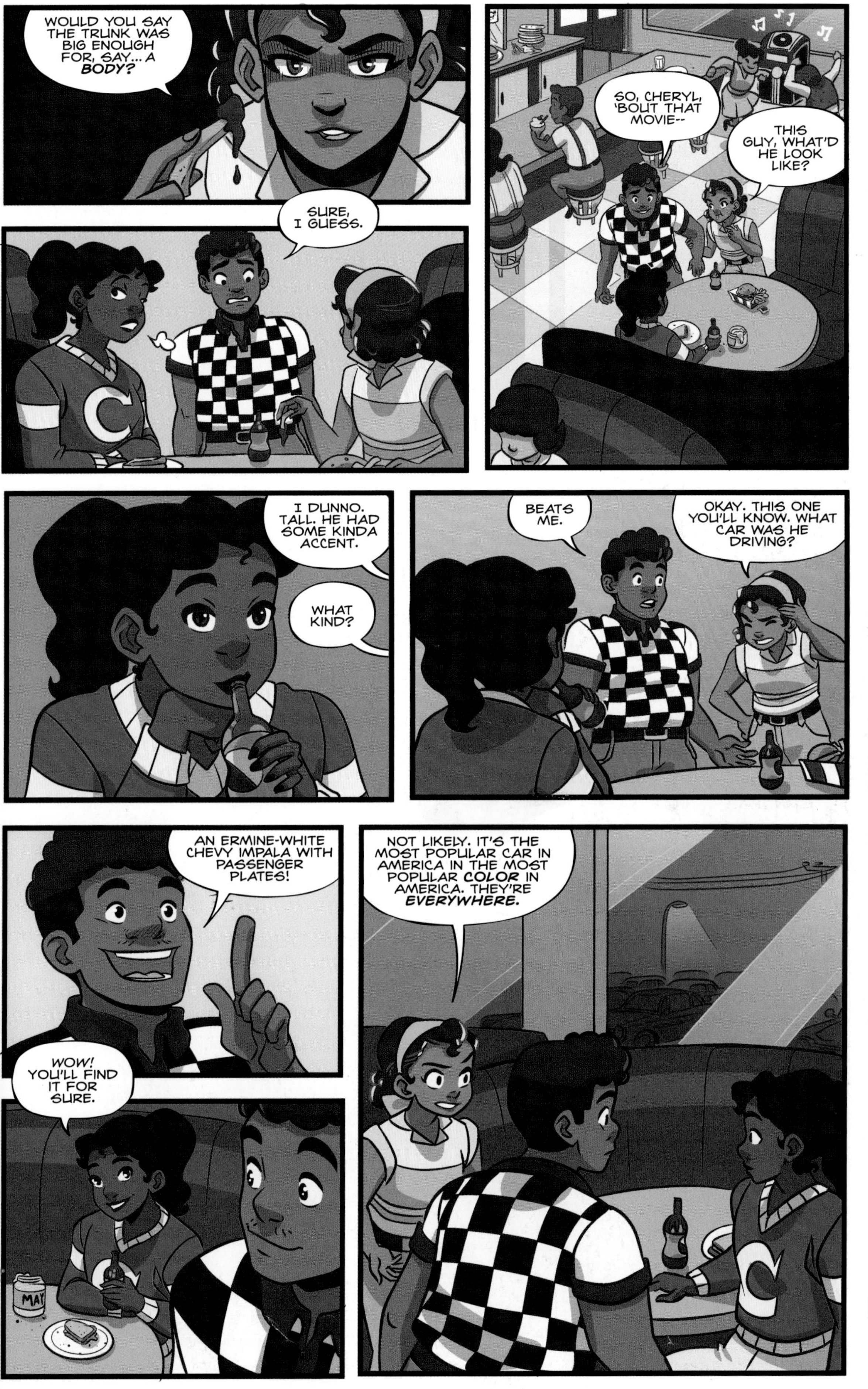
WOULD YOU SAY THE TRUNK WAS BIG ENOUGH FOR, SAY... A BODY?
SURE, I GUESS.
SO, CHERYL, 'BOUT THAT MOVIE--
THIS GUY, WHAT'D HE LOOK LIKE?
I DUNNO. TALL. HE HAD SOME KINDA ACCENT.
WHAT KIND?
BEATS ME.
OKAY. THIS ONE YOU'LL KNOW. WHAT CAR WAS HE DRIVING?
AN ERMINE-WHITE CHEVY IMPALA WITH PASSENGER PLATES!
WOW! YOU'LL FIND IT FOR SURE.
NOT LIKELY. IT'S THE MOST POPULAR CAR IN AMERICA IN THE MOST POPULAR COLOR IN AMERICA. THEY'RE EVERYWHERE.

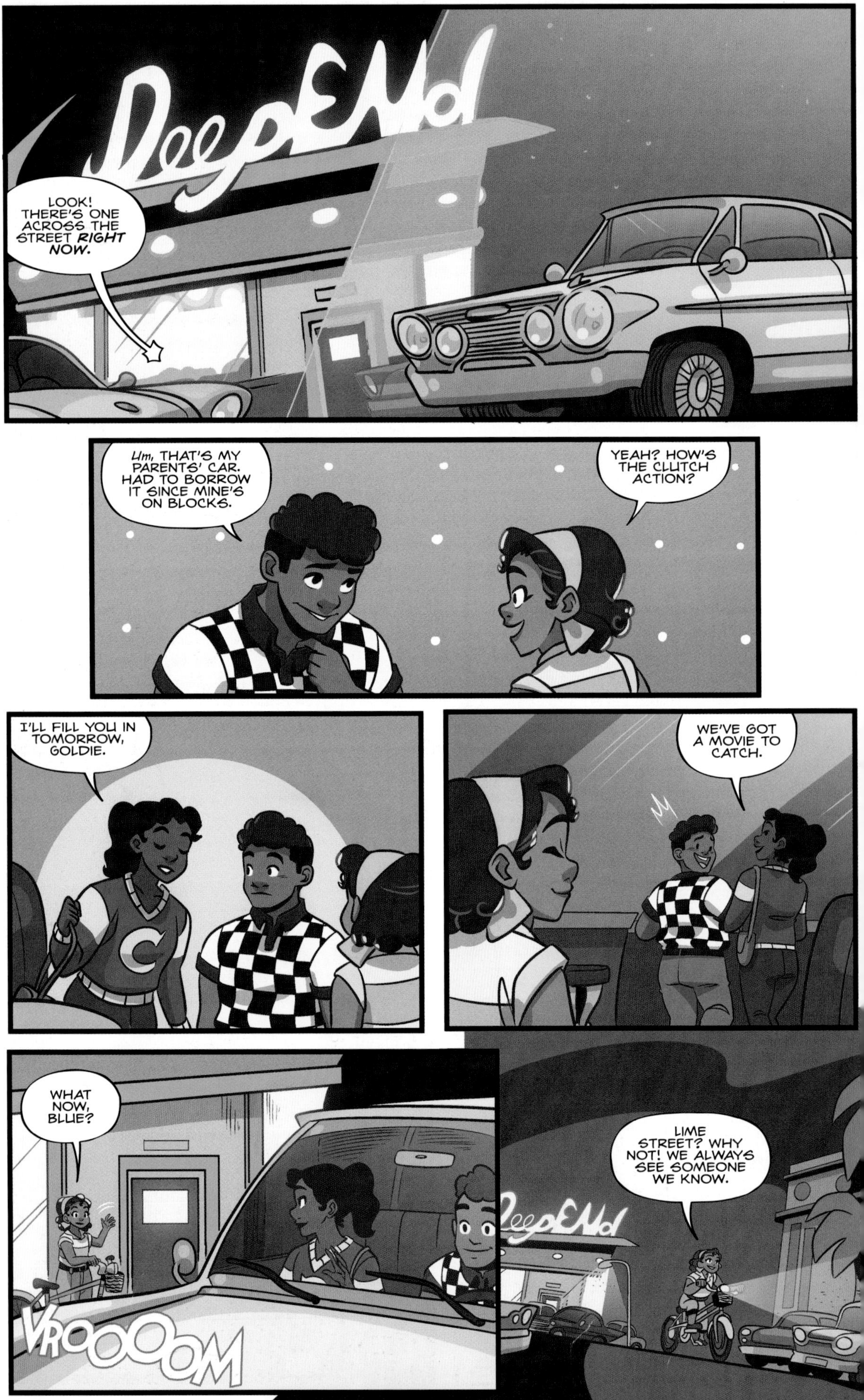

LOOK! THERE'S ONE ACROSS THE STREET *RIGHT NOW.*
UM, THAT'S MY PARENTS' CAR. HAD TO BORROW IT SINCE MINE'S ON BLOCKS.
YEAH? HOW'S THE CLUTCH ACTION?
I'LL FILL YOU IN TOMORROW, GOLDIE.
WE'VE GOT A MOVIE TO CATCH.
WHAT NOW, BLUE?
VROOOOOM
LIME STREET? WHY NOT! WE ALWAYS SEE SOMEONE WE KNOW.

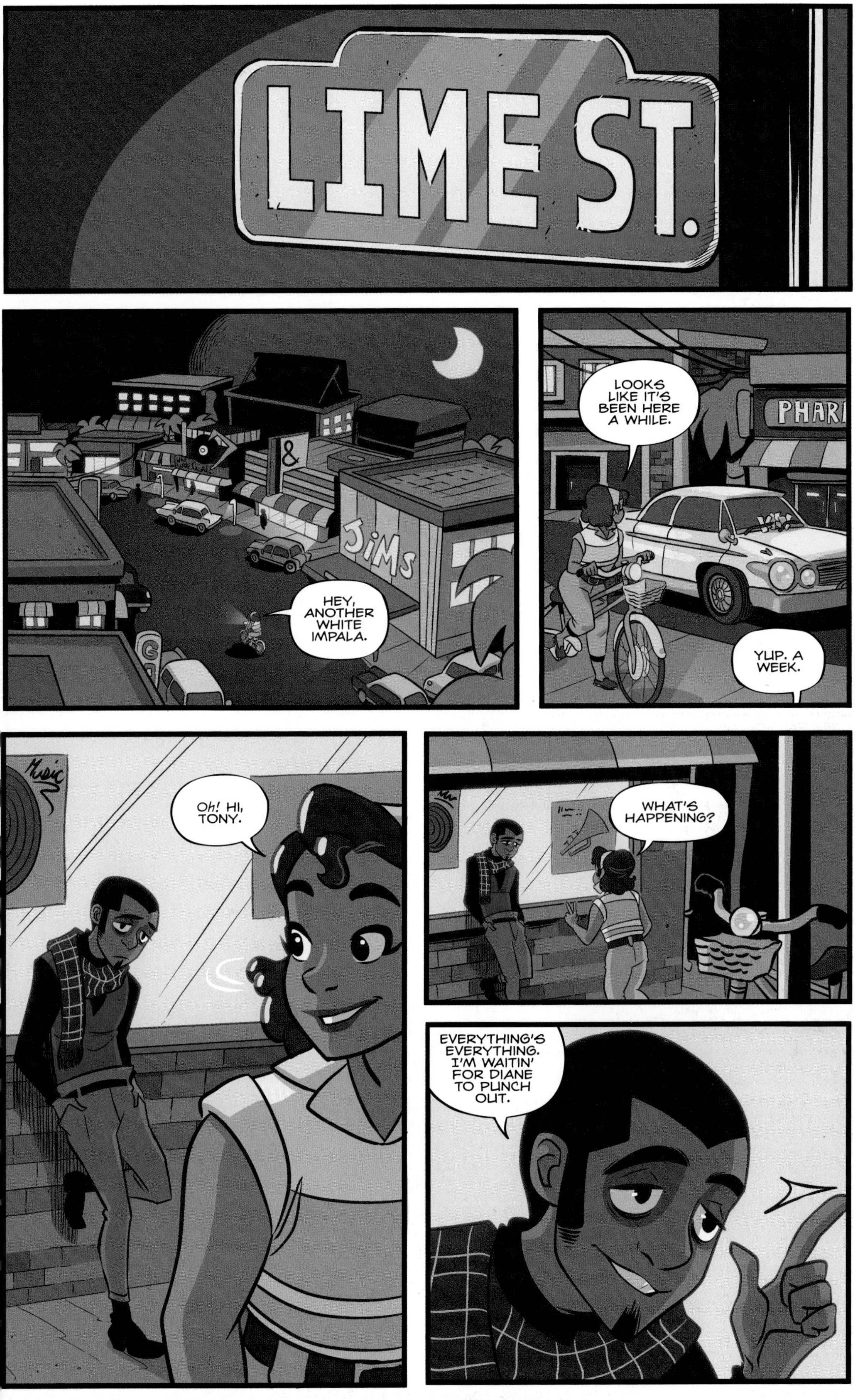
LIME ST.
HEY, ANOTHER WHITE IMPALA.
LOOKS LIKE IT'S BEEN HERE A WHILE.
PHAR
YUP. A WEEK.
Music
Oh! HI, TONY.
WHAT'S HAPPENING?
EVERYTHING'S EVERYTHING. I'M WAITIN' FOR DIANE TO PUNCH OUT.

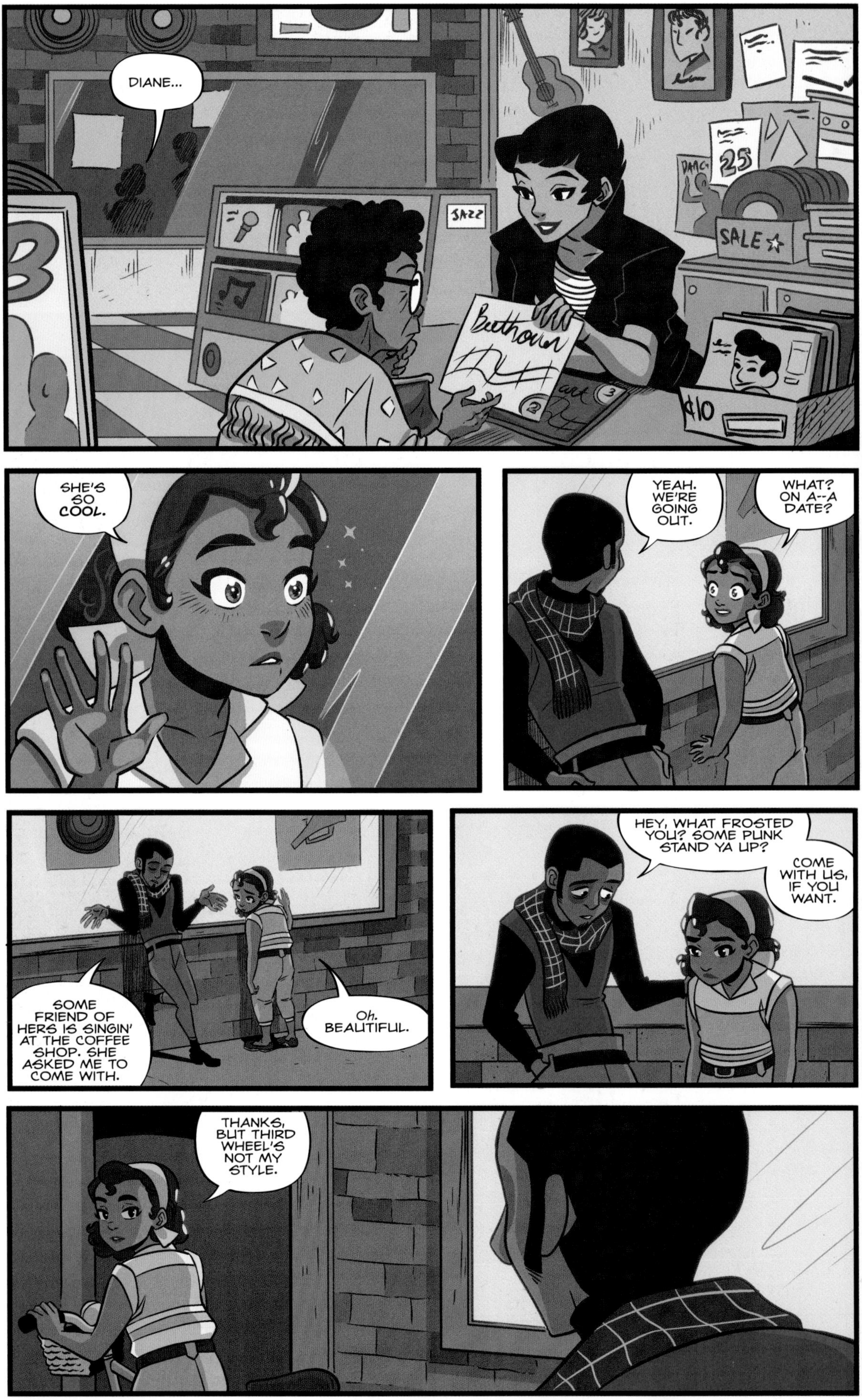
DIANE...
SHE'S SO COOL.
YEAH. WE'RE GOING OUT.
WHAT? ON A--A DATE?
SOME FRIEND OF HERS IS SINGIN' AT THE COFFEE SHOP. SHE ASKED ME TO COME WITH.
Oh. BEAUTIFUL.
HEY, WHAT FROSTED YOU? SOME PUNK STAND YA UP?
COME WITH US, IF YOU WANT.
THANKS, BUT THIRD WHEEL'S NOT MY STYLE.

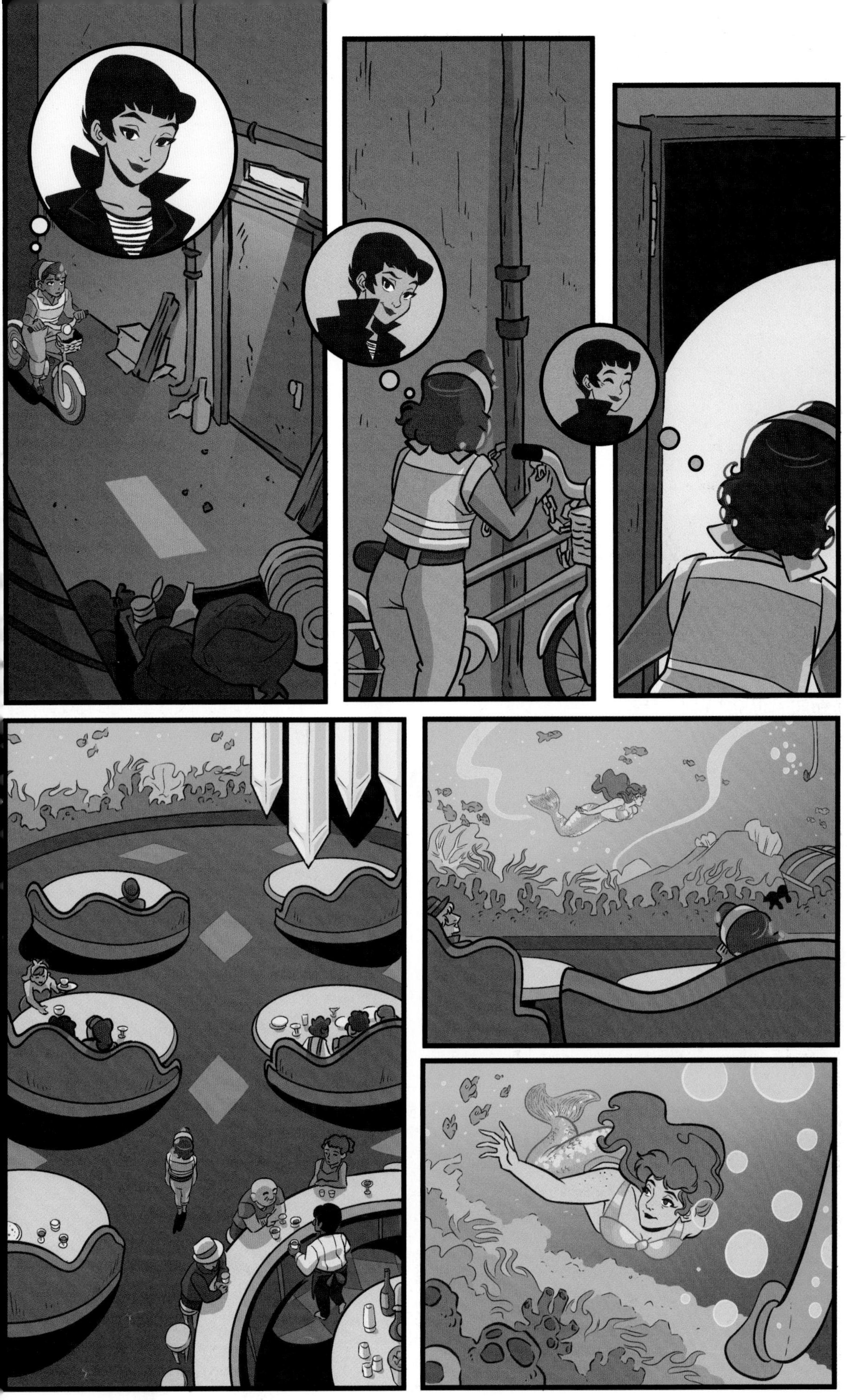

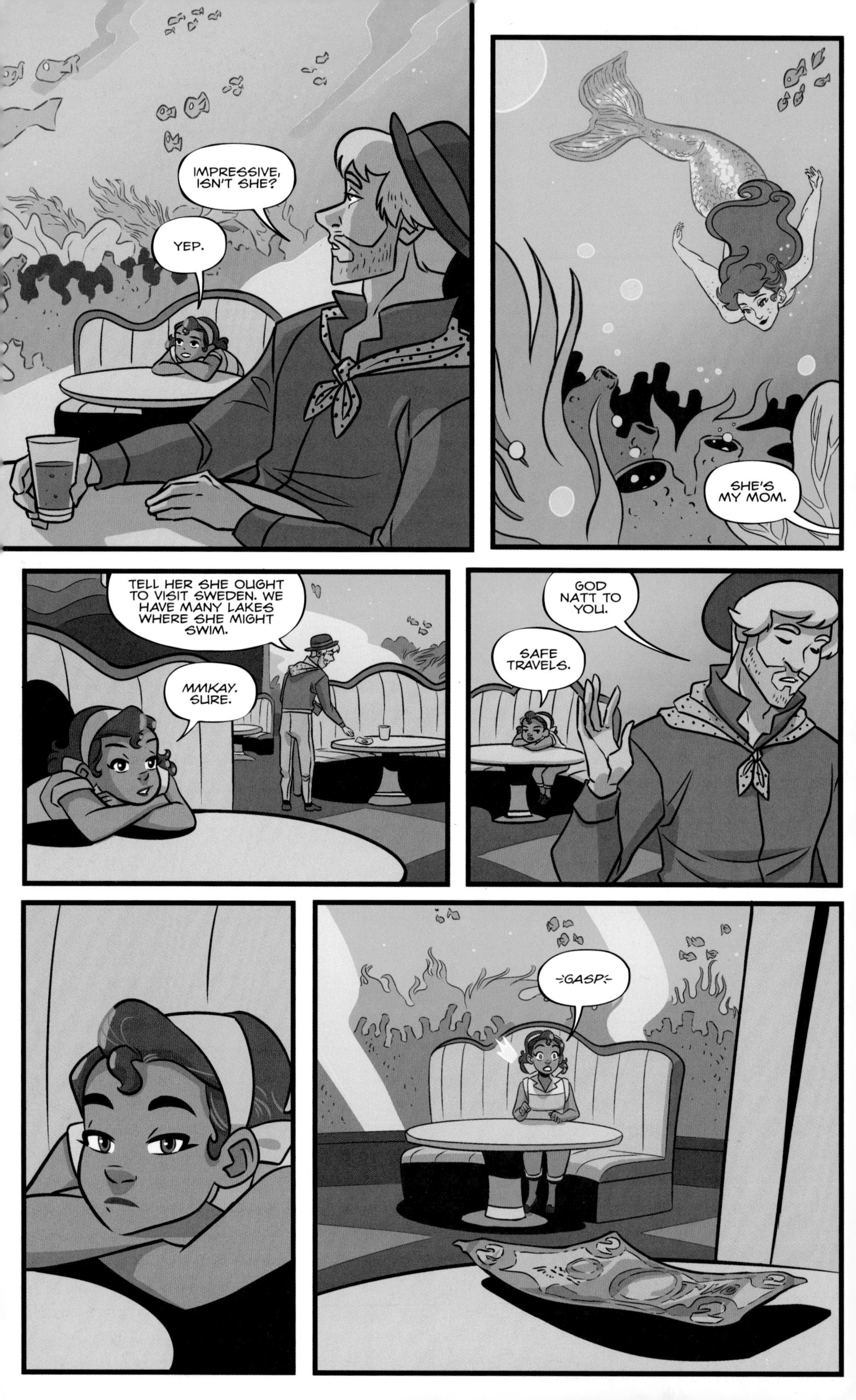
IMPRESSIVE, ISN'T SHE?
YEP.
SHE'S MY MOM.
TELL HER SHE OUGHT TO VISIT SWEDEN. WE HAVE MANY LAKES WHERE SHE MIGHT SWIM.
MMKAY. SURE.
GOD NATT TO YOU.
SAFE TRAVELS.
GASP

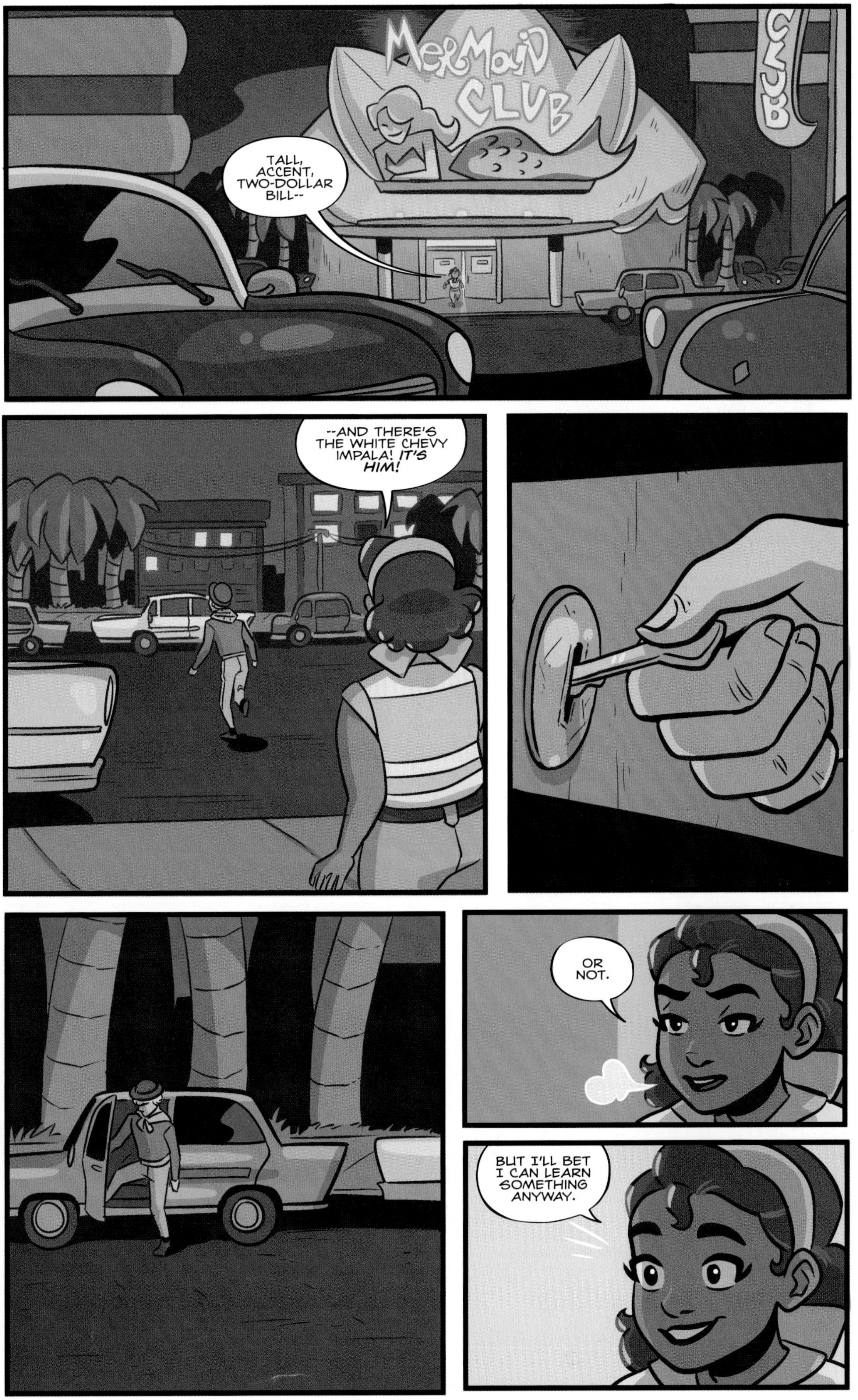
MerMaid CLUB
CLUB
TALL, ACCENT, TWO-DOLLAR BILL--
--AND THERE'S THE WHITE CHEVY IMPALA! *IT'S HIM!*
OR NOT.
BUT I'LL BET I CAN LEARN SOMETHING ANYWAY.

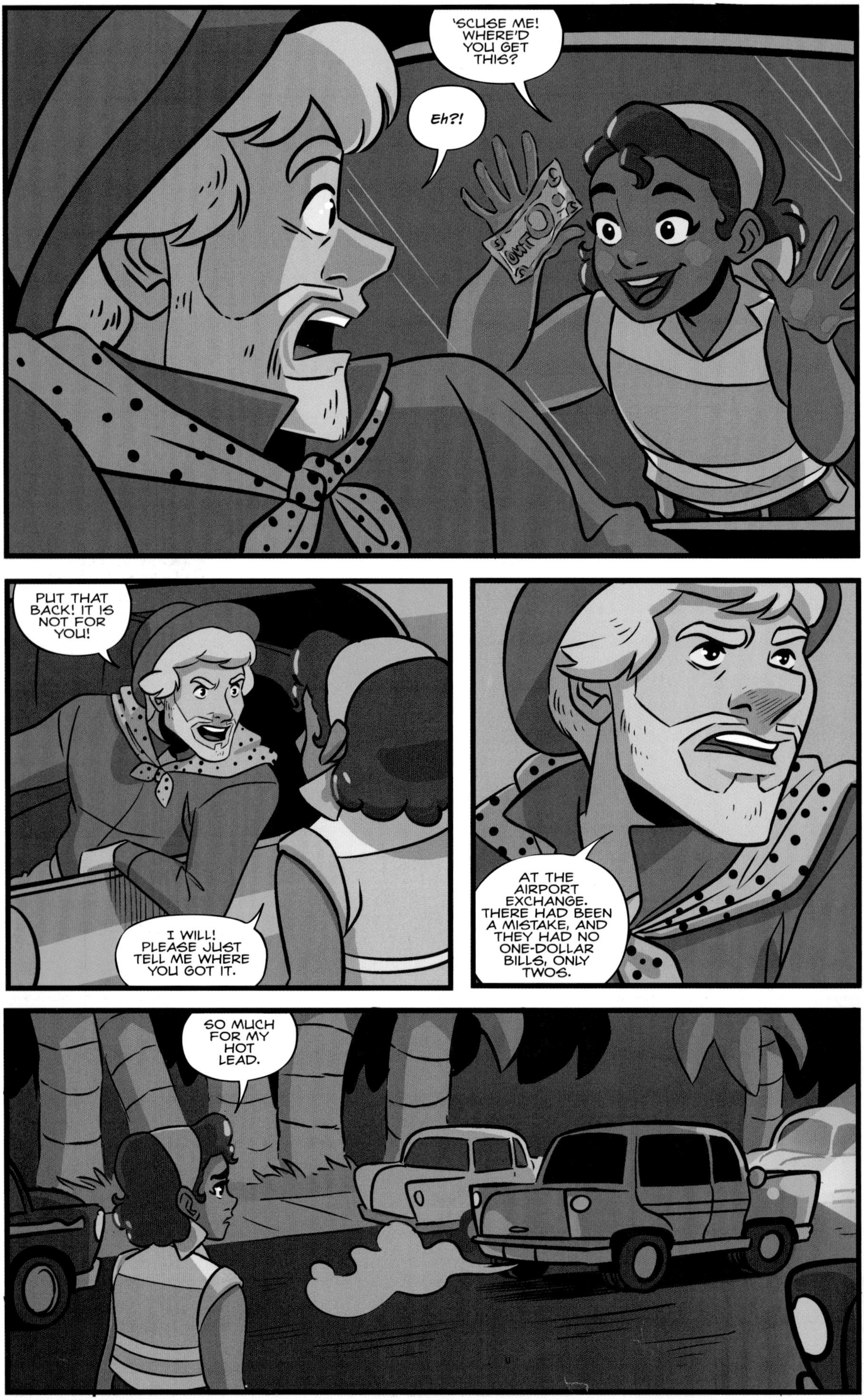
'SCUSE ME! WHERE'D YOU GET THIS?
Eh?!
PUT THAT BACK! IT IS NOT FOR YOU!
I WILL! PLEASE JUST TELL ME WHERE YOU GOT IT.
AT THE AIRPORT EXCHANGE. THERE HAD BEEN A MISTAKE, AND THEY HAD NO ONE-DOLLAR BILLS, ONLY TWOS.
SO MUCH FOR MY HOT LEAD.

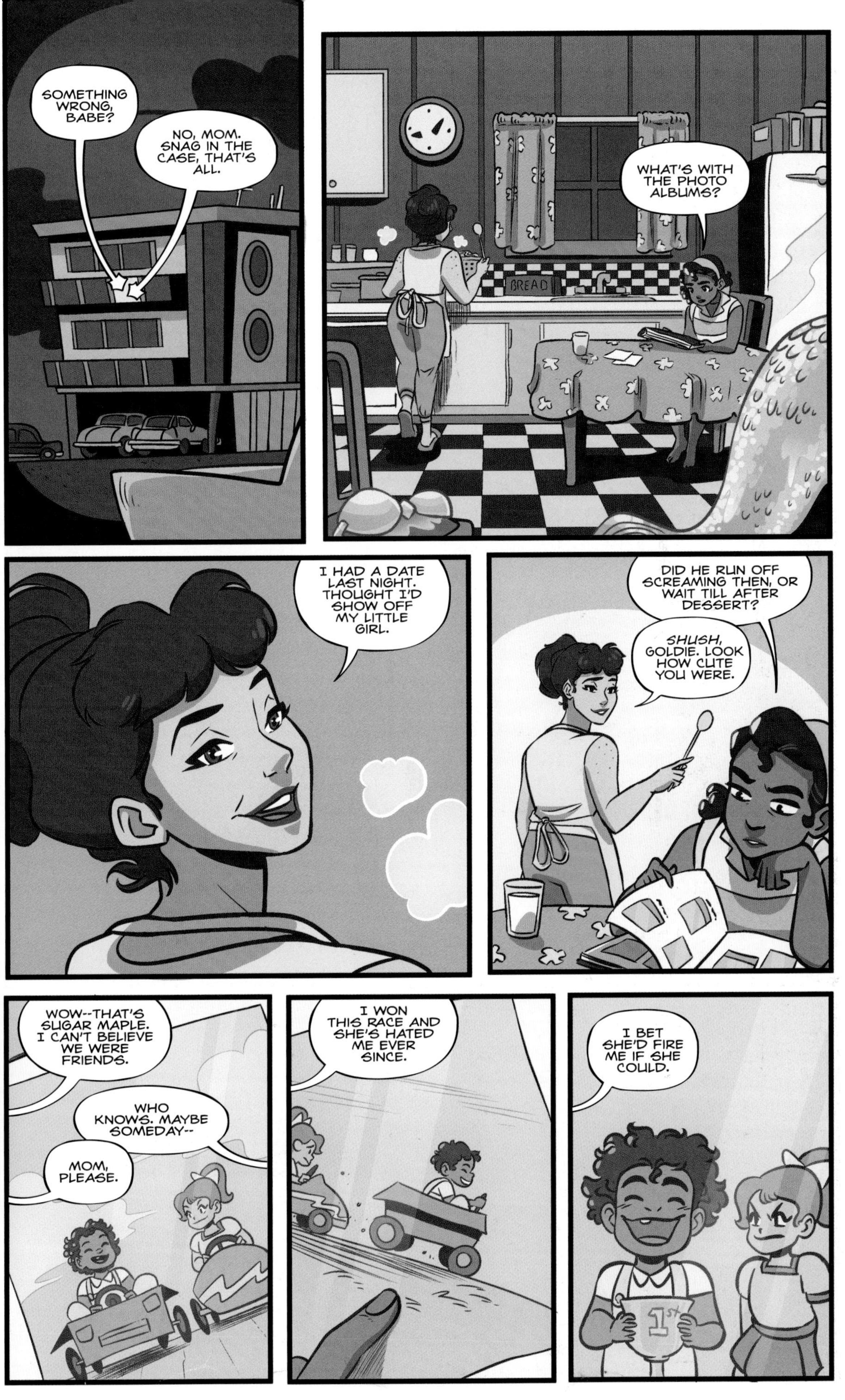
SOMETHING WRONG, BABE?
NO, MOM. SNAG IN THE CASE, THAT'S ALL.
BREAD
WHAT'S WITH THE PHOTO ALBUMS?
I HAD A DATE LAST NIGHT. THOUGHT I'D SHOW OFF MY LITTLE GIRL.
DID HE RUN OFF SCREAMING THEN, OR WAIT TILL AFTER DESSERT?
SHUSH, GOLDIE. LOOK HOW CUTE YOU WERE.
WOW--THAT'S SUGAR MAPLE. I CAN'T BELIEVE WE WERE FRIENDS.
WHO KNOWS. MAYBE SOMEDAY--
MOM, PLEASE.
I WON THIS RACE AND SHE'S HATED ME EVER SINCE.
I BET SHE'D FIRE ME IF SHE COULD.
1st

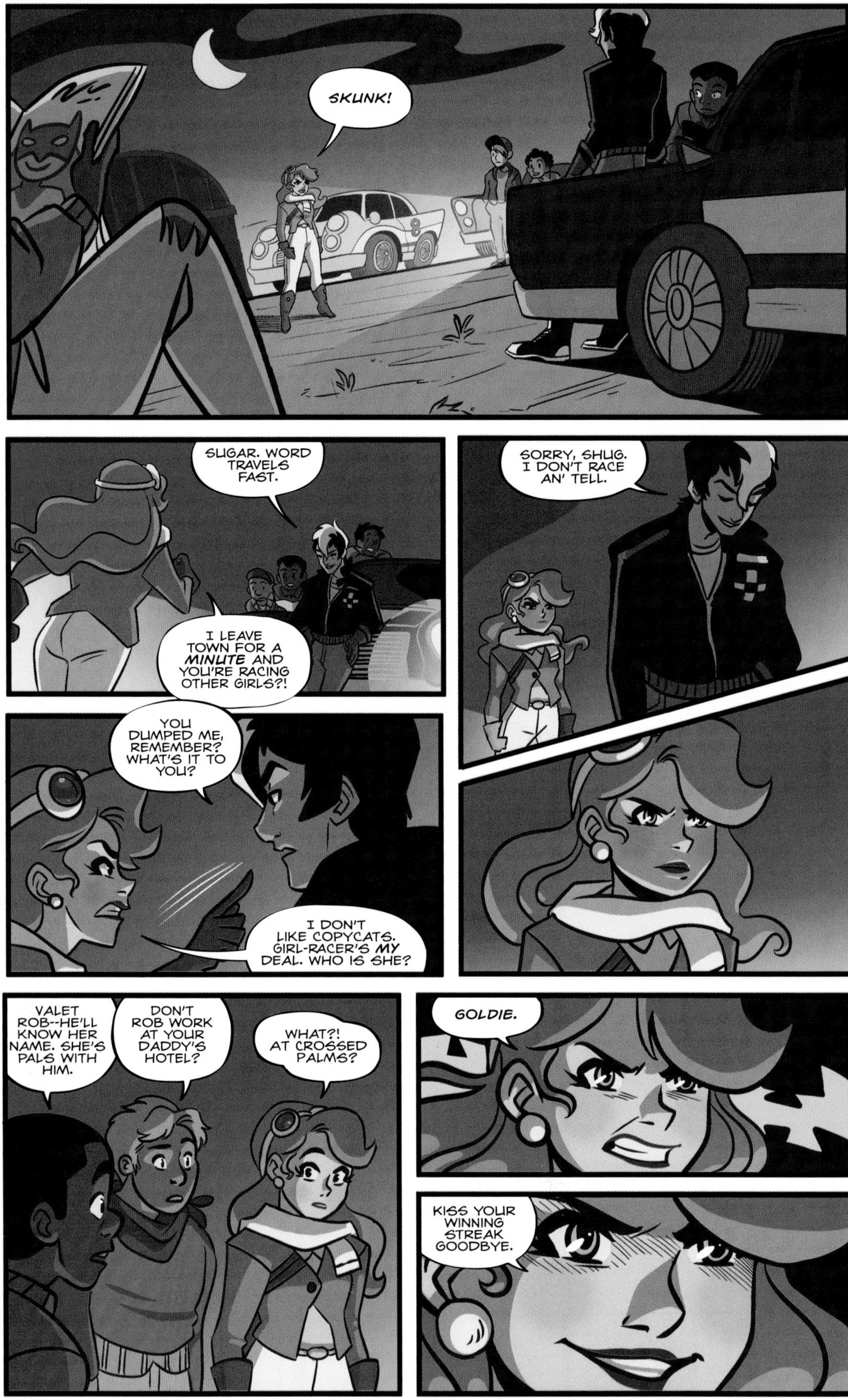
SKUNK!
SUGAR. WORD TRAVELS FAST.
I LEAVE TOWN FOR A *MINUTE* AND YOU'RE RACING OTHER GIRLS?!
SORRY, SHUG. I DON'T RACE AN' TELL.
YOU DUMPED ME, REMEMBER? WHAT'S IT TO YOU?
I DON'T LIKE COPYCATS. GIRL-RACER'S *MY* DEAL. WHO IS SHE?
VALET ROB--HE'LL KNOW HER NAME. SHE'S PALS WITH HIM.
DON'T ROB WORK AT YOUR DADDY'S HOTEL?
WHAT?! AT CROSSED PALMS?
GOLDIE.
KISS YOUR WINNING STREAK GOODBYE.

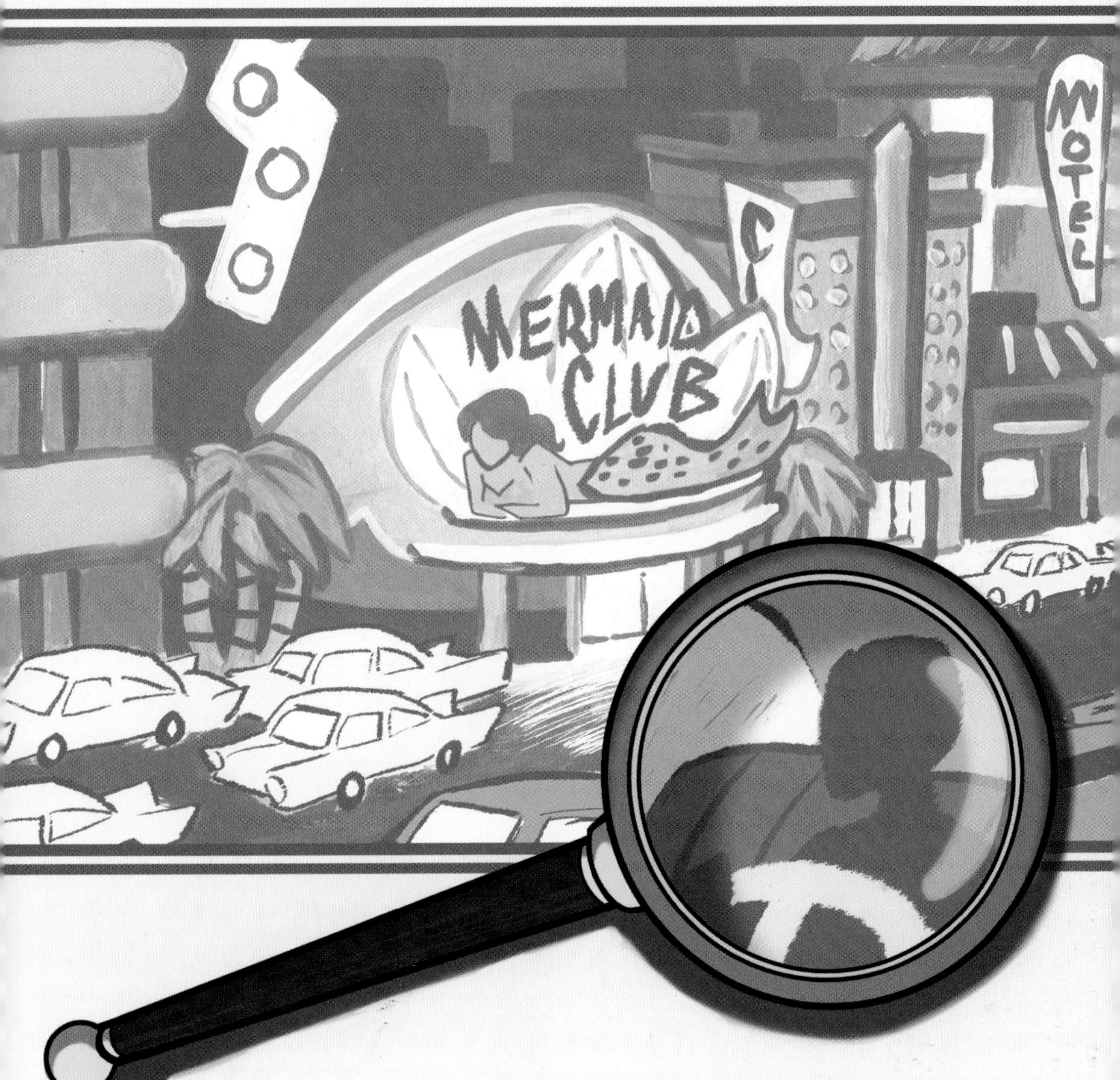
MERMAID CLUB
MOTEL

chapter

THREE

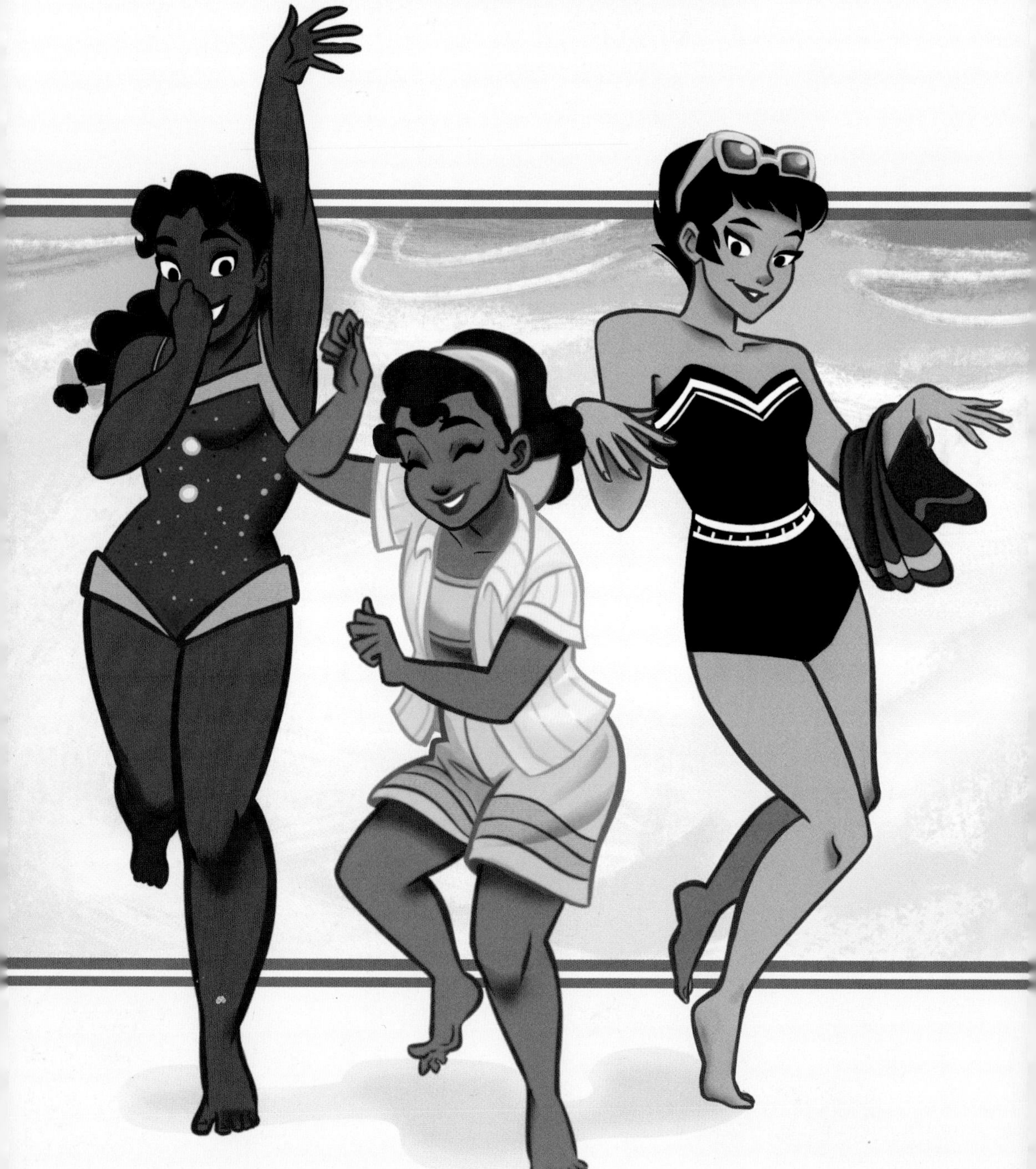

issue three cover by **Brittney Williams**

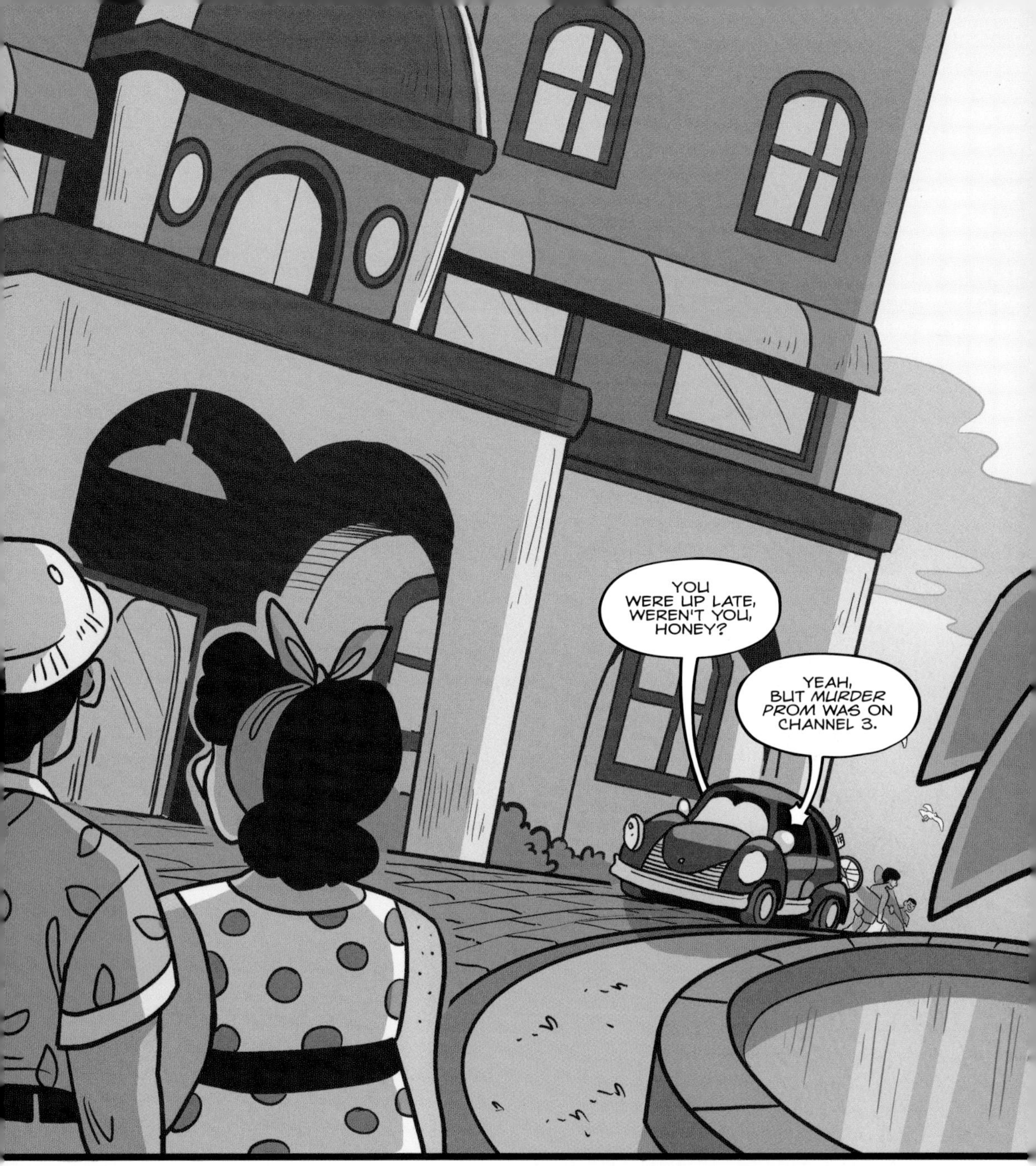
YOU WERE UP LATE, WEREN'T YOU, HONEY?
YEAH, BUT *MURDER PROM* WAS ON CHANNEL 3.

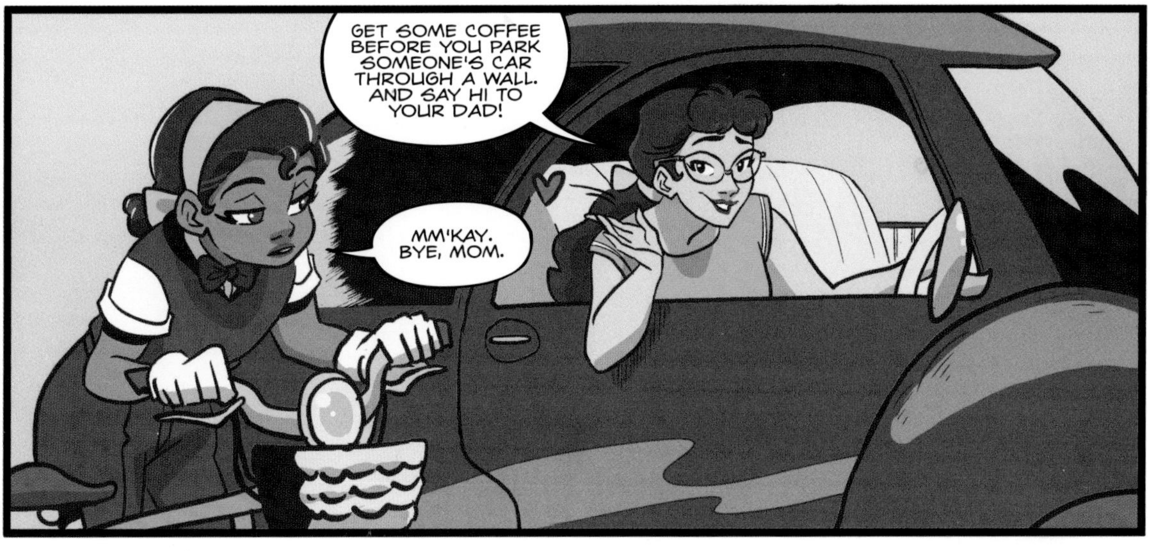
GET SOME COFFEE BEFORE YOU PARK SOMEONE'S CAR THROUGH A WALL. AND SAY HI TO YOUR DAD!
MM'KAY. BYE, MOM.

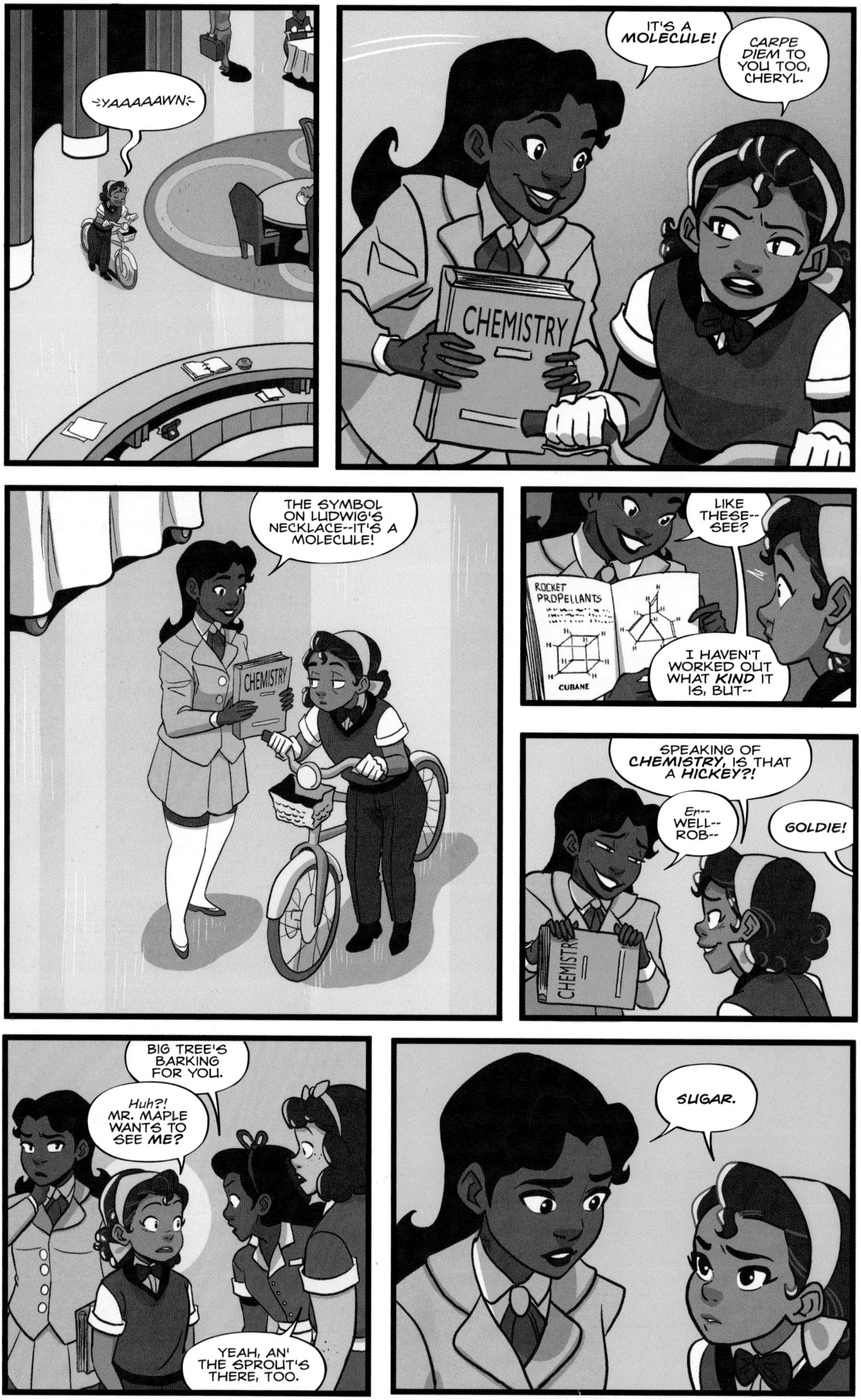

YAAAAAWN
IT'S A MOLECULE!
CARPE DIEM TO YOU TOO, CHERYL.
CHEMISTRY
THE SYMBOL ON LUDWIG'S NECKLACE--IT'S A MOLECULE!
CHEMISTRY
LIKE THESE--SEE?
ROCKET PROPELLANTS
CUBANE
I HAVEN'T WORKED OUT WHAT KIND IT IS, BUT--
SPEAKING OF CHEMISTRY, IS THAT A HICKEY?!
Er-- WELL-- ROB--
GOLDIE!
CHEMISTRY
BIG TREE'S BARKING FOR YOU.
Huh?! MR. MAPLE WANTS TO SEE ME?
YEAH, AN' THE SPROUT'S THERE, TOO.
SUGAR.

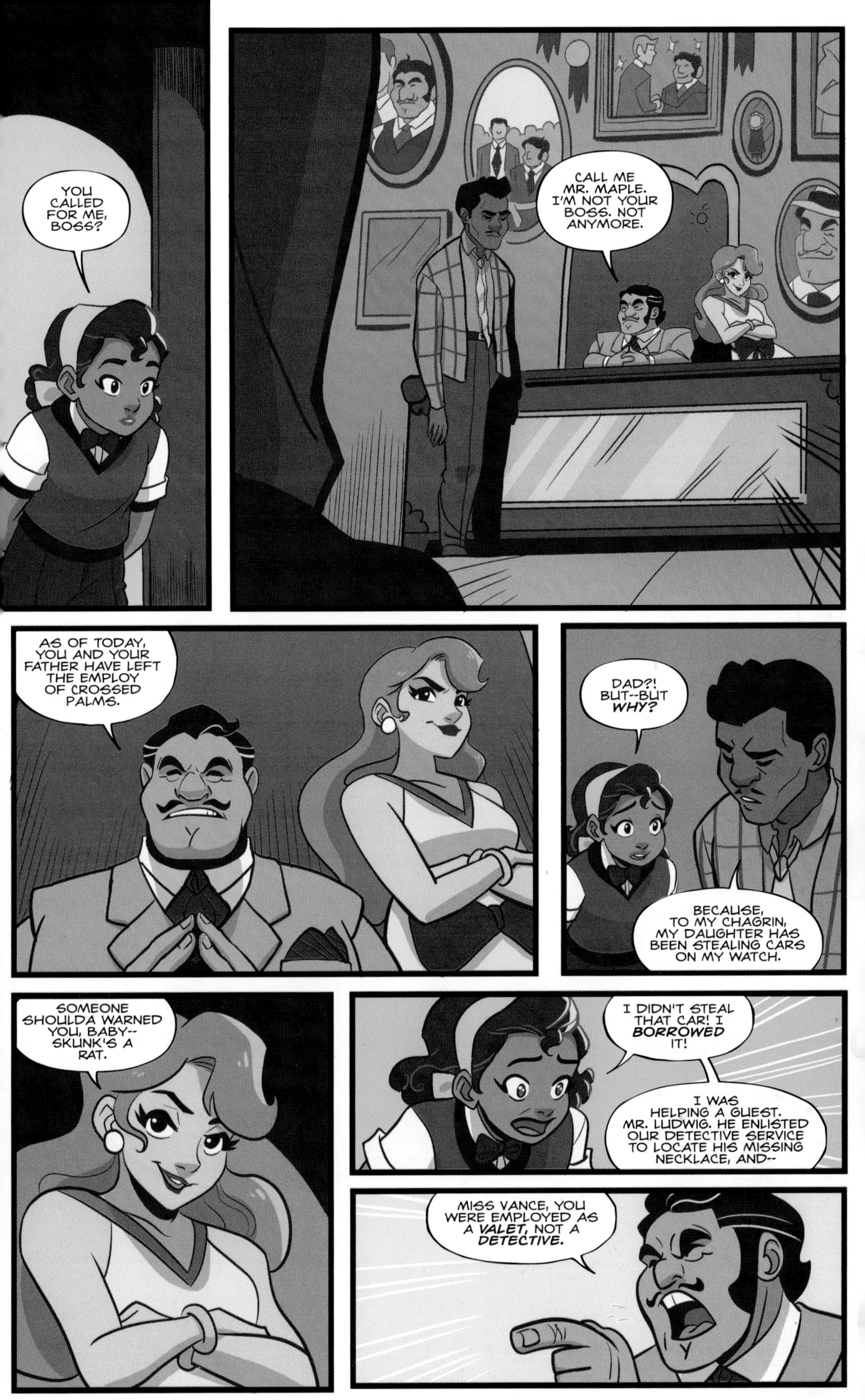

YOU CALLED FOR ME, BOSS?
CALL ME MR. MAPLE. I'M NOT YOUR BOSS. NOT ANYMORE.
AS OF TODAY, YOU AND YOUR FATHER HAVE LEFT THE EMPLOY OF CROSSED PALMS.
DAD?! BUT--BUT *WHY?*
BECAUSE, TO MY CHAGRIN, MY DAUGHTER HAS BEEN STEALING CARS ON MY WATCH.
SOMEONE SHOULDA WARNED YOU, BABY-- SKUNK'S A RAT.
I DIDN'T STEAL THAT CAR! I **BORROWED** IT!
I WAS HELPING A GUEST. MR. LUDWIG. HE ENLISTED OUR DETECTIVE SERVICE TO LOCATE HIS MISSING NECKLACE, AND--
MISS VANCE, YOU WERE EMPLOYED AS A ***VALET***, NOT A ***DETECTIVE.***

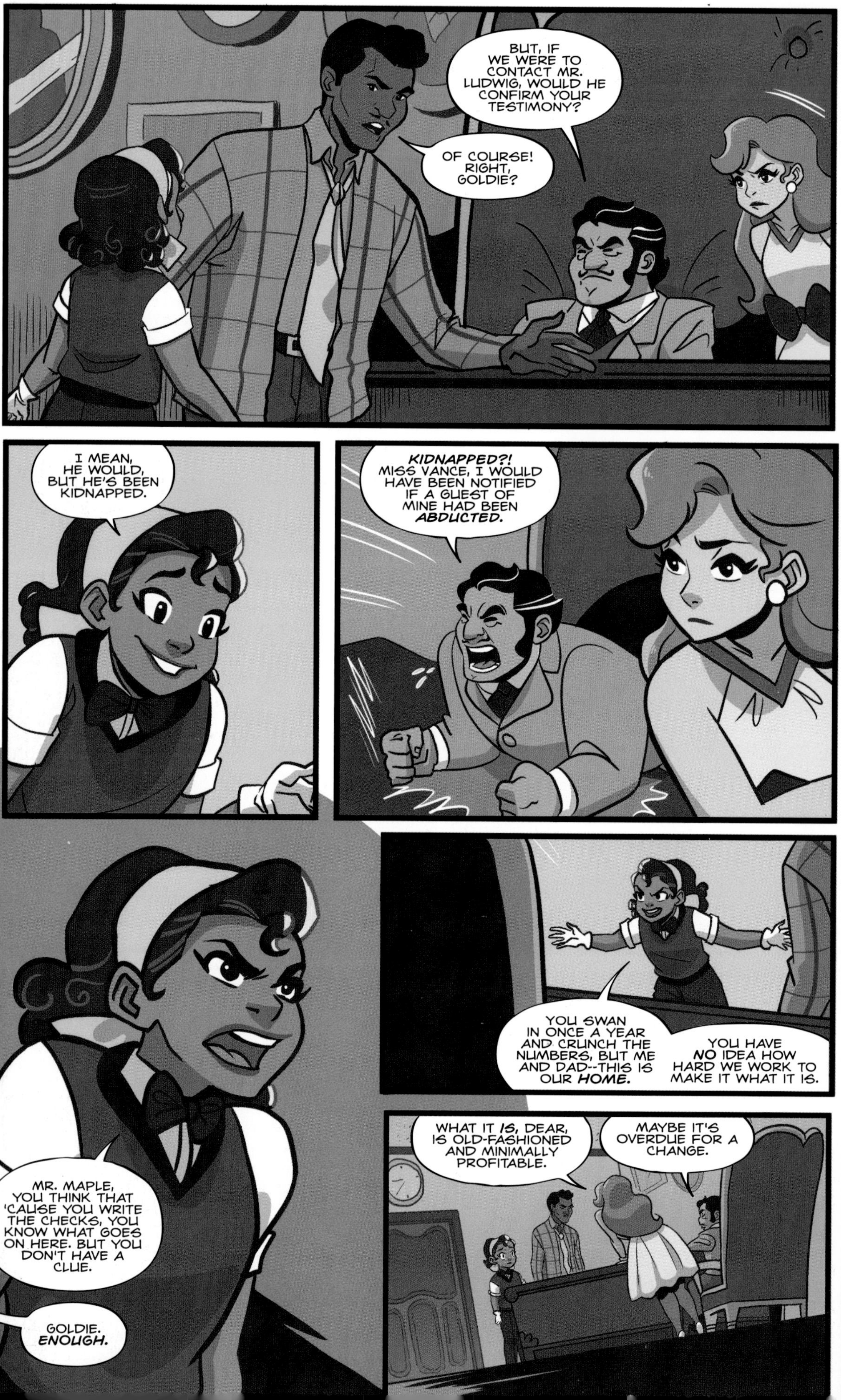

BUT, IF WE WERE TO CONTACT MR. LUDWIG, WOULD HE CONFIRM YOUR TESTIMONY?
OF COURSE! RIGHT, GOLDIE?
I MEAN, HE WOULD, BUT HE'S BEEN KIDNAPPED.
KIDNAPPED?! MISS VANCE, I WOULD HAVE BEEN NOTIFIED IF A GUEST OF MINE HAD BEEN *ABDUCTED.*
MR. MAPLE, YOU THINK THAT 'CAUSE YOU WRITE THE CHECKS, YOU KNOW WHAT GOES ON HERE. BUT YOU DON'T HAVE A CLUE.
GOLDIE. *ENOUGH.*
YOU SWAN IN ONCE A YEAR AND CRUNCH THE NUMBERS, BUT ME AND DAD--THIS IS OUR *HOME.*
YOU HAVE *NO* IDEA HOW HARD WE WORK TO MAKE IT WHAT IT IS.
WHAT IT *IS*, DEAR, IS OLD-FASHIONED AND MINIMALLY PROFITABLE.
MAYBE IT'S OVERDUE FOR A CHANGE.

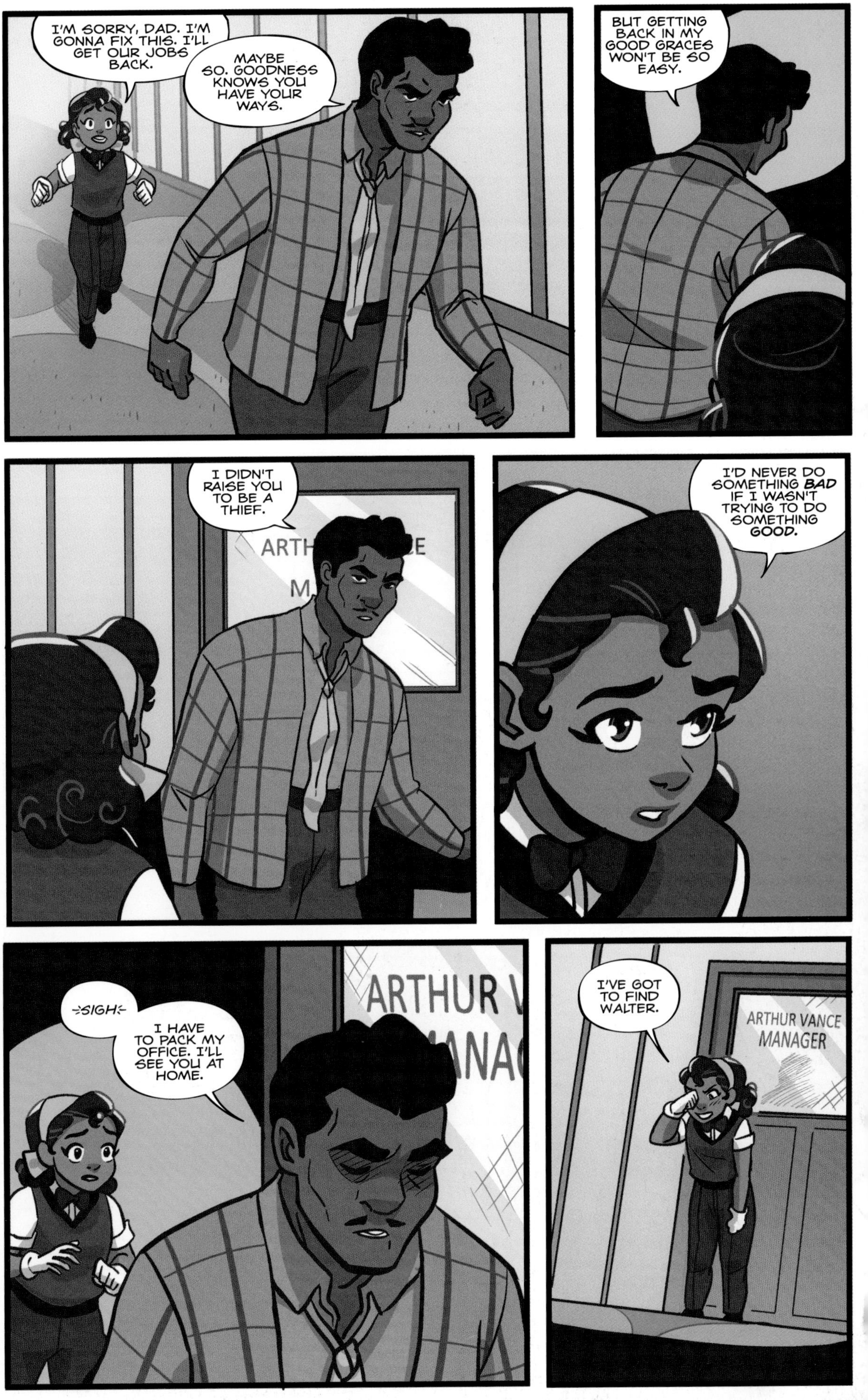
I'M SORRY, DAD. I'M GONNA FIX THIS. I'LL GET OUR JOBS BACK.
MAYBE SO. GOODNESS KNOWS YOU HAVE YOUR WAYS.
BUT GETTING BACK IN MY GOOD GRACES WON'T BE SO EASY.
I DIDN'T RAISE YOU TO BE A THIEF.
I'D NEVER DO SOMETHING BAD IF I WASN'T TRYING TO DO SOMETHING GOOD.
ARTHUR V
SIGH
I HAVE TO PACK MY OFFICE. I'LL SEE YOU AT HOME.
I'VE GOT TO FIND WALTER.
ARTHUR VANCE
MANAGER

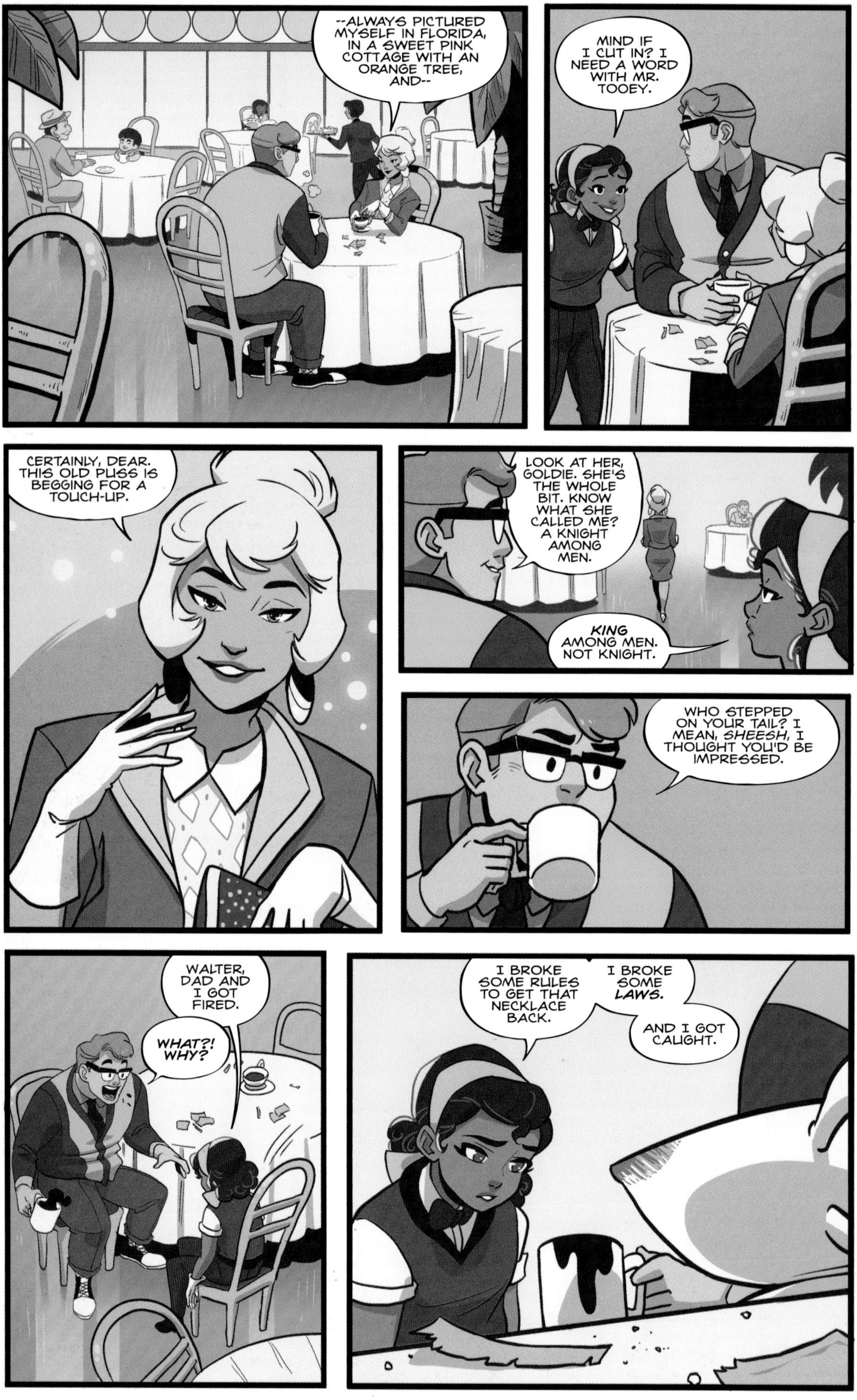
--ALWAYS PICTURED MYSELF IN FLORIDA, IN A SWEET PINK COTTAGE WITH AN ORANGE TREE, AND--
MIND IF I CUT IN? I NEED A WORD WITH MR. TOOEY.
CERTAINLY, DEAR. THIS OLD PUSS IS BEGGING FOR A TOUCH-UP.
LOOK AT HER, GOLDIE. SHE'S THE WHOLE BIT. KNOW WHAT SHE CALLED ME? A KNIGHT AMONG MEN.
KING AMONG MEN. NOT KNIGHT.
WHO STEPPED ON YOUR TAIL? I MEAN, SHEESH, I THOUGHT YOU'D BE IMPRESSED.
WALTER, DAD AND I GOT FIRED.
WHAT?! WHY?
I BROKE SOME RULES TO GET THAT NECKLACE BACK.
I BROKE SOME LAWS.
AND I GOT CAUGHT.

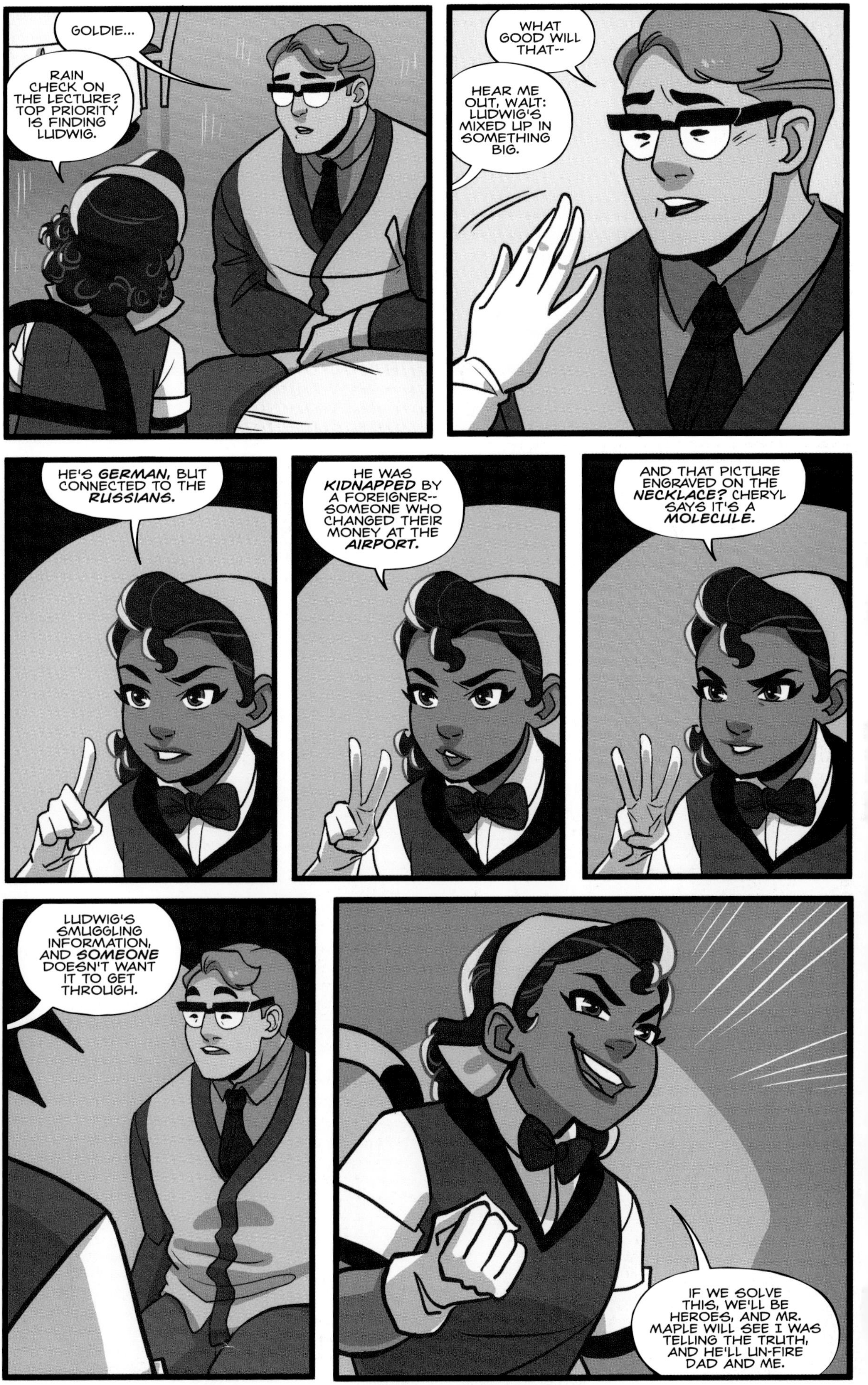
GOLDIE...
RAIN CHECK ON THE LECTURE? TOP PRIORITY IS FINDING LUDWIG.
WHAT GOOD WILL THAT--
HEAR ME OUT, WALT: LUDWIG'S MIXED UP IN SOMETHING BIG.
HE'S *GERMAN,* BUT CONNECTED TO THE *RUSSIANS.*
HE WAS *KIDNAPPED* BY A FOREIGNER--SOMEONE WHO CHANGED THEIR MONEY AT THE *AIRPORT.*
AND THAT PICTURE ENGRAVED ON THE *NECKLACE?* CHERYL SAYS IT'S A *MOLECULE.*
LUDWIG'S SMUGGLING INFORMATION, AND *SOMEONE* DOESN'T WANT IT TO GET THROUGH.
IF WE SOLVE THIS, WE'LL BE HEROES, AND MR. MAPLE WILL SEE I WAS TELLING THE TRUTH, AND HE'LL UN-FIRE DAD AND ME.

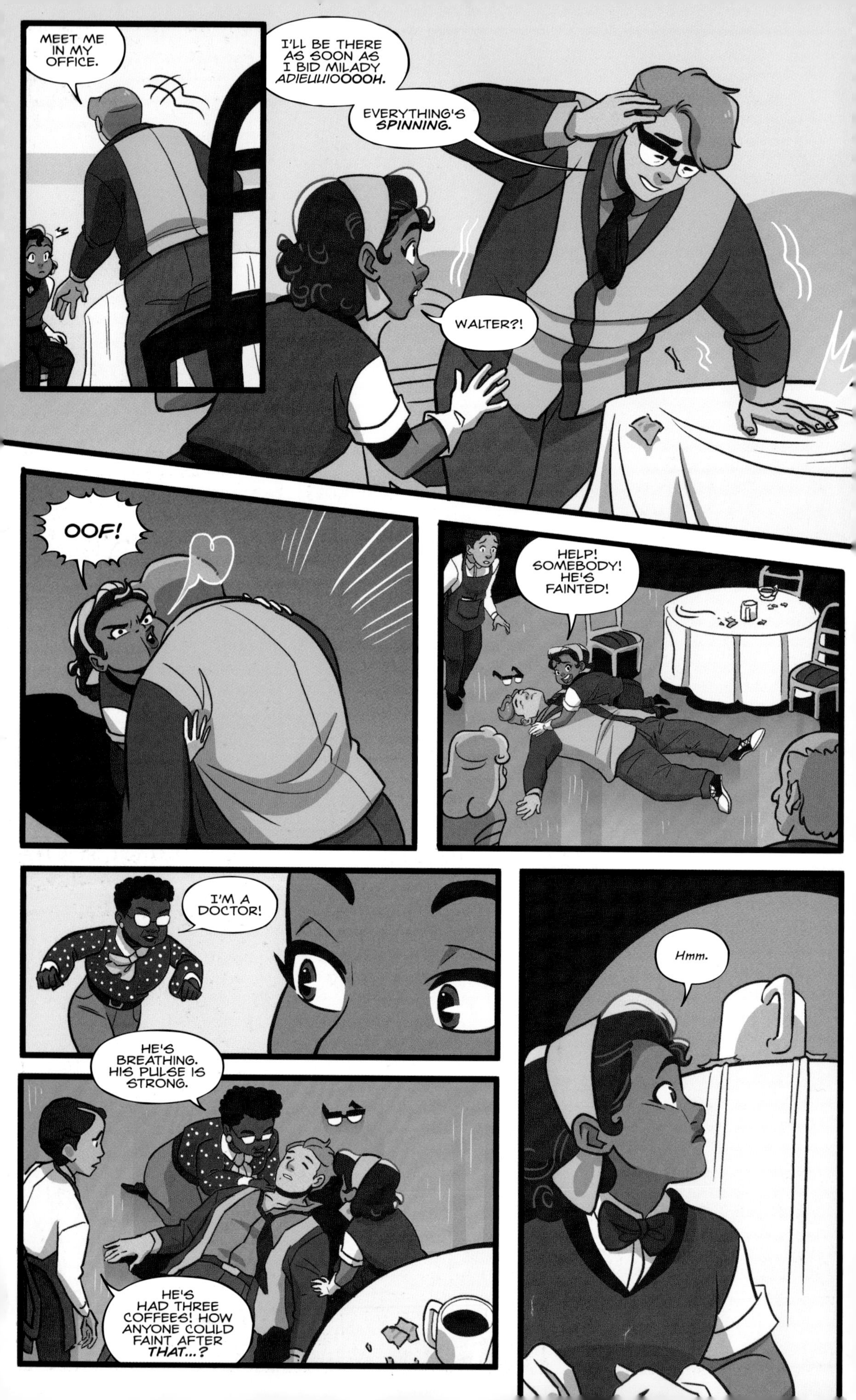
MEET ME IN MY OFFICE.
I'LL BE THERE AS SOON AS I BID MILADY ADIEUUIOOOOH.
EVERYTHING'S SPINNING.
WALTER?!
OOF!
HELP! SOMEBODY! HE'S FAINTED!
I'M A DOCTOR!
HE'S BREATHING. HIS PULSE IS STRONG.
HE'S HAD THREE COFFEES! HOW ANYONE COULD FAINT AFTER THAT...?
Hmm.

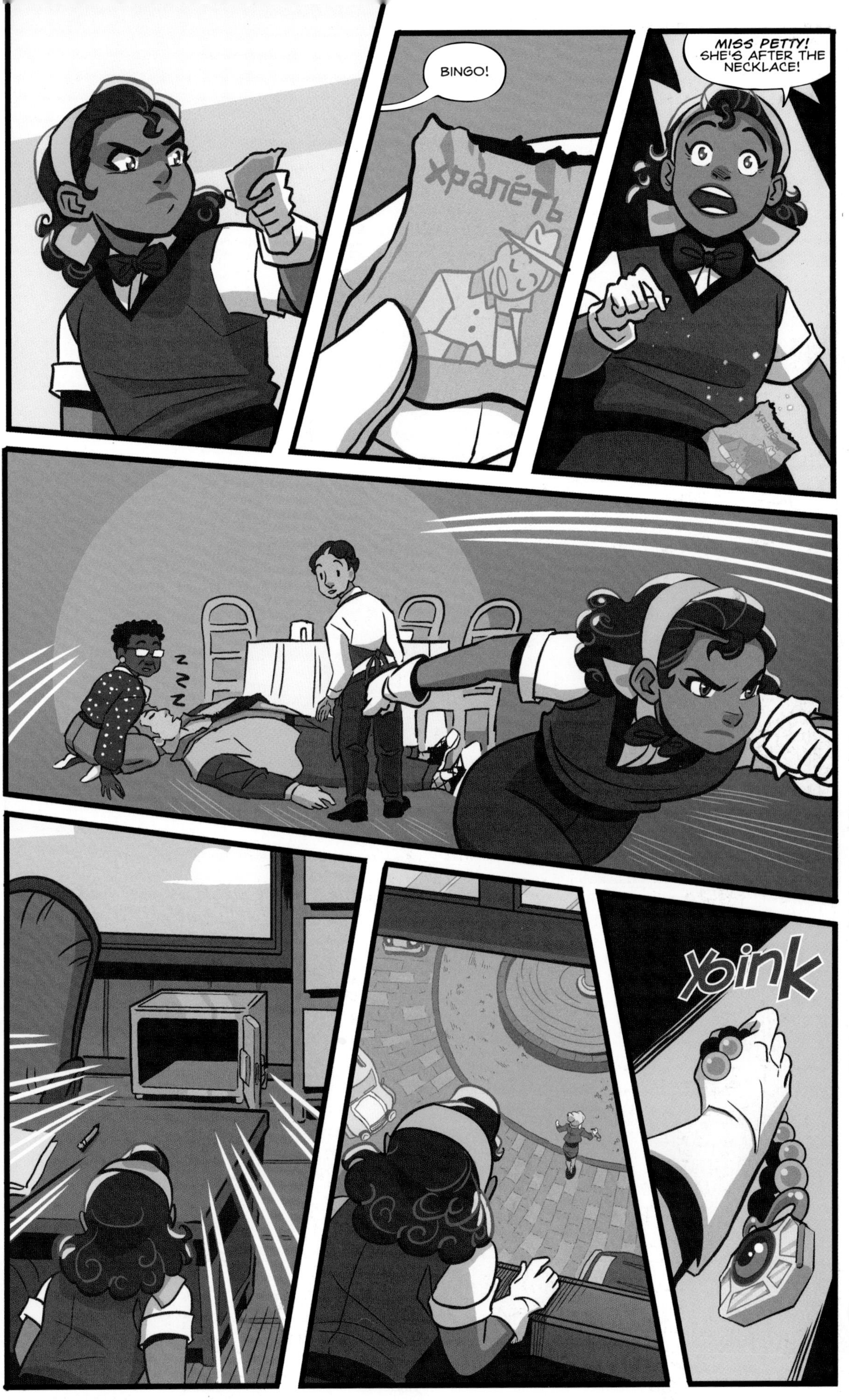
BINGO!
храпеть
MISS PETTY! SHE'S AFTER THE NECKLACE!
YOINK

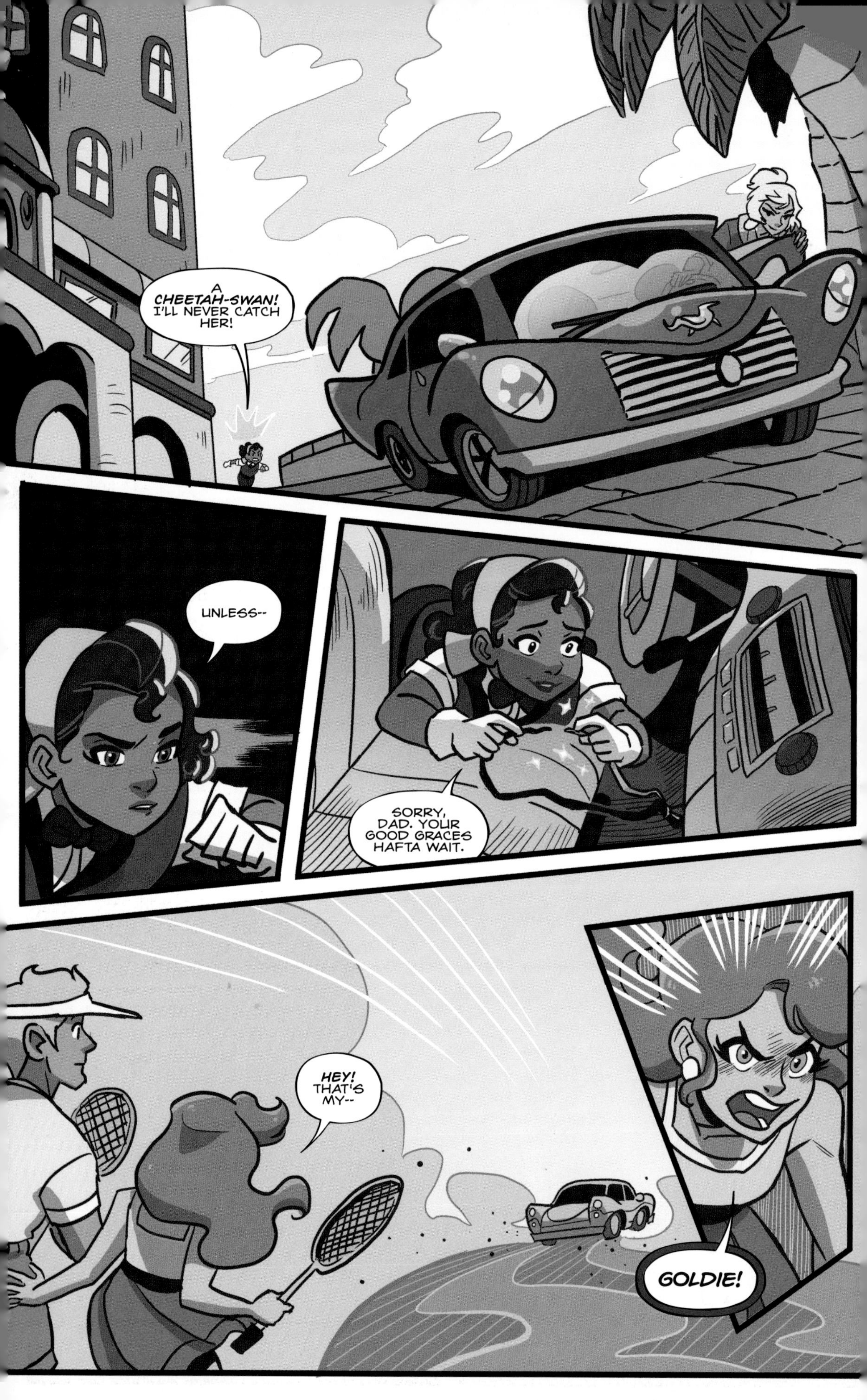
A CHEETAH-SWAN! I'LL NEVER CATCH HER!
UNLESS--
SORRY, DAD. YOUR GOOD GRACES HAFTA WAIT.
HEY! THAT'S MY--
GOLDIE!

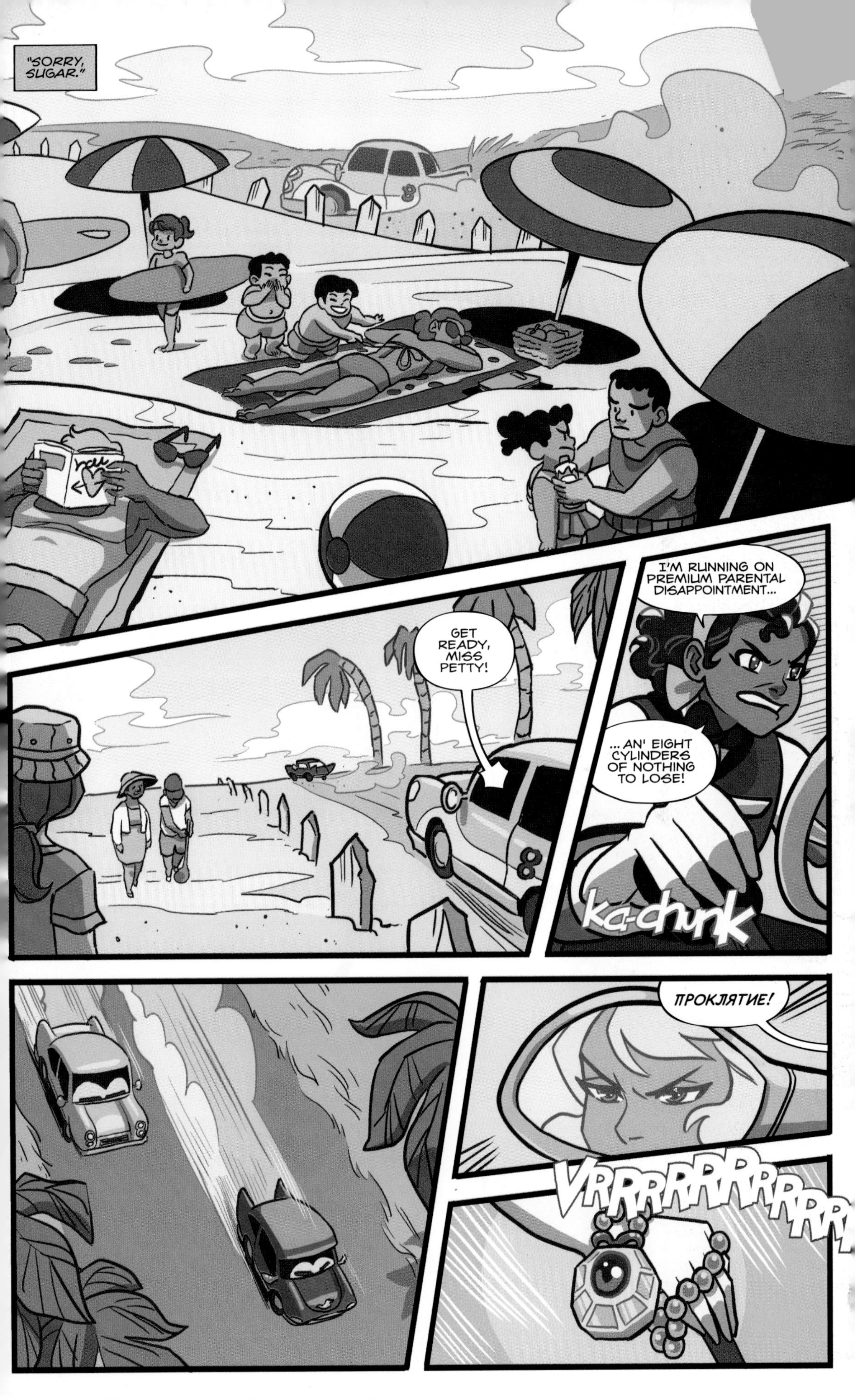
"SORRY, SUGAR."
GET READY, MISS PETTY!
I'M RUNNING ON PREMIUM PARENTAL DISAPPOINTMENT...
...AN' EIGHT CYLINDERS OF NOTHING TO LOSE!
KA-CHUNK
ПРОКЛЯТИЕ!
VRRRRRRRRRRR

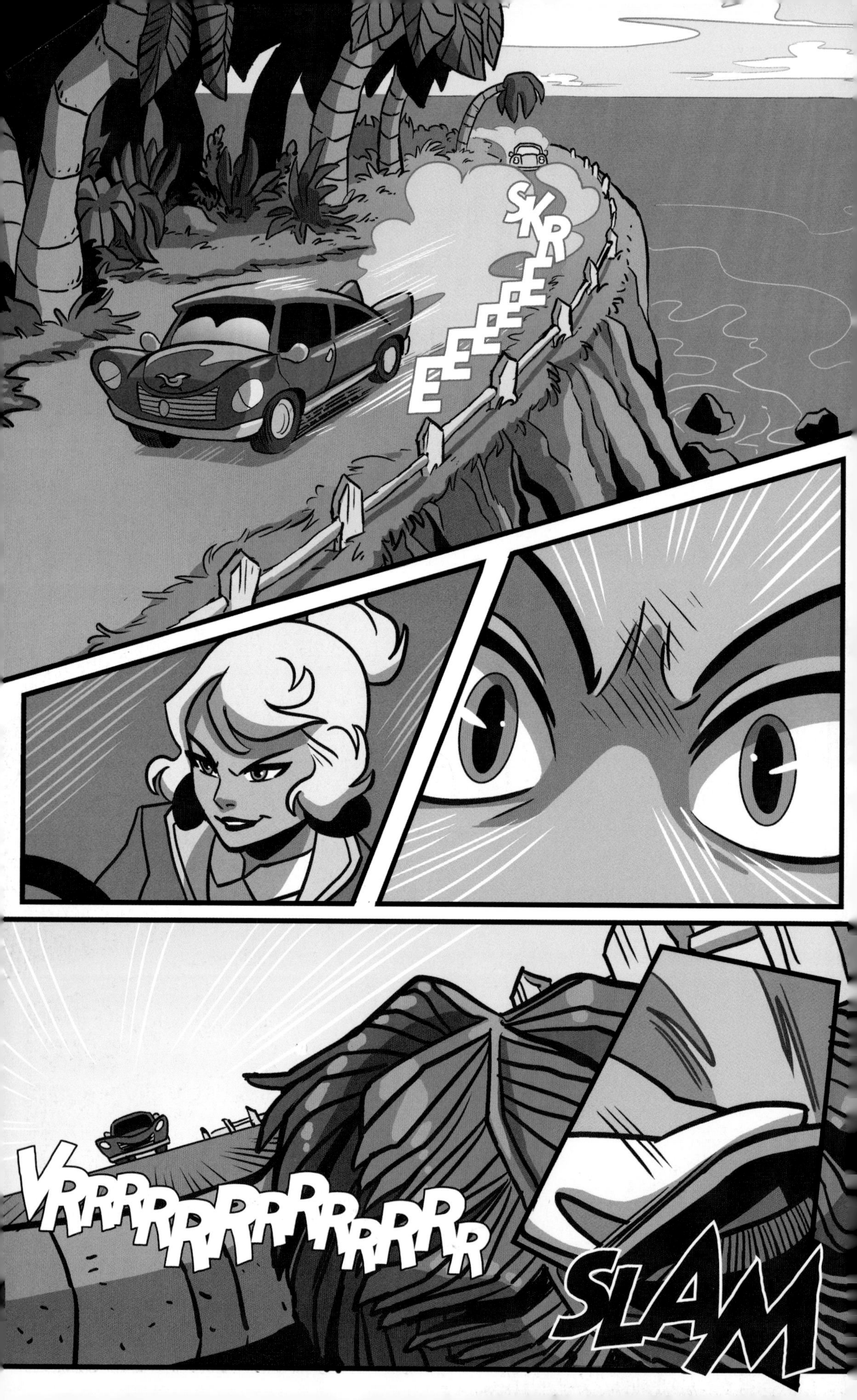

SKREEEEEEE
VRRRRRRRRRRRRRRR
SLAM

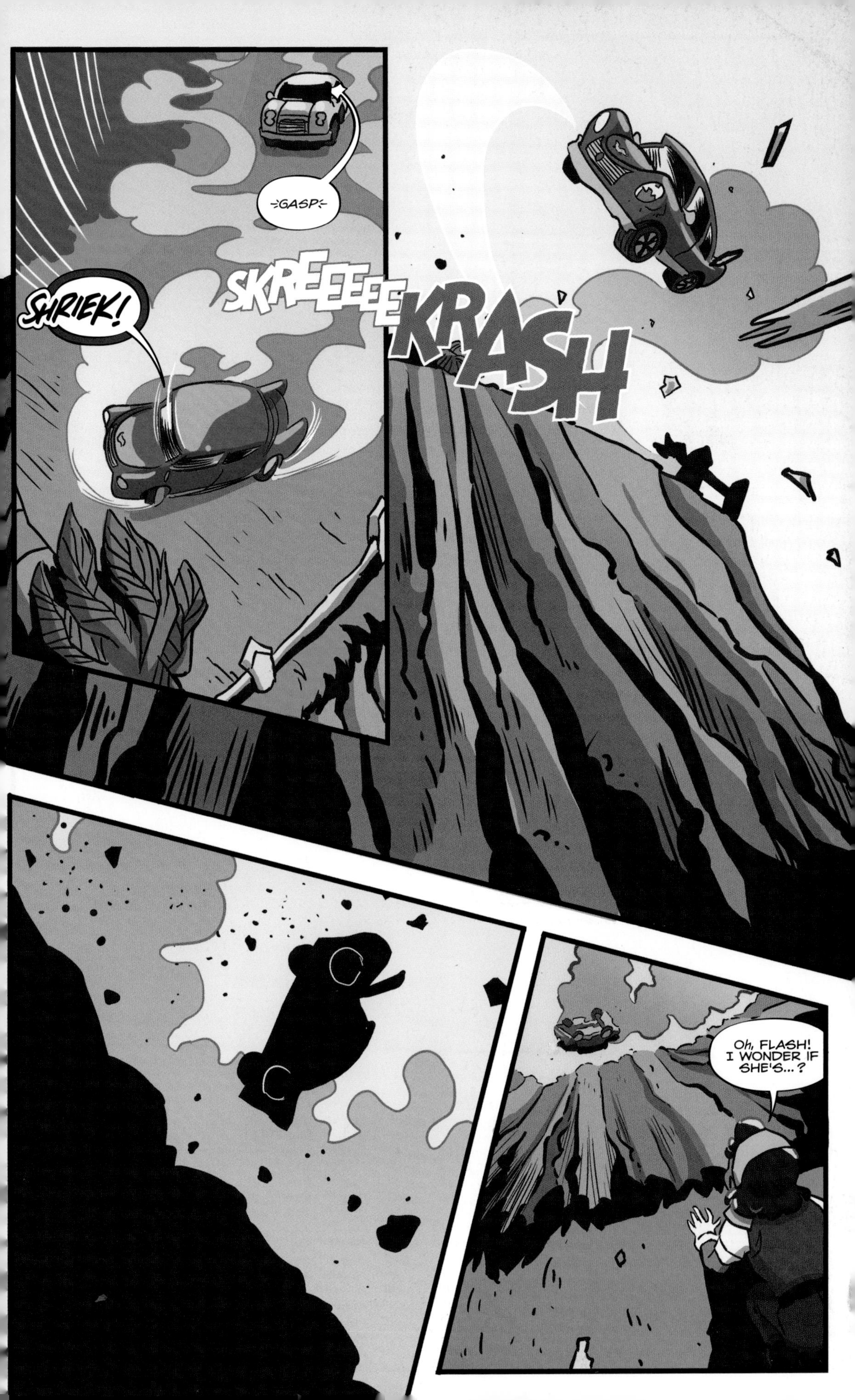

=GASP=
SHRIEK!
SKREEEEEEKRASH
Oh, FLASH! I WONDER IF SHE'S...?

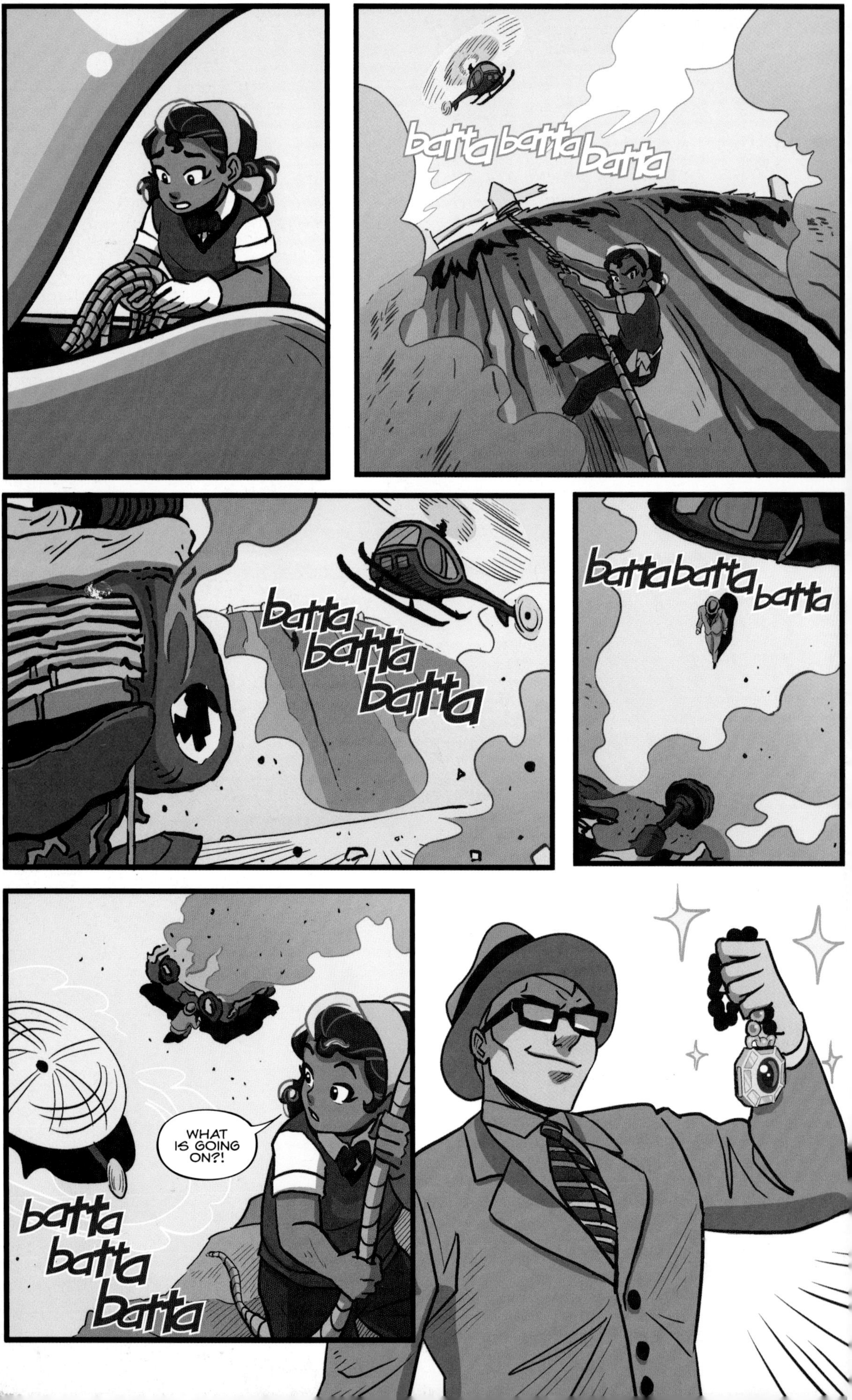
batta batta batta
batta batta batta
batta batta batta
WHAT IS GOING ON?!
batta batta batta

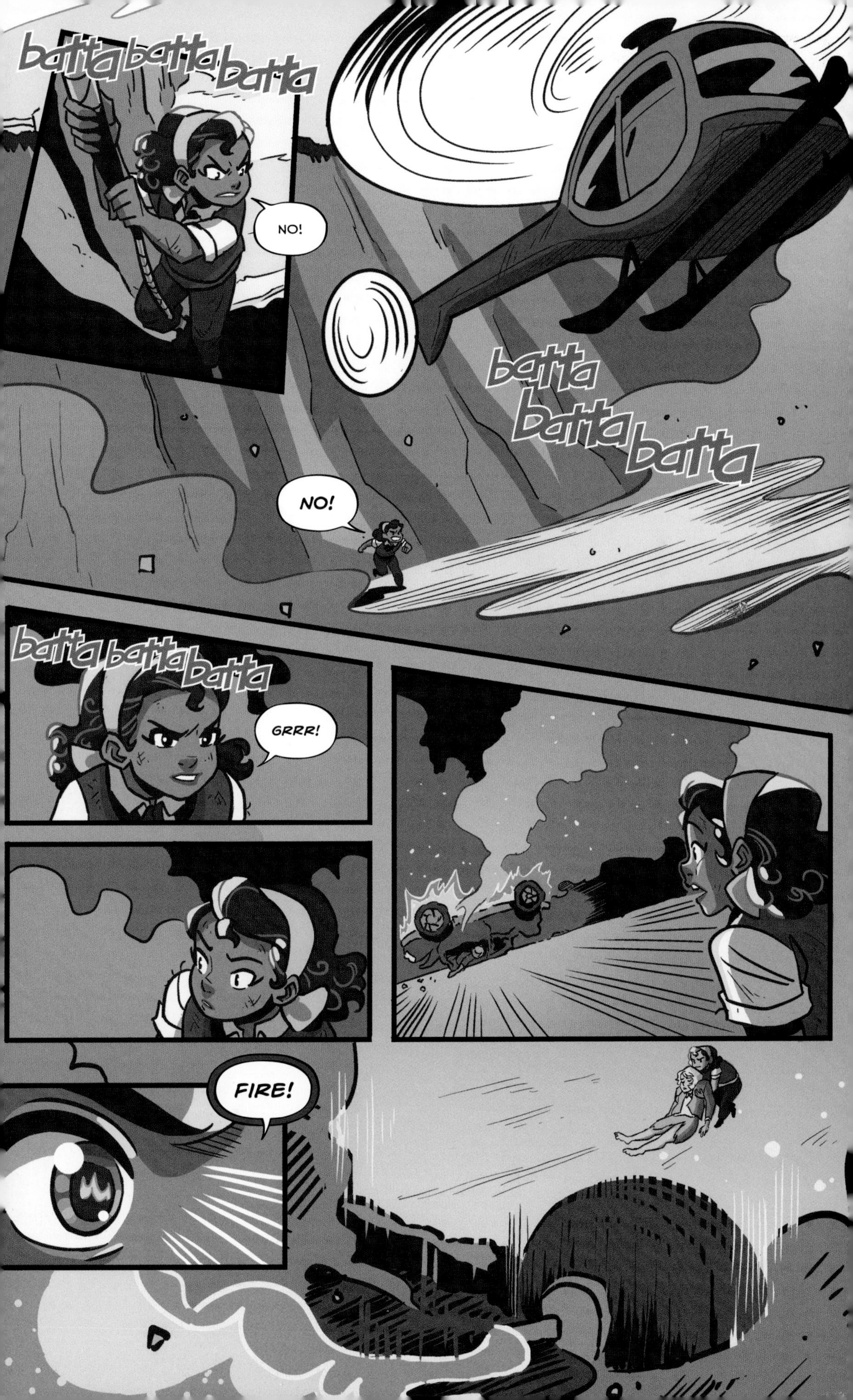
batta batta batta
NO!
batta batta batta
NO!
batta batta batta
GRRR!
FIRE!

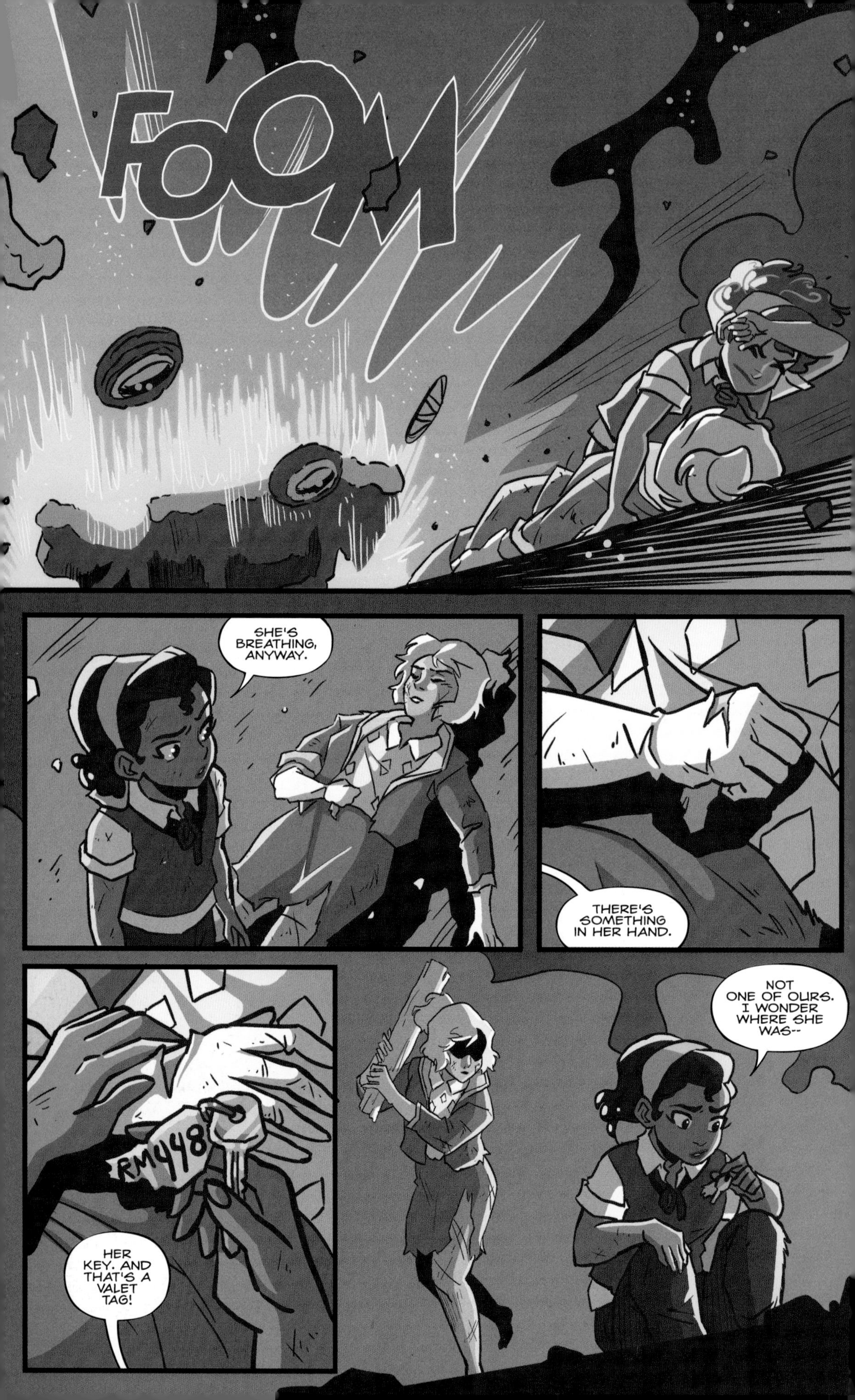
FOOM
SHE'S BREATHING, ANYWAY.
THERE'S SOMETHING IN HER HAND.
RM 448
HER KEY. AND THAT'S A VALET TAG!
NOT ONE OF OURS. I WONDER WHERE SHE WAS--

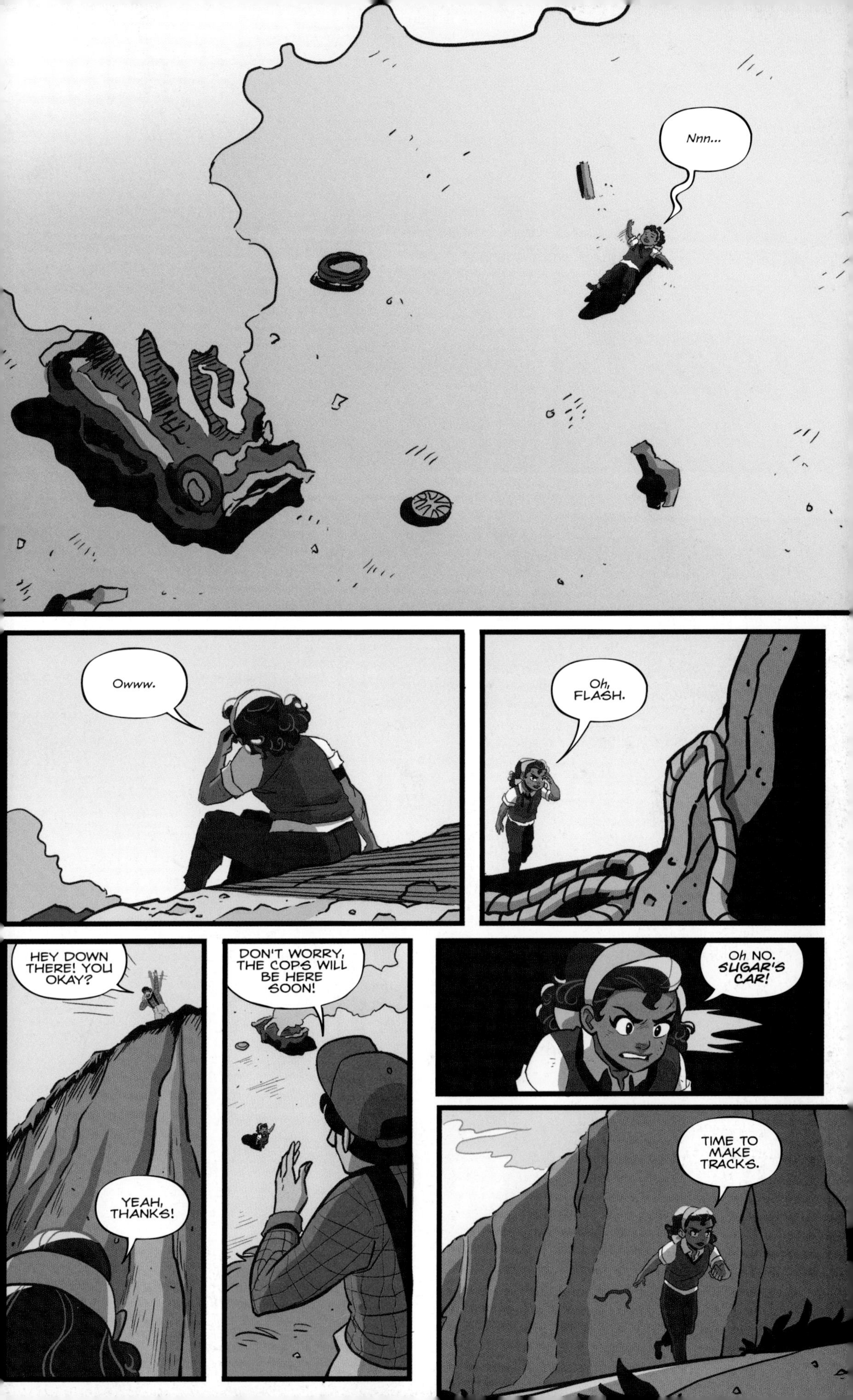
Nnn...
Owww.
Oh, FLASH.
HEY DOWN THERE! YOU OKAY?
DON'T WORRY, THE COPS WILL BE HERE SOON!
YEAH, THANKS!
Oh NO. SUGAR'S CAR!
TIME TO MAKE TRACKS.

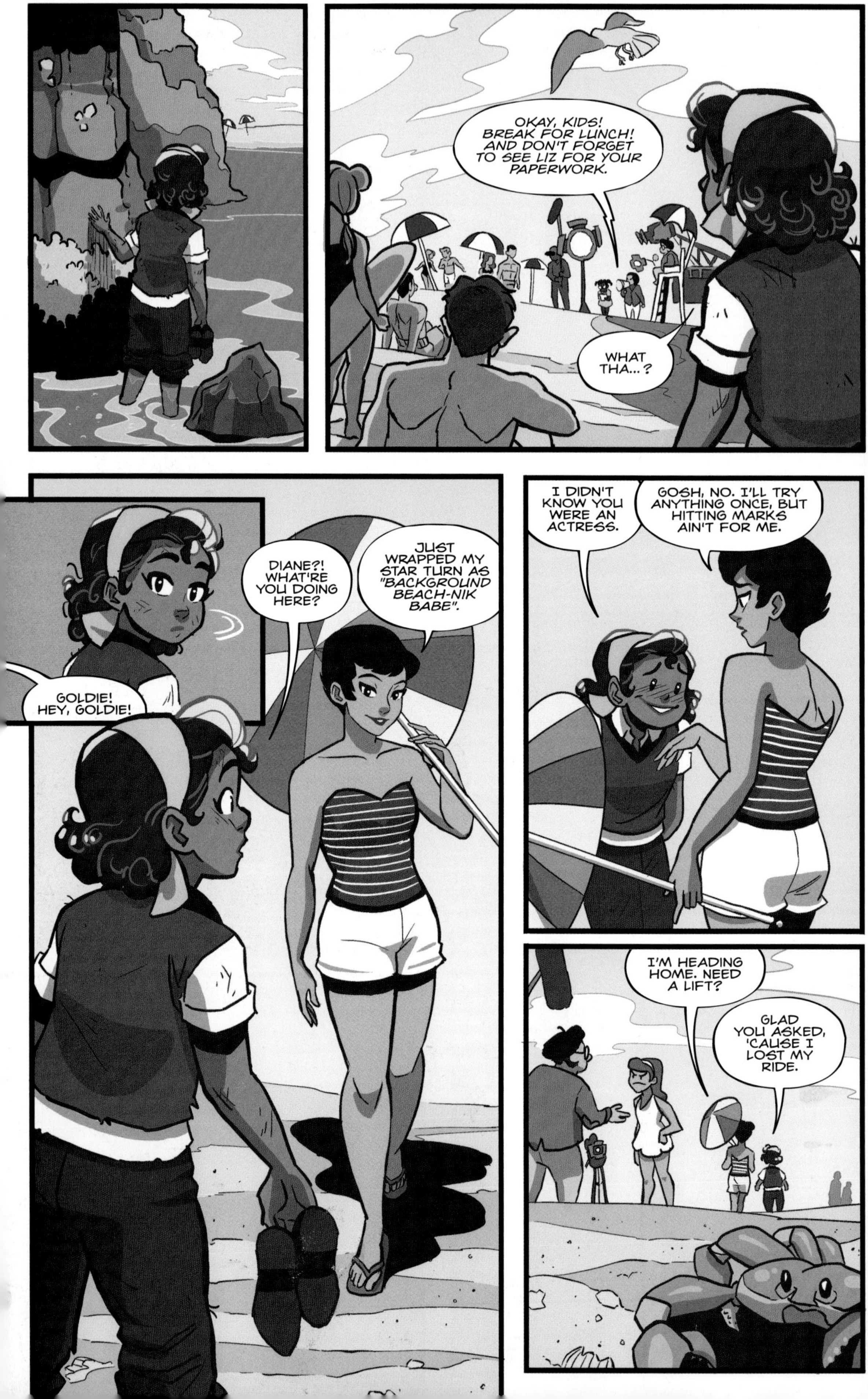
OKAY, KIDS! BREAK FOR LUNCH! AND DON'T FORGET TO SEE LIZ FOR YOUR PAPERWORK.
WHAT THA...?
GOLDIE! HEY, GOLDIE!
DIANE?! WHAT'RE YOU DOING HERE?
JUST WRAPPED MY STAR TURN AS "BACKGROUND BEACH-NIK BABE".
I DIDN'T KNOW YOU WERE AN ACTRESS.
GOSH, NO. I'LL TRY ANYTHING ONCE, BUT HITTING MARKS AIN'T FOR ME.
I'M HEADING HOME. NEED A LIFT?
GLAD YOU ASKED, 'CAUSE I LOST MY RIDE.

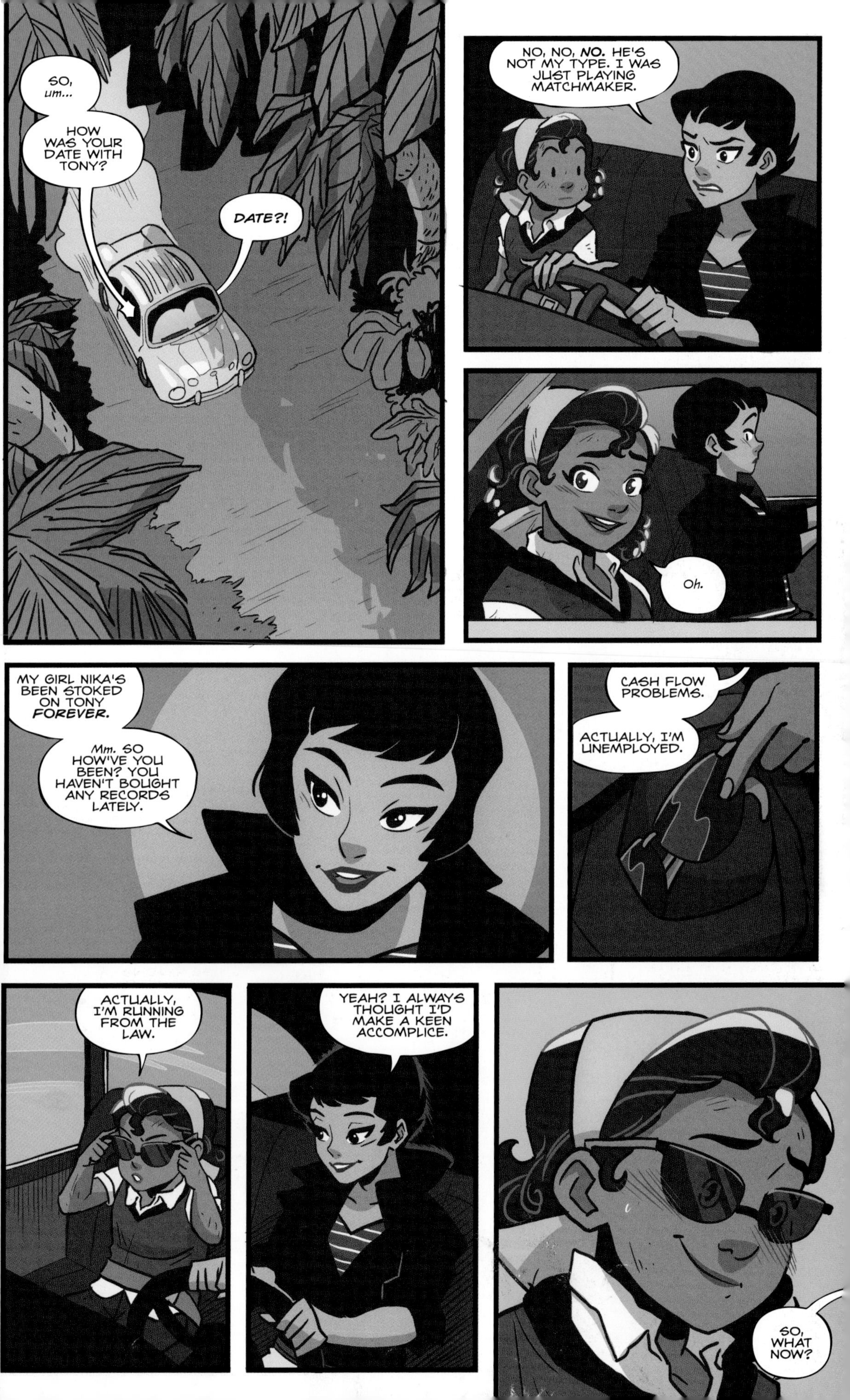
SO, um...
HOW WAS YOUR DATE WITH TONY?
DATE?!
NO, NO, NO. HE'S NOT MY TYPE. I WAS JUST PLAYING MATCHMAKER.
Oh.
MY GIRL NIKA'S BEEN STOKED ON TONY FOREVER.
Mm. SO HOW'VE YOU BEEN? YOU HAVEN'T BOUGHT ANY RECORDS LATELY.
CASH FLOW PROBLEMS.
ACTUALLY, I'M UNEMPLOYED.
ACTUALLY, I'M RUNNING FROM THE LAW.
YEAH? I ALWAYS THOUGHT I'D MAKE A KEEN ACCOMPLICE.
SO, WHAT NOW?

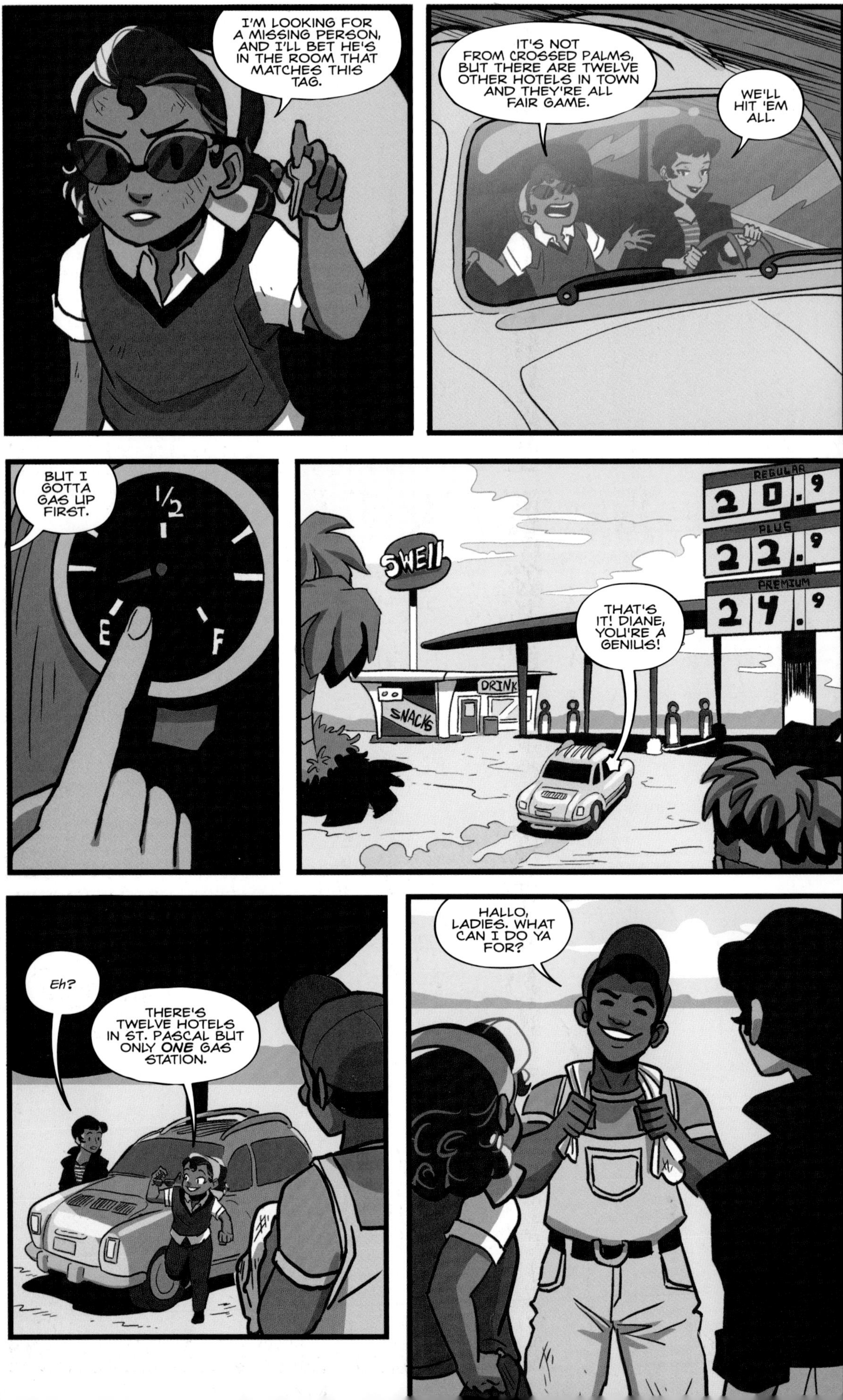
I'M LOOKING FOR A MISSING PERSON, AND I'LL BET HE'S IN THE ROOM THAT MATCHES THIS TAG.
IT'S NOT FROM CROSSED PALMS, BUT THERE ARE TWELVE OTHER HOTELS IN TOWN AND THEY'RE ALL FAIR GAME.
WE'LL HIT 'EM ALL.
BUT I GOTTA GAS UP FIRST.
1/2
E
F
REGULAR
20.9
PLUS
22.9
PREMIUM
24.9
SWELL
DRINK
SNACKS
THAT'S IT! DIANE, YOU'RE A GENIUS!
Eh?
THERE'S TWELVE HOTELS IN ST. PASCAL BUT ONLY ONE GAS STATION.
HALLO, LADIES. WHAT CAN I DO YA FOR?

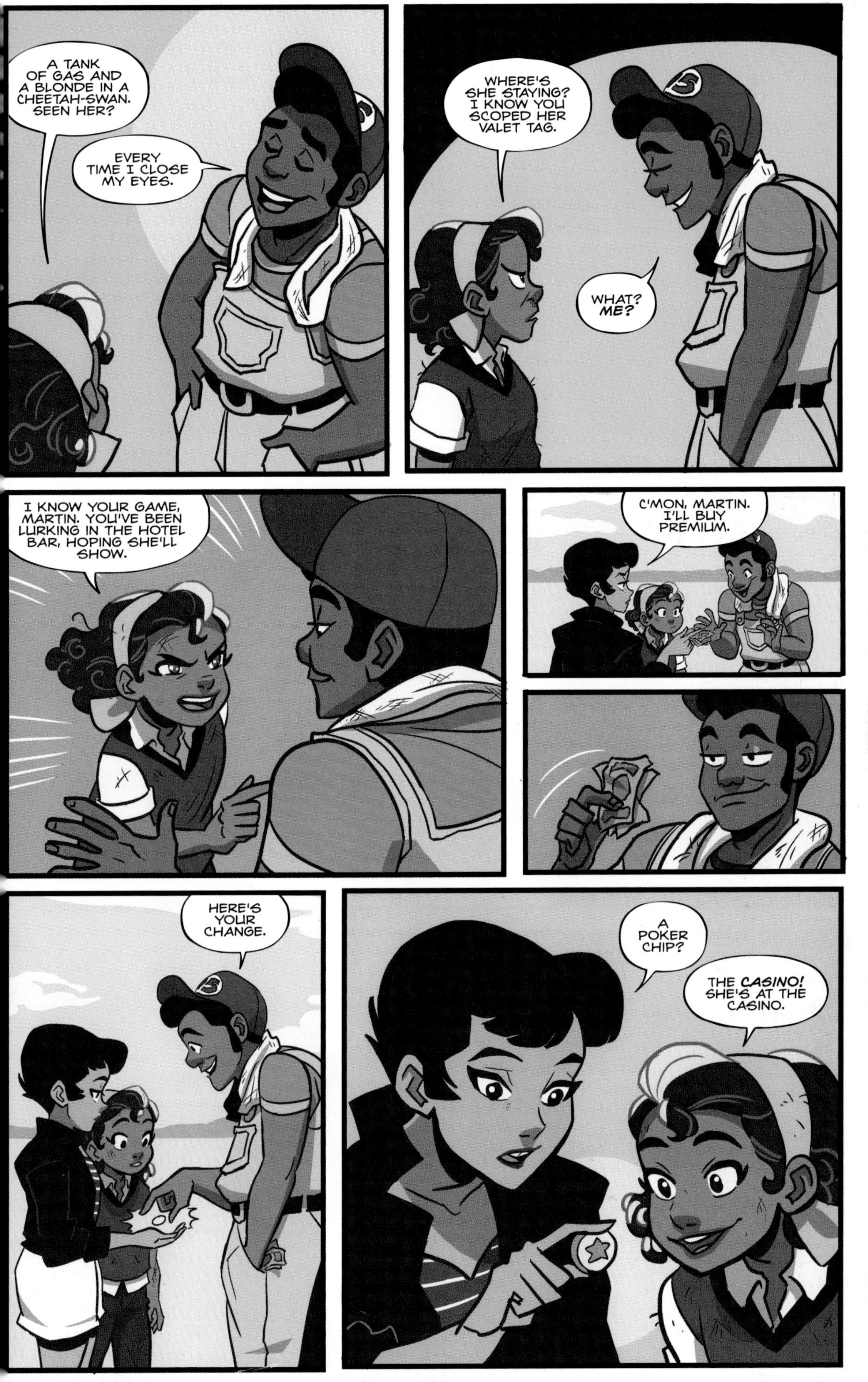
A TANK OF GAS AND A BLONDE IN A CHEETAH-SWAN. SEEN HER?
EVERY TIME I CLOSE MY EYES.
WHERE'S SHE STAYING? I KNOW YOU SCOPED HER VALET TAG.
WHAT? *ME?*
I KNOW YOUR GAME, MARTIN. YOU'VE BEEN LURKING IN THE HOTEL BAR, HOPING SHE'LL SHOW.
C'MON, MARTIN. I'LL BUY PREMIUM.
HERE'S YOUR CHANGE.
A POKER CHIP?
THE *CASINO!* SHE'S AT THE CASINO.

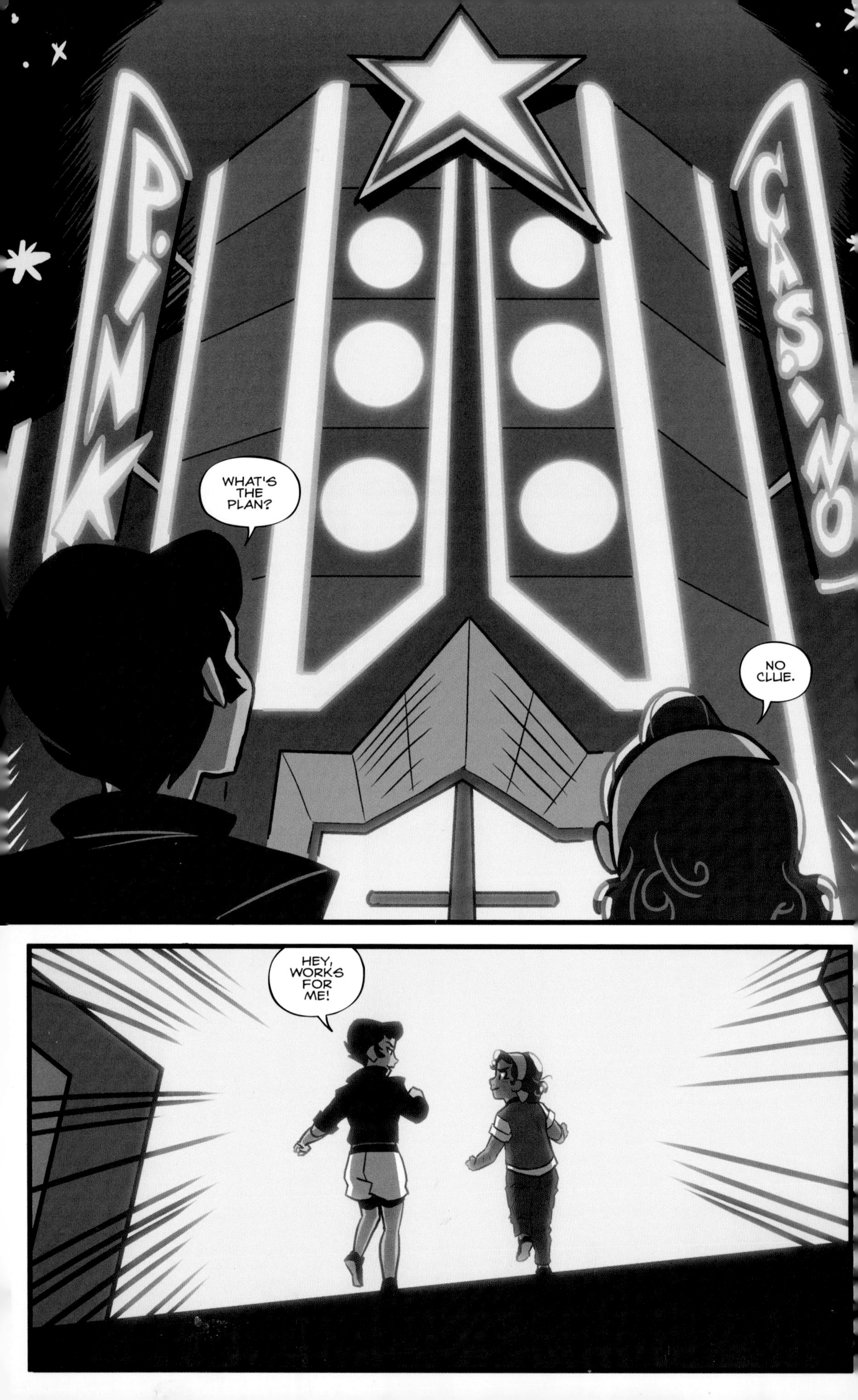
PINK
CASINO
WHAT'S THE PLAN?
NO CLUE.
HEY, WORKS FOR ME!

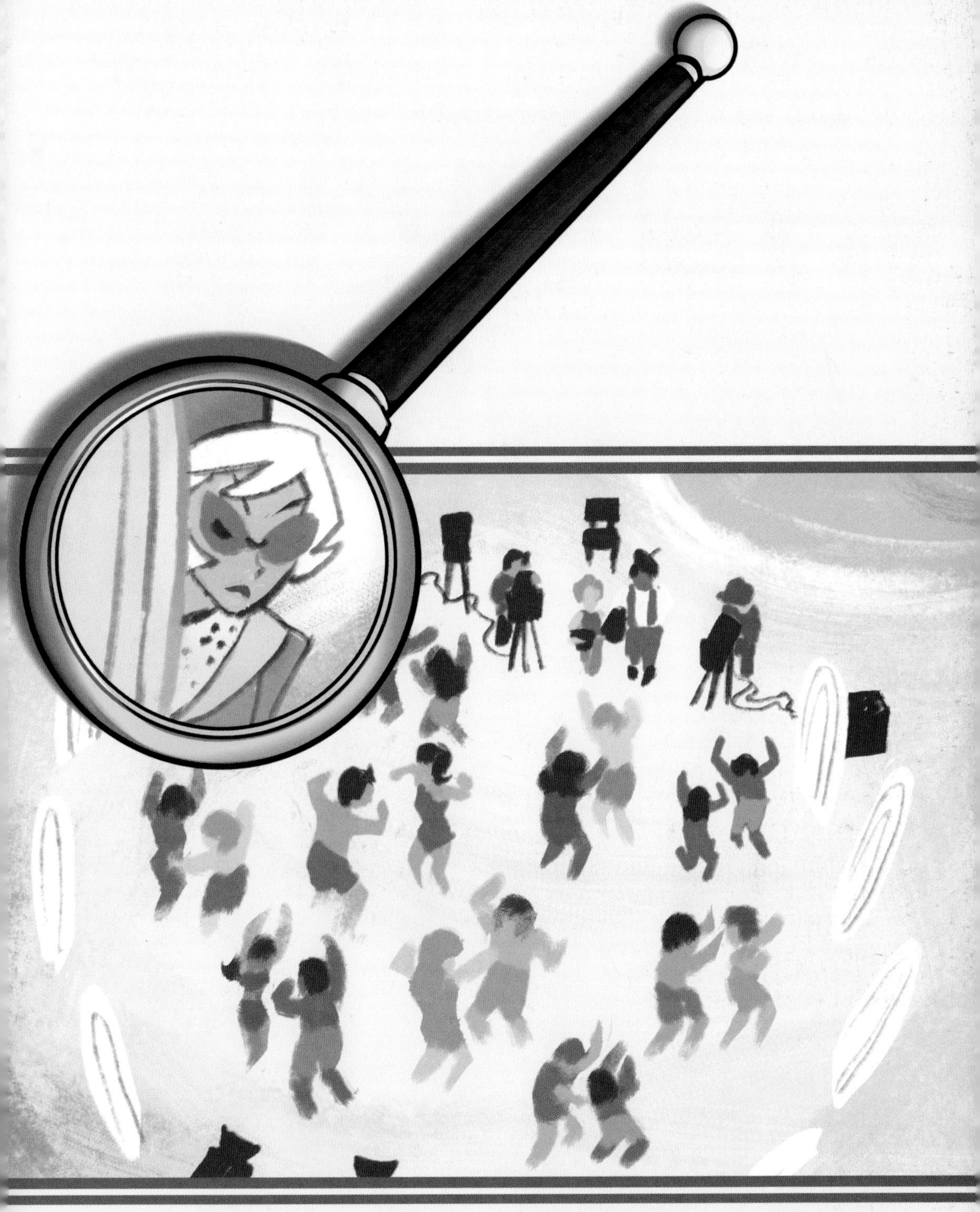

chapter

FOUR

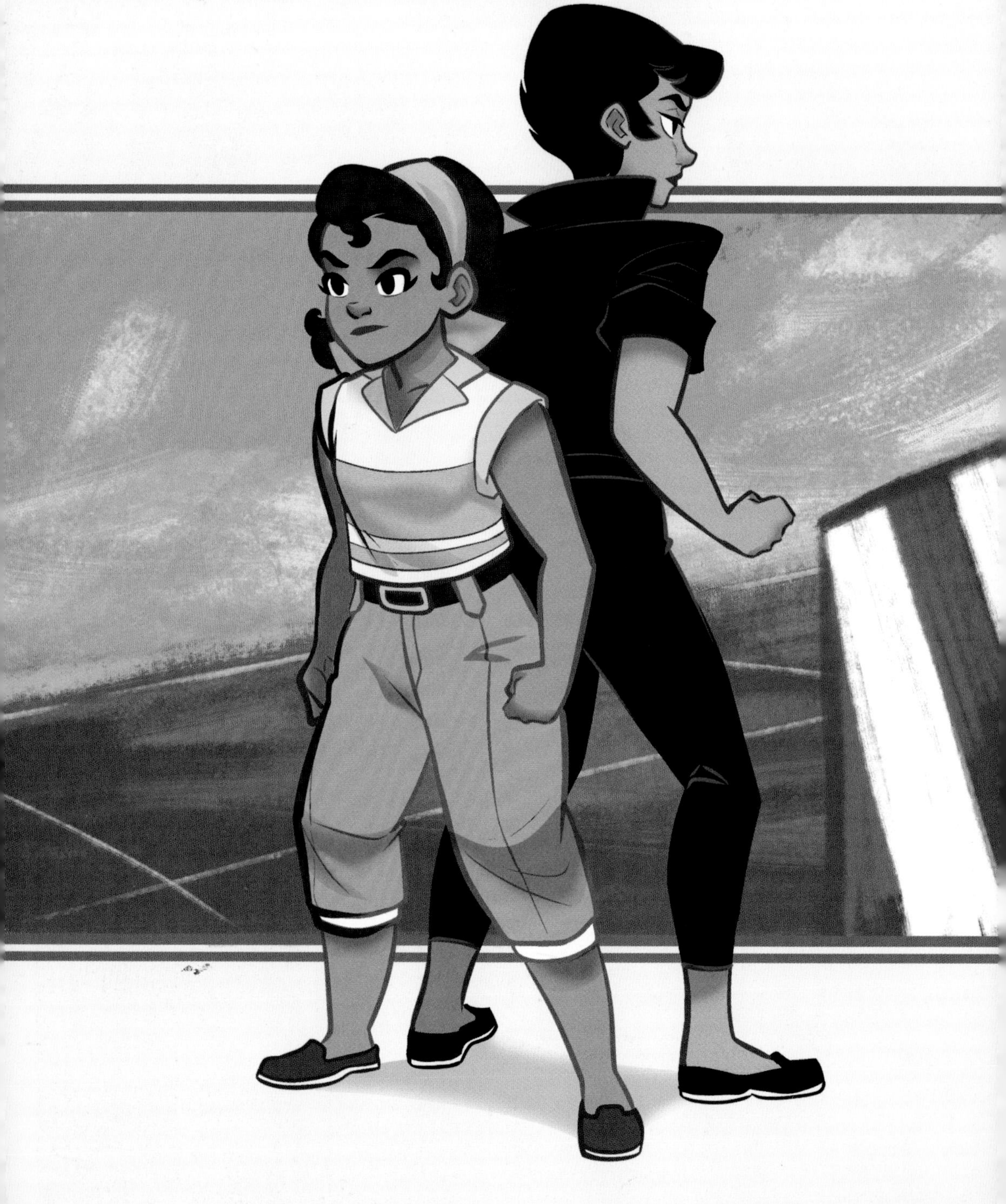

issue four cover by **Brittney Williams**

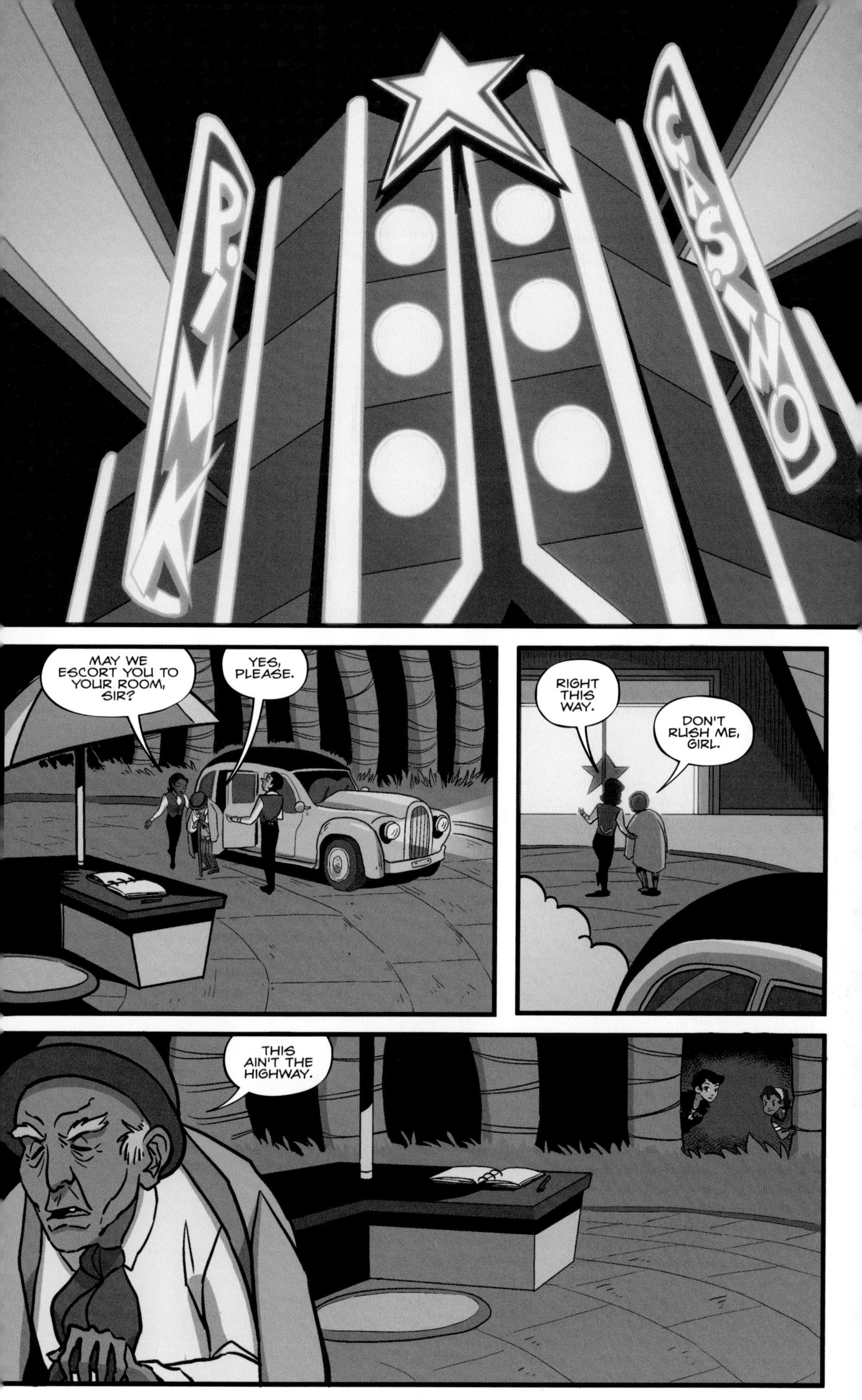
PINK
CASINO
MAY WE ESCORT YOU TO YOUR ROOM, SIR?
YES, PLEASE.
RIGHT THIS WAY.
DON'T RUSH ME, GIRL.
THIS AIN'T THE HIGHWAY.

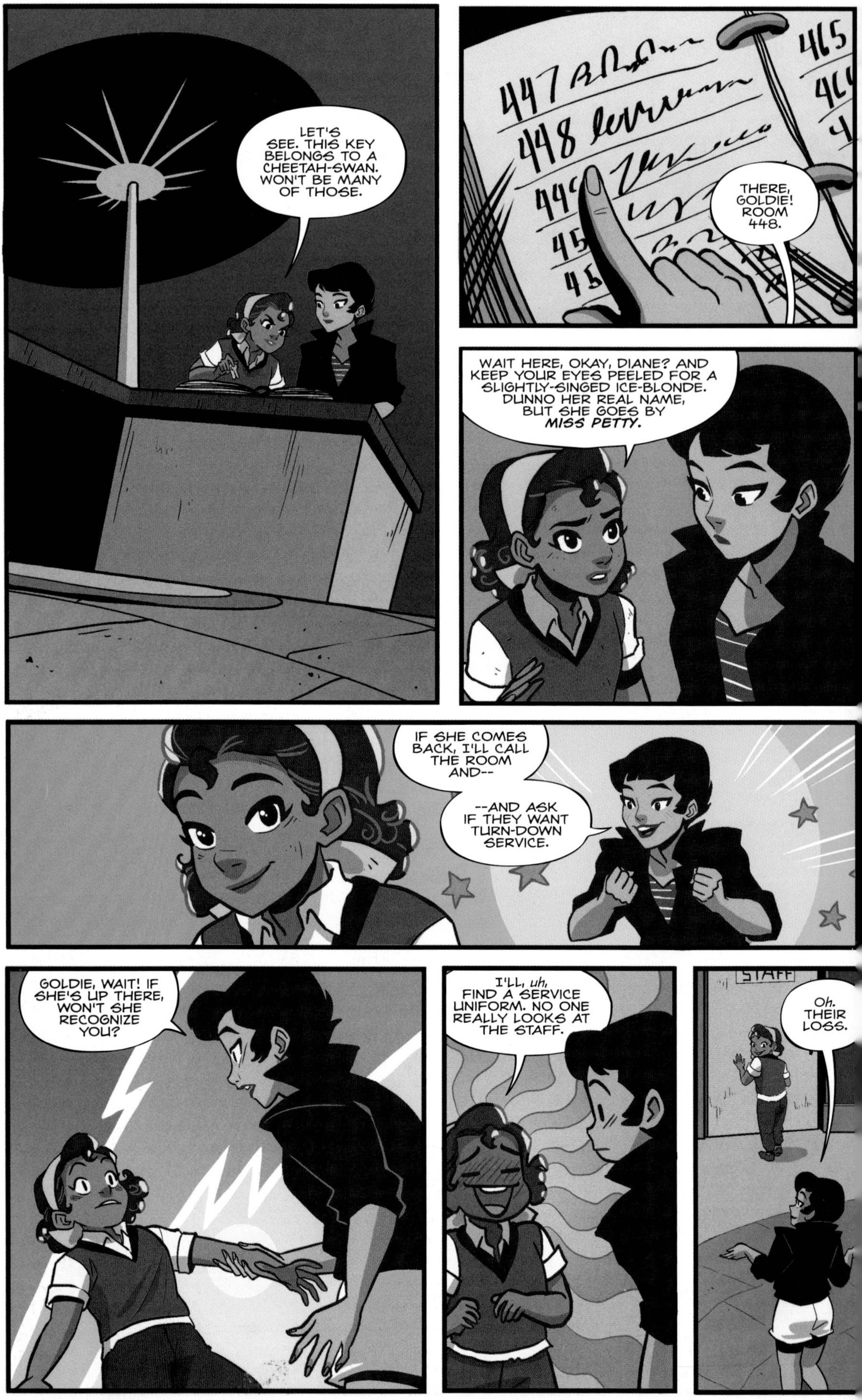
LET'S SEE. THIS KEY BELONGS TO A CHEETAH-SWAN. WON'T BE MANY OF THOSE.
THERE, GOLDIE! ROOM 448.
WAIT HERE, OKAY, DIANE? AND KEEP YOUR EYES PEELED FOR A SLIGHTLY-SINGED ICE-BLONDE. DUNNO HER REAL NAME, BUT SHE GOES BY MISS PETTY.
IF SHE COMES BACK, I'LL CALL THE ROOM AND--
--AND ASK IF THEY WANT TURN-DOWN SERVICE.
GOLDIE, WAIT! IF SHE'S UP THERE, WON'T SHE RECOGNIZE YOU?
I'LL, uh, FIND A SERVICE UNIFORM. NO ONE REALLY LOOKS AT THE STAFF.
STAFF
Oh. THEIR LOSS.

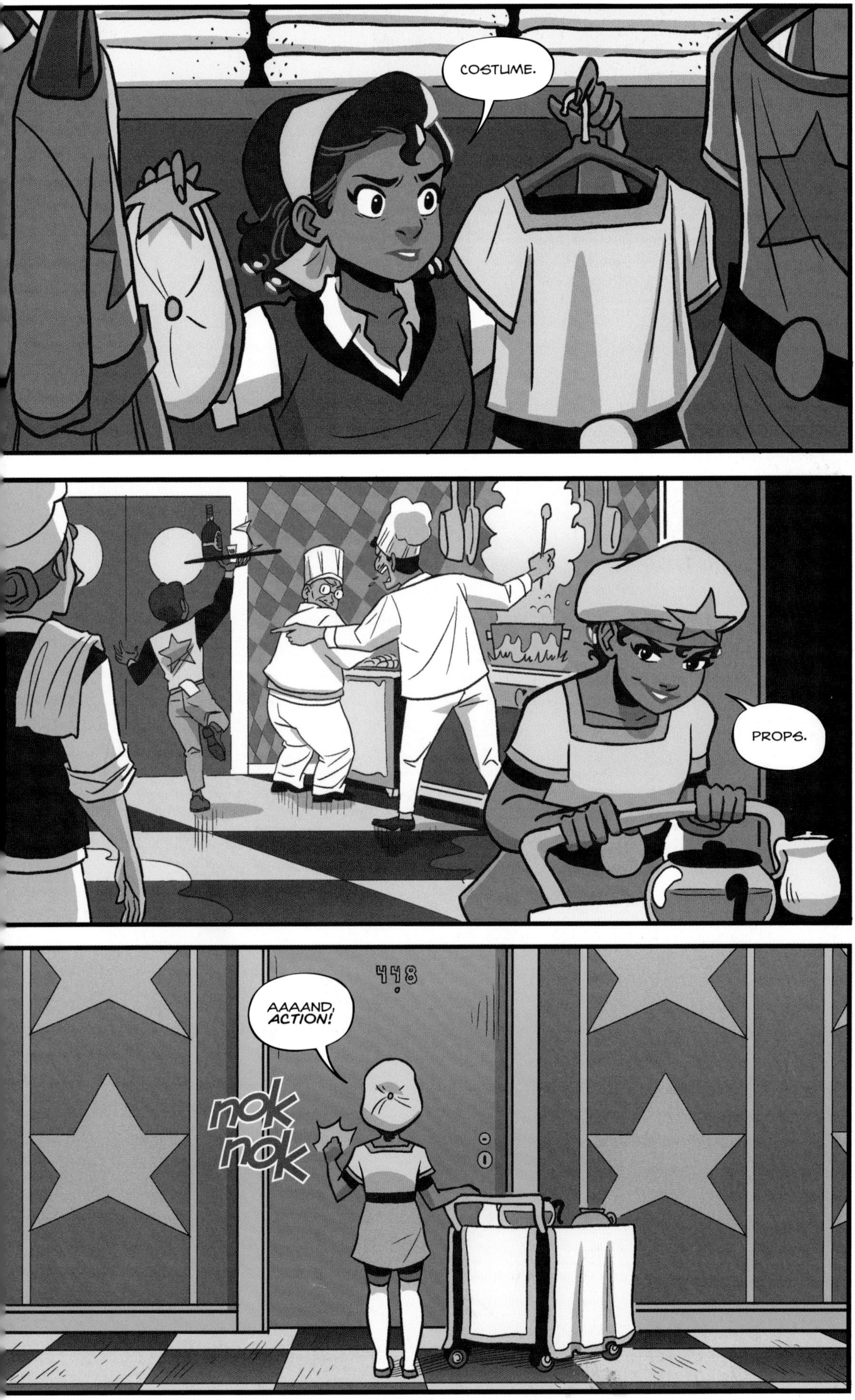
COSTUME.
PROPS.
448
AAAAND, ACTION!
nok nok

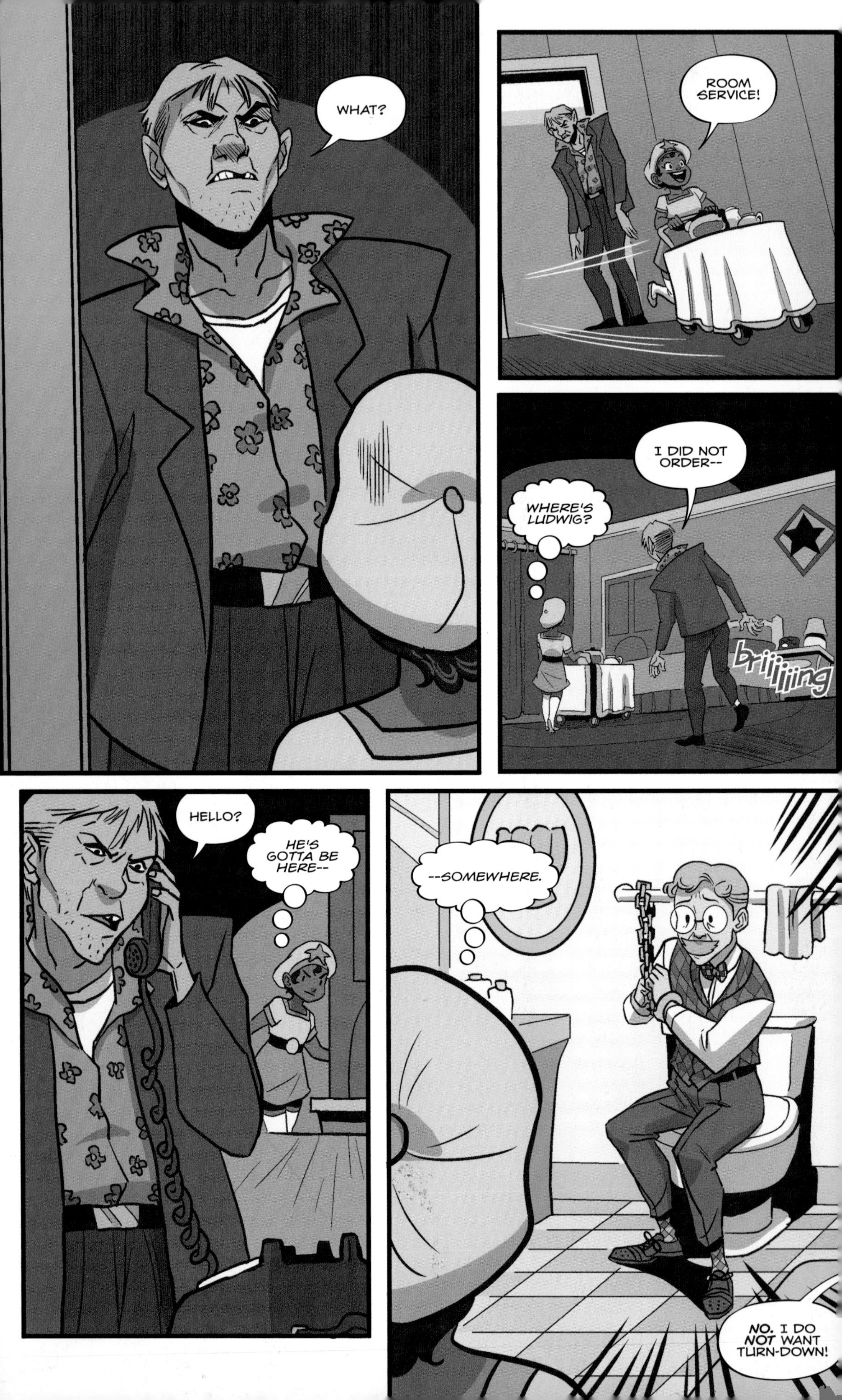
WHAT?
ROOM SERVICE!
I DID NOT ORDER--
WHERE'S LUDWIG?
briiiiiing
HELLO?
HE'S GOTTA BE HERE--
--SOMEWHERE.
NO. I DO NOT WANT TURN-DOWN!

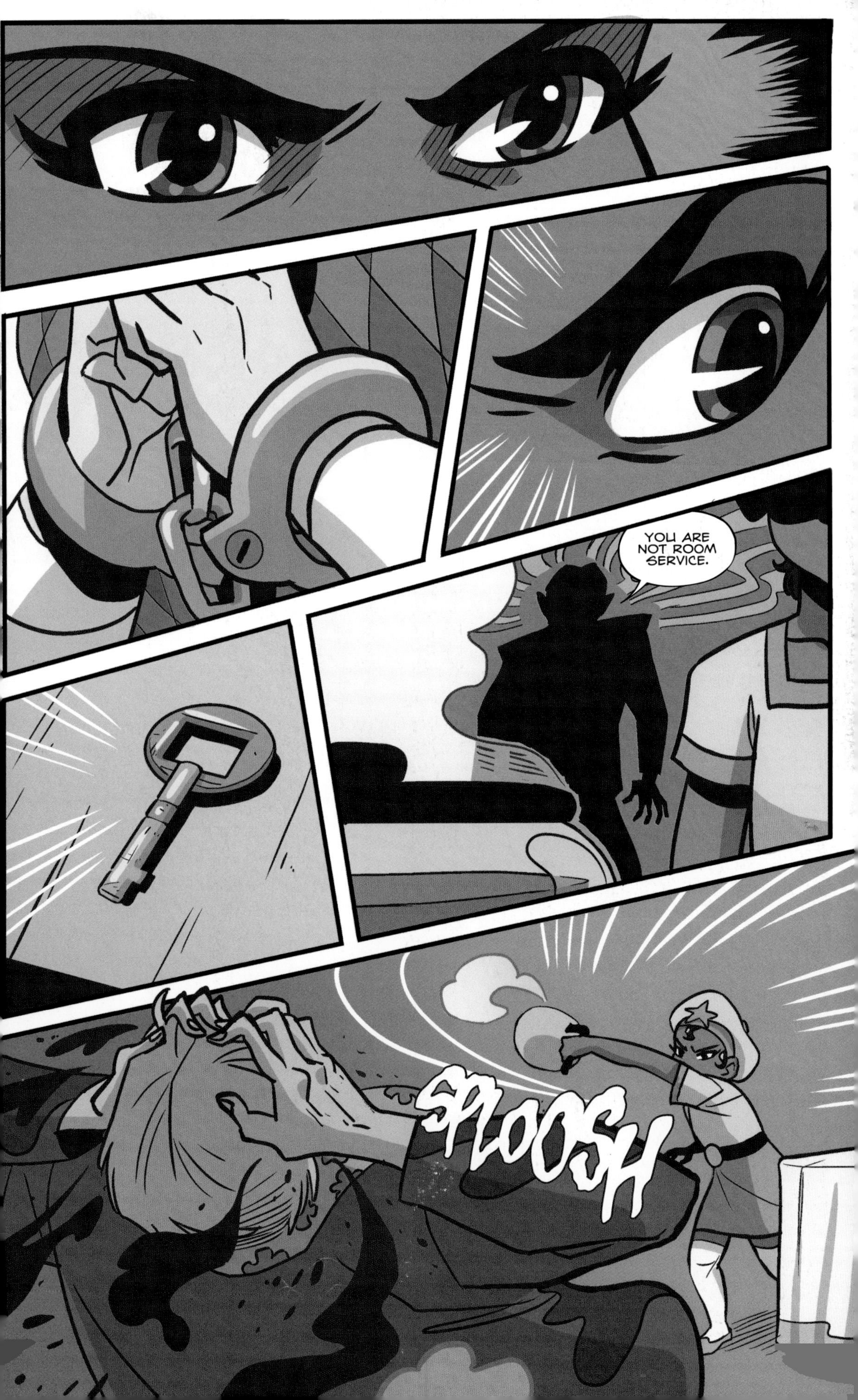
YOU ARE NOT ROOM SERVICE.
SPLOOSH

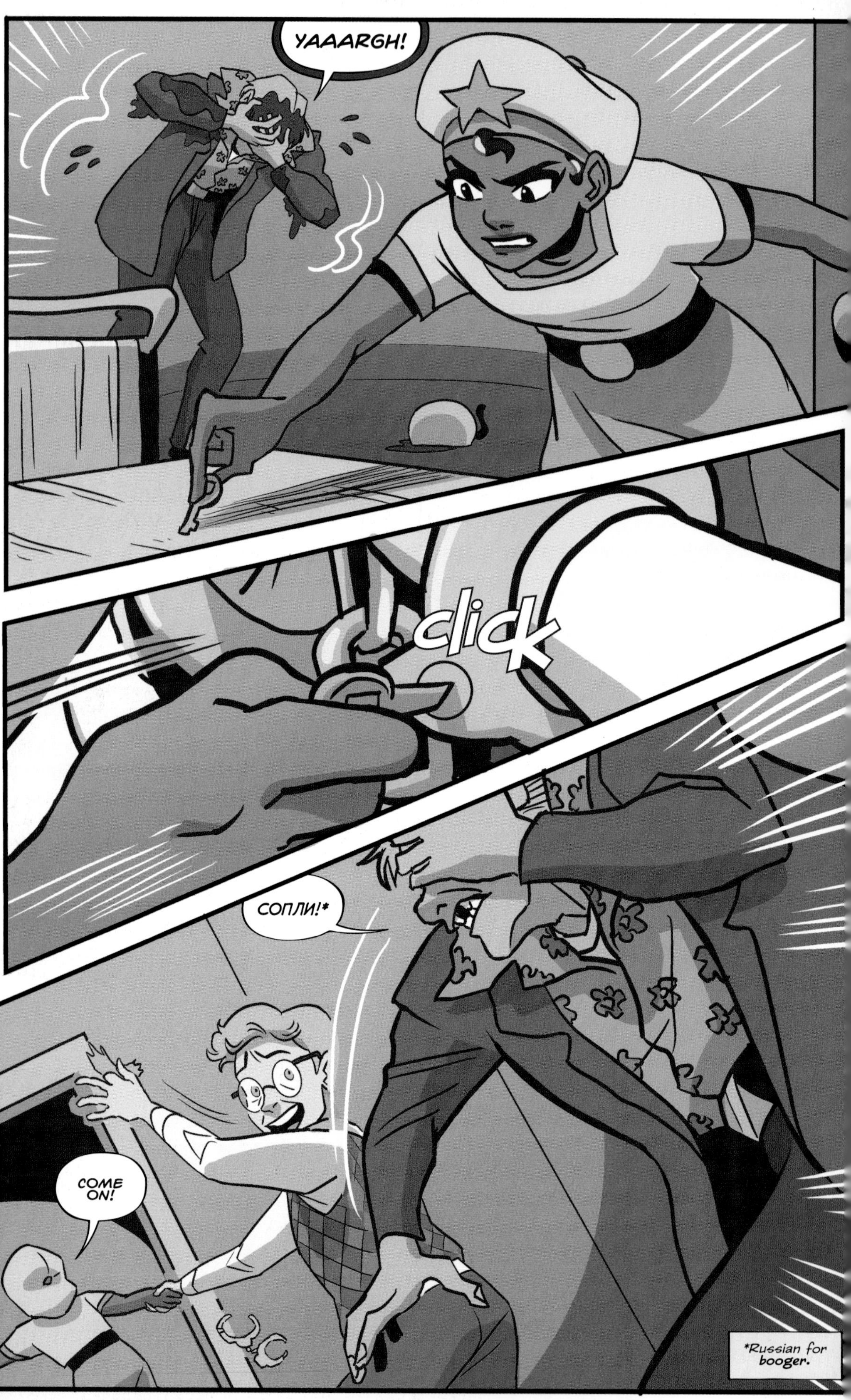
YAAARGH!
click
СОПЛИ!*
COME ON!
*Russian for booger.

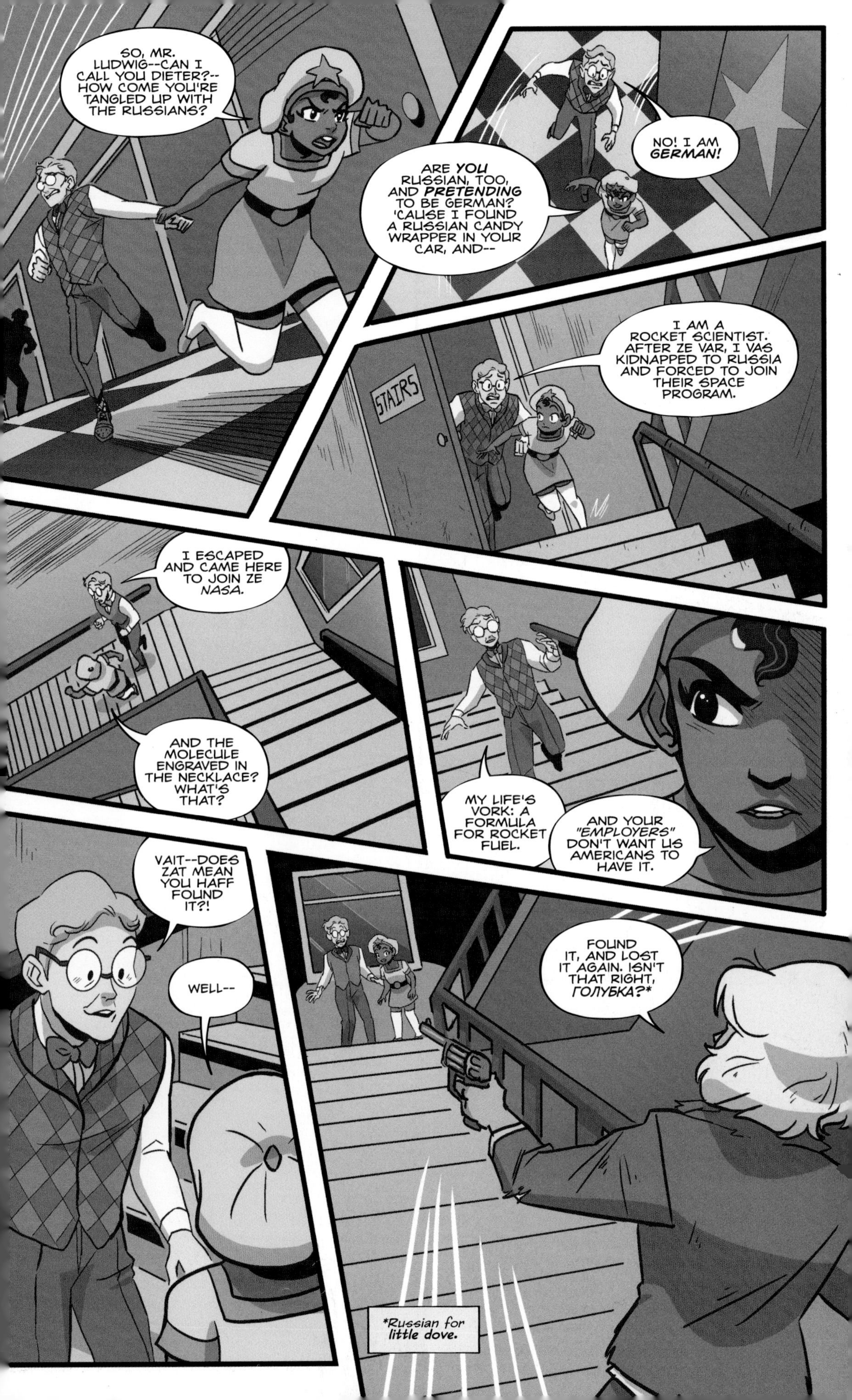
SO, MR. LUDWIG--CAN I CALL YOU DIETER?--HOW COME YOU'RE TANGLED UP WITH THE RUSSIANS?
NO! I AM GERMAN!
ARE YOU RUSSIAN, TOO, AND PRETENDING TO BE GERMAN? 'CAUSE I FOUND A RUSSIAN CANDY WRAPPER IN YOUR CAR, AND--
STAIRS
I AM A ROCKET SCIENTIST. AFTER ZE VAR, I VAS KIDNAPPED TO RUSSIA AND FORCED TO JOIN THEIR SPACE PROGRAM.
I ESCAPED AND CAME HERE TO JOIN ZE NASA.
AND THE MOLECULE ENGRAVED IN THE NECKLACE? WHAT'S THAT?
MY LIFE'S VORK: A FORMULA FOR ROCKET FUEL.
AND YOUR "EMPLOYERS" DON'T WANT US AMERICANS TO HAVE IT.
VAIT--DOES ZAT MEAN YOU HAFF FOUND IT?!
WELL--
FOUND IT, AND LOST IT AGAIN. ISN'T THAT RIGHT, ГОЛУБКА?*
*Russian for little dove.

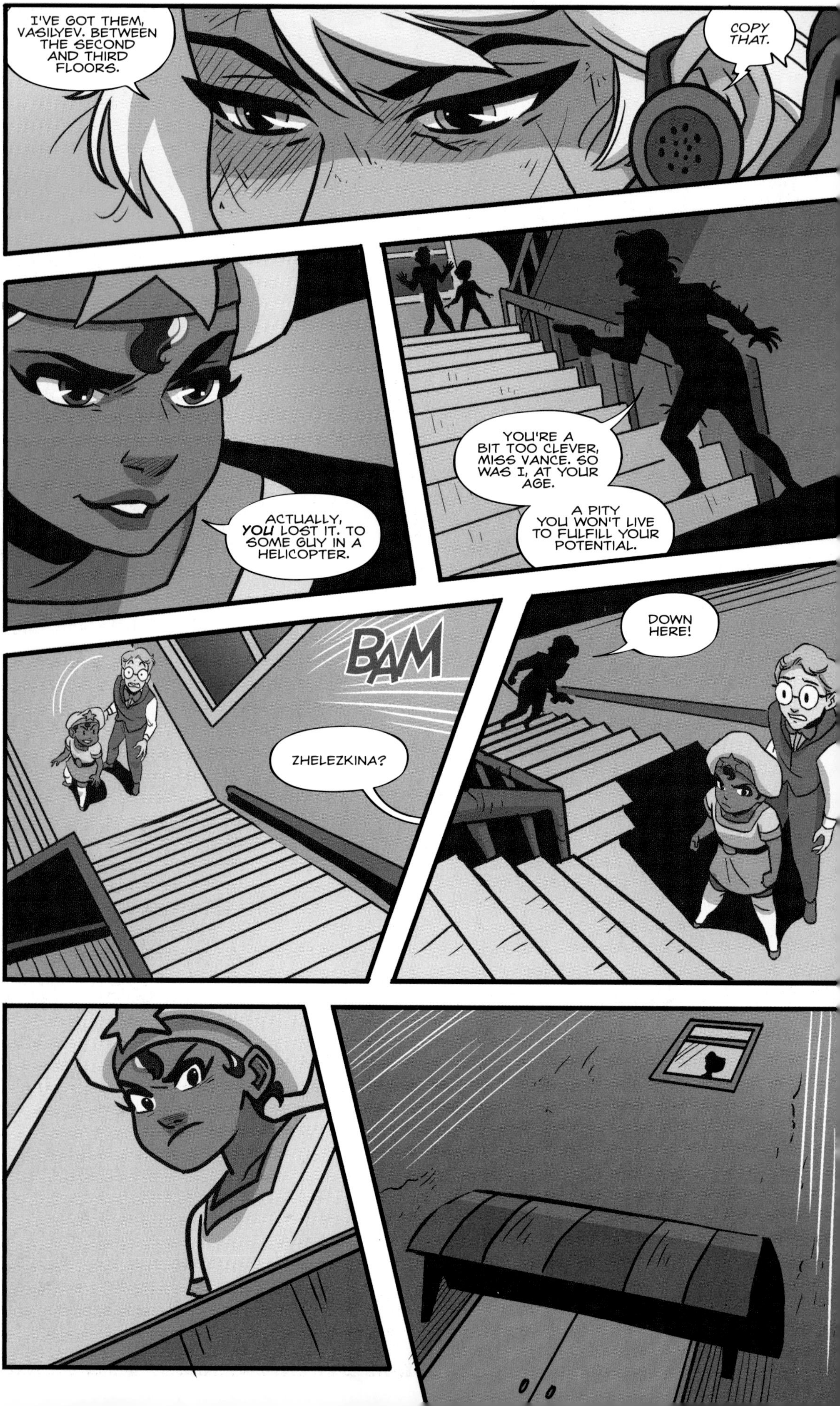

I'VE GOT THEM, VASILYEV. BETWEEN THE SECOND AND THIRD FLOORS.
COPY THAT.
ACTUALLY, YOU LOST IT. TO SOME GUY IN A HELICOPTER.
YOU'RE A BIT TOO CLEVER, MISS VANCE. SO WAS I, AT YOUR AGE.
A PITY YOU WON'T LIVE TO FULFILL YOUR POTENTIAL.
BAM
ZHELEZKINA?
DOWN HERE!

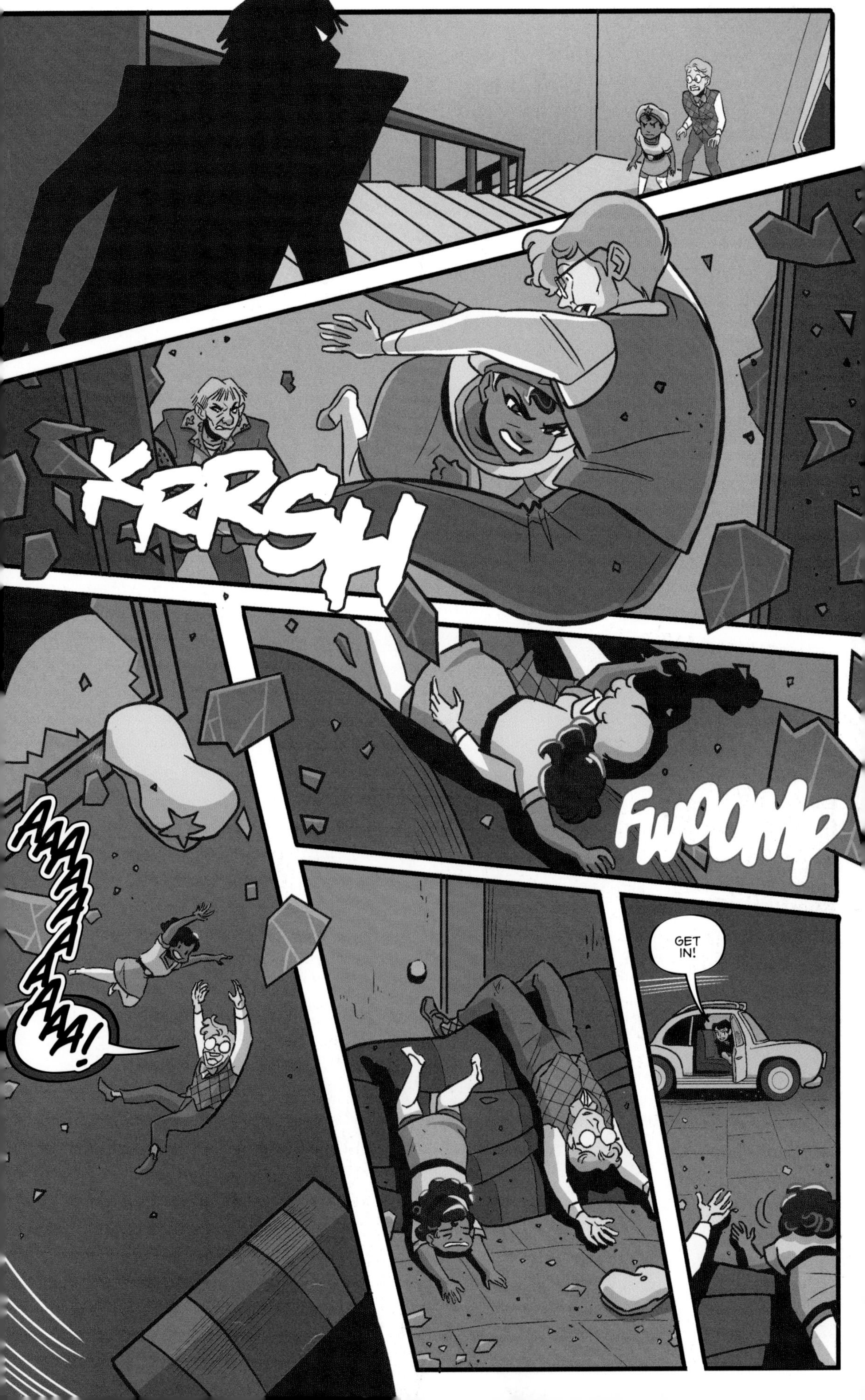
KRRSH
FWOOMP
AAAAAAAAAAAA!
GET IN!

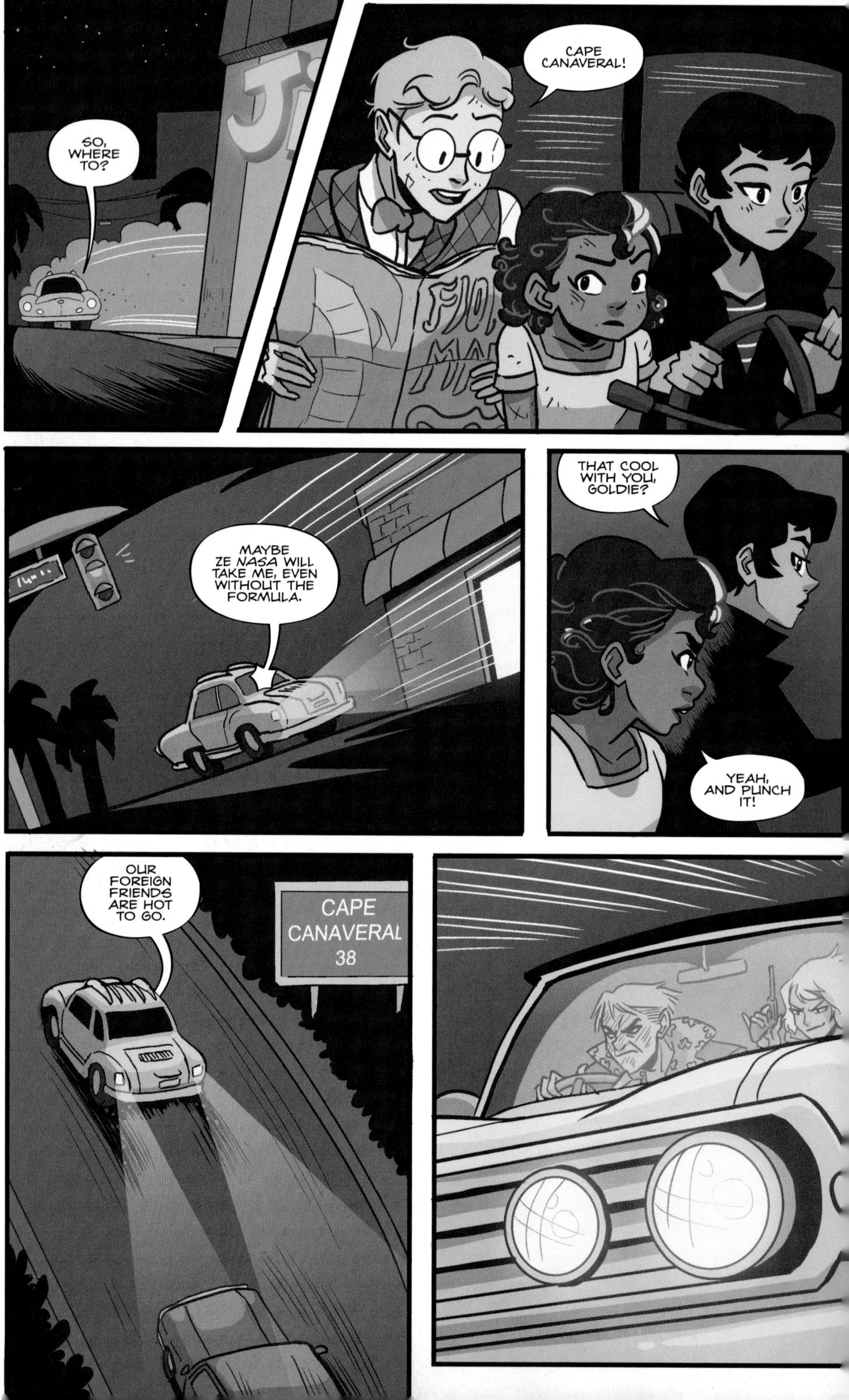
SO, WHERE TO?
CAPE CANAVERAL!
MAYBE ZE NASA WILL TAKE ME, EVEN WITHOUT THE FORMULA.
THAT COOL WITH YOU, GOLDIE?
YEAH, AND PUNCH IT!
OUR FOREIGN FRIENDS ARE HOT TO GO.
CAPE CANAVERAL 38

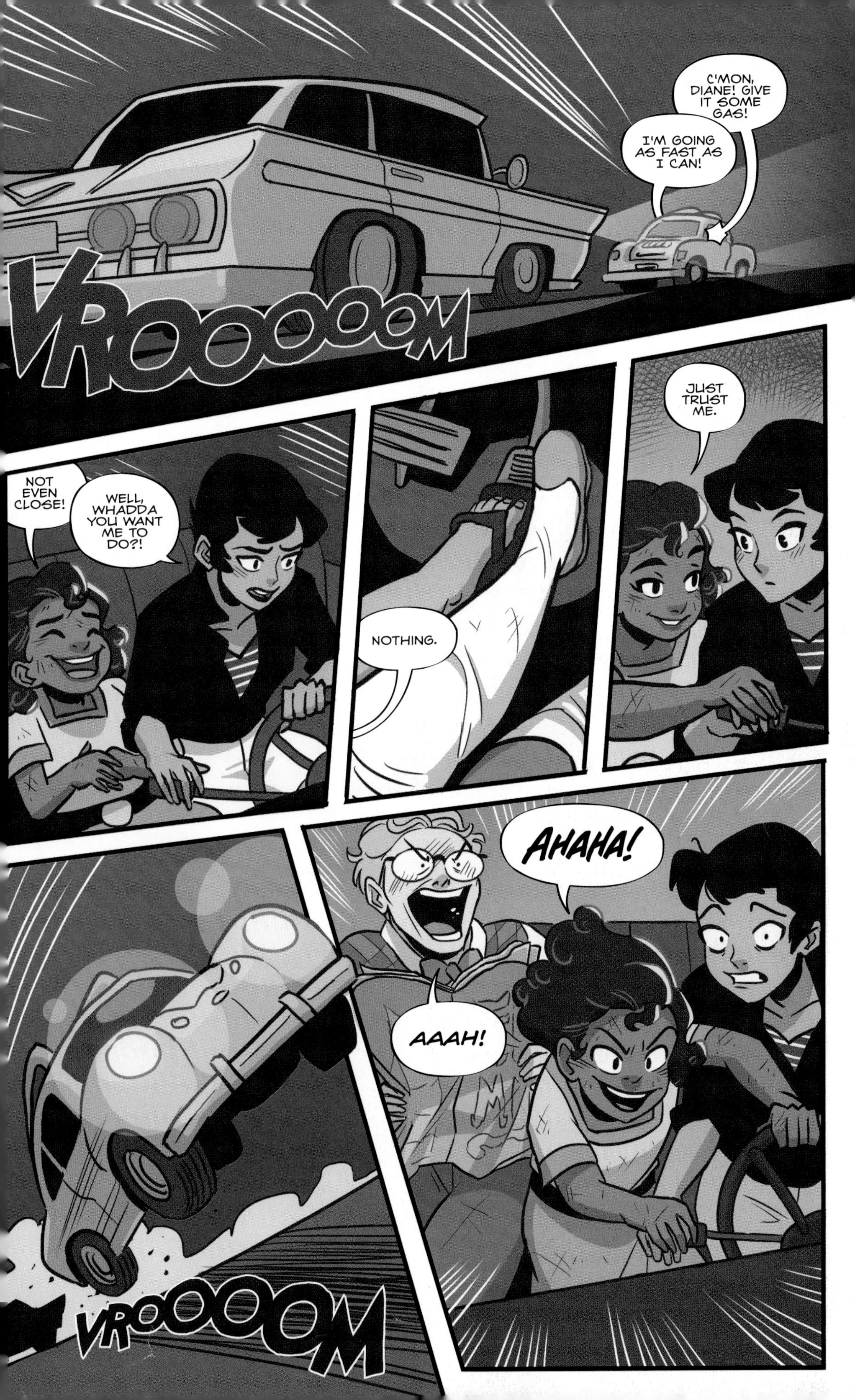
C'MON, DIANE! GIVE IT SOME GAS!
I'M GOING AS FAST AS I CAN!
VROOOOOM
NOT EVEN CLOSE!
WELL, WHADDA YOU WANT ME TO DO?!
NOTHING.
JUST TRUST ME.
AHAHA!
AAAH!
VROOOOOM

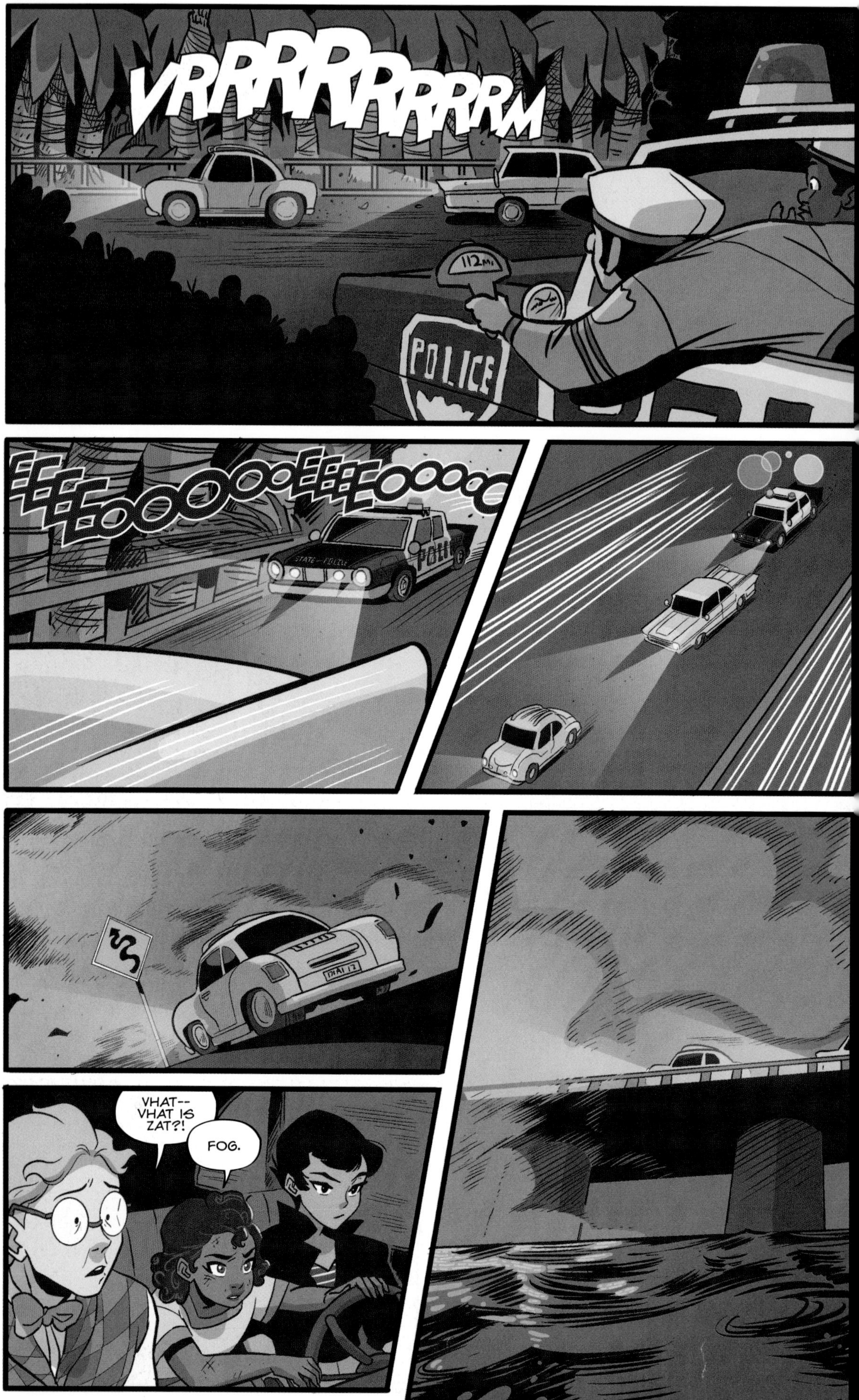
VRRRRRRRRRRM
112 MPH
POLICE
EEEEEOOOOOEEEEEOOOOO
STATE POLICE
POLICE
VHAT--
VHAT IS
ZAT?!
FOG.

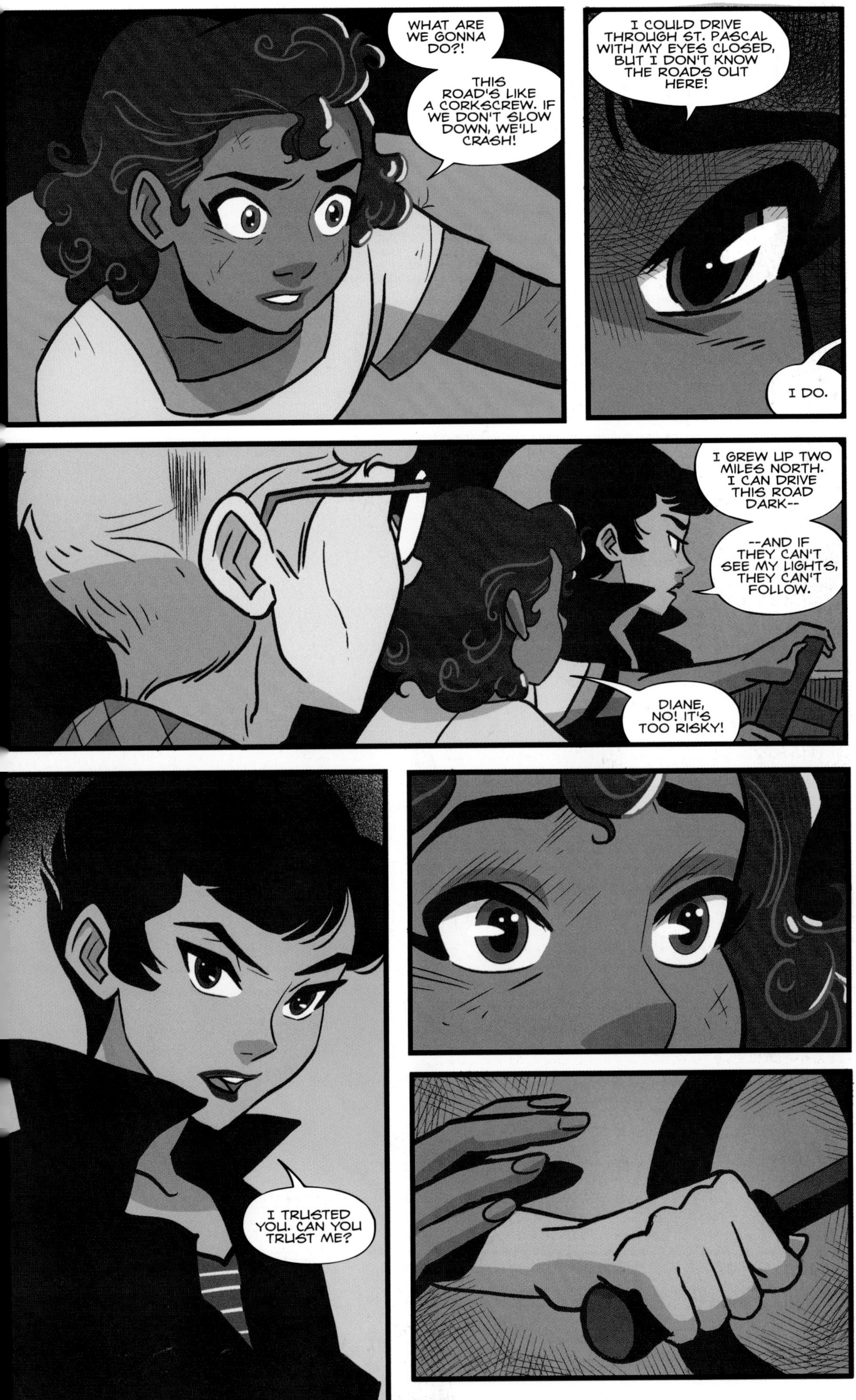
WHAT ARE WE GONNA DO?!
THIS ROAD'S LIKE A CORKSCREW. IF WE DON'T SLOW DOWN, WE'LL CRASH!
I COULD DRIVE THROUGH ST. PASCAL WITH MY EYES CLOSED, BUT I DON'T KNOW THE ROADS OUT HERE!
I DO.
I GREW UP TWO MILES NORTH. I CAN DRIVE THIS ROAD DARK--
--AND IF THEY CAN'T SEE MY LIGHTS, THEY CAN'T FOLLOW.
DIANE, NO! IT'S TOO RISKY!
I TRUSTED YOU. CAN YOU TRUST ME?

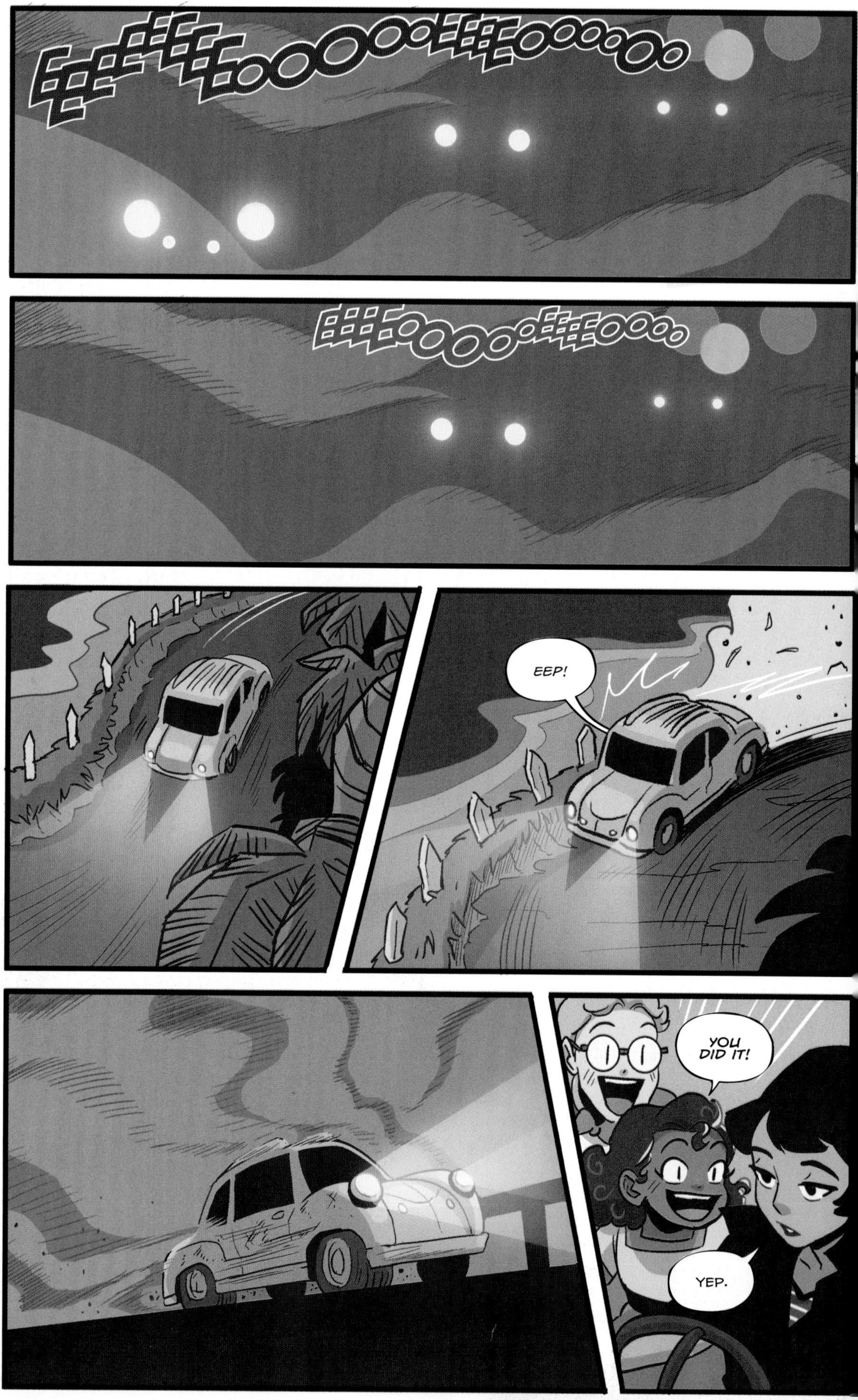
EEEEEEEOOOOOOEEEOOOOOO
EEEEOOOOOEEEOOOO
EEP!
YOU DID IT!
YEP.

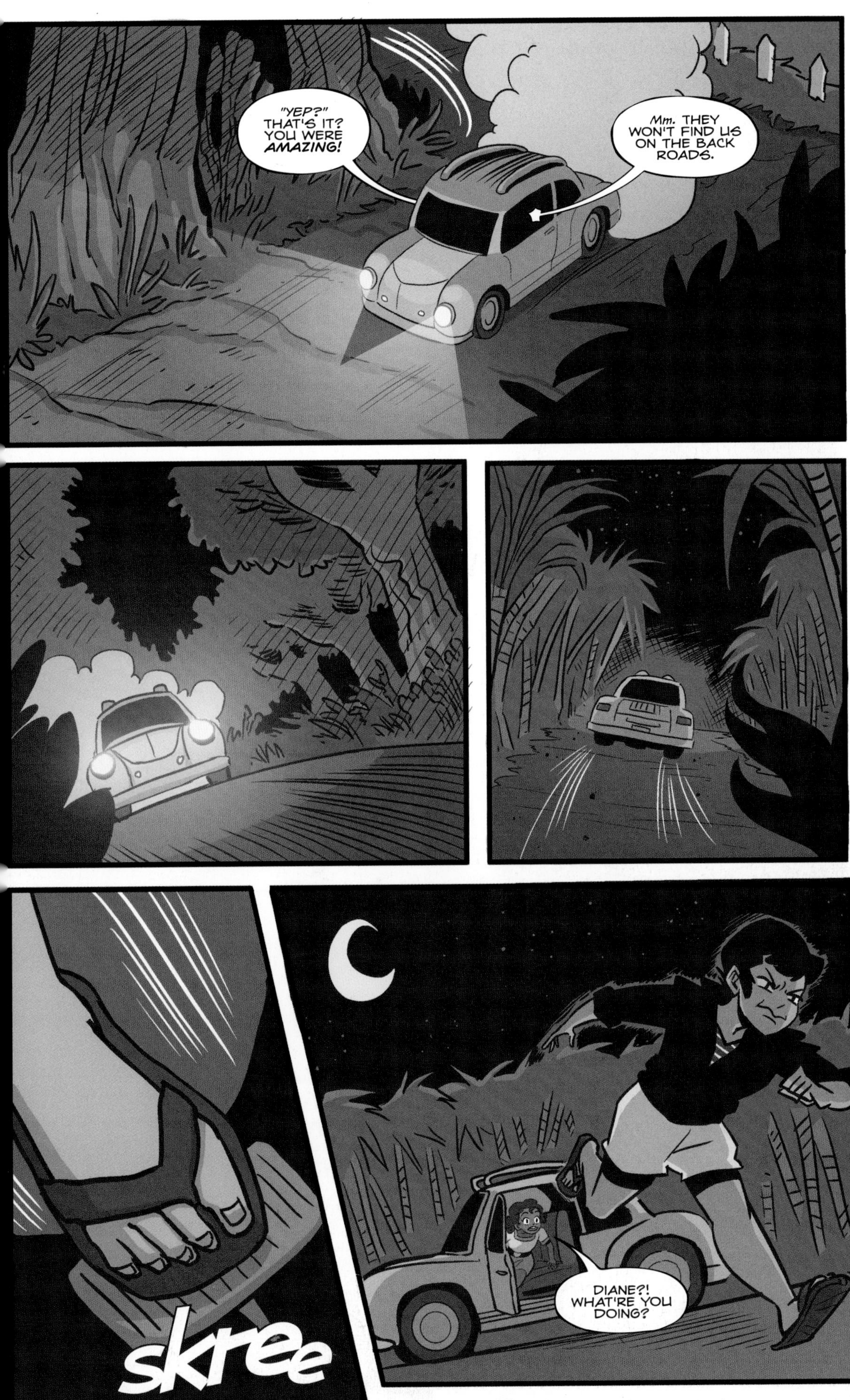
"YEP?" THAT'S IT? YOU WERE *AMAZING!*
Mm. THEY WON'T FIND US ON THE BACK ROADS.
skree
DIANE?! WHAT'RE YOU DOING?

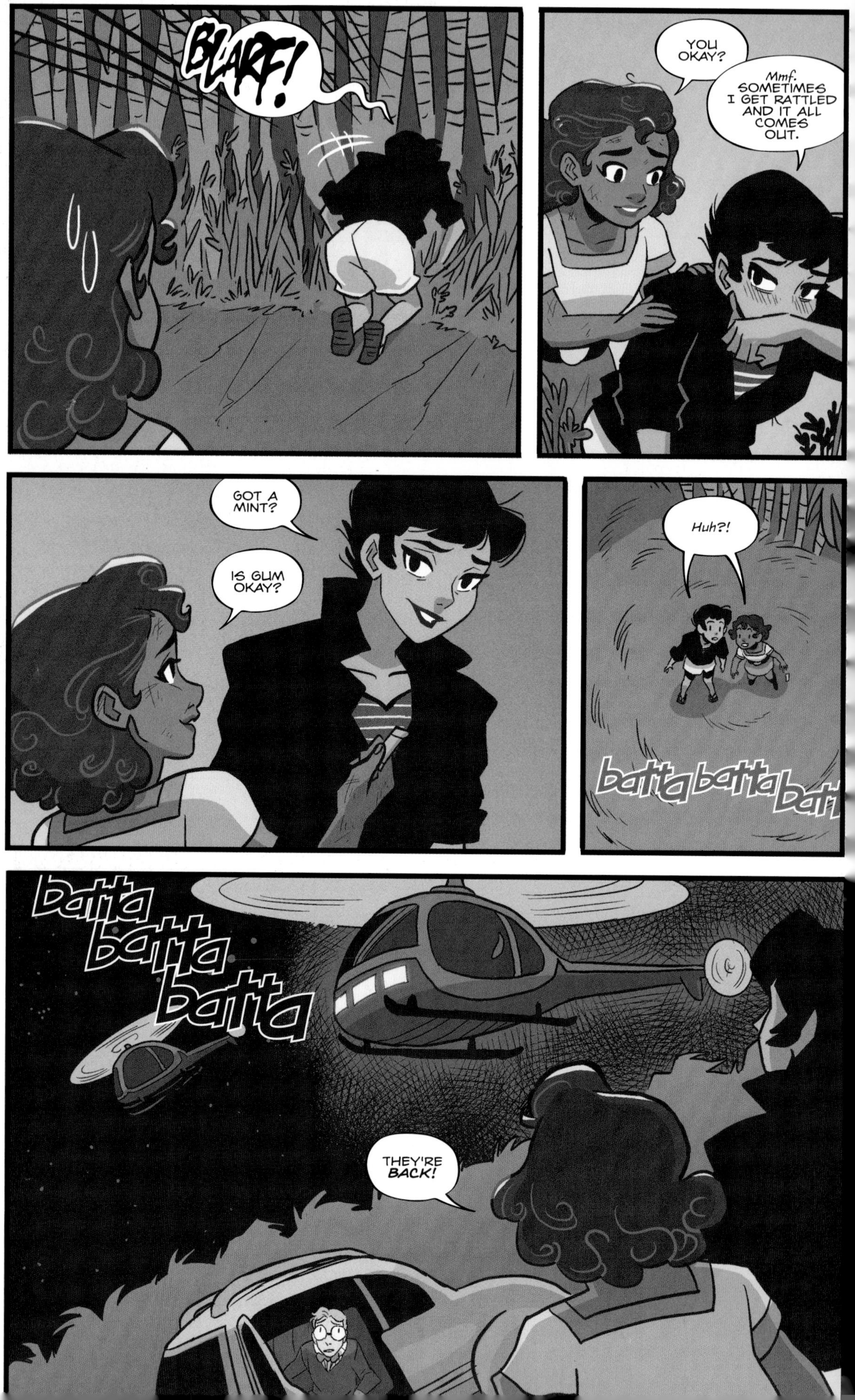

BLARF!
YOU OKAY?
Mmf. SOMETIMES I GET RATTLED AND IT ALL COMES OUT.
GOT A MINT?
IS GUM OKAY?
Huh?!
batta batta batt
batta batta batta
THEY'RE BACK!

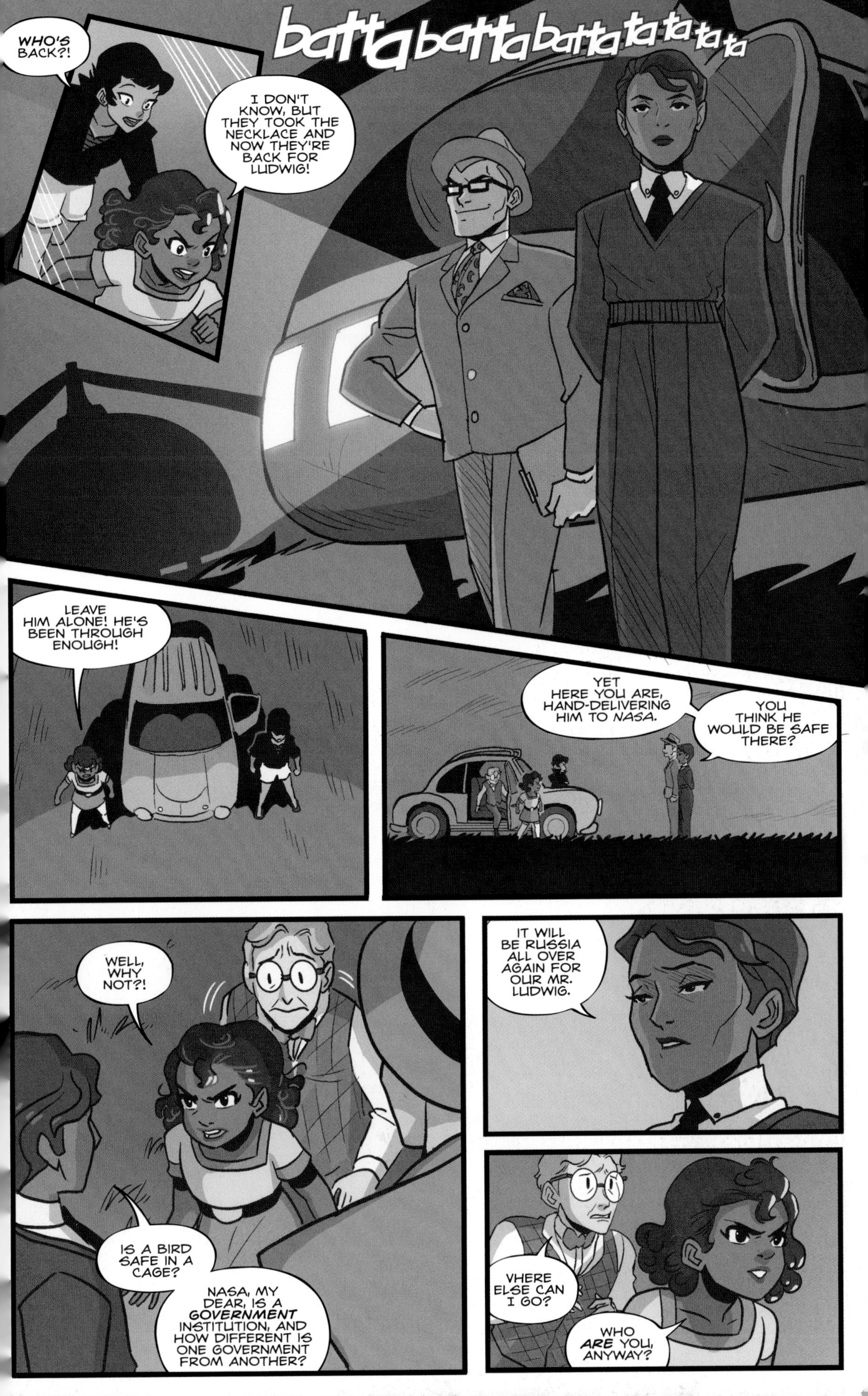
batta batta batta ta ta ta ta
WHO'S BACK?!
I DON'T KNOW, BUT THEY TOOK THE NECKLACE AND NOW THEY'RE BACK FOR LUDWIG!
LEAVE HIM ALONE! HE'S BEEN THROUGH ENOUGH!
YET HERE YOU ARE, HAND-DELIVERING HIM TO NASA.
YOU THINK HE WOULD BE SAFE THERE?
WELL, WHY NOT?!
IS A BIRD SAFE IN A CAGE?
NASA, MY DEAR, IS A GOVERNMENT INSTITUTION, AND HOW DIFFERENT IS ONE GOVERNMENT FROM ANOTHER?
IT WILL BE RUSSIA ALL OVER AGAIN FOR OUR MR. LUDWIG.
VHERE ELSE CAN I GO?
WHO ARE YOU, ANYWAY?

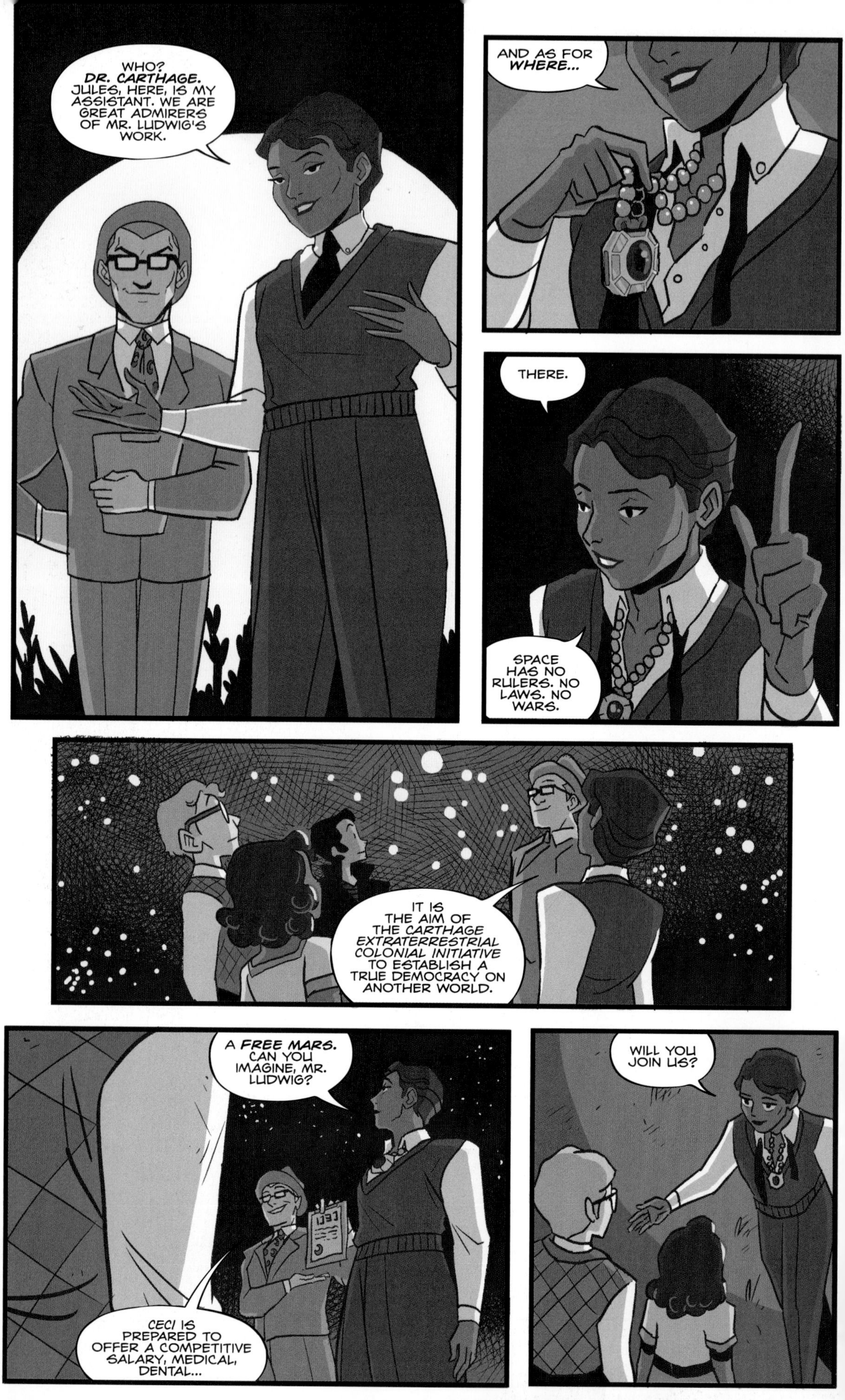
WHO? DR. CARTHAGE. JULES, HERE, IS MY ASSISTANT. WE ARE GREAT ADMIRERS OF MR. LUDWIG'S WORK.
AND AS FOR WHERE...
THERE.
SPACE HAS NO RULERS. NO LAWS. NO WARS.
IT IS THE AIM OF THE CARTHAGE EXTRATERRESTRIAL COLONIAL INITIATIVE TO ESTABLISH A TRUE DEMOCRACY ON ANOTHER WORLD.
A FREE MARS. CAN YOU IMAGINE, MR. LUDWIG?
CECI IS PREPARED TO OFFER A COMPETITIVE SALARY, MEDICAL, DENTAL...
WILL YOU JOIN US?

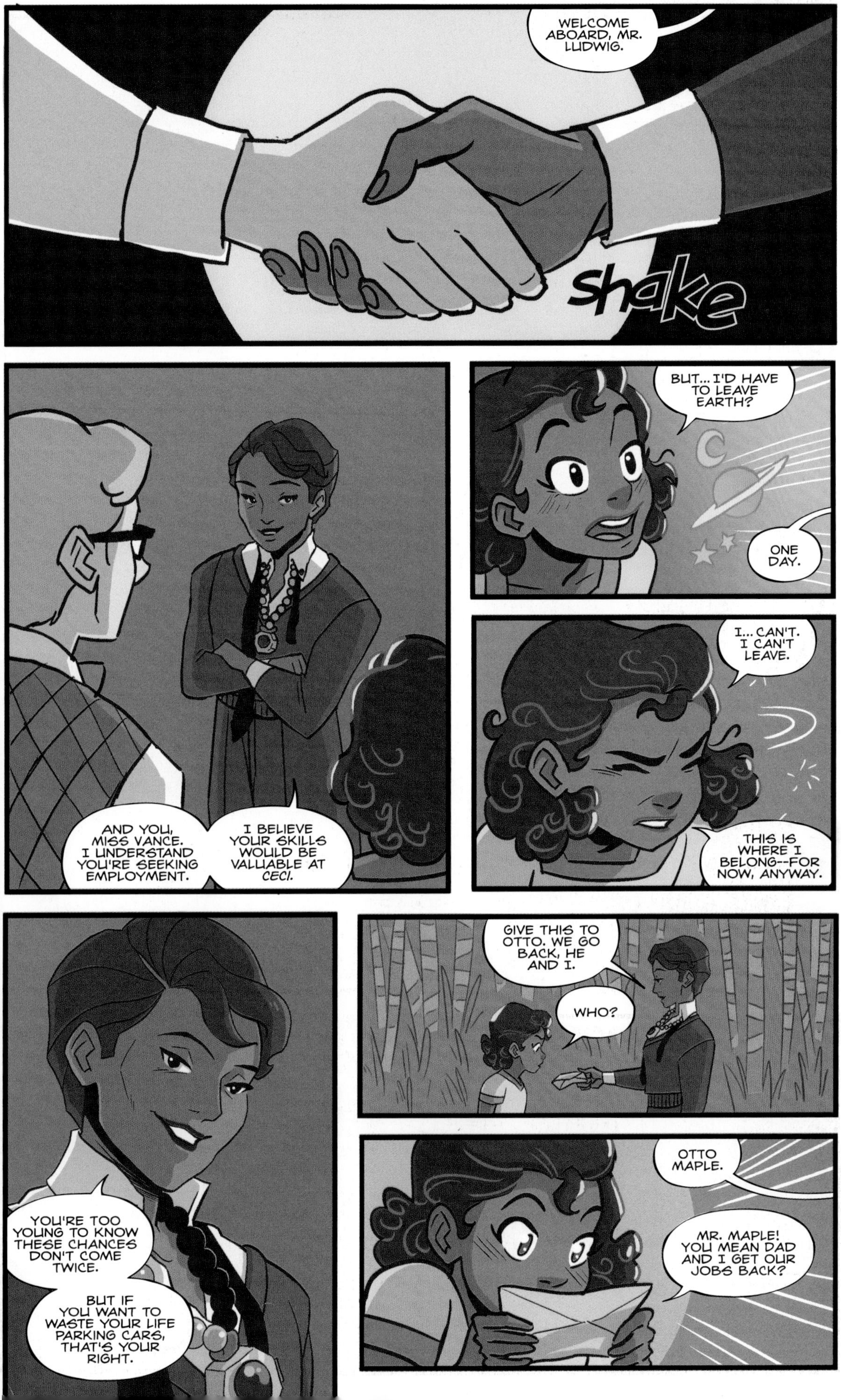
WELCOME ABOARD, MR. LUDWIG.
shake
AND YOU, MISS VANCE. I UNDERSTAND YOU'RE SEEKING EMPLOYMENT.
I BELIEVE YOUR SKILLS WOULD BE VALUABLE AT *CECI.*
BUT... I'D HAVE TO LEAVE EARTH?
ONE DAY.
I... CAN'T. I CAN'T LEAVE.
THIS IS WHERE I BELONG--FOR NOW, ANYWAY.
YOU'RE TOO YOUNG TO KNOW THESE CHANCES DON'T COME TWICE.
BUT IF YOU WANT TO WASTE YOUR LIFE PARKING CARS, THAT'S YOUR RIGHT.
GIVE THIS TO OTTO. WE GO BACK, HE AND I.
WHO?
OTTO MAPLE.
MR. MAPLE! YOU MEAN DAD AND I GET OUR JOBS BACK?

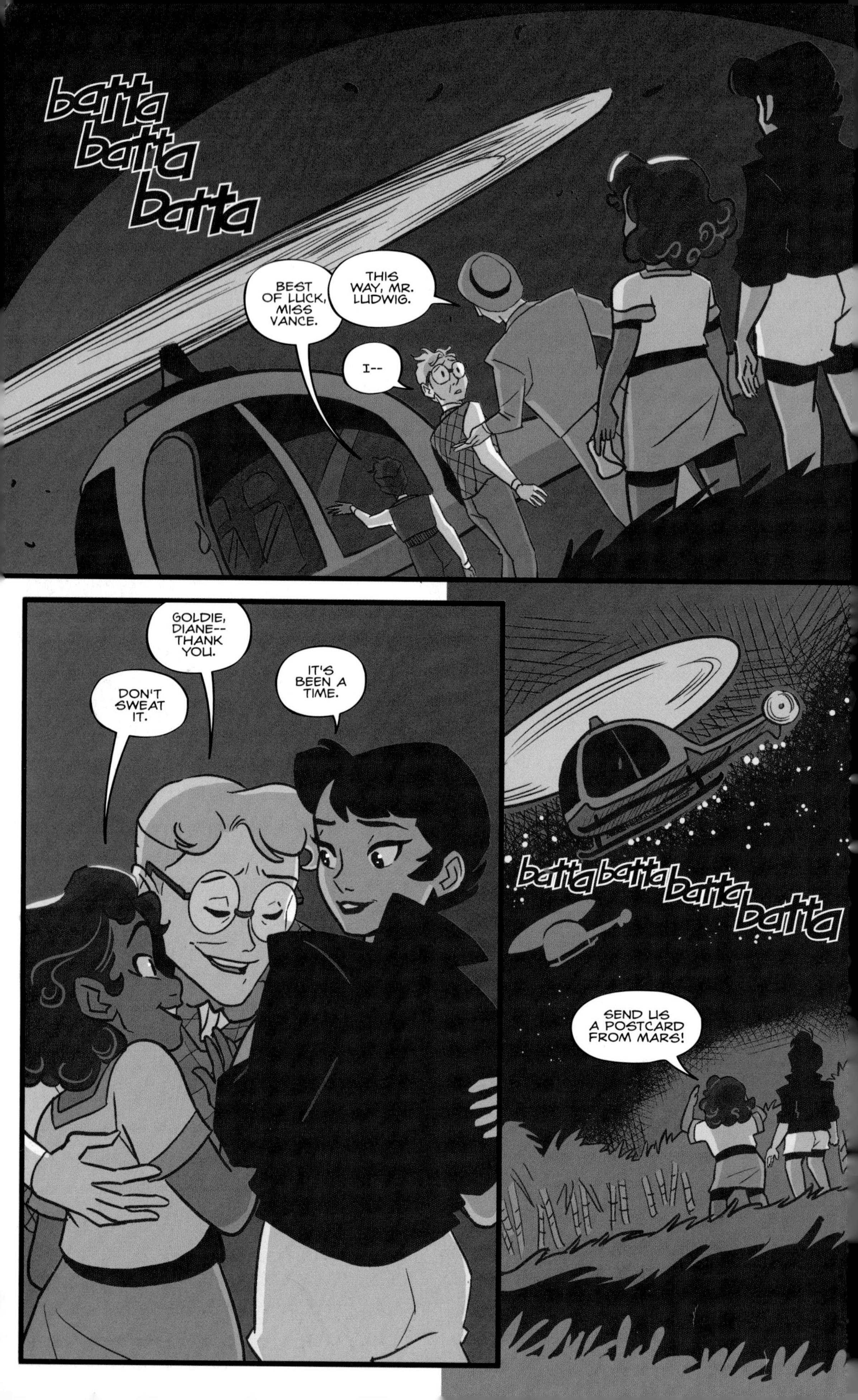
batta
batta
batta
BEST OF LUCK, MISS VANCE.
THIS WAY, MR. LUDWIG.
I--
GOLDIE, DIANE-- THANK YOU.
DON'T SWEAT IT.
IT'S BEEN A TIME.
batta batta batta batta
SEND US A POSTCARD FROM MARS!

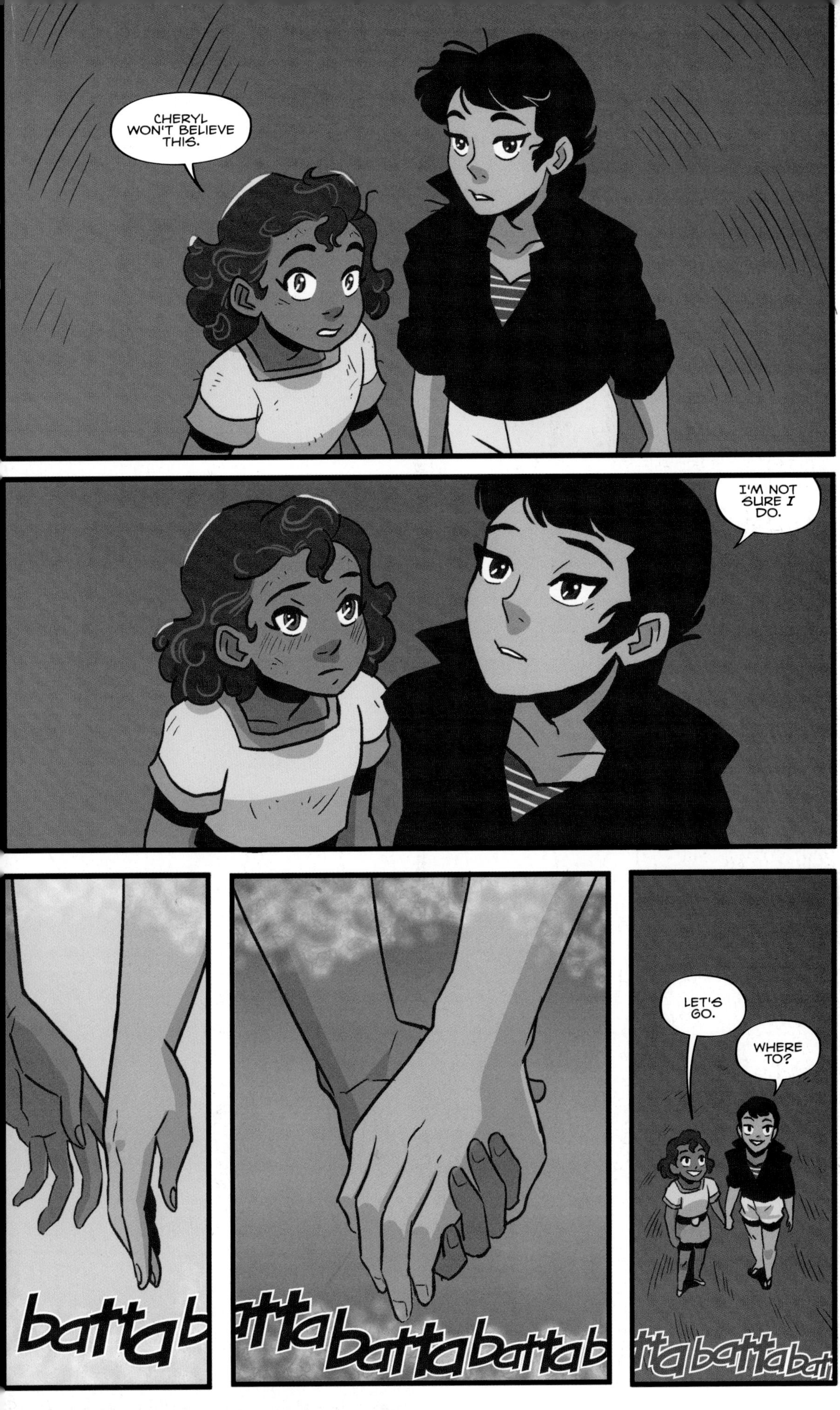
CHERYL WON'T BELIEVE THIS.
I'M NOT SURE *I* DO.
battabattabattabattabattabattabatt
LET'S GO.
WHERE TO?

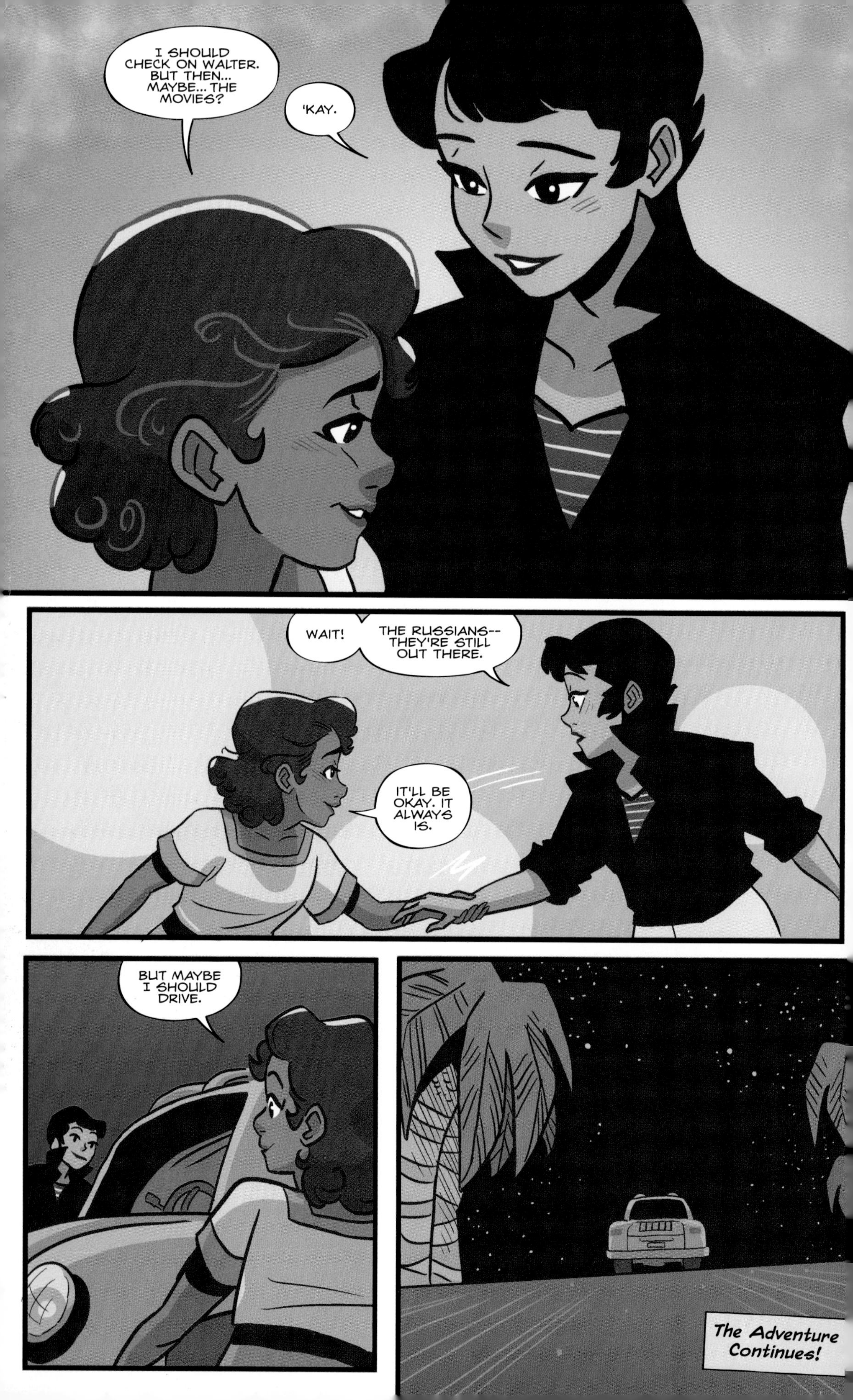
I SHOULD CHECK ON WALTER. BUT THEN... MAYBE... THE MOVIES?
'KAY.
WAIT!
THE RUSSIANS-- THEY'RE STILL OUT THERE.
IT'LL BE OKAY. IT ALWAYS IS.
BUT MAYBE I SHOULD DRIVE.
The Adventure Continues!

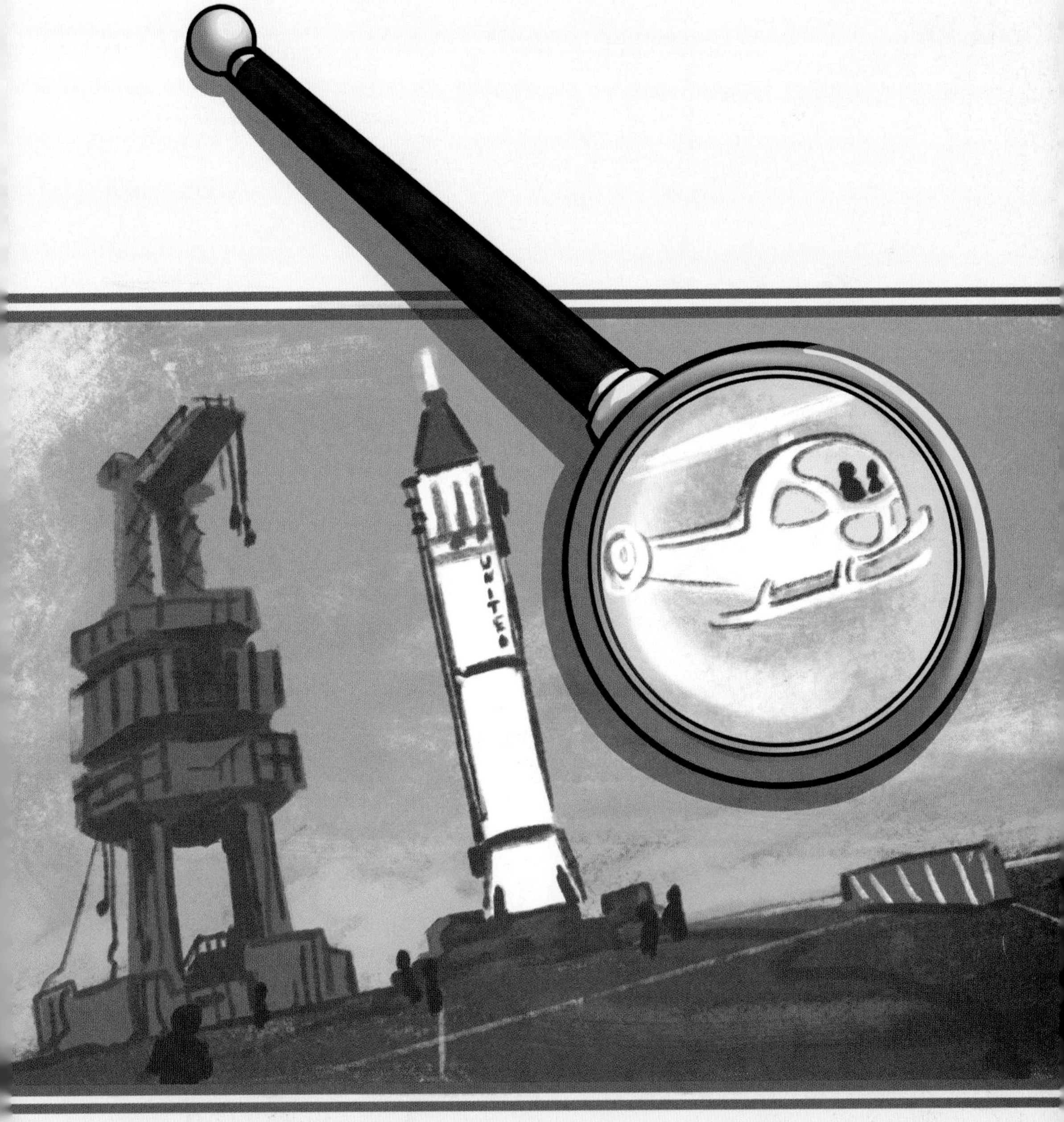
UNITED

Goldie Vance concept art by Brittney Williams

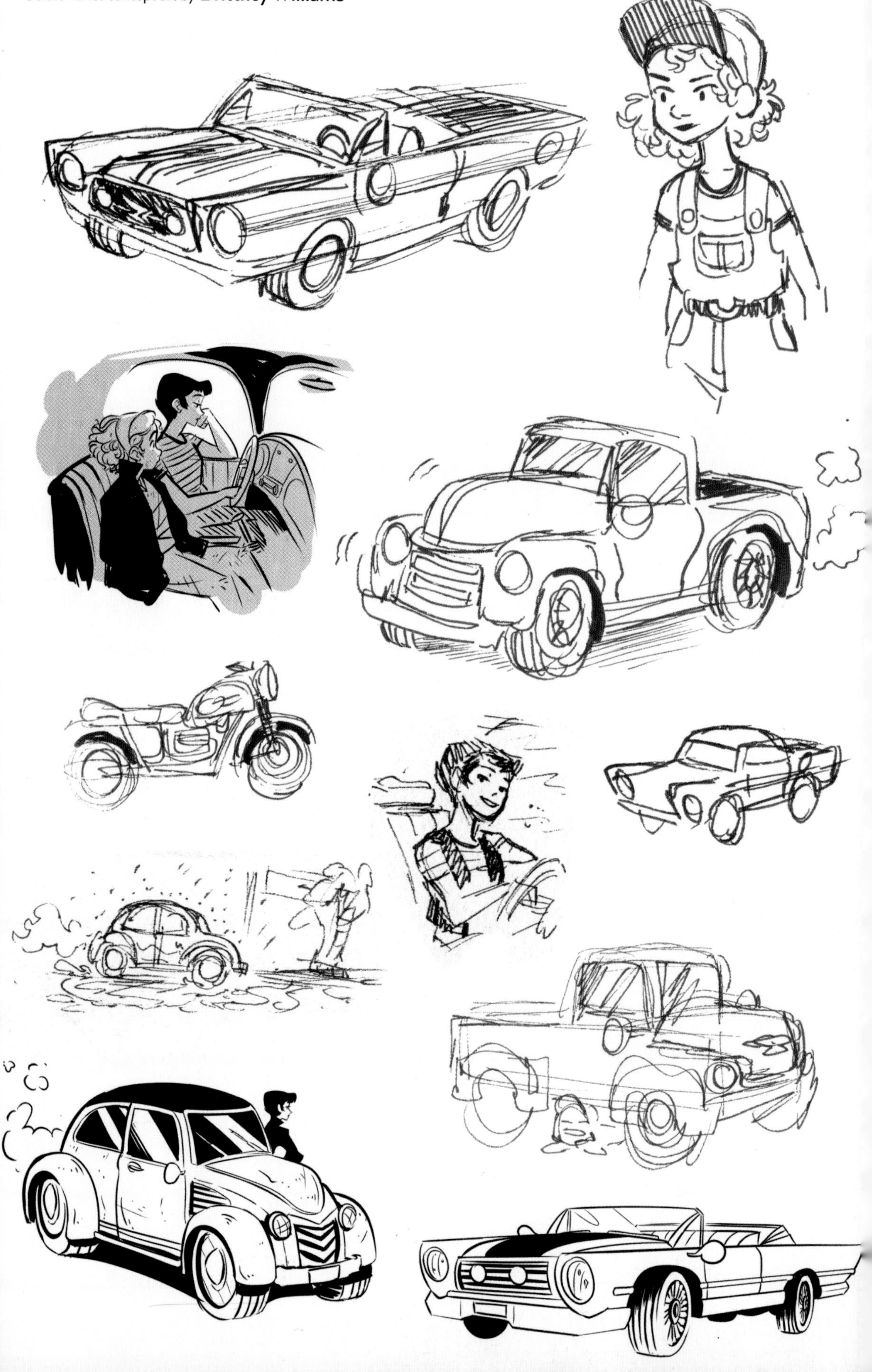

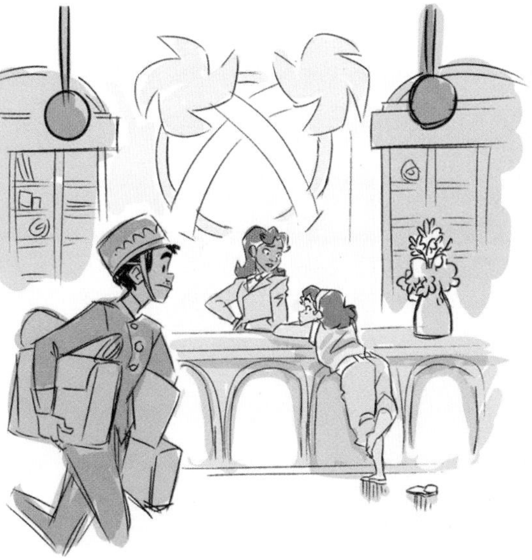

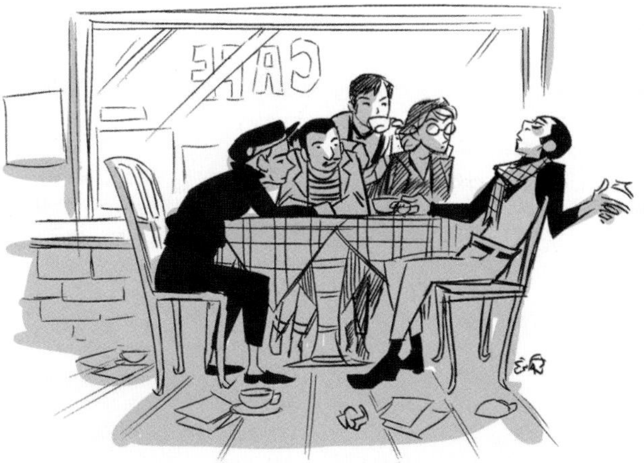

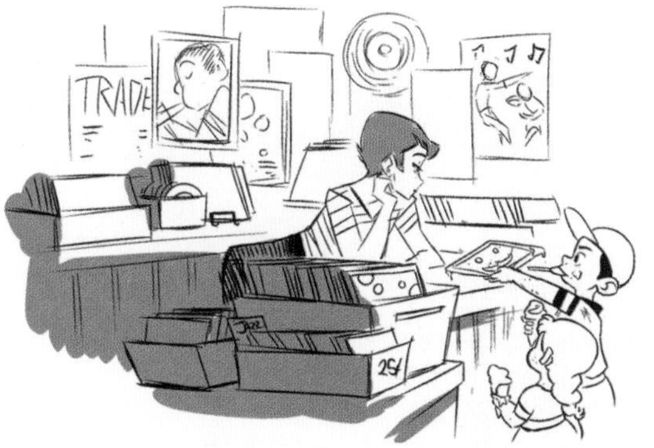
TRADE

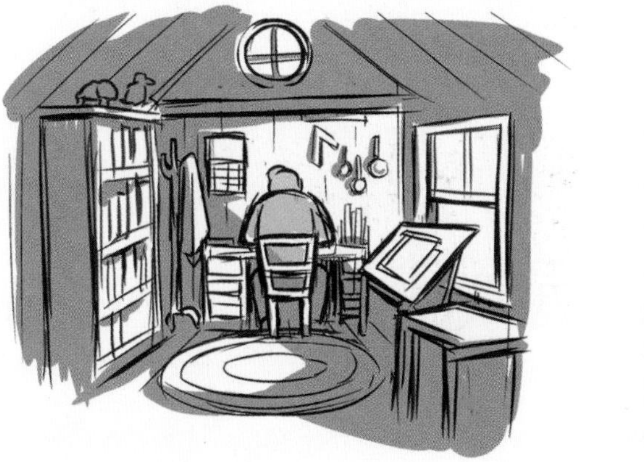

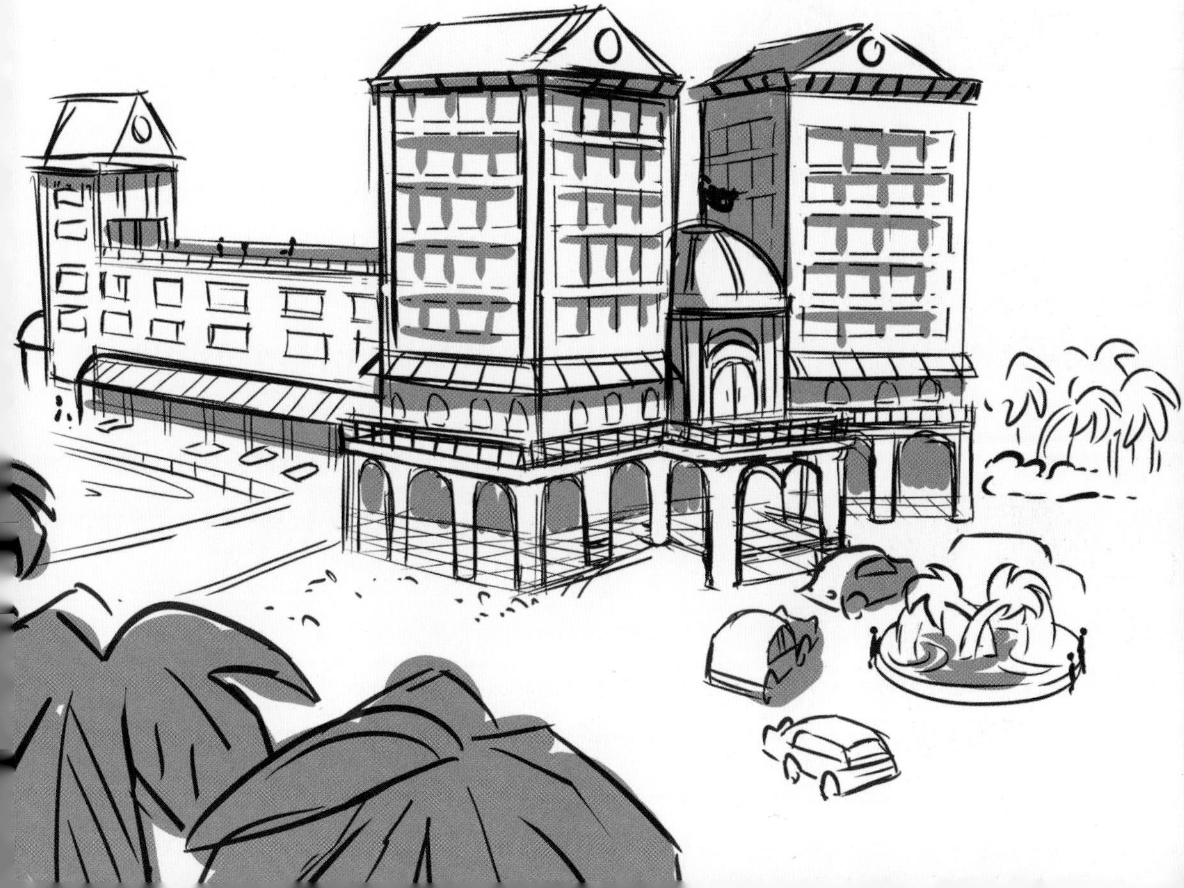

cover GALLERY

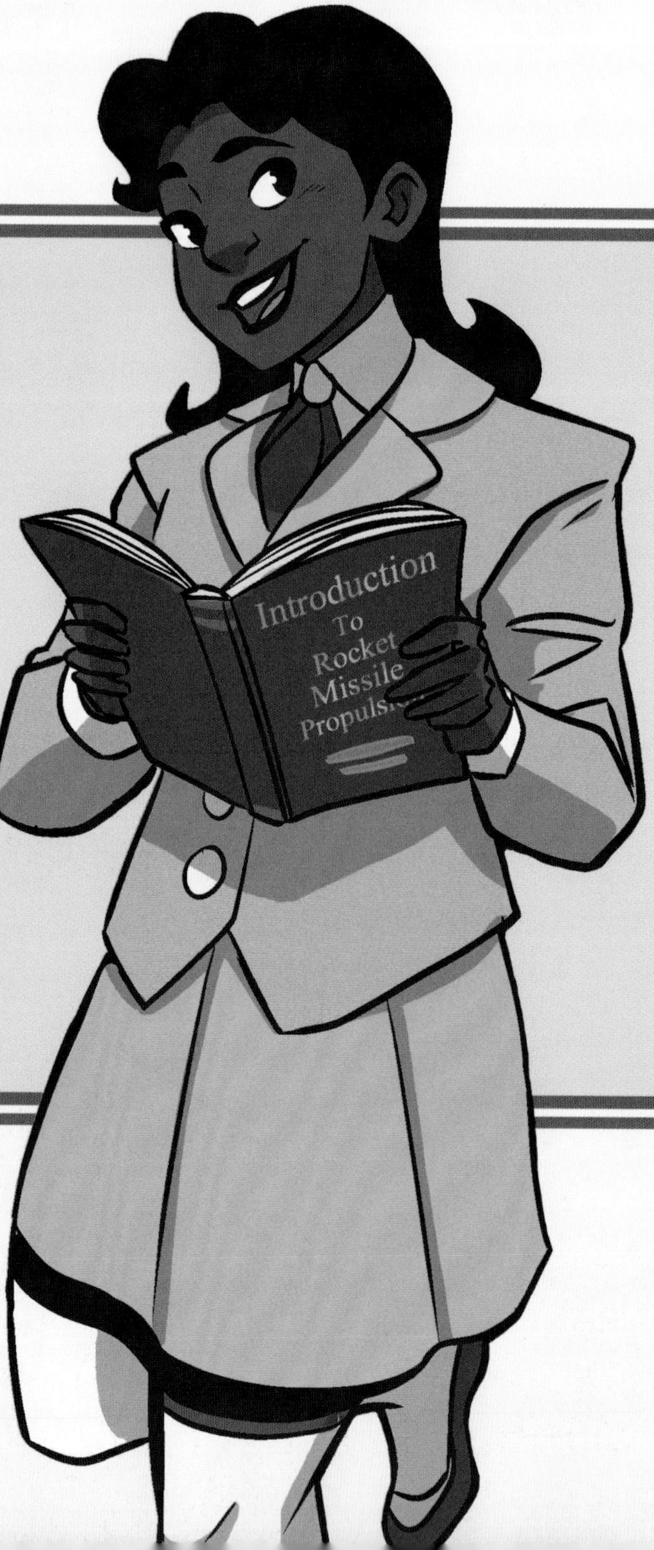
Introduction
To
Rocket
Missile
Propulsi

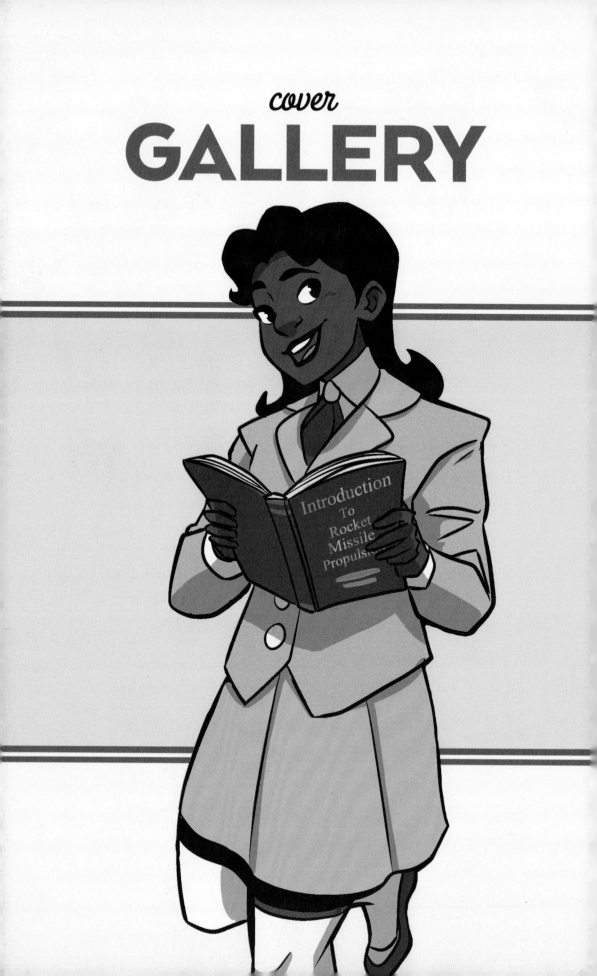

issue one variant by **Marguerite Sauvage**

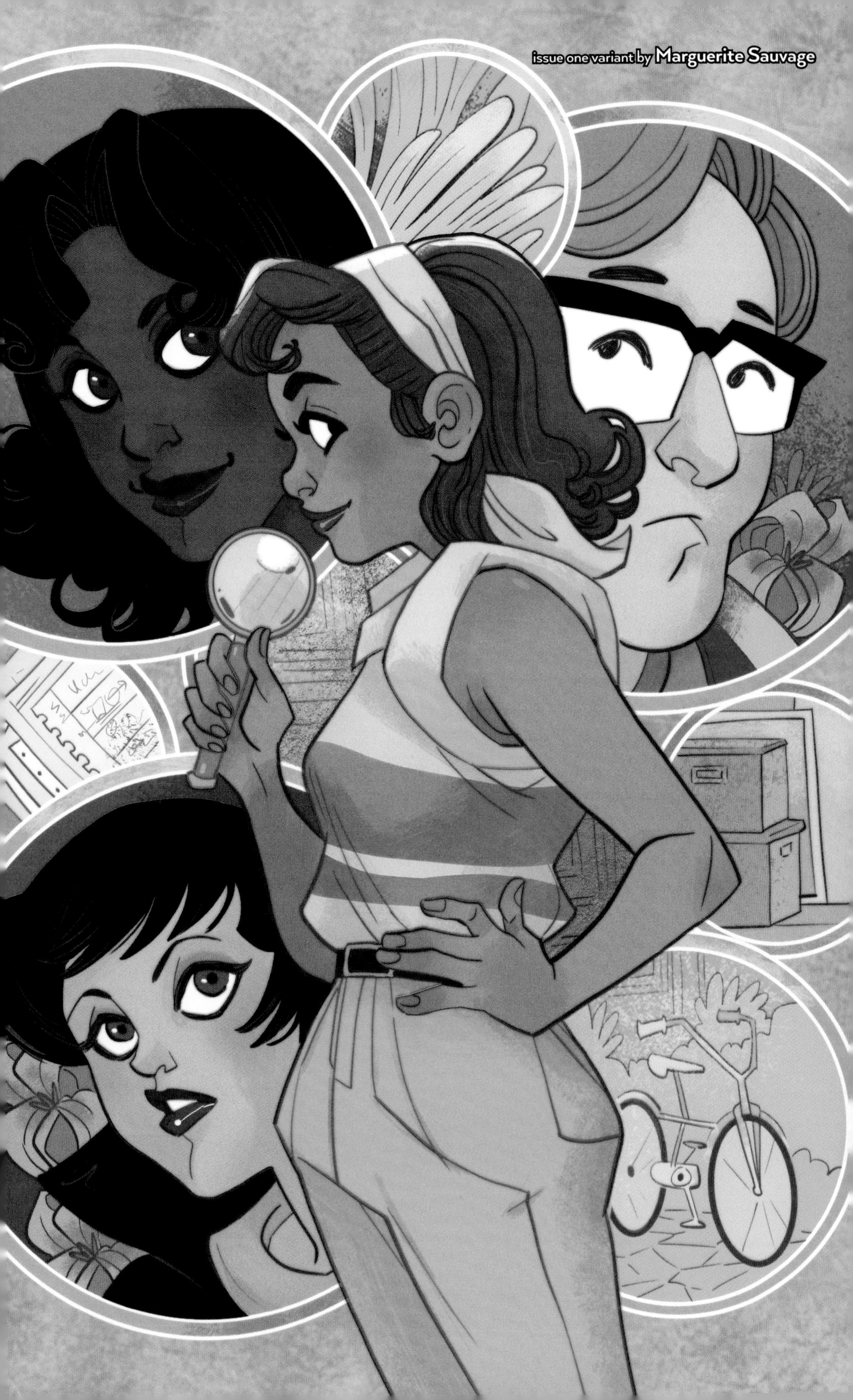

issue one variant by Jen Wang

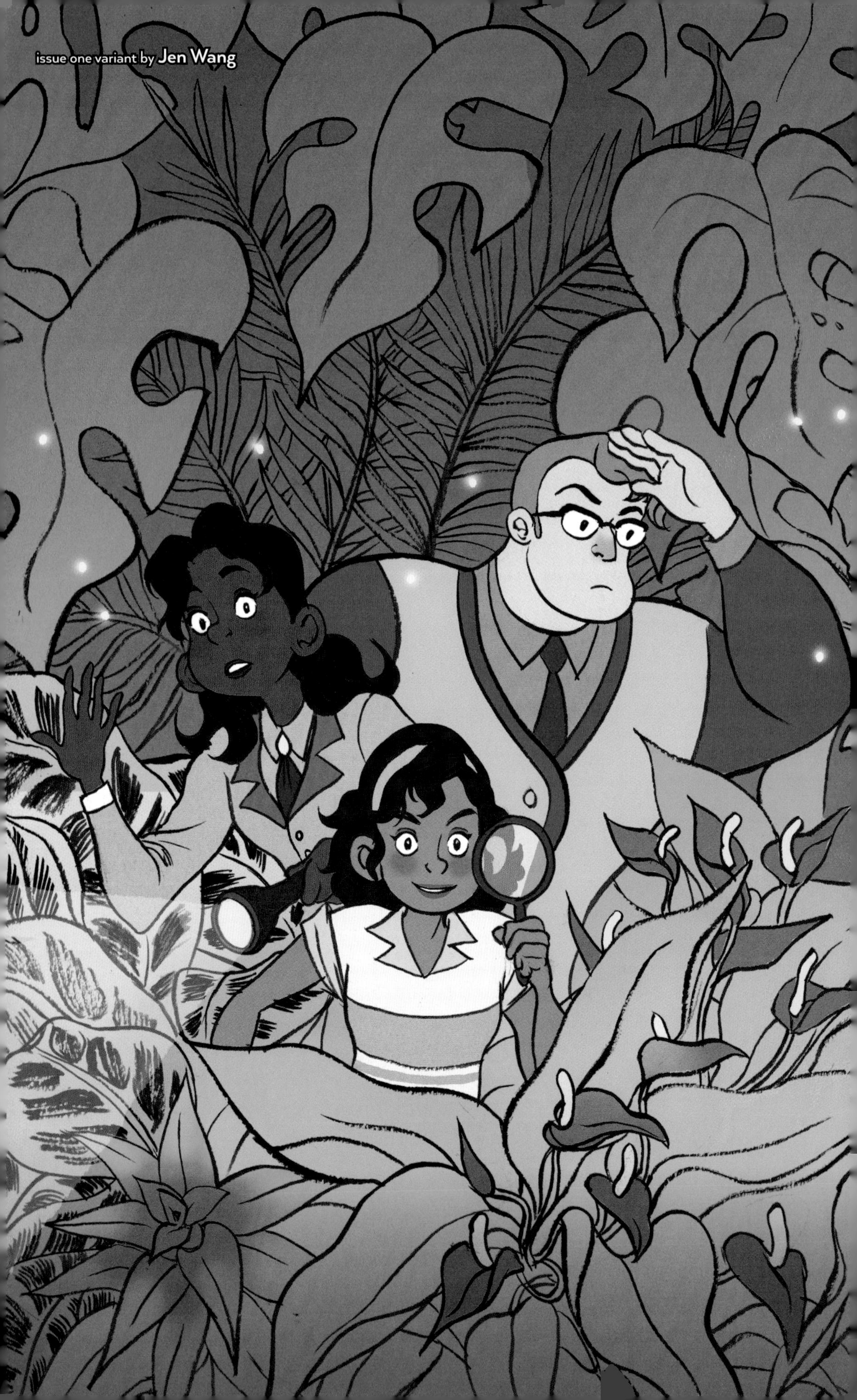

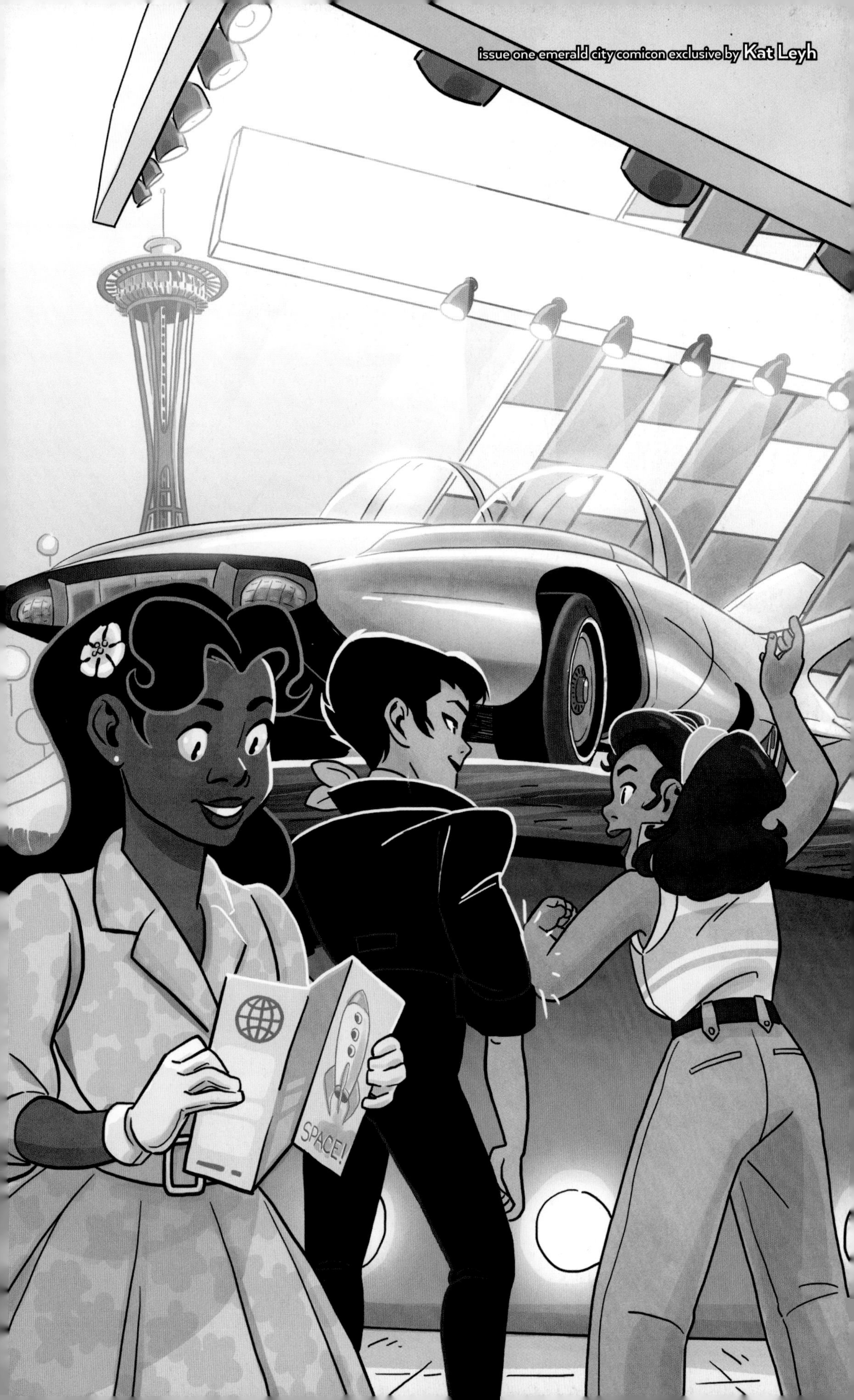
issue one emerald city comicon exclusive by Kat Leyh
SPACE!

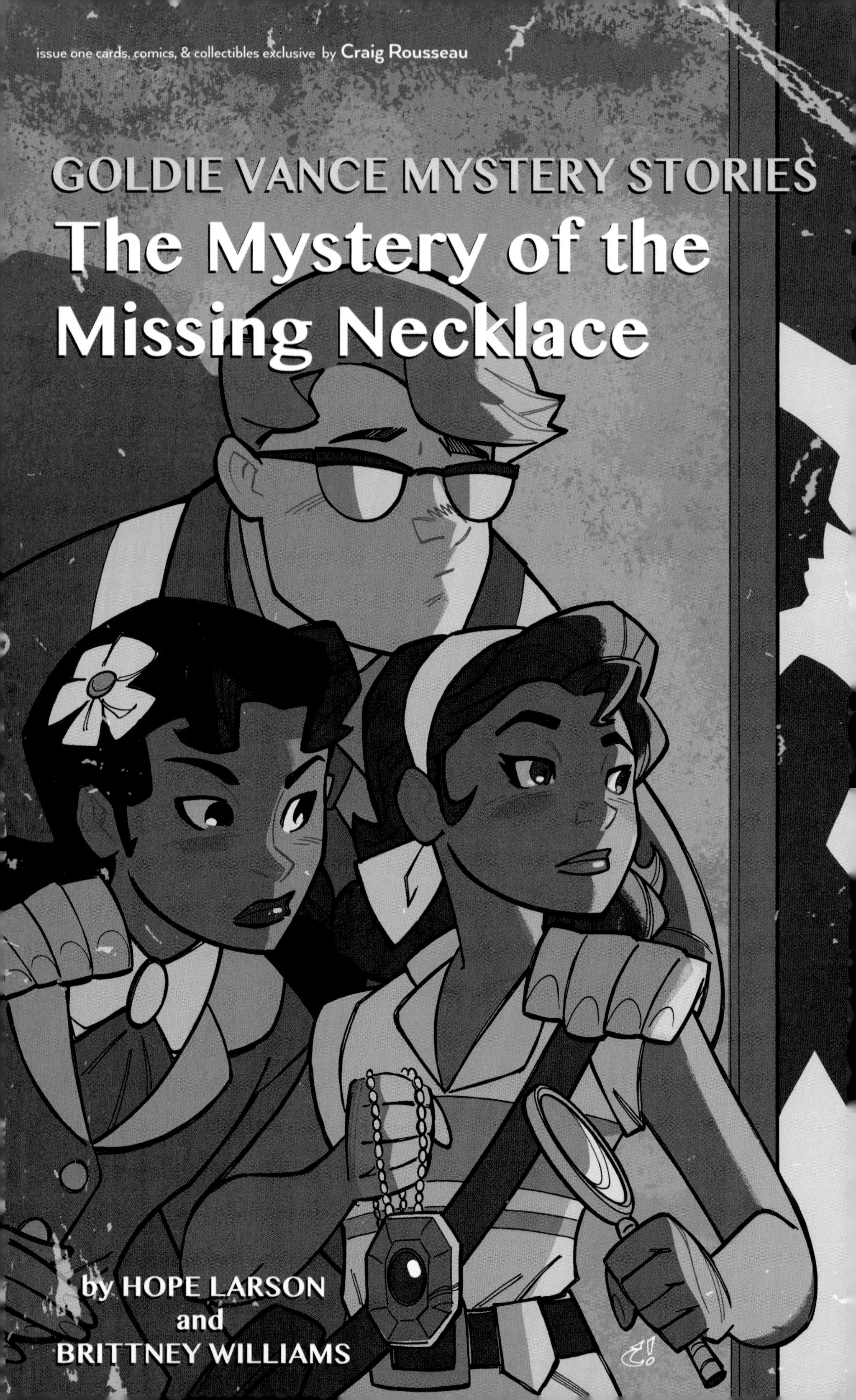
issue one cards, comics, & collectibles exclusive by Craig Rousseau
GOLDIE VANCE MYSTERY STORIES
The Mystery of the Missing Necklace
by HOPE LARSON
and
BRITTNEY WILLIAMS

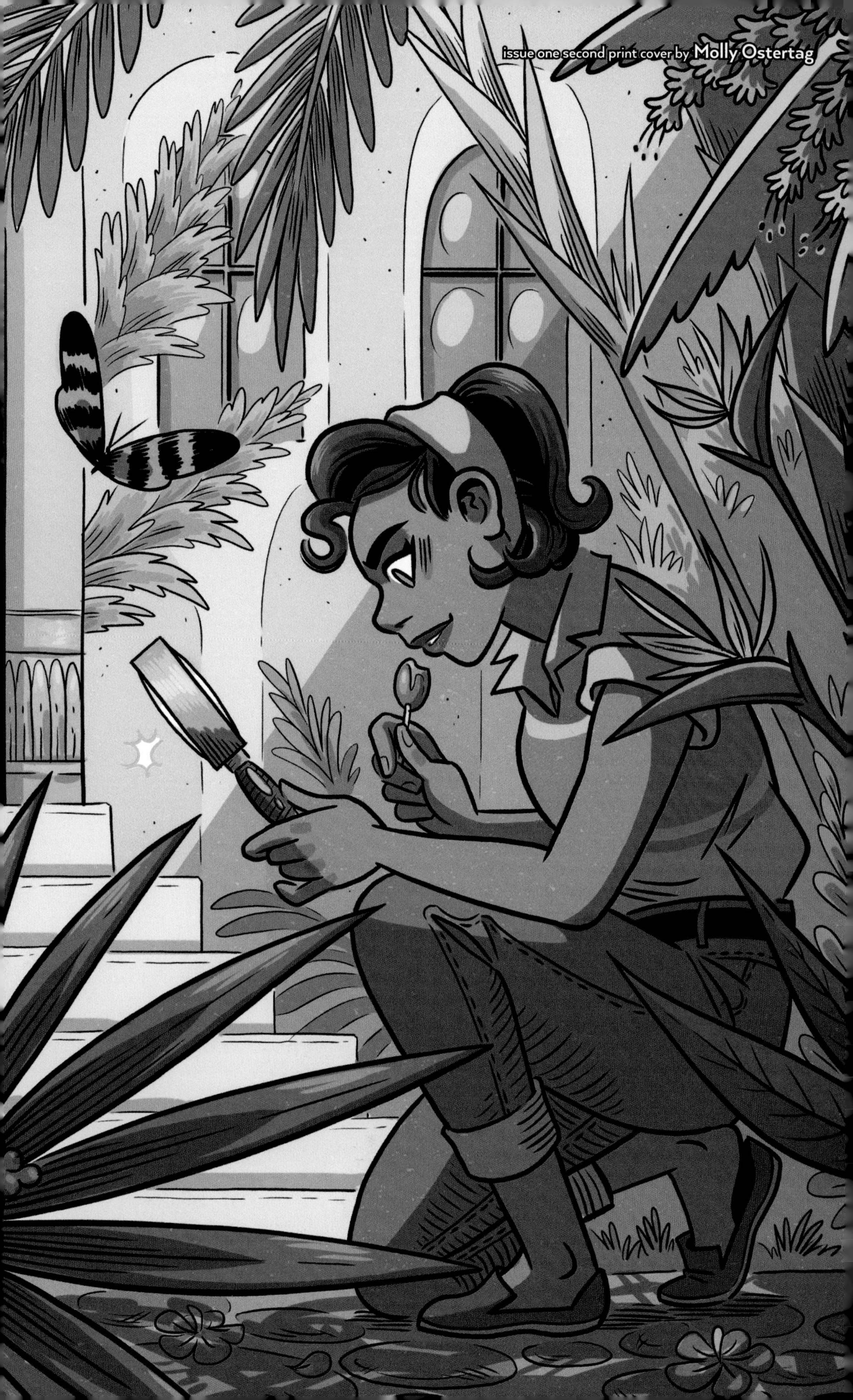
issue one second print cover by Molly Ostertag

issue two variant by **Veronica Fish**

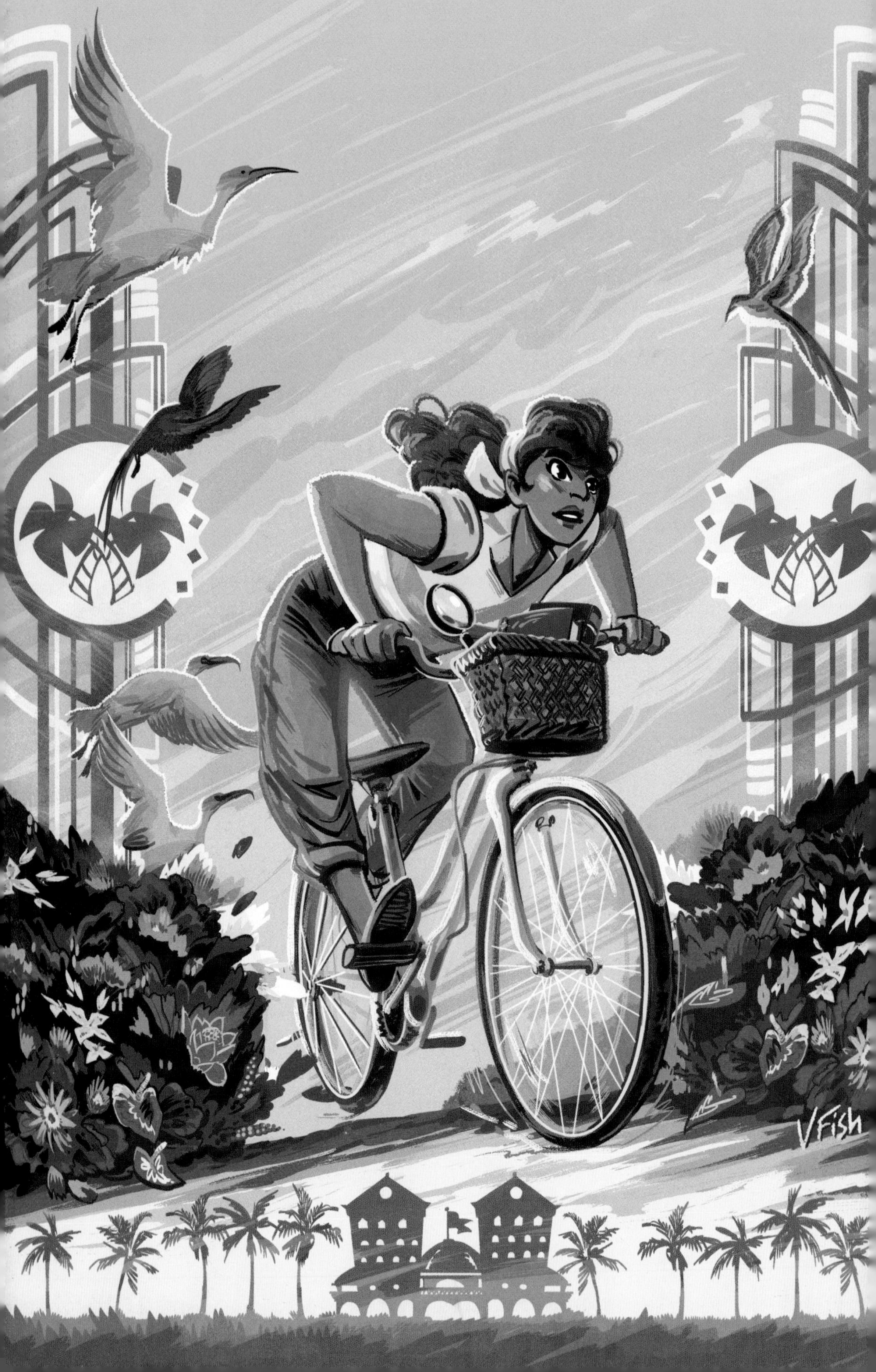
VFish

issue two second print cover by **Brittney Williams**

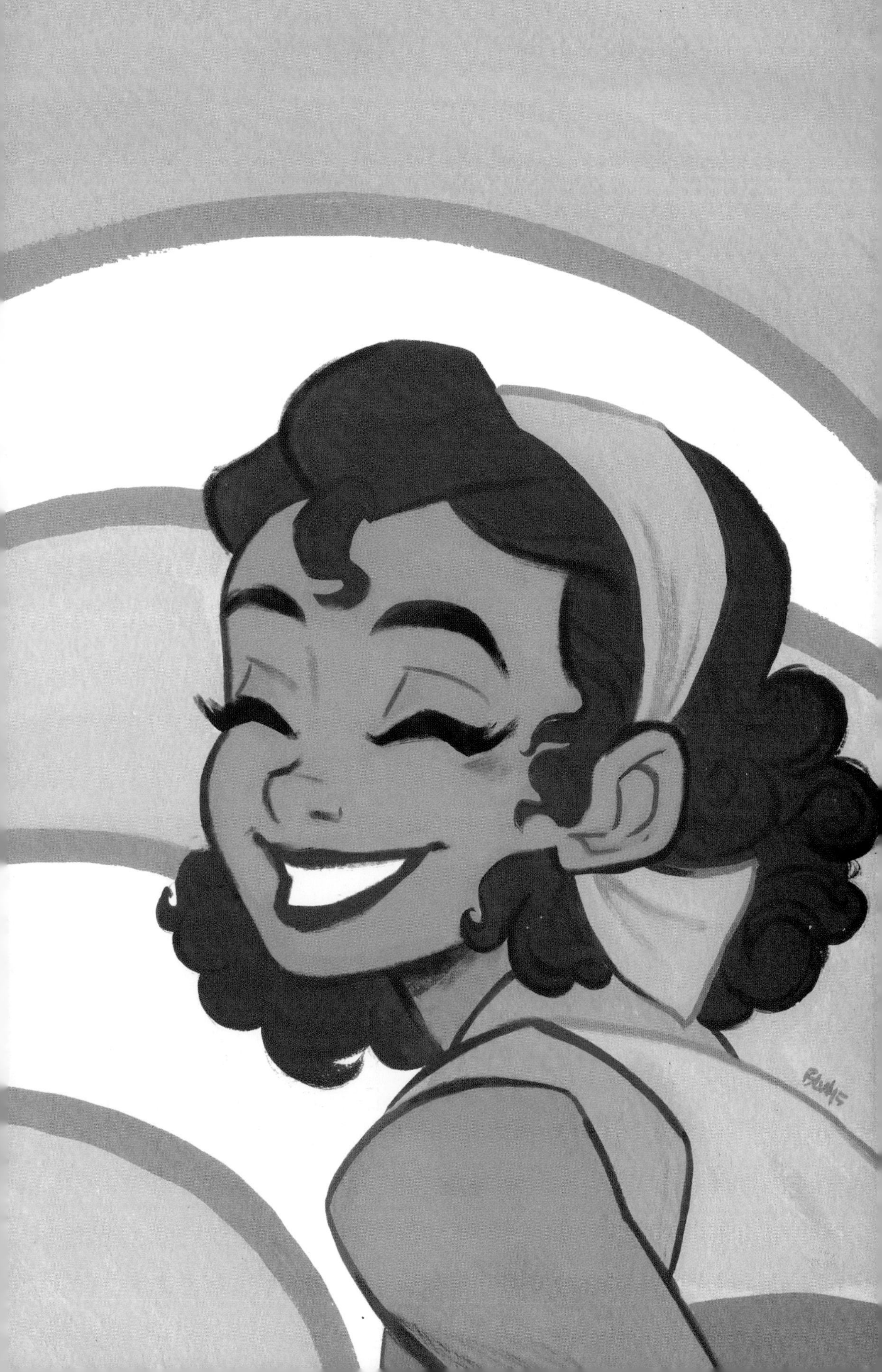

issue three variant by **Dan Parent** with colors by **M. Victoria Robado**

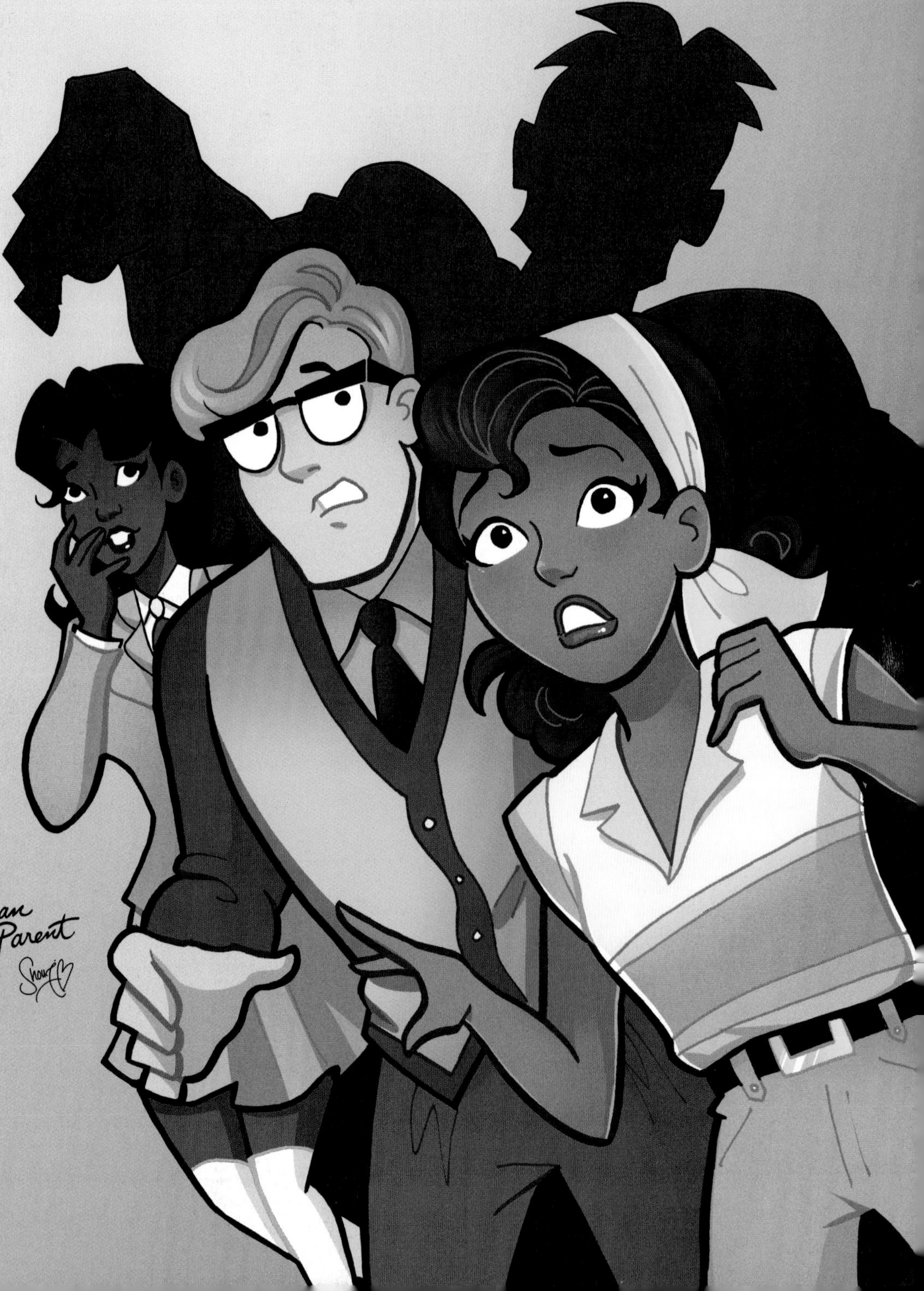
Dan Parent

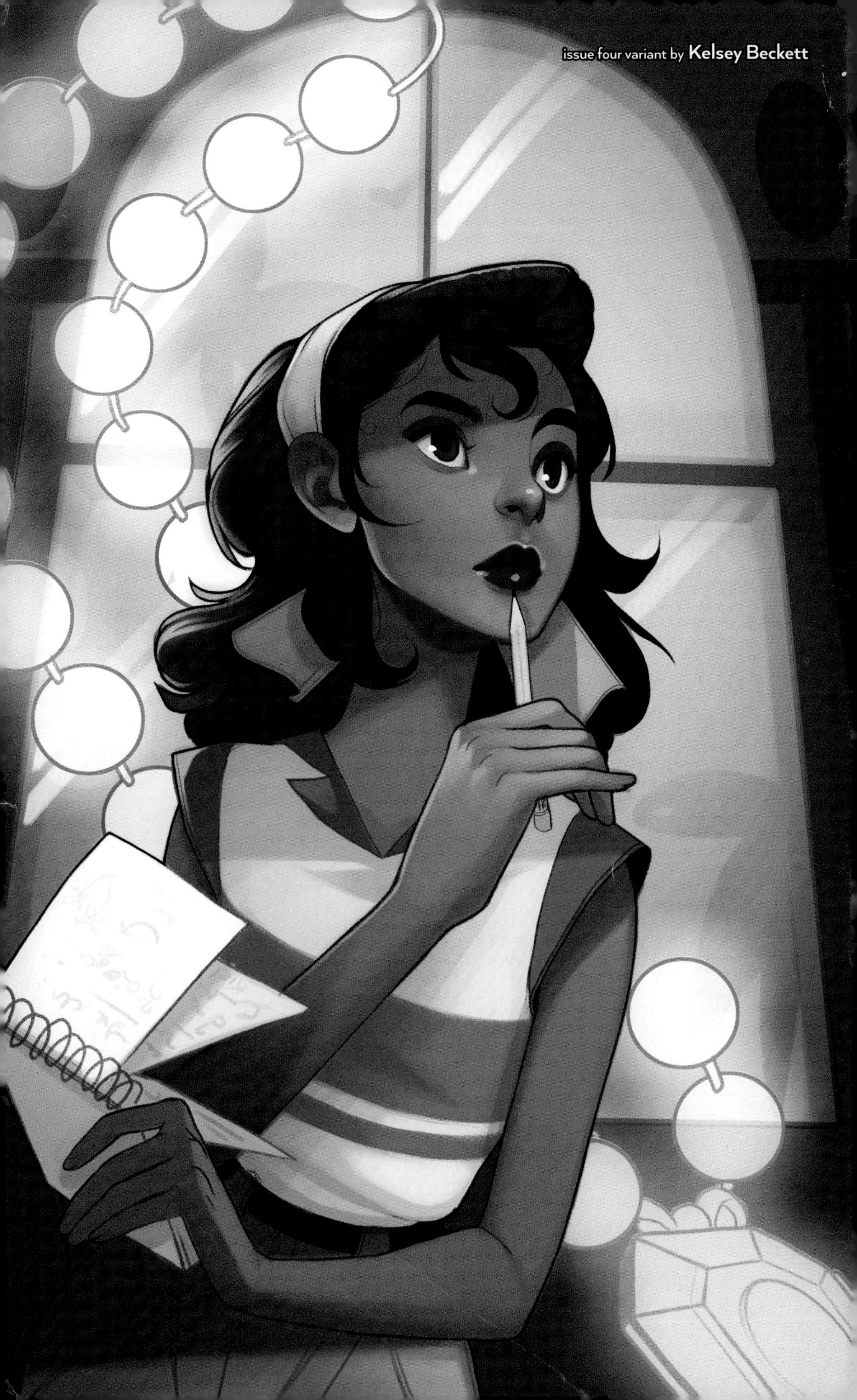

issue four variant by **Kelsey Beckett**

ALSO FROM BOOM! BOX™

FOR THE LOVE OF IT

STEVENSON • ELLIS • WATTERS • ALLEN
LUMBERJANES
BEWARE THE KITTEN HOLY

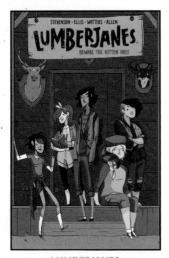

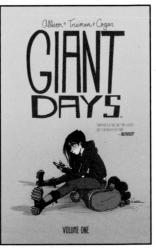

LUMBERJANES
Noelle Stevenson | Grace Ellis | Shannon Watters | Brooke Allen

Vol. 1: Beware the Kitten Holy TP
$14.99 US • $18.99 CA • £10.99 UK | ISBN: 978-1-60886-687-8

Vol. 2: Friendship to the Max TP
$14.99 US • $18.99 CA • £10.99 UK | ISBN: 978-1-60886-737-0

Vol. 3: A Terrible Plan TP
$14.99 US • $18.99 CA • £10.99 UK | ISBN: 978-1-60886-803-2

Vol. 4: Out of Time TP
$14.99 US • $18.99 CA • £10.99 UK | ISBN: 978-1-60886-860-5

Allison + Treiman + Cogar
GIANT DAYS
VOLUME ONE

GIANT DAYS
John Allison | Lissa Treiman | Max Sarin

Vol. 1 TP
$9.99 US • $11.99 CA • £7.50 UK | ISBN: 978-1-60886-789-9

Vol. 2 TP
$14.99 US • $18.99 CA • £10.99 UK | ISBN: 978-1-60886-804-9

Vol. 3 TP
$14.99 US • $18.99 CA • £10.99 UK | ISBN: 978-1-60886-851-3

JONESY
VOLUME ONE

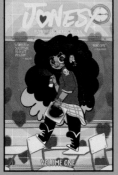

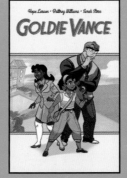

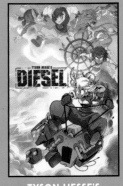

JONESY
Sam Humphries | Caitlin Rose Boyle

Vol. 1 TP
$9.99 US • $11.99 CA • £7.50 UK
ISBN: 978-1-60886-883-4

Hope Larson • Brittney Williams • Sarah Stern
GOLDIE VANCE

GOLDIE VANCE
Hope Larson | Brittney Williams

Vol. 1 TP
$9.99 US • $11.99 CA • £7.50 UK
ISBN: 978-1-60886-898-8

TYSON HESSE'S
DIESEL

TYSON HESSE'S DIESEL: IGNITION
Available November 2017
$14.99 US • $18.99 CA • £10.99 UK
ISBN: 978-1-60886-907-7

ALSO AVAILABLE

HELP US! GREAT WARRIOR
Madeleine Flores
$19.99 US • $25.99 CA • £14.99 UK
ISBN: 978-1-60886-802-5

TEEN DOG
Jake Lawrence
$19.99 US • $25.99 CA • £14.99 UK
ISBN: 978-1-60886-729-5

THE MIDAS FLESH
Ryan North | Shelli Paroline | Braden Lamb

Vol. 1 TP
$14.99 US • $18.99 CA • £10.99 UK
ISBN 978-1-60886-455-3

Vol. 2 TP
$14.99 US • $18.99 CA • £10.99 UK
ISBN: 978-1-60886-727-1

POWER UP
Kate Leth | Matt Cummings
$19.99 US • $25.99 CA • £14.99 UK
ISBN: 978-1-60886-837-7

BOOM! BOX™

AVAILABLE AT YOUR LOCAL COMICS SHOP OR BOOKSTORE.
To find a comics shop in your area, call 1-888-266-4226.
Prices and availability subject to change without notice.